FREEZE MY MARGARITA

FREEZE MY MARGARITA

A SAM JONES NOVEL

LAUREN HENDERSON

CROWN PUBLISHERS
NEW YORK

Grateful acknowledgment is made for permission to reprint "A Boy Named Sue," words and music by Shel Silverstein. Copyright © 1969 (Renewed) Evil Eye Music, Inc., Daytona Beach, Florida. Used by permission.

Published by Crown Publishers, 201 East 50th Street, New York, New York 10022. Member of the Crown Publishing Group.

Random House, Inc. New York, Toronto, London, Sydney, Auckland
www.randomhouse.com

CROWN is a trademark and the Crown colophon is a registered trademark of Random House, Inc.

Originally published in Great Britain by Hutchinson in 1998.

Printed in the United States of America

Design by Karen Minster

Library of Congress Cataloging-in-Publication Data
Henderson, Lauren, 1966–
        Freeze my margarita / Lauren Henderson.
            p.   cm.
        I. Title.
    PR6058.E4929F74   2000
    823'.914—dc21   99-39921
                                                        CIP

ISBN 0-609-80684-X

10 9 8 7 6 5 4 3 2 1

First American Edition

FOR ALL THE
GUYS WHO'VE
EVER MADE
ME TAPES,
YOU KNOW
WHO YOU ARE.

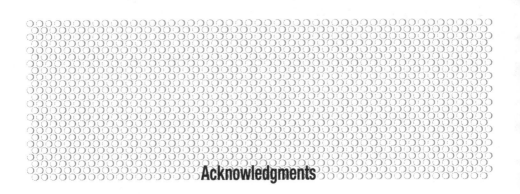

Acknowledgments

Much gratitude for their technical help to Frank Nealon at the National, Conrad at the Aldwych, Charlie the doctor and Lisa my sister, the best Helena I've ever seen. Not forgetting everyone at Questors who let me hang around and make a nuisance of myself during *Romeo and Juliet*. As always, big thanks to Sandy for her invaluable editorial services.

FREEZE MY MARGARITA

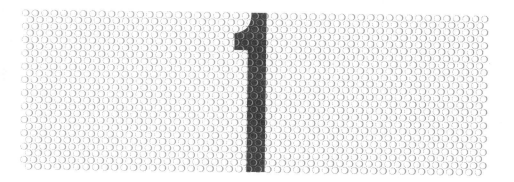

The man on his hands and knees in front of me had been there for a few minutes already, but in this establishment that was nothing out of the ordinary. I didn't realize at once that he was asking me something; the Velvet Underground were pounding lugubriously out of the speakers at a high enough volume to drown out anyone speaking in an appropriately servile tone of voice.

"Can I lick your boots clean?"

"I'm sorry, what?" I ducked my head. Rearing up on his knees, he said more loudly:

"Can I lick your boots clean?"

I shrugged. "Be my guest." His face fell. "You filthy little piece of scum," I added, not wanting to disappoint. He cheered up at once and ducked down, tongue poking out of the slit in his leather mask. But just as I turned back to the conversation he had interrupted, a horrible realization struck me.

"Oh my God, they're suede! Stop it! They'll be ruined!" I kicked out involuntarily. He curled over on one side and started moaning:

"Sorry, mistress, sorry, I'm a bad slave, do with me what you will. . . ."

"Do with me what you will?" I said sotto voce to Janey. She shrugged.

"Been reading too much Anne Rice."

"Mrs. Radcliffe, more like." I looked down at the bad slave and, feeling guilty at having deprived him of his fun, prodded his rubber bodysuit with the heel of my boot. He whimpered in ecstasy.

"I never know how they manage to let the sweat out in those things," I said to Janey.

"Probably don't."

"Ick."

"Oh well, at least he didn't claim to be the slave in *Pulp Fiction*," she said. "I've had three of those already this evening. So unoriginal. I like your dress, by the way."

"Thanks." I looked down at myself complacently. "Makes me feel like Scarlett O'Hara."

She gave me a frankly uncomprehending stare. "Ran it up out of a pair of old curtains, did you? I'd like to see the room they were hung in."

"The lacing, idiot." Without a Mammy to pull me in while I gripped onto the bedpost, I hadn't quite achieved an eighteen-inch waist, but it was still considerably restrained. And my bosom, never insubstantial at the best of times, was now resting precariously just under the top of my leather corset, propped up by what felt like most of the flesh that should have been covering my ribcage.

"Sam!"

I looked around to see a slave heading towards me at full lick, rather like an out-of-control Labrador, dragging his handler behind him on the leash. At first I didn't realize who he was; his features were obscured by two wide strips of leather, one over his eyes, the other over his mouth, secured at the back by a cross-piece. The zips that would have made him blind and dumb were hanging open, and squinting through them I began to distinguish a familiar face. He was wearing a black rubber sleeveless bodysuit, which at least allowed the air around his armpits to circulate.

"Eet's been so long!" he was exclaiming. "How are you?"

With the clue of the accent, I pinned down his identity: Salvatore, Sally to his friends, one of a gang of gay Sicilians who had for that very reason emigrated en masse to London. We had been at art school together, but our paths hadn't crossed for years.

"Hi, Sally." I did my best to kiss him hello, though the straps kept getting in the way. Janey had meanwhile struck up a conversation with some guy who'd been trying to catch her attention for the past half an hour and was now deep in a monologue about the latest power politics at Channel 4; she was a TV script editor. Disturbing her to introduce Sally would have been like breaking into the middle of Mass to ask the priest what the time was.

Sally looked round pleadingly at his handler. "Meestress, thees ees an old friend. May I harmbly talk to her for a few minutes?"

"Only if you obey her every command," said his mistress, handing the leash over to me. Her heels were so high that her calf muscles stood out like clenched fists. I took it gingerly. I've never really liked being responsible for other people.

"Um, buy me a drink," I suggested. "And that's an order."

"Two of the usual," Sally said to the barman. "On my account."

"You have an account here?"

"Not really. I give heem the merney at the end of the evening. I can't carry money een thees." He indicated the latex bodysuit. I saw what he meant.

The barman was already placing two identical concoctions in front of us, the salt rim to the glasses contrasting prettily with the pale aquamarine liquid inside.

"What's that colour?" I said warily, reminded of mouthwash.

"Blue curaçao," said the barman proudly. "Half and half with the triple sec. They're blue margaritas."

"Aren't they fabulous!" Sally enthused. "Eet's my dreenk of the year."

"Ever since the time some wally brought a bottle of crème de menthe to a cocktail party and made us Peppermint Somethings that tasted like toothpaste and cream, I've stuck to the whisky sours," I said, picking up my glass. I sipped tentatively. "God, this is *delicious*." Instantly converted, I took a good pull at my straw.

"So, tell me everysing you have been doing," Sally said.

"Oh, it's going OK, I suppose. I've got an exhibition coming up soon and I've finished most of the pieces for it. All of them, really. I'm just tinkering around now."

"Who are you weeth?"

"The Wellington Gallery."

"But that's excellent!"

"I know," I said gloomily. "It's hard to explain without sounding spoilt, but the trouble is . . . Sally, do you remember Lee Jackson, who taught us sculpture? I know you only did it for the first year—"

"How do I forget a woman like that?" said Sally rhetorically, lapsing for a moment into the traditions of his culture.

"She said once that the two responses of the hack sculptor, if a piece of work isn't going well, are either to make it big and paint it red, or make loads and fill the room up with them."

"So you are making everysing raid?"

"Nope, it's the second one. I see fifteen mobiles hanging together and I just don't know if I think they're good any more. They look really striking en masse. But anything looks good if you multiply it by fifteen and hang it from the ceiling: goldfish bowls, bits of ironmongery, even cocktail glasses—why are you staring at me like that?"

Sally's eyes were bugging out through the zips as if he were a Hanoverian king with water on the brain. The very small part of my mind which was not occupied with the misery of my artistic crisis wondered how he zipped his eyes shut without catching those long Sicilian eyelashes in the teeth. Be a waste to pull them out.

"You said you are making mobiles now?"

"That's right."

"*Guarda bene*, we must meet up and talk about thees. Can I come round to your stoodio? Are the mobiles there?"

"Yes, but—"

"I remember your work well. I liked what you did very march. *Very march*."

"Well, it's completely changed," I said instantly, not being one of those people who hoards their juvenilia. I'm the opposite: I need to keep moving on. Preferably as Juggernaut, with spikes on my wheels to shred my old work as I go. At art school our painting teacher made us bring in what we considered the best of our current work, then announced that we were going to build a bonfire in the yard with the paintings as fuel. I was the only one who jumped at the idea. Move on or die. Thank God I had a gallery and could get rid of my mobiles. I knew artists who, still unrepresented, lived with the pieces they had made years ago, unable to sell them. As far as I was concerned they might as well have been living in crypts surrounded by mouldering corpses.

Sally shrugged his shoulders, raising his hands, palm up, in a gesture I remembered well. It meant, "So what?"

"Why do you want to see them?" I asked warily.

"I am set designing now, and I am doing well." Sally had none of the English inhibitions about blowing one's own trumpet. It was very refreshing. "I am just to start—just *about* to start," he corrected himself, "to wairk on a new production of the *Dream*. That ees *Midsummer Night's Dream*, if you do not wairk in the theatre."

"Thanks, I didn't think you meant *I Dream of Jeannie*."

"*Cosa?* Anyway, we want it to be modern, modern, modern. Also we have some money, we have thees nice big theatre with a *proscenio*—the Cross—and so for instance we can permit oursailves to fly some people. I have been theenking about thees for a long time, how to do it in an interesting way, like Peter Brook with the trapezes. And now you come to tell me that you are making mobiles, and this whole idea explodes in my haid . . . They are beeg, aren't they? You always make theengs beeg."

"Pretty big. But Sally, even if you like them, the last thing I want to do is start making more for a theatre production. I was thinking about a holiday. Somewhere warm, where the boys are pretty and the drinks are cold."

"I come weeth you! I know just the place. *After* we've done the show."

"Oh, for God's sake—"

Sally's leash was abstracted from my hand.

"Was he well behaved?" his mistress asked me. Her lipstick was dark plum and so fresh that it glistened stickily, even in the dim light. Either she had touched it up recently, or she had been at the newly tapped virgin's blood in the back room.

"Not at all," I said vindictively, "he's been nagging at me and won't take no for an answer."

She drew in her breath sharply and tugged Sally's collar so hard he nearly fell off the bar stool.

"I see you still wilfully fail to respond to discipline!" she said, dragging him off with her. It was a choke leash; his half-strangled gurgle of pain wasn't faked. "Down!"

"I'll reeng you!" he croaked at me, hobbling off on all fours, and providing me in the process with a nice view of his bottom through the lacing on the back of his suit.

I stared after them, knowing that he would. Sally didn't have my number, but that wouldn't stop him; he'd just ring round everyone he knew till he found someone who did, persistent little bugger that he was. Well, he would just have to take no for an answer this time. There was no way I was making any more mobiles for a very long time, let alone ones specially customized so that people answering to the names of Peaseblossom and Mustardseed could use them as tarted-up hoists. I had my pride.

○○○

"Who was that?" said Janey later.

I gave her a thumbnail sketch of Sally and his latest brilliant idea. To my surprise, she said immediately that she considered it to be by no means a bad scheme.

I stared at her blankly.

"Are you serious? You know what kind of state I'm in! The last thing I want to do is start bastardizing my own work for a bunch of vampires in a theatre production. I want to get away, far, far away—"

"Where the boys are warm and the drinks are cold. I know, you keep saying so. And it'd do you good. You haven't had a boyfriend in ages, not since you dumped that perfectly nice one—"

"He was too straight," I said sullenly. "He wanted to take me to his parents' vicarage in Sussex for Sunday lunch, for God's sake. I know he was a nice guy, but we didn't have that much in common apart from sex. And OK," I admitted, anticipating her objection, "that was great at first, but it always tails off after a few months, you know? Familiarity breeds not a lot in that department. Anyway, I've been working. I haven't had time to think about anything else. I told you, all I need is a holiday."

"But you can't just yet. You said you had to be in London for at least another couple of months to finish things off and do the catalogue notes. Maybe this could be just the thing to get you out of a rut. You know you're happiest when you're working."

This is the trouble with friends who've known you for too long; they are unanswerably well informed on your best interests. (Also they remember your entire sexual history better than you do, and are all too willing to fill in the lacunae that you were hoping would be left blank by posterity.)

"What production is it?" she was asking.

"*A Midsummer Night's Dream*, at the Cross."

"Really!" Her blue eyes widened into saucers. "Helen auditioned for that! Wouldn't it be nice if the two of you could work together?"

Janey, bless her, was an eternal optimist. She would never see that Helen, her girlfriend, nursed a cordial loathing for me which was her normal response to someone she couldn't influence with her personal brand of synthetic charm. I wasn't that fond of Helen either, but I had more justification for my dislike, including the episode where Helen had left Janey for a TV producer called Kurt (a man, *nota bene*) and the promise of a leading role in the series he was then working on. The part hadn't materialized and Helen had come back to Janey, not noticeably sadder or wiser but definitely contrite, promising to be faithful from then on. I suspected that Helen's definition of faithfulness was looser than the elastic on Mick Jagger's underpants, but had not shared this observation with Janey, not wishing to destroy the friendship. A lack of this kind of maturity and judgement had imperilled relations with another good friend of mine recently, and I try never to make the same mistake twice.

"What part was she up for?" I asked.

"She wants to do Titania. She thought she gave a pretty good reading, but she couldn't tell what the director was thinking. It's Melanie Marsh. I haven't met her, but she's supposed to be very good. Helen said she was a cold fish."

Which, translated, meant that Melanie Marsh hadn't responded when Helen had flirted with her. Maybe she would cast her as Helena, the girl nobody fancied.

"Anyway," Janey was saying with quiet persistence, "it won't hurt you to show this Sally guy round your studio. What have you got to lose?"

I shrugged. "I'm just so sick of my work, Janey. I feel completely burnt out. Sometimes I wonder if I've just been busking along on one good idea up till now. After everything happened with Nat, I started working hell-for-leather to distract myself, and now I feel like my energy's run out."

"It's been a while." Janey looked concerned. Nat's wasn't a name I mentioned very often.

"A couple of years. Sometimes it feels like a couple of weeks . . . If it hadn't been for him I'd never have been making mobiles. I should tell the whole story to this idiot who's writing the catalogue."

"For God's sake don't!" Janey went pale under her powder. She had the prettiest, plumpest little eighteenth-century face, with rounded cheeks and cupid's-bow lips. Her hair was fair and wispy, her skin like expensive white velvet worn to the softest of downs. I always imagined her in a gilt-framed portrait reclining on a chaise longue, fanning herself, wearing blue silk and eating fairy cakes. Even the rubber frock she was wearing tonight was so layered with chiffon and draped with necklaces that you could hardly see its origins. She was one of my best and oldest friends and just now she was giving me her special elder-sister, concerned-about-my-soul look. I wilted under the force of her solicitude.

"That's why you haven't been seeing anyone, isn't it? You've gone all morbid. You've been thinking about him."

"How could I help it, Janey?" I said simply, abandoning my defences. "For the past few months I've been in my studio, working non-stop, living like a hermit . . . and sometimes it seems to me that making the mobiles is just a way of balancing out what happened with Nat . . . How could I not think about him?"

But Janey was looking so worried now that I promptly reneged on my last words. I've never had much time for confiding in people; either that, or it's never seemed to work. Which comes to much the same thing in the end.

"I didn't mean it," I said lightly. "I'm just sick of my work, that's all."

"Don't worry. My writers go on like this all the time." Janey twisted one of her many silver bracelets and gave me a sibylline look. "What you need is a complete change of project. You'll see. Something to get your teeth into."

"What I need," I corrected, "is another one of these." I waved my glass at the barman. "Two more blue margaritas, please."

"Two more *what?*"

"You'll like them. I guarantee it."

○○○

I hadn't had people round to my studio in so long I had forgotten what kind of effect it usually has on visitors, even without fifteen very large silver mobiles hanging in clusters from the ceiling, moving gently in the breeze from the open door. The heap of power tools, welding masks and work gloves below the mobiles looked as though it was growing up to meet them: stalactites and stalagmites. Never tidy at the best of times, the studio had completely let itself go over the past few months, as, indeed, had I. At least I had been forced to shower regularly, remove the metal shavings from my hair and cleanse my face after long stints with the welding mask. The kitchen hadn't been so lucky; I had been living off takeaways to avoid having to clean work-related debris off the surfaces. That's the trouble with these open-plan spaces: everything goes everywhere. . . .

"You leeve here too?" was the first thing Sally said, in an incredulous tone of voice. I had heard this from too many people already to find it offensive; and, besides, he had been standing for a very complimentary length of time with his head cocked backward, staring at the mobiles.

"Up there." I gestured to the sleeping platform, built twelve feet up the far wall. "I wake up in the middle of the night and my head's on a level with most of the mobiles. It's beautiful, particularly when there's moon-light, but I can never get away from them either. Sometimes they'll be moving, because there's a wind through the skylights, and I imagine they're talking to each other. I always think they're alive, once I've hung them."

That was a particularly badly structured sentence, I reflected. Still, Sally didn't seem to have noticed. Melanie Marsh, introduced by Sally as MM, said nothing either, but although I had only known her for five minutes or so, I was beginning to suspect that this was her modus operandi: speak only when you have something to say. The cowboy ethic.

"Can I go up the ladder to see them closer?" Sally asked eagerly.

"Sure. Just don't look at the sheets. I know your sensibilities are delicate."

Sally spent the next few minutes hanging off the ladder that led up to my sleeping platform, squinting at the mobiles nearest to him, looking like a monkey with a new set of toys. Feeling it incumbent upon me, I went over to what was now euphemistically known as the kitchen area and put on the kettle. One thing I always had in stock was tea.

Having people round was making me step back and take a good look at the scuzzy, bachelor-boy lifestyle—empty beer cans, takeaways and dirty sheets—which I had elected recently. Enough was enough. As soon as the mobiles were out of here I would do a major clean-up. Perhaps I should hire one of those industrial cleaning hoses and blitz the place.

"Do you want some tea?" I said to Melanie Marsh.

"Yes please." She remained where she was, in the centre of the room, surrounded by mobiles, her feet squared apart, hands in her pockets, rocking slowly backwards and forwards, eyes still, almost blank. Her looks were nondescript—mousy hair pinned at the back of her head, average-to-thin figure—and her clothes equally so. She wore jeans, work-boots and layers of sweaters. If I had had to describe her it would not have been by a list of physical features but her aura, the sense she gave of calm and control, of harnessed energy. She was someone who knew what she was doing, and if she didn't, she knew at least which path she needed to take. I couldn't help being impressed by her.

I brought the tea over and we stood together, sipping from our mugs, looking at the sculptures. Through some strange osmosis of Melanie

Marsh's aura I found myself relaxing in her company, able to detach myself for the first time from this batch of work; I felt the first faint fraying of the cord that tied me too close to them, the beginning of the process of letting go. Until Sally clambered down from the ladder and bounded over to us we didn't say a word.

"Tea's over there," I said, nodding.

"Thank you, I do not dreenk tea all the time," Sally said haughtily, "I have my coffee een the morning and *poi basta.*"

"You wait till we start work properly, Sal," Melanie Marsh said affectionately. "You'll be at the tea with the rest of us."

She turned to me for the first time, cradling the mug in her hands.

"I like these a lot," she said. Later, watching her in rehearsals, I was to realize that this was probably her highest unit of praise. "I can see exactly where Sally's going with the idea."

"We raise them for the scenes at the court, so they become like *lampadari,*" Sally cut in excitedly. "How do you say—hanging lights—"

"Chandeliers."

"Chandeliers. Maybe remove some, I weell have to see. Then for the scenes in the wood, they come down, the lovers find their path through them, they lose themselves—maybe Puck comes down on one. With the lighting eet weell look like magic."

"We have a respectable budget for this one," Melanie Marsh explained to me. "An old benefactor of the theatre left a legacy for them to put on one Shakespeare a year, so we hit the jackpot. We can afford to fly the fairies—Puck at least. It would mean designing a mobile for him to ride on. Quite a challenge, I imagine. I don't even know if it's feasible."

"Oh no, it should be fairly straightforward," I reassured her. "Obviously the design would be very much simplified anyway—you can't have all those contraptions round things that are going up and down and might get caught." I gestured to the silver wire, like planetary rings, which surrounded most of my mobiles. "We'd have to strip them down and stylize them. Puck's would have to be strengthened and I'd beat the surface flat around the chain, or maybe have two long dents for him to put his feet into."

"But would it look like the other mobiles? Because it would be good if the audience didn't guess in advance what was going to happen, seeing one that was a bit different."

"No, there's no reason for it to show at all. The dents would be on the top, near the chain, so to see them you'd have to get much closer than an audience would be. I can sketch it out for you if you'd like. . . ."

My voice tailed off. Sally was grinning at me, showing most of his teeth and quite a lot of gum.

"Well, I'm very pleased," said Melanie Marsh, having finessed me so neatly I had only seen the trick once she had taken it. "The best thing initially would be for Sally and you to put your heads together for the design, and then he can draw up something for me to see." She crossed over to the kitchen and put the mug down. "You could do the work in the theatre workshop, if you want. It might make sense. We can clear most of the room for you. After all, the mobiles will form a large part of the set. Though if you'd prefer to work on your own, that's fine, of course. It just occurred to me that you're rather out of space here. . . ."

Strangely enough, it was the idea of working in company, a group of loud, busy people in a constant flurry of activity, that swung the decision for me; that, and the escape route it offered from the studio. The mobiles would have to remain here for quite a while until the gallery was ready to take them, and the less time I spent with them now, the fewer doubts I could have about whether they were really finished, and the better I—and they—would be.

"No, that would probably work very well," I said slowly, feeling my next few months swirl around me and reform into a new and interesting pattern.

"Great. I'll look to see something from the two of you by the end of next week, say. Why don't you come to the read-through? We can talk afterwards, and you might find it interesting. Sal will tell you when. I'm very glad to have you on board, Sam." She shook my hand. Her face was round and pale and as smoothly inexpressive as a nun's, but now it broke into a smile. She moved towards the door. Looking back, she said:

"And call me MM, won't you? Everybody does."

Helen, I learnt in a phone call from Janey, had been cast as Titania. I resigned myself with the reflection that we were unlikely to see overmuch of each other. There were about twenty people in the cast; it wasn't a Beckett one-woman show with Helen's mouth spotlit for the entire performance. Not that the idea of seeing Helen buried up to her neck didn't appeal to me.

"I've even had to read the play," I complained to Janey over the phone. "I thought I'd better, it's years since I've seen it. But I'm so bad at imagining it coming to life. The words just stay firmly on the page. I don't know how you do it."

"It's a knack," Janey said. "Comedy's the hardest."

"And the organization required to get everyone on and off in the right places! It'll be like marshalling troops for a small war."

"Same as farce. Directing on stage is terrible: you're responsible for everything. Unless you're Peter Hall and have seventeen assistants, and Melanie Marsh isn't there yet."

"Yet?"

"I told you, she's supposed to be good. She did a very successful *Marat/Sade* on the Fringe earlier this year and she's been on a roll ever since. I think she's booked to do her next production for the National."

"So she's made it." I found to my surprise that I was rooting for her.

"Well, no. This is really the testing time. Young directors often do one good production; that starts a buzz going, they get booked all over the place, and then it turns out that the original success was a fluke and they're completely out of their depth. It's obvious quite quickly, too. They start rehearsal and pretty soon people know things aren't going well. Then word gets round that the production's a disaster—gossip travels so fast you wouldn't believe it. . . . Still, the play staggers on somehow. It has to."

"But what about the places that've booked them next?"

"Nothing they can do. Contracts already signed and sealed. The poor directors bounce round for a while, cannoning from one catastrophe to another, and then fade into complete obscurity. It's awful for them, too. They know they're not ready for what they're doing, or simply not good enough. Lots of nervous breakdowns."

"Can't the theatres sack them if they see early on that they've got a disaster on their hands?"

Janey's sigh echoed down the wire. "It's very difficult. . . . What they might do is bring in someone else. At the Cross, for example, it'd be the artistic director, Philip Cantley. He'd take over and knock the show into some sort of shape, but he'd leave Melanie's name on the credits. Not that it would matter much, because the entire industry would know what had happened. They'd have known weeks before the show opened."

"Janey, you're scaring the shit out of me!"

Janey's voice lost its detached, speculative tone. "Look, don't worry, Sam," she said, snapping to attention. "That hardly ever happens, and I'm sure it won't now. Helen's in it, after all."

I wondered whether Janey meant that Helen's presence in the cast guaranteed the play as a sure-fire hit.

"And like I say," she continued, "the buzz around Melanie Marsh is really good. I've heard it from lots of people. So don't panic, OK?"

This would have been considerably more reassuring if she had not just sketched out for me a doomsday scenario involving an incompetent director buzzing like a beehive in the mating season. But I didn't point that out to her. What would I gain by frightening the pants off both of us?

○○○

Belief in Melanie Marsh as a director radiated from most people gathered for the read-through like star quality from the young Lauren Bacall. This group, it quickly became clear, was composed of the members of her team, the ones who followed her from one production to another. Its primary members were Sally; a girl called Sophie who did the costumes, and was trying to mortify her own extreme prettiness by wearing an ankle-length A-line skirt, huge trainers and a cut-off sweater with batwing sleeves which could equally have been knitted by Sophie's well-meaning grandmother or Issey Miyake; and the tame composer, a serious type with a heavy fringe and big NHS glasses. In the whole time I was working on the production I never heard him say a word.

All of them—save the composer—talked to Melanie Marsh as respectfully, voices slightly hushed, as if they were postulants and she their abbess. She even had her own acolyte. Not long out of his teens, he compensated for his youth by aping a solemnity of manner so exaggerated that it would have been overdone if his idol really had been an abbess. He even carried a clipboard, bless him. Melanie Marsh treated him with tremendous respect, which was very good of her. The others teased him ruthlessly for his earnestness but, apart from a few blushes, he didn't care. He was the chosen squire to Melanie Marsh's knight and that was worth every bit of mockery they could throw at him. He was called Matthew and he was very sweet. I decided that I needed a Matthew of my own. In her shoes I would have picked someone prettier, but doubtless she was above that kind of petty aesthetic snobbery.

In this observation, I was later to learn, I had sorely misjudged her.

I had been called to the rehearsal venue, a church hall in Belsize Park, half an hour before the cast was due to arrive, and was late by at least that much. This seemed to be standard procedure. The actors trickled in over the next hour, complaining about the walk from the station (ten minutes), the weather, and the difficulty of finding the church hall in which we were meeting (on the main road, right next to the church. Duh).

Meanwhile, Sally and I showed our sketches to Melanie Marsh. We had planned eight mobiles, two of which would be designed so that Puck could ride on them. I had suggested to Sally that all four fairies make their initial entrance on the mobiles, but he had laughed me to scorn. Apparently it took one operator—or flyman, as he called them—to raise or lower each mobile, plus one extra to guide each person, or flyer. And they could afford four flymen at the most, not eight. Besides, he added airily, and not quite convincingly, he wouldn't have flown them even if finances permitted: it would cheapen the effect if all the fairies rode the mobiles as well as Puck.

MM, as I was learning to call her, nodded approval and gave us concrete proof of this at once by showing the designs round the group. Sally, better at line drawing than me, had added a couple of sketches, one showing the effect of the mobiles hanging high up as chandeliers for the opening scene at court, and another one with the lovers winding their way between them, maze-like, in the wood.

"I thought at a certain point of having columns for them to rest on, to make them trees. But then I theenk eet weell be too clarmsee," he announced, finding the last word with great satisfaction.

"I like them as they are," said MM. "Remember the effect in Sam's studio? Why mess around with that?"

"Absolutely, MM," muttered Matthew at her shoulder, scribbling something on his clipboard. I couldn't imagine what.

"He'll grow out of that," Sophie said in my ear, seeing the direction of my gaze. "They're all like that in the beginning—just out of university and desperate to seem grown-up."

Behind us the double doors banged, indicating a new arrival.

"Marie!" MM said. "Come over here and have a look at your fairy carriage!"

Marie, a small, slight girl clad in a tiny padded Chinese jacket and the Lycra layers of an off-duty dancer, bent over the drawings. She had a nondescript face with the button nose and wide mouth of a rag doll.

"Great," she said enthusiastically. "Do I get to fly on my own?"

"Don't know yet," MM said. "I did wonder about you taking a jump down—the mobile stops halfway and you leap off it. Maybe onto Hugo. We'll have to see what Thierry thinks."

"Oh, is Thierry choreographing again? Excellent. I want to do a lot of acrobatics and he's brilliant for that." Marie, who was playing Puck, unwound her jacket and threw it on a chair. Without its padding, she was even smaller than I had thought, her waist snappable between finger and thumb. "Any coffee going?"

"Matthew's got a kettle rigged up in the flower-arranging room."

"The what?"

"Well, this is a church hall, darling," drawled a new arrival. "What did you expect, a Gaggia machine staffed by one of those dark and brooding boys from Bar Italia?"

"Hi, Hugo," chorused most people in unison without turning their heads.

I bucked the trend. Hugo was tall and slender, fair-haired, grey-eyed, with a long patrician nose down which he was looking at the moment. It seemed his habitual expression. He was swathed in a dark overcoat and silk scarf, both of which he discarded with something of an air to reveal the black polo neck and stripy trousers underneath. He was one of the few men I'd seen who could wear the latter successfully; despite being slim, he had a nice little bottom to round them out. Stripy trousers didn't work if they drooped in puddles where the buttocks should be.

"Coffee first, socializing afterwards," he said decisively, following Marie into the flower-arranging room. "Who is this young stripling in charge of the brewing up?"

"Matthew, hi," said the young stripling, holding out an eager hand.

"Called after a disciple, no less! How appropriate. I'm Hugo."

"Oh, I know. I saw you in *Ghosts* at the RSC. You were great."

"*Great.*" Hugo propped himself against the wall as Matthew put the kettle on. "Well, I expect that's better than 'neat,' which is Kevin Costner's famous compliment to Madonna after her show. I think she made a vomiting gesture, didn't she? Always the lady . . . Are you from Oxford, Matthew?"

"No, Cambridge."

"Sidney Sussex?"

"King's."

"Well, there's no accounting for the paucity of your vocabulary then, is there? Or maybe just a little."

"Oi, keep off Sidney Sussex," called MM, and for the first time I saw her grinning.

"And you've got a nerve having a go at King's," added the composer. "You were down the bar the entire three years."

"That's right, darling, I couldn't stay away from all those girls in baggy black with poorly applied lipstick. Like Robert Smith clones. So fetching."

"This is a bit of a Cambridge mafia," Sophie informed me. She seemed to have taken it upon herself to guide me through the maze of interconnected relationships. "Hugo and MM and me all met there, and MM gets her assistants sent up by our old tutor. He picks them out for her."

"But you can't have studied costume design at Cambridge," I said. "I was under the impression they thought modern languages was a dangerously advanced subject."

"It is," said Hugo from across the room. "For years Classics dons insisted on speaking Latin in Italy, not to mention Ancient Greek in Greece. Very cross they were too when Johnny Foreigner didn't know what the hell they were on about."

"No, I did history of art, with Hugo," Sophie said, ignoring this. "Then I apprenticed myself to a tailor for a couple of years. I never really studied design."

"A much more sensible procedure," Hugo commented. "I despise the cult of the expert."

"You went to drama school for three years, Hugo!" Sophie pointed out gleefully. I noticed that Hugo's entrance had lifted everyone's spirits.

"I, of course, am above such petty generalizations," Hugo responded smoothly.

The doors were banging now with regularity as the actors trooped in, making without exception straight for the kettle.

"No cappuccinos, I expect. I couldn't find *anywhere* near the station to get a mocha latte," said one fretfully. "I really thought I'd be all right in Belsize Park. I mean, it's practically *Hampstead.*"

"Perhaps we could buy young Matthew a milk frother," Hugo suggested. "I'm sure he pumps a nice head of foam, don't you, Matthew?"

The young stripling, struggling to refill the kettle from a leaky cold tap, a dozen people now waiting impatiently for their mugs of coffee, flashed a quick smile at Hugo. Clearly he was so glad to hear his name issuing from the august lips that whatever other words surrounded it were of minimal importance.

"You know Sally from art school, right?" Sophie said to me. I was continually surprised by how very pretty she was, her big eyes with spiky lashes set in a little heart-shaped face, and how wilfully the current fashion seemed designed to conceal it. I had never been interested in that particular game of double bluff. No-one was going to prise me out of my miniskirts and into an A-line which skimmed the ankles and looked as if it were made out of a carpet sample.

I nodded. "We met up again last week at the Torture Garden."

"No prizes for guessing what Sally was wearing," Hugo drawled. "Or rather, where he wasn't wearing it."

"Any time, *carino*," Sally said to him, flapping his inch-long eyelashes.

A large, red-faced forty-year-old, carrying a substantial beer belly as proudly as if he were an expectant mother, turned his head at this interplay and gave Sally a full-throttle baleful stare. Sally remained unaffected, either blissfully unaware of this kind of would-be moral disapproval or so used to it that it passed right over his head. Hugo, on the other hand, picked up on it at once and saw that I had too.

"Endearing, isn't he?" he observed to me, nodding at Beetroot Face. "Such a charmer. And how well he carries that *embonpoint!*"

"Time to get started," MM said. Her voice was hardly raised, but everyone snapped to attention. Within a few minutes we were gathering ourselves round the long and rather wobbly trestle table which Matthew had set up in the centre of the hall. Each person had pulled out their copy of the play, already dog-eared and scribbled-on, and set it in front of them like hymnals in church.

"It's pretty draughty in here, isn't it?" said Helen, drawing up a chair opposite mine at the table. "Oh, hello, Sam!" she said, noticing me. I was surprised to hear genuine pleasure in her voice. Usually Helen greeted me with as much warmth in her voice as an ice floe drifting off the coast of Greenland. My mighty brain deduced that she was feeling insecure among all this camaraderie and was so glad to see a familiar face that she didn't care whose the personality was behind it.

"Are we all here?" said MM.

There seemed, to my inexperienced eye, to be enough people round the table for a full-scale production of *War and Peace*, battle scenes included, but Matthew said importantly:

"Well, George Bradley couldn't be here, because he's filming this week."

"Lucky George," someone said.

"It's just *The Bill*," Hugo observed. "He's a positive fixture as the porky inspector from Hicksville-in-the-Marsh."

"And Violet Tranter's not here either. I don't know why."

"Bugger Violet," said MM placidly. "And don't make one of your clever remarks, Hugo. Matthew, ring her up. If you can't get hold of her, ring her agent."

"Who's Violet Tranter?" I said to Sophie. "The name sounds familiar."

"Oh, she's the girl who was Fuchsia."

I blinked, then realized what she meant.

"*Gormenghast?* I saw that on TV. It was a while ago, wasn't it?" I had in my early years identified with Fuchsia, the sulky, rebellious, passionate teenage heroine whom Sting had once famously been in love with. To my disgust, Violet Tranter, all big blue eyes and cloudy hair, had played her instead like a maiden in a tower waiting for the prince. I pulled a face.

"Yes, Vi was miscast," Hugo said, noticing this. "The girl who was Fuchsia," he added meditatively. "I rather like that. Sounds like a title for a detective novel, don't you think? She'd be dead before it started, of course."

"Like *Laura*," Matthew volunteered.

Hugo and I opened our mouths, paused for a moment, and closed them again in such unison we could have been synchronized. Why ruin the film for everyone?

"That was a lovely goldfish impression you just did," I said to Hugo mischievously.

"Darling, you should have seen yours," he retorted. "You positively goggled."

MM was looking at her watch. "We can't hang around waiting for Violet. Tabitha, you read Hermia for now. Right, let's go round the table. Everyone say their name, what they're doing on the production, and what they had for breakfast. I'll start: I'm Melanie Marsh, I'm your director, and I had Weetabix with milk. Matthew?"

Matthew stammered out something about toast and jam ("Tut tut," Hugo murmured, "a growing boy needs more than that in the morning") and we were off. Beetroot Face, sitting next to Matthew, declared himself to be Bill, playing Bottom; simultaneously, he directed a glare round the table as if signalling his intention to head off any jokes on this subject which might come his way in the future. I noticed that he fixed his stare on Hugo particularly, for which I could scarcely blame him. In the half-hour I had known Hugo I had already learned to tell when he had an observation trembling on his lips; now, meeting Bill's eyes with his own limpid grey ones, he wiped his face suspiciously clean of all expression. As Bill guided us through the various courses of his own breakfast—juice, grapefruit, fry-up, cereal, toast— Hugo, instead of observing that there was no food shortage about to be announced in Greater London as far as he knew, or wondering dulcetly how Bill managed to pack so many victuals into his slender frame, remained silent. He did not withdraw his gaze from Bill, however, even as the baton of introductions passed around the table; indeed, he favoured him with the sweetest of smiles. Bill became increasingly fidgety.

The list of characters seemed endless. Sally, sitting next to me, showed me how he had used different colours in his script to break the play down into three different strands: scenes between the fairies—Oberon and Titania, Puck and Titania's four attendants—the court, with the two pairs of lovers, and the group of rustics who provided, all too obviously, the comedy interludes. I borrowed his coloured pens and did the same myself, hoping it would make me feel more professional.

After the roll of names, MM announced that she would like everyone to stay for the reading if possible but would understand if non-actors left. Would they please do so between acts to avoid disturbing the cast. Afterwards the rehearsal schedule would be distributed and we would break for lunch.

Having nothing better to do, I stayed. I originally meant to drop out after an hour or so, but to my surprise I found myself unwilling to leave;

even though I knew, I wanted to see for myself how it all came out. Afterwards Sally said that it had been an exceptionally good read-through. My lucky streak again.

Violet Tranter did not materialize. Matthew reported that he had tried her flat, to no avail, and her agent, who hadn't spoken to her for a few days but was sure that he had told her about the read-through. Halfway through the doors banged and everyone looked up, but it was only Steve, the stage manager at the Cross theatre, a large, bulky, no-nonsense man dressed completely in black, who bustled in with an air of being busier than the rest of us put together.

Hugo, doubling as Theseus, king of Athens, and Oberon, king of the fairies, was extremely good already, authoritatively regal: all-powerful, malicious, selfish and decidedly world-weary, an Oberon suffering from such eternal ennui that he was scarcely amused even by Puck's antics. Helen's cold little voice matched him so nicely that I realized why MM had cast her. Still, she needed help with the long speeches, which she delivered in tones as flat as her own chest. Marie, as Puck, was plainly feeling her way into the part; she didn't seem a natural for Shakespeare and I suspected she would be much happier when she was cartwheeling across the stage and shouting out her lines when upside down. Bill was a surprisingly funny and poignant Bottom, all bluster and insecurity.

The fairies were a cluster of pretty, lithe young things, two boys, two girls, and all of them very much on the make, eager to catch MM's notice. One of the girls was Tabitha, who was reading in for Violet Tranter, dark and narrow-limbed with a long mane of silky black hair, an ethnic mix that could have been anything from Spanish to Asian. I saw why MM had told her to read Hermia, one of the lovers; Hermia was required to be small and dark, in contrast with her rival Helena. Nervous at first, Tabitha gained in confidence as she went and by the time of her big scenes was acquitting herself reasonably well.

It wasn't enough to make her stand out, however. The young men—Lysander and Demetrius—were average, but the revelation was a girl called Hazel Duffy, playing Helena. Usually this was a thankless, whiny part: the girl neither of the boys wants who wakes up to discover that, through magic, both of them are suddenly enchanted with her, and refuses to believe them. But next to Hazel Duffy the other three lovers looked like cardboard cut-outs. She played Helena's lines to the full, with all the passion and misery of unrequited love, and later the frustrated conviction that everyone else was ganging up to make fun of her. After her first long speech all eyes in the room were fixed on her, and there was absolute silence: no fidgeting, no sipping of coffee, no slipping out to the loo.

An initial glance round the table, despite her position at the head, would have passed over MM completely; she was so quiet, so colourless, a peahen among all these bright birds preening their plumage, constantly calling attention to themselves. And yet without her the room would have had no centre; she was the still fulcrum around which everything revolved. She had been maintaining an almost stolid calm, reading in the absent George's dialogue and whispering the occasional note to Matthew, whose clipboard was always at the ready, his head bobbing importantly every time he wrote something down.

But after Hazel made her declaration of love for Demetrius and determination to follow him into the wood sound as fresh as if it had been written last week, with none of the cod-Shakespearian mannerisms on which the other three lovers, less confident than she, were relying, even MM raised her head and gazed at Hazel for a long time with a clear and approving eye. It was noticeable that she said nothing to Matthew: there was nothing she needed to say.

After a pause the man who was playing Quince cleared his throat and began the next scene. The momentary fizz of tension subsided, but was not forgotten. Heads dropped thoughtfully to the scripts in front of them. And, looking round the table, I wondered if I were the only person who was thinking that Violet Tranter might live to regret not turning up for the read-through.

"Her real name's Susan Higson, you know," Sophie said as we strolled down to Belsize Park to have lunch. "She thought Violet Tranter sounded more romantic."

"Well, I can't fault her there," I commented. "I disapprove of this new trend for actresses being called by their real names. In the Forties they'd all have been renamed. I mean, Jeanne Tripplehorn, Renée Zellweiger, Michelle Pfeiffer—they sound about as glamorous as brands of pork pies."

"Couldn't agree with you more, darling," Hugo said from my other side, having caught us up. "Speaking as someone whose real name is Brian Dumpster—"

Bill chortled. "Brian Dumpster!" he repeated. "Funny, that! Was your dad American, then?"

"Well done, Bill, you win the Hugo Fielding Credulity Award for 1998. I'll present you with your silver-plated pen later," Hugo said acidly.

Bill made a huffing noise and muttered something about pretentious ponces which made Hugo's eyes narrow.

"Darling," he said in the campest of tones, falling back to put an arm round Bill's ample shoulders. "I'm so sorry. You can call me by any name you want to, any time you want to, anywhere . . . and talking of which, I hear we're sharing a dressing room! Practically the intimacy of the boudoir. I can't *wait* to be alone with you."

Sophie rolled her eyes at me. We had reached Haverstock Hill and turned down towards the parade of shops.

"We're going to the caff, Huge, are you coming?" she said.

To my disappointment, Hugo shook his head. "Too cliquey, sweetheart, don't you think? My regrets to you and the lovely Sam. I shall hang out with the actors." He drew out the last syllable to rhyme with drawers.

"Hugo's very good about that kind of thing," Sophie said as we waved the others goodbye and headed down towards the café. "It's true, we can get very cliquey. Not meaning to, but we've all known each other so long. And it's always a bit actors-versus-the-rest-of-the-world when you're doing a play."

"You mean they've got to bond?"

"Exactly. MM'll get them all playing silly games this afternoon, warming them up. Hugo's quite right; he can't be seen to be hanging out with the director's gang the whole time. No-one in the cast would be relaxed around him."

I pushed open the door of the café, which was probably the one remaining down-to-earth eaterie in the whole of Belsize Park. The tablecloths were red-and-white checked plastic, the lighting stark. Everything on the menu came with rubbery white toast, whether you'd ordered it or not, and a few limp leaves of iceberg lettuce placed at one side of the plate for garnish. I found it comfortingly familiar.

MM, Matthew and Sally were already assembled round the table, together with Steve, the Cross stage manager. I had gathered from Sophie that there was a policy movement underway to subsume Steve firmly into their, or our, side; his loyalties would naturally lie with the theatre itself rather than any individual production, and a hostile stage manager would be an enormous hindrance. To this end Sophie seated herself next to him and used her big eyes to tremendous effect. Sally nobly restrained the excesses of which I knew he was capable, and by the end of lunch Steve, who had sat dourly through the reading, had softened slightly towards us.

"I'm always a bit suspicious of young Oxbridge types," he said to MM. "Just out of college and think they know it all. But I must say that you lot seem to know what you're doing. I didn't see your *Marat/Sade*, but Philip says you did a nice job there."

Philip, I remembered, being the artistic director of the theatre. Steve's tone of voice was patronizing enough to have put even the Queen firmly in her place; she might be Elizabeth Windsor but he was the stage manager of the Cross theatre. It was clear which he would consider more important. He had the absolute self-satisfaction of the man convinced he's the only one who knows how things should be done. To get round him, MM would need to butter him up rather than challenge his authority. A petty tyrant, made worse by the fact that his authority was limited to only one sphere of operations. If we stepped on Steve's toes he'd be drawing in his breath sharply at every little thing we asked for and saying that it couldn't be done. He was overweight and had the pallor of someone who spends all his daylight hours inside a darkened theatre. I later learned that the Cross was Steve's entire life; he was in at ten every morning, even when it was totally unnecessary, often staying till late at night.

"I look forward to working with you, Steve," MM was saying simply. "It's a wonderful space, the Cross. I'm very lucky to have the opportunity to use it."

Steve puffed his chest out proudly, pulling his shoulders back. His short, steel-grey hair was cropped close to his bullet head, and suddenly I saw him as an NCO, working under a series of commanding officers half his age and twice as posh. What had they said to young officers new to the Front: "Pray God you get a good sergeant major"? I realized the advantage of having Steve on our side. He would throw spanners in the works of anyone of whom he didn't approve, but once committed to something, he would move mountains to get it right.

"We've got a very good set of flymen," he assured MM. "Trained 'em myself. They'll do a nice job for you. No strings attached!"

After a few seconds it dawned on us that he had made a joke. Everyone laughed dutifully. Sophie went as far as to pat him on his pudgy white hand.

I decided it was as well that Hugo hadn't joined us for lunch.

ooo

"Still no answer from Violet?" MM said to Matthew as we walked back up the hill, full of scrambled eggs and mushrooms. On toast, of course. Now that Steve had left us, the conversation flowed much more freely.

"I'm afraid not. Do you want me to go round to her flat?"

MM shrugged. "No, don't worry. If she's not answering the phone, she's unlikely to come to the door. By now she's probably picked up the messages and is busy making up some complicated excuse, which I'll have to sit through and pretend to believe. . . ."

"Violet is a nuisance," Sophie observed. "I warned you, MM."

"You did, I know. But she'll do a nice job, all the same."

"What if she doesn't turn up?" Matthew said. "Would Tabitha do it?"

"Oh, Violet'll turn up." MM's voice was certain. "She can't afford a reputation for that kind of behaviour. But no, I wouldn't ask Tabitha to step in. She's too lightweight."

Sally nipped into the tobacconist for some cigarettes and we waited outside, Sophie lighting up.

"Hazel's excellent," she observed. "A real find."

"Isn't she?" MM said with emphasis. "Practically fresh out of drama school. She'll put Violet on her mettle. I don't want her resting on her laurels; she's got to feel that she needs to prove herself. That fight between them has to be done properly. We'll get Thierry to work out something really good. Nice and physical."

"Catfight!" I said. "Dress 'em in PVC bikinis and drop them in a mud bath."

Sophie started giggling. "Like Alexis and Krystle on *Dynasty*, do you remember?"

"Wasn't that a swimming pool?"

"But their hair! Always the same, even when eet was wet!" Sally said, emerging from the shop. "They must have changed the weegs very often."

"I was surprised Violet agreed to do Hermia at all," Sophie said. "After all, it's not a star part. When I worked with her at the Almeida last year she was already getting a swelled head. And then that TV commercial and *Gormenghast*—"

LAUREN HENDERSON ○○○○○○○○○○○○○○○○○○○○○○○○○○○○○○○○

"Her agent rang me," MM observed. "She chased the part."

"That's right," Matthew said, keen to make his contribution to the discussion. "I remember that."

"Probably fancies someone in the cast," I chipped in.

Everyone focused intently on this idea; the atmosphere fizzed with speculation.

"The Lysander is very pretty. If you like them ginger," I remarked.

"He is, isn't he?" said Sophie and Sally practically in unison.

"I love those freckles," Sophie added. "I wonder if he touches them up?"

"And those leettle boys who play the fairies are to die for," Sally observed.

"They'd be two a penny to Violet, though, those boys," said Matthew. "I bet she likes them rich or influential. Or both." A shade of wistfulness coloured his voice for a moment.

"Sexual obsession," I said portentously, "is of necessity unfathomable."

"Unlike Sally's fundament," said Hugo, coming up behind us and groping Sally's buttocks one-handed with an accuracy that spoke of past experience. The other hand was occupied by a pale blue Sobranie.

"I theenk eet's very true." Sally sighed. "Eef I understand you."

"Unfathomable," I said, "means you can't get to the bottom of something."

"No-one complains about that weeth me, I can assure you," Sally said. "Can I have one of your cigarettes, Hugo? They are so preety."

"Primrose yellow or pastel pink?" Hugo said, offering Sally a silver cigarette case. "I must say," he added with satisfaction, "I can't wait to see Bill's face when we walk back in smoking these. *What* a raving old reactionary that man is."

"Disgusted of Tunbridge Wells," I offered.

"He is, isn't he? That's perfect," Hugo said appreciatively, blowing a smoke ring in the direction of Hampstead. "I shall call him that from now on. Between ourselves. To his face, of course, he will be Billy-boy."

"Hugo," said MM warningly. Still, she was smiling.

"Don't worry, lord and mistress," Hugo said, rather too airily.

"I'm sure things will be all right," I commented. "I can't really imagine Hugo doing anything that would interfere with Bill's Bottom."

○○○

Sally came round a few days later to help me load my tools in the van and take them over to the theatre. He reported that Violet Tranter had still neither shown up nor phoned; her agent declared himself as baffled as everyone else.

"Has anyone called her friends?" I said.

Sally shrugged his elegant little shoulders. "Violet ees not one of those who has friends, you know. Not girl friends who know what she ees doing."

"A man's woman, I take it."

"*Al massimo.* She has some fags, the type who don't know they are fags yet, you know, or maybe they are just Eengleesh men," Sally said reflectively. "Sometimes I do not know the difference . . . in any case, they are her friends. But I do not think they know where she ees."

"Maybe Hugo was right," I suggested. "Maybe she *is* dead. Stretched across her bed in a flimsy chiffon negligée with a dagger of strange Oriental design driven into her heart . . . Has anyone been round to her flat?"

"Oh yes, her agent. He went at once," Sally said, deflating my lurid imagination. "He has a key, I theenk. Or maybe he asks a neighboor. But there ees no body een the bath."

"So what's going to happen?" I said curiously.

"Well, eef she has not shown herself live soon, MM offers the part to someone else. Not Tabitha."

"Does Tabitha know that?"

"I doubt eet." He picked up my MIG welder and started to wrap the cord around it. "I am sure they have one just like thees at the theatre," he observed.

"Oh no they don't," I said coldly. "Though it may look the same to an untrained eye."

Sally had done sculpture at college for the minimum time required; as soon as possible he had concentrated on making exquisite scale models of his set designs, cut perfectly with the finest of Stanley knives, painted and varnished within an inch of their lives. He had no capacity to understand how a power tool, through years of use and wear and self-customization, could become as familiar to you as your own hand. And there was no point explaining it to him.

"I'm taking everything, OK?" I emphasized, cutting off strips of orange gaffer tape and wrapping them round each expensive, beloved gadget I possessed. Then I wrote "SAM'S. KEEP OFF." on each bit of tape in black marker pen. They wouldn't be able to say that they hadn't been warned.

"The boys at the theatre are very—disposable," Sally volunteered.

"*What?*" Sally's English was very good, but occasionally betrayed him into the hands of the enemy. I started sniggering. He looked cross.

"I mean, they are—they 'elp a lot."

"They're helpful," I corrected, still sniggering. He drew himself up to his full height.

"If you need to be helped," he said, pronouncing his h's slowly and carefully, "they weel help you."

"You mean what's-his-face, the master carpenter? I met him a couple of days ago when I went by to check out the workspace." I threw my respirator, goggles and work gloves into a stained and battered canvas bag, and looked round. "Where's the hand cream?"

"Here." Sally fetched it from the kitchen table. "I see you care for your skeen."

"Idiot, it's for my hair." I tossed it in the bag. "I grease it down before I start welding, or grinding. Otherwise it gets full of metal filings, wood chips, bits of steel, God knows what . . . it all tangles up and I can never get my hair clean again." I pulled at a long, dark, curly strand by way of illustration. "Also it dries out like straw."

Sally was looking rather horrified.

"That's nothing," I said, grinning at him. "I lost clumps of hair years ago because sparks landed on my head. The teachers don't warn you. You might call it trial by fire. Someone in my class was forge-welding steel once—it dribbles and melts into slag, did you ever see us doing it? He got some on a frayed rip in his jeans and caught on fire. We rolled him over and put it out. Nothing too spectacular, he was hardly burnt. But still . . ."

In silence, Sally passed me the arc welder he was holding. I put it into another bag.

"I do not theenk," he announced, "that I weell be coming to see you work very often."

"That's all right. I'm sure I'll have all the disposable boys down there hanging over my shoulder giving me would-be helpful advice. Like in the gym."

"The cheem?" Sally said blankly.

"Oh, you know. Men can't see women operating machinery without wanting to chip in. Unless it's of the domestic variety, in which case they can't work it and need you to help them. Funny, that."

I opened the front door and started carrying the bags down the steps and into the van. My studio is in Holloway, an extension of the huge warehouse next door, on a back street without a single other dwelling in sight, just one run-down industrial complex after another. Of course I live here quite illegally—the building isn't approved for residential use. But to quote a catchphrase overused by Bob, next door's night watchman, "Who the hell cares?" He himself practically lives in his snug little den over there; he's fixed it up with a camp bed, a stove, a nice warm heater and his cat, Fat Shirley.

Sally followed me with the lightest bag, the one containing my respirator and protective gear, stumbling and complaining bitterly about the weight. No wonder he had looked so vacant when I had mentioned the word "gym."

The van, a red Ford Escort whose state of dilapidation perfectly matched its current surroundings, was due for its MOT and produced, for Sally's benefit, a series of alarming creaks and rattles. In order to engage third gear I had to execute a complicated, wrist-twisting manoeuvre which was automatic to me by now but caused Sally to draw in his breath sharply and shrink back in his seat. Mercifully for his refined sensibilities, not to mention the continued health of the van, the theatre was only a quarter of an hour's drive away, in an undistinguished back street near King's Cross, just close enough to the Angel for the marketing people to be able to call the location Islington.

I dog-legged over to the Pentonville Road with my current favourite tape blaring happily away; it was a thrash metal compilation, with occasional sentimental interludes, designed for cruising down American freeways in an enormous pick-up rather than scrambling through narrow London backstreets. The sun was shining, Sally had brought chocolate croissants for breakfast, and a series of male American voices were screaming a combination of abuse and endearments ("I'm just a BAD PENNY! I always come BACK TO YOU! Should have KNOWN you couldn't TRUST me—far as you could THROW ME!") over a raging flood of angry guitars and metallic reverberations. I couldn't have been happier. I just wished that the guy who'd made me the tape had bothered to list the tracks; I didn't know who half of the groups were. I was too busy getting into his jeans to make him do it. Just shows how sex can screw up your priorities.

Sally was very affronted. I knew he preferred groups composed of exquisite, clone-beautiful black girls with perfectly applied lipliner, singing banalities in such glorious harmony that for a while you didn't realize that the lyrics were entirely composed of three short, inane statements, repeated ad infinitum ("Don't Walk Away. While I'm Crying. Be Cos I Love You, Baby"). They always thanked God first in their sleeve notes ("U R the 1 where all love flows!"), straightened their hair, had Barbie-perfect figures and were probably dubbed by their fat, gospel-singing, Weather Girl lookalike aunts.

Anyway, Sally didn't like the Circle Jerks. Another good reason for him not to come down much while I was working in the basement of the theatre; I had brought my portable stereo as well.

"One way, or another, I'm gonna find you, I'm gonna get you get you get you get you—" Debbie Harry was threatening as we pulled up behind the theatre. Sally had cheered up slightly on hearing a girl's voice. I pulled out the tape and put it in my pocket.

Bez, the master carpenter, was leaning against the wall by the stage door, smoking a roll-up, squinting his eyes into the pale streaks of sun.

"All right?" he said in a friendly way as I swung myself out of the van. "Want a hand?"

Sally excused himself on a flimsy pretext while Bez and I lugged the bags through the narrow entrance and down a series of equally cramped corridors and lino-floored staircases to the basement. When I had dropped in the day before yesterday, we had had the usual macho standoff about whether I knew what I was doing: we had folded our arms and stood with our feet apart while Bez grilled me on my knowledge of carpentry, welding and power tools while smoking endless roll-ups, tobacco bulging out of the end like stuffing from a Chinese pancake. Fortunately I had passed the test and we had bonded. The formalities quickly concluded, he had not only agreed to set aside for me a big section just next to the carpenters' workspace, bristling with power points, but offered me the services of his charge hand, a lanky, spotty youth, much as a Roman patriarch might have lent out one of his indentured slaves. ("Get Sextus to fetch and carry for you. He's not much cop—one of a batch, only cost six sesterces the lot—but he's willing, I'll give him that. If he starts pissing around, tell me and I'll have him whipped.")

Sextus emerged now from Bez's office. Tall and thin as a rotting cadaver, he had the complexion of a glue sniffer, though not the voice.

"Oi, it's Lurch," said Bez. "Get in a brew for me and Sam, will you, Lurchie?"

I had to admit that the unfortunate youth did bear a strong resemblance to the Addams Family's butler. Plugging in my portable stereo, I dropped in the tape.

"I want a boy . . . a tough boy, a rough boy . . ." squealed the Go-Gos. "I'm searching for a boy, a real boy, a strong boy."

"That's all right, that is," said Lurch articulately, emerging from the kitchen with a mug of tea in each hand. "Who's that, then?"

"The Go-Gos," I said, adding: "Belinda Carlisle," when his face remained blank.

"*Belinda Carlisle?*" Lurch said, dropping his jaw but not the tea.

"Nice one, Lurchie," said Bez, handing me a mug. "Not quite 'Heaven Is a Place on Earth,' is it? Representative sample of the youth of today," he said to me satirically, indicating his charge hand. Bez couldn't have been over forty-five. "Thick as a two-by-four. At least your being here'll extend his musical boundaries a bit."

As we drank our tea, Bez brought me up to date on the shopping list of materials I had left with him.

"Should have everything in by the day after tomorrow. I'll give you a bell when it's here and you can start work."

"Nice one," I heard myself saying. Bez's stock phrases were infectious.

Just then "A Boy Named Sue" came on, the live version, Johnny Cash sounding like a dead ringer for John Wayne. I turned the volume up.

> *Well, my daddy left home when I was three,*
> *And he didn't leave much to Ma and me,*
> *Just this old guitar and an empty bottle of booze.*
> *Now, I don't blame him because he run and hid,*
> *But the meanest thing that he ever did*
> *Was before he left, he went and named me Sue.*

Roars of laughter billowed from the audience, not only the one in the background of the tape. Halfway through, Sally tripped downstairs and started to say something.

"Sssh!" we said in unison.

"But there ees—"

"Shut *up!*"

Sally subsided. Lurch was tapping his foot happily and swinging from side to side.

"Be doing a bloody hoedown in a minute," Bez muttered.

As the song rollicked to a halt, a voice behind Sally said repressively:

"Well, I'm glad to see you all enjoying yourselves."

The voice was chilly enough to freeze the grins to our faces with rigor mortis, but Bez remained no whit abashed.

"Cut the music, Lurchie. All right, Mr. C," he said cheerfully. "Nice to see you back. Had a nice break from it all, I hope. Cup of tea?"

"No thank you," said Philip Cantley, the artistic director of the theatre, as Lurch shambled over and turned the tape off. Not that this courtesy was necessary. Philip Cantley had been an actor for most of his life and had a voice that was diamond sharp; it could have cut glass. He looked me up and down, his eyes cold and dark as chinks in marble. "You must be Salvatore's sculptor."

"Sam Jones," I said, rather envying Bez's union-protected, builder-to-client nonchalance. "Has Sally shown you the designs?"

"I'm sure Melanie will in due course," Philip Cantley said, in what was clearly a rebuff. "It would scarcely be appropriate for me to be peering over her shoulder in the meantime."

He exchanged a few words with Bez, then turned on his heel and left in the direction of the chief electrician's office. I raised my eyebrows at Bez, who shrugged.

"Horses for courses," he said. "Mr. C likes young ladies to look feminine, know what I mean? Everyone knows that in the business. You should see the way some girls come in to audition when he's directing something himself. Skirts nearly up to their waists."

I snorted with laughter, looking down at the stained jeans and cropped layers of sweaters I usually wore for work; at my boots, so worn that the steel caps were showing through the toes.

"What was he expecting?" I said. "Jennifer Beals?"

"'What a feeling! Keep believing!'" Lurch wailed in an unexpected, falsetto Irene Cara impression. We all stared at him.

"See what I mean?" Bez said. "Let's have that Johnny Cash on again."

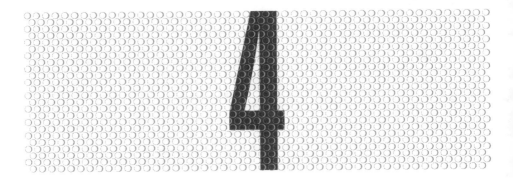

4

Hugo made a similiar crack when he dropped into the theatre a few days later. Through my goggles I could just about see that someone had come down the stairs—the green lenses always reminded me of the night-stalker glasses from *The Silence of the Lambs*. Identification of people across a large and cluttered basement, however, was beyond their capacity, and besides I was concentrating much too hard on what I was doing to squint.

"I thought you were scrambling eggs down here," Hugo said when I flipped the mask back.

"Sounds like that, doesn't it?" I put down the MIG welder and took a deep breath, standing back to look at the work-in-progress. "You didn't look directly at the flame, did you?"

"Don't worry," Hugo said, "if I were going to go blind it would have happened a long time ago, believe me. Cigarette?"

"No thanks."

He tapped out a Gauloise and lit it with one of those ancient pinwheel lighters that sends out an inch-high jet of flame.

"I thought you smoked pastel Sobranies," I observed.

"Not today. They don't go with the outfit." One white hand loaded with a fistful of silver rings indicated his black-and-white check trousers, white shirt and leather jacket. "I know what you're going to say next, and you're quite right; they didn't go with what I was wearing at the read-through either. I sacrificed my exquisite aesthetic sensibilities on the altar of annoying Bill, rabid old out-of-condition homophobe that he is. God knows what he's doing in the theatre. I see him more as the leader of a telesales team." Lounging against the carpenters' work bench, he blew out some smoke rings and stared at me assessingly. His fair hair was slicked back today; his cheekbones and the bridge of his nose, thrown into relief, caught and held the light.

"I'm rather disappointed," he said. "I thought when you pulled that thing off your head, all your hair was going to cascade down like something out of *Flashdance*, but you've got it pinned up instead."

"I think Philip Cantley shares your disappointment."

I checked the gap I'd just filled in; it looked pretty smooth to me. Hugo strolled forward and squinted at it.

"Impressive," he said. "I think. No, our Philip likes them so *femme* they make Marilyn Monroe look like the Marlboro Man. Whereas at this moment you're more Gina Gershon in *Bound*."

"Really?" I perked up.

"Mm. Normally I'd have said Jennifer Tilly. But those leather jeans are very butch, darling."

"I shouldn't be working in them, really. They were very expensive about a decade ago, but they're so old now they're hanging off me."

I poked at them dispiritedly. The knees had gone, which was always the beginning of the end. The bottom would be next.

"Get a pair custom made," Hugo suggested. "Girls need to, really, especially ones like you. All those curves to fit. I know a great little man in Brick Lane; I could give you his number." He tilted his head. "Brown would be nice on you, a really dark bitter chocolate brown. Go with your hair and eyes."

"Hugo!" Sally called down the stairwell. "Are you down there?"

"Absolutely. I'm doing my raving queen impression and giving Sam some fashion advice. Not that she needs it." He favoured me with a matinée idol smile. "What is it?"

"Come up! You weell never guess who cet ees who has just come een!"

"I can, actually," Hugo drawled. "It was about time." He stubbed out his cigarette and looked at me. "Come on, darling. Your first sight of the flower of our cast."

I had a lot to do, but as always my curiosity won out. How could I resist being present at the return of the prodigal daughter?

○○○

I could see at once how Susan Higson had selected her stage name. If she had been a green-eyed blonde, it would have been Primrose; a vivid brunette, Poppy; but, with the cloud of dark hair that made her tiny frame seem even more fragile, and her huge eyes, the colour of pansies under water, Violet was the perfect choice. She wore a clinging cardigan which was the exact blue-purple of her eyes, half its pearl buttons undone to show the lacy body underneath, and a pair of beige boot-cut trousers which clung to her flanks with loving attention. The silk scarf knotted around her neck perfectly echoed the colour of the trousers. Her heels were high and square, and she was so hung about with delicate silver jewellery that she reminded me of an Asian friend of mine: the same exiguous build and mane of hair, not to mention the trembling wristfuls of slender bracelets.

"I'm so, so sorry," she was saying to MM, clasping the latter's hands between her own. They were on the stage, which was occupied by the set for the Cross's current production of *Who's Afraid of Virginia Woolf?*, raked high and filled with bookshelves, fake fur rugs and leather recliners. Bez and the chief electrician, whose name I had forgotten, were sprawled in a couple of armchairs, watching the action appreciatively. "I feel *terrible*. I just had this awful, awful *crisis*—I don't know if I can even *explain* it—"

"Try," MM suggested. Her voice was at its most calm and friendly. I doubted this would mislead Violet, whose eyes widened, her gaze zooming onto MM's face like the focus on a rifle.

"I know you're angry with me," she said contritely. "How couldn't you be angry with me? I *should* have rung, I know I should. It was just the world felt like it was closing in on me"—she made a wide sweeping gesture, bracelets tinkling against each other—"and I *had* to run away. And it wasn't that easy to phone from Goa," she added more prosaically.

"Vi's jingling like Santa's reindeer," Hugo muttered in my ear. We were standing by the deputy stage manager's desk in the wings, stage right. I could see part of the scene round the corner of one huge black masking flat; Hugo, more enterprisingly, had his face pressed against the black gauze window inserted in the flat for the benefit of the crew. It was invisible to the audience but as easy to see through, close-up, as a tinted window in a car.

"Is there someone there?" Violet said, swinging round. Her hearing must have been as sharp as a cat's.

Rather sheepishly Sally emerged onto the stage, followed by Hugo and then me. It was the first time I had stood here, though Bez had shown me round days ago; the rake was so steep that I was glad I was in my work boots. How the actors managed not to break their ankles was beyond my comprehension. Violet, in her three-inch heels, seemed totally at home. She said a brief hello to Sally and Hugo and stared pointedly at me.

"Vi, this is Sam Jones, our artist-in-residence," Hugo said. "She's making the mobiles for the sets."

"Oh right," Violet said, sweeping me with the purple searchlight of her gaze and discarding me in my battered jeans and T-shirt as someone who wasn't worth shooting down. She favoured Hugo and Sally with dazzling smiles and then returned her attention so thoroughly to MM that the rest of us were immediately relegated to the status of a shadowy mass behind the footlights. It was to MM that she was playing the scene. I noticed that although her accent was Received Pronunciation, the actors' and BBC presenters' standard, she had a trick of emphasizing certain words in a way that was the trademark of upper-class, public-school-educated girls.

"I absolutely *assure* you, *promise* you, that it won't happen again. God, on my *life*. I really want to do this show, I've been so looking forward to working with you. . . ." She let her breath out in a long sigh. "How can I convince you? What can I *say?*"

She scanned MM's face; remaining pleasant and blank, it offered her few clues. But at that moment a voice said from the auditorium:

"Violet? Long time no see!"

Violet pivoted on her heel, giving a small extra toss to her head so that her long tresses would swing round and resettle in a luxuriant mass.

"Practising for a hair advertisement," I said to Hugo and Sally.

"Philip?" she was saying, peering out into the auditorium. "Goodness, it's been *ages*. I'm afraid you've turned up in the middle of a terrible ticking off. I've been *so* naughty and MM is *awfully* cross with me. I went AWOL for a week at the beginning of rehearsals." She lifted her hands and crossed them protectively over her breastbone. "I *know* how bad that is, really I do."

Philip Cantley came round the first row of seats and up onto the stage via a couple of steps half-concealed by the frontage of one of the boxes. Holding the stage not only with his presence as an actor but with all the authority of the status conferred on him by his title of artistic director, he might as well have been wearing a big gold mayoral chain round his neck.

Quite properly, MM was the first person he favoured with a nod.

"Everything all right, Melanie?"

"Yes thanks. We were having a set meeting." She gestured to Bez and the chief sparks.

"And Violet?" He turned to her.

"I just got here. Practically from the *airport*."

"This simply isn't on, Violet," Philip Cantley said sternly. His greying hair was gathered in the shortest of ponytails at his nape, and he had a silk ascot twisted loosely round his neck in the style of an eighteenth-century dandy. All he needed was the silver-handled cane to twirl. His eyes, dark and flat as the pips of some poisonous fruit, came to rest on her. She shrunk back slightly against one of the bookcases as he continued:

"Unprofessional behaviour is frowned on in this theatre. Melanie would have the perfect right to throw you off the production and I wouldn't be able to stop her. She's the director, not me, and she has complete authority. I couldn't interfere."

"I know, Philip." Violet hung her head.

"Well, Melanie?" Philip Cantley turned to MM. How neatly she had been finessed; by stressing her autonomy, he had made his own wishes clear. And yet I didn't believe that MM would let herself be pressured into making a decision that was not her own. I was already becoming one of her shield-bearers.

I slid my eyes sideways to Hugo, who was watching the interplay with open appreciation. He raised one brow at me and I knew that our thoughts were running in tandem.

"Violet, you're on probation," MM said easily. "One week. I expect you to be early for every call. I'll have a look at the schedule and we'll try to blitz your scenes this week. After that I'll decide."

"Thank you," Violet said so humbly that I expected her to genuflect.

"Thank Philip for pleading your case," said MM with more than a hint of amusement.

Philip Cantley, unsure of how to react, very sensibly did nothing at all; Violet looked blank.

"I'm off the book," she said proudly.

"Learnt your lines in the taxi from the airport?" Hugo suggested.

"Good. So's Hazel," MM said calmly, ignoring him. "That will help a lot."

"Who's Hazel?" said Violet casually.

"My *dear*," Hugo observed happily. "*What* a treat there is in store for us."

○○○

"Something about Philip Cantley," I commented later on, in safer sur- roundings, "makes me want to take two steps back and string some garlic round my neck."

"He is a nasty piece of work, isn't he?" Hugo agreed. "Shivers down one's spine."

"I see him as something from a Ben Jonson," I observed. "Venom behind the wit."

"As long as he doesn't compete with me for the Restoration dandies," Hugo said carelessly. "I have that market pretty much sewn up." He flourished a deep and elaborate bow so perfect that I could almost see the brocade tails of his frock coat and the lace cascading from his cuffs. "Still, Edmund at the National next. I heard this morning."

"Well done!" Sally gave him a big sloppy kiss. "Congratulations!"

Hugo looked quietly smug. "Always nice to have the next thing planned out. God stand up for bastards! I shall look forward to playing an evil young stud after the Queen of the fairies—sorry, loves, *King*." He shot a sidelong glance at me.

We crossed York Way onto the promontory of King's Cross station, the frontage of WH Smith and burger bars half-obscured by kids hanging out, beggars with scrawny dogs tied to half-chewed pieces of string, officious policemen, confused tourists, *Big Issue* sellers and people milling around the bus stops. The sun was shining, which only made the place look dingier. Perversely, I found the near-squalor comforting. It reminded me of home. Hamburger wrappers skidded across the pavement, caught in the crossfire of breezes and hot exhaust from the passing buses. Hugo strolled through the crowds like a weary aristocrat.

"Well, I must love you and leave you," he said. "Back up the bowels of the Northern Line to Belsize Park, oh the excitement of it all. Are you coming, Sally?"

"No, I am going home. I must go to the launderette."

"Oh God, so must I," I said, a cold, sinking feeling at the pit of my stomach like a badly digested meat pie as I thought of the state of my sheets. I would just boil-wash everything and see what happened. At least that way it would be disinfected.

"Not coming to rehearsal, Sam? MM doesn't mind at all if you want to sit in. I have a rendezvous with my Titania, the divine Helen. Face that sunk a thousand ships."

"She's the girlfriend of one of my best friends," I said reprovingly.

"Poor best friend," said Hugo, unabashed. "That girl'd shag a can of baked beans for a part. Probably has. Probably," he added, drunk on his own invention, "been filmed doing so."

"How's she doing as Titania?"

"Oh, MM's getting something very nice out of her. Or not nice at all. I've never seen Titania as such a nasty piece of work before. Mind you, so's my Oberon. Corrupter of children and despoiler of innocence. I *am* having fun."

He flashed us a lovely smile and was gone, descending the stairs to the underground as graciously as if they led down to a ballroom. I stared after him thoughtfully. It was very unsound to say you hoped someone might not be gay, even if you were speaking from a purely selfish perspective, so I didn't voice my thoughts; but that didn't mean that they weren't there.

Which was quite an achievement, given my recent disinclination even to speculate about the sexual predilections of any attractive male who happened across my path.

○○○

To my distinct surprise, I woke up the next morning with a feeling of promise and new possibilities. It was so unfamiliar to me that I lay there for a while, breathing in the equally unaccustomed scent of fabric conditioner which still clung to my sheets, and savoured it to the full. Janey had been right, up to a point; I had needed a new project to sink my teeth into. Still, the technical challenge of the mobiles for the set wasn't enough to account for this wellbeing. It was the company, the emergence from my self-imposed isolation into the surroundings of the theatre workshop, the easy, perhaps too easy, camaraderie of the cast and crew as they began to pull together, to find their stroke and row in unison. It might be too unforced, the facility with which they bonded with newcomers who would be already half-forgotten by the time the next production was underway, but for the moment the immediate, unreflecting friendships I had formed suited me perfectly.

Who knew, after all, where I'd be in a month's time? Or a year? I could go anywhere I wanted. Duggie had mentioned a joint exhibition in Berlin, and he had an associate in New York who was interested in what he was pleased to call my concept. From being so rooted in my studio that to see anyone, even answer the phone, had seemed too much of an intrusion on my work, I saw myself swinging away in a wide, exhilarating, centrifugal curve, the studio still at its hub but shrinking in the distance as new places came suddenly into focus.

I swung myself out of bed, straightened the duvet and plumped the pillows. Padding down the ladder that led from my sleeping platform to the main studio floor, I ran through a schedule for the day, so absorbed that for the first time I hardly favoured with a glance the mobiles clustered thickly below the ceiling. Shower, coffee, gym—that last was more than overdue; if it weren't for the physical aspects of my work I would be horribly out of condition. Twice a week at least from now on.

The gym was in Chalk Farm, just down the hill from the church hall in Belsize Park. Maybe, after my work-out and some form of refreshment, I would drop in on the rehearsal; I seemed to remember that today they were running through the first two acts. Then I could see if anyone wanted to come for a drink afterwards. Clearly I had developed an unslakeable thirst for company. Not to mention gossip.

○○○

I slipped through the doors in the middle of an impassioned scene between Hazel and Fisher, who played Demetrius; she was pleading with him not to go, while he was desperate to follow Hermia. In an effort to stop him, she clung to one of his legs and he had to drag her half across the room before he could shake her off. Finally, he made his escape and Hazel, crying plaintively: "I'll follow thee, and make a heaven of hell,/To die upon the hand I love so well," ran off in the direction Demetrius had taken. MM, leaning against the wall where the audience would be, was nodding. Matthew, behind a trestle table piled with papers and copies of the script, conferred in whispers with Steve, the stage manager, and an assistant of his. I was impressed; Hazel was as excellent as she had promised to be, and Demetrius, who had been rather flat before, was now firing on all cylinders. Hazel was pulling him up to her level. I clapped, a flat and lonely sound in the large empty space which nevertheless drew a wide and beautiful smile from Demetrius. Hazel swung round to look at me, her face flushed, her eyes glazed with concentration, still half in another world.

"I brought chocolate Hob-Nobs," I said, coming forward. "Plain chocolate, none of that wishy-washy milky crap."

"Brilliant!" Fisher, a tall, West Indian–looking boy, attacked the packet at once. He held it out to Hazel, who shook her head rather wistfully.

"I'm always on a diet," she said, "and if I start I won't stop."

I noticed that Fisher didn't try to persuade her, or tell her she looked fine; he simply nodded understandingly and took a few biscuits himself. Actors took their weight as seriously as if they were teenage girls.

"Well, I think it works very nicely now we've put all the bits together, don't you?" said MM, munching a Hob-Nob. "I still want to go over your speech at the end of the first scene, Hazel—you know: 'How happy some o'er other some can be'—if we have time today. Though I imagine I'll have my hands pretty full with Violet."

"Violet?" Hazel echoed.

"Yes, we have her once more among us," MM said with a hint of irony. "She swears she's off the book, which would be a help."

"Well, I'm glad to hear she's at least learnt her lines," Fisher said sarcastically. "Where's she been?"

"In Goa. But don't make an issue of it, please, for your own sake. We have a lot of catching up to do and it won't be helped if everyone's at daggers drawn."

"Don't have a Goa at her," called Matthew from across the room. Everyone smiled politely.

"But—" Hazel said, her hesitant manner contrasting powerfully with the passion she had just exposed on stage.

"What?" MM said, turning to her. There was a subtle intensifying of MM's quality of attention as it centred on Hazel; MM might not even be aware of it herself, but I noticed it, and it was unlikely that I was the only one.

"I think Tabitha assumed she was coming along this afternoon," Hazel said. "It's on the rehearsal schedule, and she's been reading in Hermia."

"Only in the opening scene, for blocking," MM said. "I hope you're wrong, Hazel. But I did tell Matthew to call her, just in case. Matt?"

Her loyal slave had already pricked up his ears at the mention of his name.

"I did, honestly, MM," he called from behind his desk. "I left a message yesterday and two this morning."

"Well, let's hope she's got them." MM looked at her watch. "We've got fifteen minutes. Fisher, have a cup of something or a cigarette break while Hazel and I polish up this speech, will you? Right, Hazel, come over here."

They strolled across the room to the far corner and stood, MM propped against the wall, script in her hands, reading out lines here and there to illustrate her point as Hazel nodded, her body almost standing to attention with the effort of concentration. Occasionally she repeated a line back. I watched, fascinated despite my inability to hear what they were saying. Fisher and I made coffee and further inroads on the Hob-Nobs. He asked me abstractedly how the set was going, to which I returned a suitably neutral answer; politeness satisfied, he went outside to smoke. I quite liked Fisher, but he did not allow himself to be known easily. He stood slightly to one side, watching the antics of others without really joining in. I had the sense that he was cleverer than most people and easily bored by inanities.

When the doors banged a few minutes later, I thought it was Fisher returning. Instead Tabitha bounced through, glowing with excitement, her lustrous dark hair falling around her face so silkily that she must just have washed it. I hoped for her sake not in honour of the rehearsal.

"Hi everyone!" she sung out, dropping her bag by the door. "All right, Matthew?" She waved at him. "Oh, sorry!" she added, realizing that MM and Hazel were conferring in the corner. "I'll just warm up a bit, OK?"

Bounding over to one of the windowsills, she swung a leg up to rest on it and grasped her foot in one smooth motion. It was showy, but I'd taught weight training and I could see she knew what she was doing. MM shot a look at Tabitha and then at Matthew, who pulled an agonized face and mimed holding a phone to his ear. Meanwhile, Fisher re-entered the hall, eyes wide, flapping his hands at MM as Tabitha, blissfully unconcerned, completed her stretches and wandered over to MM and Hazel. She was rotating her shoulders, her hands clasped in the small of her back.

"I can't wait to get started," she said enthusiastically. "There's this lift we did in ballet I thought I could use for the bit where Hazel goes for me, you know? Where's Fisher—oh, hi, Fisher. You know the lift where you get my calf and hoist me up, yeah—Fisher and me did dance classes together—anyway, I thought—"

At that moment the reason for Fisher's agonized gesturing became clear. Violet, dressed surprisingly sensibly in head-to-toe Ralph Lauren Sport—fleecy jacket, polo-neck sweater, narrow leggings and deck shoes—came through the door with the air of a diva and stood poised just inside, waiting for all eyes to turn to her. Her smile of satisfaction faded a moment after the desired effect had been produced as she realized, her instincts sharp as a cat's, that it had happened for the wrong reasons.

"Hello everyone," she said slowly, her voice very sweet and carrying beautifully. She walked towards the little knot of people at the centre of the hall. "I'm Violet. I'm terribly sorry I wasn't here before. I'm going to work like a *dog* from now on, I absolutely *promise*." Her great purple eyes swept the group. "You must be Hazel," she said in perfectly friendly tones.

Next to Violet and Tabitha, both of them tiny slips of things, Hazel, five foot eight at the most, towered like a monolith. I could see why she was concerned about her weight; she had the kind of raw-boned frame that showed every pound it carried. She ducked her head involuntarily, looking deeply embarrassed by the situation, and muttered a hello at Violet.

Tabitha, however, was more than standing her ground. She had even taken a few steps forward and was doing her best to stare Violet down. Her eyes were flashing, her hands on her hips; she looked like one of Joaquin Cortes's flamenco dancers challenging another for the honour of a solo with Mr. Skinny-Shanks himself.

"Well, I'm Tabitha," she said, "and I didn't know you were going to show up. No-one told me."

Violet, taking the situation in at a glance, dealt with this smoothly. "I'm so sorry," she said. "I'd have a go at poor Matthew if I were you. What's your name?"

"Tabitha. But—"

"Thank you *so* much for keeping my part warm for me, Tabitha—I remember Anthony Cavendish saying that once to his understudy, who he was madly in love with. It was the funniest thing." She took off her jacket and looked around her, clearly considering Tabitha dismissed. "I haven't been here before. Is there any chance of getting a coffee? I'll make it for everyone," she added quickly. Violet was on her best behaviour. "Fisher, darling, just point me in the general direction, will you?"

Looping her arm through Fisher's, she went through to the kitchen area, chatting away. The message was clear; she had no need to stay and defend her territory from someone as insignificant as Tabitha. Hazel, with surprisingly bad timing for so good an actress, said pensively:

"She's even prettier than she was on TV, isn't she?"

Tabitha gulped. Tears of rage and frustration sprang to her eyes.

"Tabitha," said MM, forestalling an explosion, "come outside for a minute, would you? We need to have a little talk. I think between us we may have got our wires crossed."

Tabitha, angry and upset, followed MM out into the fresh air. I wondered if MM were taking her into the cemetery for their little talk; it would be unpleasantly appropriate, if heavy-handed. And I wondered, too, if Hazel had really made that comment in all innocence. It had flicked Tabitha on the rawest spot conceivable. If Hazel were a stirrer—and often the quietest types were the worst—she would have plenty of material to work with on this production. The more unpleasant side of my nature anticipated fireworks.

I didn't foresee a murder, though. I can report no anticipatory shivers down my spine. But I have a good excuse for lack of belief in psychic phenomena: once you've lost your virginity on a tomb at midnight, unscathed by anything but stubble rash, it's hard to summon up the necessary frisson which belief in the supernatural requires.

Her talk with MM concluded, Tabitha flounced back into the hall, picked up her bag, tossed her hair, did the flashing-eye thing again at Violet, and flounced out, all limbered up with no place to go. Violet, meanwhile, treated the whole affair as if it were quite beneath her notice, a highly accomplished tactic and one I made a note of for the future. Her air of unconcern also had the side-effect of impressing Hazel so thoroughly she hardly said a word. Until they started rehearsing. Nothing could cow Hazel then.

Watching the scene between the four lovers take shape, tentatively as yet, I realized how much the success of a play depends on its casting. Violet, as Hermia, was a spoilt girl used not only to getting her own way, but to having every man around in love with her; she larded Hermia's sheer incredulity, on waking to find that both her suitors had changed allegiance to Helena, with tremendous petulance. And Hazel was genuinely upset and distressed, sure that everyone was playing a nasty joke on her and becoming angry in her turn when they wouldn't admit it. The two boys had a more difficult time, as their roles were almost interchangeable. I thought Fisher was much better than Paul, the Lysander, who had a tendency to strike attitudes and had been visibly disappointed on being informed that Tabitha was not to play Hermia. She was another attitude-striker; their styles had chimed perfectly.

After an hour or so I went outside and curled up on a bench in the cemetery, sketching ideas for the mobiles. The cyclorama at the back of the *Virginia Woolf* set was thickly hung with fake ivy, dimly lit to represent the garden wall seen through the back window. Bez, showing me round, had mentioned how much that quantity of plastic ivy cost—nearly a thousand pounds—and after I had recovered from the shock I had asked if I could re-use some when they took the set down. Creative recycling. I wanted to spray-paint it silver and drape it around the mobiles, even drill holes and thread the ivy through so it looked as if it were growing out of them.

The gravestones were set into a thick green carpet of grass, so perfectly clipped and trimmed that it looked like expensive Wilton. Beyond them imposing and doubtless ancient oaks spilt great shadows over the lawn. Sunlight dappled through the leafy branches onto the worn grey stone of the church and tombstones, catching flashes of colour off the stained-glass windows and, from the grass, streaks of a green so bright it was almost emerald. It was a tourist's idea of England in microcosm, but none the less beautiful for that, a green thought in a green shade. Inspired by my surroundings, I was experimenting with some effects that were meant to look like the boles of trees, copied from the oaks, when someone tapped on my shoulder.

I jumped as much as it is possible to jump when you're sitting cross-legged on a garden bench.

"Sorry, darling, did we startle you?" Hugo said, staring over my shoulder at my sketchpad. "Hmm, interesting. Not that you draw terribly well, but the idea's intriguing."

"Piss off." I swatted him with the pad.

"Can I see?" Sophie took it from me. "Oh, I think that's great," she said enthusiastically. "It's like a surreal forest. I was going to give the fairies wreaths, and maybe I can tie them in to this ivy thing you're doing. I want them to be quite spooky."

Sophie, with her short ragged haircut and tiny pointed ears, looked like an escapee from a Dali-inspired forest herself. She was wearing a tiny Muji vest and over-large combat trousers; the former strained over even her narrow torso and the latter sagged below her waist, barely held up by her hips. It was a look that played with proportions, flaunting thinness: look, I must be really skinny to be able to wear these grotesquely enormous trousers!

"As long as I don't have to wear a toga, I don't care," Hugo was saying firmly. "When MM asked me if I'd do Oberon, I said fine, as long as no-one tries to get me into a bloody sheet."

"Bloody sheet sounds more *Macbeth*," I observed.

"The Scottish play named, and in a cemetery too! Turn three times widdershins and copulate with the vicar," Hugo advised. "Otherwise we're all doomed."

I stood up, dusting off my bottom. "Well, I think I'll go back inside," I said, adding with studied carelessness, "though the main excitement of the day has been and gone."

I could almost see Hugo's ears pricking up. "Sam? I smell gossip in the air."

He jumped ahead, barring me and Sophie from passing through the cemetery gate. "Neither of you crosses this divide till Sam tells me what's been happening. Soph, I know you're as curious as I am. Make her tell, go on. Tickle her or something."

Under this duress, I brought them up to date with the Tabitha/Violet encounter. Hugo smacked his lips as if he were savouring a fine wine.

"Lovely," he sighed. "This one will run and run. . . ."

A stout form could be seen plodding down the path towards us. Hugo swung round, his voice becoming silky.

"Bill, my sweet! Walk with me a while. It's been two days since I saw you and I swear every minute has been a torment without sight of your smiling face. . . ." Linking his arm through a reluctant Bill's, he strolled off towards the church hall.

Sophie was giggling. "Huge is too much," she said. "You either love him to death or want to brain him. Once he's got his knife into someone, he just keeps twisting it in the wound."

"Fun for the rest of us to watch."

"As long as Bill doesn't try to throttle him."

"Well," I pointed out, "that could be amusing too."

Sophie stared at me. "You don't mind Hugo, do you?" she said, concerned.

"On the contrary. I just meant it would be fun to see Bill lose it completely."

"He might, if Huge keeps going like this. His tongue is a lethal weapon. Shit, we'd better go in. I've got to measure everyone."

More people were coming down the path: three of the fairies, Tabitha conspicuous by her absence, and Helen, who wiggled her fingers at me in a half-hearted wave. Clearly her pleasure in seeing me was wearing off. They followed us in through the doors. Hugo, having let Bill escape for the moment, was chatting to Violet, who was working her way through a packet of custard creams with an air of dedication.

"So how *was* Goa, darling? I hear it's full of tourists now."

"Oh, it wasn't that bad," Violet said dismissively through a mouthful of crumbs.

"I must say, I don't quite see you in Goa, darling. I always think of your tastes as being distinctly European. Italian food and all the creature comforts."

"The weather was wonderful this time of year," Violet said, shrugging off the subject. I had the strong impression that she really didn't want to talk about Goa.

"You don't look very brown."

"Oh, I *never* go in the sun without smearing sun cream all over me," she said immediately, horrified. "Think of the damage!"

"Very wise," Hugo said approvingly. "We girls must be careful of our complexions, mustn't we, Bill?"

Bill, pouring himself some coffee, gave what sounded like a snarl and moved away to talk to Helen. She greeted him enthusiastically, even going so far as to offer him sweetener from her own container, a mark of high favour.

"Be careful," Violet said reprovingly. "He has a heart condition."

Hugo raised his eyes to heaven. "Now tell me, darling," he persisted, "did you see Mr. Edwards on the beach? Everyone must be asking about him."

"Who?" Violet said blankly, extracting yet another custard cream from the packet.

"Tut tut, you're out of touch. Richey Edwards, the guitarist of the Manic Street Preachers, the one who was supposed to have flung himself to a watery grave in Wales of all places—mind you, he was Welsh, I dare say that explains it—and then was spotted hanging out in Goa. Hirsute, I imagine, with beads plaited everywhere. And talking of which—"

"No, Hugo, I didn't get beads plaited *anywhere*," Violet said, laughing. "And I've never heard of this Richey person."

"What about the girl who followed in his tracks—threw herself off the same bridge? They're probably shacked up in a shack in Goa, eating freshly caught lobster as we speak. I must say it sounds very tempting. Almost heaven, if it weren't for all the hippies. And the lack of proper plumbing."

"Shirley Lowell," said Hazel, so quietly that I could hardly hear her.

"What?" Violet said, swinging round immediately to include her in the conversation. She really was on a major charm offensive with Hazel.

"Shirley Lowell, the girl who killed herself," Hazel said. "I was at college with her. She wanted to be an actress too."

"Ow, Bill!" said Sophie crossly. "You trod on my foot!"

Bill, having his measurements taken, mumbled apologies.

"Well, don't jump around like that!" Sophie drew the tape measure once more up his inside leg.

"I'm sorry," Hugo said to Hazel. "Here I go, frivolling away—did I upset you?"

"No, it's OK. It was a while ago now," Hazel said composedly. "And she wasn't a very happy person."

I could see the words: "Oh well, that's all right then," trembling on Hugo's lips, but to his credit he restrained them.

"It must have been a shock," Violet said compassionately.

"Well, I wasn't around at the time," Hazel said simply. "And I don't shock easily."

Violet stared at her, sympathy frozen off at its source. Hazel, summoned by Sophie to be measured, crossed the room, and Violet hissed at us:

"I can't *believe* that girl! She's like a block of wood till you give her someone else's words to say. *Extraordinary*. She's terribly good, you know, Hugo. I'm going to have to pull my socks up."

"Hard to imagine you in anything as mundane as socks, Vi," Hugo said. "I think it's your turn." He nodded at Sophie.

"I gave my measurements in *ages* ago," Violet said fretfully. Walking over to Sophie, she held her arms out to the side with the air of a martyr preparing herself for crucifixion.

"Hang on a minute, Vi." Sophie took a long pull at her mug of coffee. "Sorry, but I'm on these anti-histamines for hay fever and if I don't keep drinking coffee they knock me out completely."

"Well, at least you're not sneezing all over me," Violet said in resigned tones.

"God, Vi, you have the tiniest waist," Sophie said enviously.

"She won't have for very much longer if she keeps mainlining biscuits," Hugo observed. "I'm eating the last one, Vi, to save your waistline."

"Bastard. I was saving that. Anyway, I'm inoculated against biscuits." Bending over, she said to Sophie: "I've got this *miracle* diet, darling. I'll tell you about it sometime in *private*." She shot a look of mock anger at Hugo. "Works like a treat, you can eat what*ever* you want."

"What's it called, the pig-out diet?" said Paul, the Lysander, braying with annoying laughter.

"You should hang out with Matthew," I said to him, "you've got exactly the same sense of humour."

Violet, not having been present when Matthew had made his awful pun on Goa, but realizing that I had taken her side, flashed a friendly smile at me. I was charmed despite myself.

"Why *do* you have to measure me all over again, Sophie?" she asked.

"I always double check," Sophie said, scribbling on her notepad, "since I discovered the hard way how optimistic people are about the size of their hips."

"Lucky you don't work for the Inland Revenue—think what would happen if you didn't take any self-assessments for granted," I observed.

Everyone in the room, self-employed to a man or woman, paled visibly at the fatal words "Inland Revenue." "Now that was *much* worse than saying *Macbeth*," I murmured to Hugo, who was rooted to the spot in horror himself. "What was it that I had to do with the vicar?"

"Only if I can watch," Hugo said, perking up immediately. "And I insist he wears his cassock throughout."

ooo

"Helen said she was going to be a bit late, so not to wait for her," Janey said, sliding into a seat opposite me.

"Shall we order for her? The church hall's just up the hill—she won't be that long."

"That means you're starving," Janey said. "All right. Just remember that I can see through your pathetic little attempts to deceive me. Let's have a look."

She opened the menu. I had already decided what I wanted ten minutes before while working my way through a bottle of Tsing-Tao beer. We were in a Chinese restaurant on Haverstock Hill, which specialized in vegetarian cuisine to the extent of offering mock-meat made out of gluten which the menu assured us was practically indistinguishable from the real thing. As Janey had deduced, I was very hungry, too hungry to risk a punt on a wild-card food choice: I intended to play safe. Janey, on the other hand, proceeded to run the gamut from mock-prawn sesame toast to mock-duck fillet. She was probably intending to finish with mock-banana fritters. We handed our menus back to the waiter.

"Bet yours is weird," I said supportively when he had gone.

"Change is necessary to the soul," Janey said gnomically. And indeed she looked different herself; her usual draperies of scarves and necklaces were missing, replaced by a single pendant at her neck, and instead of her equally loose, flowing shirts and shawls, she wore a fitted jacket and matching trousers.

"You look great, Janey," I said, leaning forward to examine her pendant, a moonstone.

"It's my birth stone," she said, fingering it and blushing slightly. "A present. I know you don't go in for astrology, but I think it suits me anyway, don't you?"

"Absolutely. And that yellow's lovely with your hair." I indicated the jacket.

Janey looked down at her suit. "I'm smartening up, aren't I? It's this new job."

"Oh, that explains the new light in your eyes."

It was true; she was positively glowing, her blue eyes shining like turquoises. Janey, who had been a script editor, had just moved to the BBC as a commissioning editor, a job she had been coveting for a long time now.

"It's the light of power," she said, grinning at me. "Look on my works, you mighty, and despair. I think I'm going to get my first drama serial green-lighted. There's this brilliant producer I've just met, really dynamic, a ball of fire, and she loves the idea. I got her to read the book it's based on over the weekend, and she rang me up today, very excited about it. We're going to meet and talk tomorrow."

"Janey, that's brilliant! A toast!" We clinked beer glasses.

"What's all this?" Helen said, pulling up a chair.

"Darling!" Janey, flushed, leant over to kiss her. "Have some beer, we're toasting to my meeting with Gita tomorrow!"

"Good luck," Helen said dutifully, raising her glass.

"How was the rehearsal?" Janey squeezed Helen's other hand. I had never seen her this affectionate with Helen, in public or in private. She was on cloud nine today.

"Oh, good, I think. I'm happy with what I'm doing. Hugo's really getting up my nose, though. He thinks he's so clever."

"He *is* clever," I was unable to resist saying.

"Oh well, if you like that kind of Oxbridge smart-arse messing around . . ." Helen drank some more beer. She had a bird-like face: her eyes were narrow greenish slits, her nose a sharp little beak, her mouth thin-lipped. By some alchemy of the camera this combination of features was very photogenic and she worked often in TV and commercials. "Hugo doesn't seem to take anything seriously."

"He's a good actor, though," Janey observed. "I saw him in *Ghosts*."

Helen's eyes narrowed still further. I didn't yet realize that actors loathe being told that people they don't like, or find difficult to work with, are good, no matter how self-evidently it may be true.

"He's all *right*, I suppose," she said vindictively. "Very mannered, though. And he's making Bill's life a misery. I like Bill, he's so down-to-earth. Our scenes are going really well."

"Bill is an awful old homophobe, though," I commented.

Janey raised her eyebrows.

"Well, he's fine with me," Helen said, "which is all I really care about. Have we ordered yet?"

The starters arrived. I polished off my hot and sour soup in a matter of minutes and nibbled through some spring rolls while Janey and Helen tackled the lettuce wraps of mock-minced pork and the mock-prawn toast.

"This is odd," Helen said after a mouthful of the mock-pork, "what is it?"

Janey pulled a shut-up face at me. "It's vegetable gluten. *Very* low calorie and good for you," she assured Helen.

"Oh really?" Helen took a big bite. "Since I haven't got the benefits of Violet's miracle diet, I've got to be careful. No biscuits for me." Helen was exuding venom from every pore this evening, but Janey seemed blissfully unaware of it, overwhelming her with affection and reassurance.

"Don't be silly, you're as slim as she is," she said soothingly. "You're looking lovely—isn't she, Sam? You could have anyone you wanted."

I blinked. "Absolutely," I said.

"Well, I think Philip Cantley likes me," Helen said, regaining her enthusiasm. "I dropped into the Cross yesterday morning and happened to bump into him, and he was very friendly."

"Why did you go round to the theatre?" Janey asked innocently. It seemed obvious to me that Helen had already given us her reason, but I waited with interest to see what excuse she would concoct.

"Oh," she said in her best elaborately casual tones, "I wanted to get an idea of the space. And I thought Sally might be there."

"Was he?" I chipped in evilly.

"No, actually," Helen said, shooting me a look which was for my consumption only. "But I thought he might be. Anyway, I was wandering round and I passed Philip's office, and the door was open, so I said hello, and he knew who I was at once, and asked me in for a coffee. Very friendly, like I said. He'd seen me in that *Peak Practice* episode I did."

"The one where you died?" I inquired.

"I lapsed into a coma," Helen corrected. "Very slowly. Anyway, he said he really liked my work. He was charming. Did you know that he's directing *A Doll's House*, the show after next?"

This question was clearly addressed to Janey, who shook her head.

"You know I'm not that up on theatre stuff."

"Well, anyway, he is." Helen pronounced this very significantly. One had to admire her tactics: she had obviously tracked Philip Cantley down to his office, waited outside till she was sure that he wasn't with someone or talking on the phone, contrived a meeting, and elicited the piece of information of most interest to herself. In her underhand way, Helen was a smooth operator. I doubted there was much she would rule out in the pursuit of a good role. Look at the affair she had had with Kurt.

"Do you think I'd make a good Nora?" she was asking Janey now. There was only one possible response, and Janey duly made it.

"Darling, of course! You'd be wonderful."

We were onto the main course now. Yielding to an impulse of gastronomic research, I leaned over and tried the mock-sweet and sour pork, which wasn't too bad, probably because all I could taste was the sauce, and then the mock-duck, which resembled its original so eerily, even to the texture, that I could hardly get it down. Ditto with the mock-lemon chicken. I returned to my crispy deep-fried tofu roll-your-own pancakes with all my prejudices confirmed.

"I might read the play," Helen said thoughtfully. "Of course I told Philip I had already. He's a very charismatic person."

Janey, rather than exhibiting any understandable jealousy, was positively beaming on Helen's industry. After what had happened with Kurt, I was surprised. But then I reflected that perhaps Janey considered that the more open Helen was about her stratagems, the less likely she was to be planning a *Doll's House*–inspired affair with Philip Cantley. It wasn't my business, in any case. All I could do was hang around, cock my shoulder for Janey to cry on—should it become necessary—and try hard to avoid saying either "I told you so" or "I saw it coming from the start."

"I can't really remember the play," Helen was saying. "But it's the name part, anyway. I mean, that's got to be good."

It would be interesting to see the limits of Philip Cantley's susceptibility. Certainly, he had come at once to Violet's rescue when MM might have sacked her; but the lead part in a play he was directing and Hermia in a production helmed by a freelance director are two very different things.

The waiter passed close to our table.

"Could we have another couple of beers, please, and some egg-fried rice?" I said. I was getting back into the swing of society with frightening ease. Why, I might even have some plum wine later on. There was no end to my excesses.

"And *this*," said Bez with what seemed to me disproportionate pride, "is the fly floor."

It was a narrow gallery, running along one wall high up above the stage. Along its edge was a wooden parapet nearly as high as my shoulder, topped with a rail as thick as a balustrade. It was like standing in a pit. Just to be able to crane over it I had to hop up onto a shelf built onto the parapet, on which were stacked large quantities of what looked like iron ingots. Actually they were steel and lead, each one of the latter nearly half my weight, which made me feel positively fragile for a change.

"Right," Bez was saying. He indicated the series of cables running down the wall side of the gallery as if they were part of a giant musical instrument, tightly strung and taut as piano wire, thickly woven and strong. "These run up to the ceiling grid. Each one goes through a pulley and then down to the bars."

"The bars the scenery's slung on?"

"Yeah, you could put it like that. Have a look over the pin rail again."

Obediently I clambered up onto the shelf once more and looked down through the maze of hanging bars to the stage below.

"Those are aluminium. We call 'em ally bars," Bez said, leaning over and flicking with his fingernail one of the many poles which were slung on hawsers, running from this gallery to the other one on the opposite wall. Most were empty; the set for *Virginia Woolf* was fixed, and the only thing suspended was from the cyclorama, a curved bar which ran round the rear of the set, holding the backdrop with its thousand-pound load of fake ivy. From time to time the bars trembled slightly, light catching then slipping off their sides, finding little purchase on the dull metal. It was oddly mesmeric.

"Those are lead," Bez said prosaically, pointing out the thicker ones. "Gas barrels, they're called. You might as well learn the lingo."

I was concentrating more on the two fixed bridges that ran from one side of the pin rail to the other, a couple of feet below the rim. Steel hawsers ran along each side, attached to metal uprights which were soldered to the grid high above our heads. The whole effect reminded me of the rope bridge in *Indiana Jones*; it looked just as flimsy and precarious.

"This is what Marie will use to reach the mobile?" I said, walking over to where one of the bridges was bolted on to the parapet.

"Yeah. But she'll have her own line, already attached to the safety harness. She climbs onto the mobile and goes down with it, but she's on a separate line. Got to be that way for safety, see?"

"But she can't hold onto this cable as it goes down," I said, fingering one of the hawsers, "even if it's inside a hemp rope. She'll cut her hands to pieces."

"No, we'll pad that up for her, don't you worry." Bez continued: "Right, so the flyman up here takes the mobile down by pulling on the hawser it's attached to."

"How does he see when it's in the right place? I mean, he'll have his back to the stage. He won't be looking at anything but the hawser, and those are all against the wall."

Bez looked surprised. "The flymen've been doing this for years, haven't they? It's second nature to them. Still, they've all got headsets, so if they do cock up the DSM can shout at them, get them to adjust a bit. That's the deputy stage manager. I keep forgetting you're new to this. All right. Then if Marie's travelling on one of 'em, the mobiles I mean, her line's operated from down below, on the deck."

"The deck." My head was swimming.

"The stage. Last century, y'see, all the flymen were sailors. Well, they were used to hauling on ropes all the time, weren't they? Makes sense. So a lot of the terms are from on board ship."

"Why isn't Marie's personal line being hauled by the person—fly-man—standing next to the flyman who's moving the mobile she's holding onto? That way they'd be in perfect synch."

"No way!" Bez looked shocked. "When people are flying it's always done from down on the deck. That way you can see your flyer coming down. It's much safer. Still, the bloke from the stage crew who's control-ling her line will be talking on his headset to the bloke who's doing her mobile, right? So they're working together. Is she just going to come straight down, or go at an angle?"

"I don't know," I said, leaning over the pin rail, trying to imagine the vertiginous descent Marie would soon be making, through a maze of ally bars and gas barrels with their attendant lines, past the blazing lights, through the dark and down onto the stage at last. The mere thought sent the adrenaline racing through my veins. "Thierry, the choreographer, will work all that out. Why?"

"Cos if she's coming down at an angle, she'll need someone else on deck. One to take her down, one to haul her from side to side."

"Jesus, it's complicated," I sighed. "I had this idea that everything would be done by computer nowadays."

"No frigging way!" Bez looked very amused. "Cost a fortune and it'd break down all the time. Only place you'd get a computerized system would be at Covent Garden, something like that, and it's a bloody night-mare, I can tell you. You should hear some of the stories."

"I thought we could take all four fairies down on mobiles, but Sally explained that'd be eight flymen at least."

"We've got five at most," Bez said, "and that's not bad."

"It's like bell-ringing," I observed, "standing here through the perfor-mance, hauling ropes up and down."

"I don't think you'd get many of 'em taking that up as a hobby," Bez said. "Too much of a busman's holiday. Seen all you want to up here?"

I looked at him, biting my lip.

"Do you know," I said slowly, "I'd really like to get on one of those bridges for a moment. Would that be OK?"

"Don't get vertigo, do you?"

"Only when I take it out on video."

"Very funny. Don't go too far, will you, or I'll get into trouble. You should really have a harness, but the lads don't usually bother."

Bez having warned me yesterday to wear sensible shoes, I was in my rubber-soled Timberland rip-offs, which squeaked on the steel beneath me but held reassuringly firm. Having swung my legs over the pin rail and onto the bridge, I took hold of the hawsers on either side and started walking, at first warily, then with increasing confidence. The steel plank wavered only slightly under my weight. Squatting down, I leaned over the edge. The blood rushed to my head, which was spinning with elation, the thrill of heights, of risk. The lights around me beat on my face, heavy as the tropical sun. I stood up and turned around—look, no hands—feeling like a tightrope walker, or a trapeze artist, suspended thirty-five feet above the stage, a tiny speck in the middle of nothing. Looking down at the bars level with my feet, I wanted to dive through them, swinging from one to another like a gymnast.

"Oi! You're enjoying that too much!" Bez called, leaning over the rail with a shit-eating grin on his face.

"Sam?" yelled a familiar voice from below. "I can see right up your skairt."

"No way, you liar," I called back smugly. "It's too tight."

With reluctance, I made my way back to the gallery, swinging myself over without the aid of Bez's helping hand. Lycra miniskirts were one of the greatest inventions of the twentieth century.

"Pervert," I yelled over the edge at Sally.

"I know, *cara,*" he called back. I was sure he was batting his eyelashes; I was just too high up to see them.

"Right, that's settled that," said Bez, "I'm not taking you up to the grid, you'd be climbing all over it like a monkey." He pointed up to where it hung, just below the ceiling. "But that's where we rig up the lines, OK? That's where the pulleys are."

"Nothing could go wrong, could it?" I said, still half-delirious from my catwalk on the gantry. "Get caught, I mean. Stuck."

. Bez looked horrified. "No way. No way. I mean," he said more carefully, "if a bar wasn't properly rigged, say, it could get caught on another bar, or the fly rail."

"Or a mobile, or a person? Could they get caught?"

"Well, technically someone could get stuck," Bez said, with extreme reluctance. "But—and this is a big but, OK—it just wouldn't happen. I check all the ropes before every performance. The flymen'd know at once, too, by the feel of the rope, if it was too heavily weighted, say. There'd be too much friction on it. It's never happened. So let's not worry, right?"

"Right, Cap'n Bez." I saluted.

He indicated the Jacob's ladder, made of iron and a mere foot wide, fixed to the far wall, running from floor to ceiling. This was one of the main access points of the theatre; on it the crew climbed right up to the grid, fifty feet above the ground, or down through a hole in the gallery, past the hawsers, down onto the stage.

"Down you go," he said. "Don't have to worry about your head for heights, do I? Like a duck to water."

○○○

I jumped the last few rungs and landed square at the bottom, enjoying the effort. In front of me were Sally and a young man about my age with a nice square face and a sensible manner. He wore wire-rimmed glasses and his mouth was pleasantly curved.

"Hi, I'm Ben Sabot," he said, shaking my hand. His own was as square as the rest of him, with spatulate fingers, the kind pig-ignorant people always refer to as sculptor's hands. Not that this was his fault. He wore a turtle-necked sweater and battered old chinos, and projected the same kind of reassuring air of competence as MM did, though at a lower wattage. "I'm the AD here. Assistant director," he added helpfully. "I'm sort of Philip's second-in-command."

"Ben did this latest piece of crap," Bez said, coming down the ladder behind me and nodding to the *Virginia Woolf* set. "Managed to con most of the papers into giving him good reviews, as well. Don't know what the world's coming to."

Ben grinned. "Bez's been at the Cross since the dawn of time," he said cheerfully. "He won't take me seriously till I've been here for at least ten years."

"Practically my first job, this was, when I finished my apprenticeship," Bez said proudly. "Charge hand to the master carpenter, worked my way up to deputy—we had one in those days, before the cuts."

"So Lurch'll have your job in a decade or so?" I suggested.

Bez gave me an appreciative look. "Perish the thought. Perish the frigging thought. Not unless I spend most of the time kicking some sense into his thick head."

"I saw you up there on that gantry," Ben said to me, shoving his hands into his pockets and rocking on his heels. "Didn't you get dizzy?"

"I loved it," I admitted. "It made me want to take up trapeze."

"Had to yell at her to make her come back," Bez said. "She'd be a great rigger if she hadn't been born the wrong sex."

"Piss off, you old dinosaur. I'm pretty strong," I said, unoffended.

"Not like you, eh, Ben?" Bez said, teasing each of us in turn. "Talk about vertigo—he makes Jimmy Stewart look like Sylvester Stallone in *Cliffhanger*."

"I have problems with the Jacob's ladder," Ben confessed, looking as abashed as a schoolboy. He had a good way with Bez, I noticed, confident enough to allow Bez to take the piss a little. There was no sense that he was standing on his dignity as AD. I could see that Bez liked him and I understood why. "Got to be done every so often, but that's my limit. Just as long as I don't look up or down."

"Bet you scamper around like a monkey," Bez said to Sally. "You look enough like one."

"Say that to me een Sicily and see what 'appens," Sally said, playing up his accent for dramatic effect.

"Ben? Ben!" called a voice from the stage.

"By the desk," Ben called back. "Just coming."

Philip Cantley rounded the masking flat and stood there, staring at us. He had an extraordinary ability to make innocent people feel as if they had been caught out in a misdemeanour; what his effect would be on a criminal discovered in the act, I could only speculate. He would have made an excellent policeman, inquisitor or headmaster of a boys' school—racking and caning a speciality. His black eyes snapped angrily; his voice was dry.

"I've been looking for you," he said to Ben as if no-one else were present. "We need to have that casting conversation."

"Coming, Philip," Ben said, with almost stagey deferentiality. "Shall we get a coffee?" To the rest of us he said: "Catch you round," and as Philip Cantley turned on his heel he gave us a wink before darting after the great man. They went into the little stage manager's office, just offstage, laid out with the props for that evening's performance, but also supplied with the only decent coffee machine the theatre possessed.

"This is where Marie's controller'll stand," Bez said to me and Sally, indicating a spot a few feet back from the deputy stage manager's desk, from which most of the show was run. "He'll have a headset, like I said. The hawser'll come down from the fly floor and he'll hook it to the wall when it's not in use."

"What happens to her line when she's down on deck?" I said.

"She undoes the clip that's holding it to her harness and it gets whipped up, straight out of sight. Fast as winking." He mimed pulling back a line with a sharp tug of both hands, whistling through his teeth to simulate the sound of a steel hawser shooting up to the grid.

"All right," I said slowly. "I think I've got the basic idea."

"Nice one," Bez said. "When's Marie due in?"

"This afternoon. I'd better get down to the mole hole and finish off the prototype. Then we'll sling it up there, just a few feet off the floor, so she can do some jumps on and off and see how it feels."

"Rather her than me," Bez said dryly.

"Oh, Marie's done everysing," Sally said. "Trapeze, saircus school, acrobatics. Thees'll be peess eeeesy to hair."

Sometimes Sally's fluent English, coupled with his accent, produced unintentionally comic effects. Bez and I doubled up with laughter, Sally staring at us resentfully.

"I said eet right, deedn't I?" he said crossly.

Still laughing, Bez and I nodded in unison.

"Then what ees so funny? *Bastardi che non siete altro.*"

Sally flounced away. I followed him, giggling.

As I walked past the stage manager's office, I pricked up my ears. Ben and Philip were discussing the casting of *A Doll's House*.

"Actually, there's someone in the *Dream* cast who'd be very good," Ben was saying. "The Helena. She's called Hazel Duffy. I saw a rehearsal and was really impressed. So's MM."

"Never heard of her," Philip Cantley snapped.

"I think she's just out of drama school," Ben said easily. "But give her a chance to audition, anyway. You'll be surprised. I know you've already got the Nora pretty much worked out, but she'd be just as good as Christine."

"Hmm. She's not the only one in that cast we're auditioning, you know."

"Of course. I've got her down already. Look, I had a great idea for Krogstad. . . ."

The voices faded as I passed the door. Ben's self-assurance was impressive; like Bez, he wasn't intimidated by Philip Cantley's blustering manner. But I was more interested in who, out of the *Dream* cast, Ben had already noted down for the *Doll's House* auditions. The way he had spoken indicated that there was only one other actress worth considering. Had he seen Helen in rehearsal too? Or did she know that Ben might be a useful person to cultivate? Helen hadn't mentioned bumping into Ben when she'd dropped into the Cross yesterday; in fact, she hadn't mentioned him at all.

○○○

I was halfway down the stairs to the basement when a woman put her head out of a door on the landing. She looked like a cross between a head librarian and a local councillor: dressed by Jaeger, neat Tory wife haircut, her glasses suspended round her neck on a gold and tortoiseshell chain. Her manner was brisk and pleasant.

"You must be Sam," she said. "I've heard all about you. I'm Margery Pickett, the administrator here. Nice to meet you."

She shook my hand. Hers was cool and dry. "Would you mind just popping into my office for a moment?" she continued. "It really won't take long."

Margery Pickett had clearly been lying in wait for me. Curious, if rather wary, I followed her into the office. It was such a contrast to the chipped linoleum flooring and bare fluorescent light of the corridors that I stopped on the threshold, blinking with surprise. The Margery Pickett Luxury Suite had a state-of-the art workstation, a coffee table rich with magazines and bordered by two very comfortable-looking armchairs, a window onto the outside world lined with beautifully kept plants, a yucca tree in one corner of the office and a fitted carpet in a warm shade of peach. Through a door on the right I could see a storage room which was neatly stacked with files from floor to ceiling and looked entirely dust free. In the far corner was a small and spotless kitchen area, equipped with a microwave oven, cafetière and electric kettle. She probably kept the food processor and mouli-légumes under the sink.

"Wow. This place is *House Beautiful*," I said. "I feel like I just walked through a magic door into a showplace for the *Homes and Gardens* exhibition."

She laughed. "How kind of you to say so. Would you like a cup of coffee? I make it fresh."

"I expected nothing less. No thanks, I'm fine."

"Well, do sit down." She indicated one of the armchairs. "I like your outfit. So practical."

I blinked; in my tight T-shirt and Lycra skirt I had about as much in common with Jaeger Woman as I did with Nancy Reagan. Usually I have a highly developed sense of irony, but the Pickett threw me off-balance; I certainly wasn't going to ask her whether she'd meant that as a compliment. Giving her a cheek-creasing smile, I sat down as decorously as possible and waited for her to make her point. Already I was sure that there would be some kind of point.

A few minutes of small talk followed, during which I was informed that Margery Pickett had popped downstairs to see Puck's mobile and thought it looked wonderful, though she understood of course that it was still a work in progress. She did hope I didn't mind her having taken a look. Having collected the necessary reassurances, she progressed to a series of pre-planned questions about my career to date, explaining that she had heard that I had an exhibition coming up and thought that it would be useful to put me in touch with the theatre's publicists. My collaboration with this production sounded like it would be perfect for an article in the *Guardian's* theatre section.

By this time, I had some inkling of where the chitchat was heading. In an attempt to cut through any more circumlocutions, neatly executed though they were, I said:

"They might want to pull out an article about me in the *Herald*, about six months back."

"Oh, the *Herald* did an interview with you?" Margery said, putting on her glasses and making a note of this. I thought this was over-egging the pudding slightly, but it made a neat touch.

"Not quite. I'm surprised no-one's told you about it."

I stared at her. Behind the lenses, her eyes, slightly magnified, flickered slightly, and I knew that she was perfectly well aware of what I was talking about. Clever woman that she was, she made the decision not to feign complete ignorance.

"I must admit I did hear something I was wanting to confirm with you. A rumour, really . . . I didn't read the article. I don't normally get the *Herald*. But it was about a sculpture of yours, wasn't it? A mobile like the ones you're making for us."

Margery Pickett took off her glasses and looked at me. Her eyes were hazel, carefully made-up, and very clear.

"It killed someone, didn't it, this mobile, after you had installed it? It was hanging in place when it fell on someone's head and killed him."

○○○

Margery Pickett was absolutely within her rights. If I had been a theatre administrator and found out that there was a sculptor on my premises who had made a mobile which had smashed someone's head in—a sculptor who had now been commissioned to make some near-identical mobiles for a production in her theatre—I too would have wanted to be reassured about health and safety standards.

But I would have asked straight out. I wouldn't have pitty-patted around the subject in ever decreasing circles, made anodyne remarks about the sculptor in question's fashion choices or feigned more ignorance on the subject than I really possessed. Naturally it was a sore spot with me, and talking about it was like digging a thumb into the bruise. That granted, I still violently disliked her chosen method of approach.

"The mobile was dropped deliberately on someone's head," I snapped. "Not by me. The police proved that to their own satisfaction. It was perfectly well secured and the bank where it happened didn't sue me. The *Herald* article covers most of the ground, and has a photograph of me looking artistic and meaningful to boot. Does that cover all your questions?"

I stood up. Margery Pickett got to her feet, looking concerned.

"I'm terribly sorry," she said, "I seem to have offended you."

"You should have asked me straight away."

She looked at me. "Yes, I should, shouldn't I? I see that now. But I've been at this theatre for probably almost as long as you've been in the world, and I tend to think of its reputation as synonymous with my own. It's been a very large part of my life. That's no excuse for putting my foot in it, of course. Will you accept my apologies?"

Frankness like this went some way towards melting my resentment. I nodded.

"You shouldn't have any problems with the insurance," I said shortly. "And the publicists will have a field day, if they tackle it right."

"Sensation junkies wanting to see if a mobile drops on anyone's head?" Margery Pickett suggested, smiling. "They always say that most people go to circuses in the hope that the tightrope walker will fall. Not a mentality I like, particularly." She coughed. "It must have been rather distressing for you at the time. The accident, I mean. Or rather, not an accident."

"Actually, it wasn't a problem for me," I said coolly. "I knew the mobile was safe. When I hang something, it stays hung."

Hearing those words issuing from my mouth was the last straw. Not only had I taken up an attitude with my arms folded across my chest and my legs akimbo, but now I was sounding as macho as John Wayne crossed with Tank Girl. To Margery Pickett's considerable surprise, I lost it completely.

"Sorry," I said through my giggles, "I just *heard* myself. . . ."

And, to my great surprise, I found myself wishing that Hugo were here to take the piss out of me. Making an idiot of yourself lacks a certain spice if there isn't anyone present who can be counted on to remind you of it later, preferably when you're drunk and vulnerable.

The total collapse of any pretensions I had to dignity settled matters nicely. Margery and I made peace. She would be setting the publicists on my heels in the near-future, and also, I had no doubt, checking up on what I had told her. In that too she was absolutely within her rights. She stressed that I should ask her if there were anything I needed, and drop in for coffee any time I wanted to. I thought I might exercise the latter option every so often. After all, she made her coffee fresh. And I had seen a biscuit tin on the counter top. Not much gets past me, not when biscuits are involved.

In fact, she offered coffee once more, but I declined regretfully. I really had to do some work on Puck's mobile before Marie started trying to execute *jetées* from it.

"Well, any time you're passing," she said. "And I do like your T-shirt, by the way. I could tell you didn't believe me before."

I looked down at my front. Across my bosom was plastered the slogan: "Faster, Pussycat! Kill! Kill!" Margery was smiling at me as a tolerant aunt would at a rebellious member of the younger generation. I would have blushed if I'd known how.

I just hoped that, in the course of her researches, she didn't find out about the time I had killed someone. For some reason I had the feeling that it might make her suspicious of me all over again.

The linoleum in the corridor and the dirty paint peeling from the walls were a culture shock after Margery's cosy little den. Reflecting how quickly we become used to bourgeois comforts, I trotted downstairs to renew my acquaintance with the living standards of the proletariat. Lurch was playing my tape again, "A Boy Named Sue" blaring out from the speakers. The sound was good quality and there was more than enough of it; in common with many other theatres, the Cross had scored heavily on lottery funds a few years previously, with the usual proviso that the grant be spent on structural improvements. This had been interpreted loosely enough to include a violently expensive, super-powerful stereo for the crew, not to mention new sofas in the staff room.

> *Well, he must have thought it was quite a joke,*
> *And it got lots of laughs from lots of folks*
> *It seems I had to fight my whole life through.*
>
> *Some gal would giggle and I'd get red,*
> *And some guy would laugh and I'd bust his head,*
> *I tell you, life ain't easy for a boy named Sue.*

The studio audience was hooting with laughter by this time.

> *(Well,) I grew up quick and I grew up mean,*
> *My fist got hard and my wits got keen.*
> *Roamed from town to town to hide my shame.*

> *But I made me a vow to the moon and stars,*
> *I'd search the honky tonks and bars*
> *And kill the man that give me that awful name.*

At this point Lurch, seeing me come in, turned down the volume and said earnestly:

"I made a copy of your tape, Sam. Put it back on your workbench. That's all right, innit?"

"Of course it is, you twat. I'll bring in some more you might like."

Lurch beamed. I had already worked out that, due to some flaw in his upbringing, he felt most at ease when people were swearing at him or getting him to do unpleasant tasks. Maybe, on reflection, it wasn't a flaw at all, and his parents had programmed him deliberately; certainly it made him eminently employable.

"I like this one best," he said.

"You won't know that till you've listened to the others, will you? Stupid prat."

Lurch's beam was now at full wattage.

"Um, is there anything wants doing?" he said. "Bez said you was up against it."

I got him to do some routine and boring soldering. He was better at it than I was, anyway. I wondered if Bez would sell him to me when I had finished here. Or maybe we could do a swap: I got Lurch and Bez got—well, I had an old oxyacetylene torch kicking round the studio somewhere which was probably worth a bit as an antique by now. . . .

"Hello? Sam?" Faintly, through the great rolling chords of Depeche Mode on a particularly miserable day—the members of the band had probably forgotten to stagger the timing of their overdoses—I could hear a little voice calling my name.

"Oi! Lurch!" I waved my hands in front of my face to attract his attention and mimed turning the music down. In the resultant silence the voice called again:

"Sam? Are you down there?"

"Marie!" I squinted at the mobile and shrugged. We were out of time: it would have to do. "Yeah, working away. Come down."

"Fancy a cuppa?" Lurch said to Marie as she appeared round the side of his workbench. I favoured the boy with an approving smile: his manners were shaping up very nicely.

"Not yet, thanks. Maybe after I've finished jumping around."

She came right up to the mobile, which we had hung over a convenient RSJ. It was low, only a couple of feet off the floor, and Marie walked all the way round it without saying a word. Lurch's gaze met mine; we were waiting for her verdict.

She started to unwrap her usual layers of jackets and wrap-over cardigans. Marie was like an onion: all outer skins and very little core.

"Um, what do you think?" I said finally, when she was down to leggings and leotard.

She looked at me blankly. "Of what? Oh, the mobile! I won't know till I'm on it. I find that with most equipment. You can't tell that much by looking at it."

Behind her back, Lurch made the gesture of someone strangling a chicken. He had been working very hard on this so-called piece of equipment for the past couple of hours, down to nicking me some strands of ivy from a corner of the cyclorama, spray-painting them silver and drilling holes in the structure through which to weave them. Clearly there was no point explaining to Marie that I had been asking for an aesthetic judgement. That was provided a short while later by Sally, who came in just as Marie had stepped from a chair held by Lurch to the mobile itself. Twining herself experimentally around the hawser, she looked like another piece of ivy, as delicate and strong.

"Beautiful!" Sally exclaimed, with gratifying conviction.

"Really?" Marie said, untwisting herself. "Did that look good? Or should I lean back a bit when I do that?"

"I meant the mobile, Marie. But what you are doing ees lovely too."

"Does it feel comfortable?" I asked. "I mean, as comfortable as you could feel in the circumstances."

Marie lifted one foot, then the other, from the indentations I had made for her, till she was hanging by her hands from the cable. We had wrapped gaffer tape around it to protect her palms.

"Yes, it feels quite well balanced," she said, setting her feet back into place. "I've known worse. Much worse."

I decided to take this as a compliment. Marie was leaning back now, one foot set into its groove, the other stretched out in a wide and generous arabesque behind her. She removed one hand from the cable and caught the foot of the outstretched leg, pulling it back into an exaggerated curve which was echoed by the cable itself, bending under the tension like a bowstring. Lurch watched, jaw dropped, all antagonism forgotten, as she swarmed up the hawser, her feet in their flimsy ballet slippers wrapping around the cable as if they were pliable as rubber. Now she was bent right back, hanging almost upside down, knees locked around the cable, her limbs as strong and flexible as the tensile steel core of the hawser itself.

It was as if she were quite unaware of our presence; she executed the moves with complete disregard for any audience she might have, interested solely in exploring the limits of the equipment and of her own body. Finally she slid back down the rope. Poised on the mobile like a bird on a branch, she spread her arms wide as if she were about to make a swallow dive, and jumped off.

It was not a success. The mobile, though secure enough, offered little purchase as a launching pad, and the jump turned into a sort of twisted hop. She landed half on her hands, springing up again almost at once, but ruefully.

"I really need a line to take me down," she said. "If I work it right, whoever's pulling me can take me up and a bit sideways, so it looks like I'm jumping off."

"Are you all right?" Bez said. I hadn't noticed him come in. "It looked great up there."

"Thanks. I'll have to get Thierry in as well, to work out stuff. But it's basically fine, Sam. You've got the ivy low down enough so my feet don't get caught in it."

"That was the idea." Lurch and I exchanged a glance of mutual congratulation.

Marie pushed her hair back from her face and then gasped, fiddling with the lobe of her ear.

"My earring! I've lost one of my earrings . . . Oh God, I don't believe it. I know I had it on this morning—"

"I heard something drop when you was up on the mobile," Lurch volunteered. "Didn't think nothing of it at the time. It was sort of over here. . . ."

He ducked to the ground. In a flash, Marie was on her knees beside him.

"It looks like this," she said, turning her head so he could see the remaining pearl stud. "They were my grandma's. I practically never take them off."

"Must've come loose when you was hanging upside down," Lurch said. "OK, if it was going to roll, it'd've gone over here. There's a bit of a slope."

They shuffled across the filthy floor on their knees, heroically ignoring the sawdust, iron filings, offcuts of wire and general debris except to filter through them in a search for the earring. At last Lurch let out a cry of triumph.

"Look there! It's caught in the hinge. Hold on."

Near the far wall there was a wooden trap, set flush to the floor, its metal rim dulled with age. The earring had lodged itself between the hinges; Lurch must have very sharp eyes. I would never have seen it.

"What's down below?" I said to Bez.

"Just the sump. Bloody great basement down there, be great for storage. But we can't use it, can we, cos it's flooded the whole time. We're too close to the canal. Stinks of drains, too, and I wouldn't be surprised if there were rats. I hear a bit of scrabbling every now and then."

"Lovely. Sounds like something out of *Quatermass and the Pit.*"

The earring was firmly wedged in the hinge. Lurch was trying to prise it out with a bit of wire, but to no avail.

"I'll lift the trap, so's to ease the hinge up a bit," he said to Marie. "You fiddle it out with this, OK?"

Suiting the action to the word, he unbolted the trap, swearing as he forced back the rusty catch.

"Put a bit of wrist action into it, Lurchie," Bez recommended, "it ain't been opened since the dawn of time."

Lurch heaved up the trap, balancing it uncomfortably on his wrists.

"Weighs a ton!" he panted. "Get a move on, will yer?"

Taking a piece of wood from Bez's work-bench, I shoved it under the trap, wedging it open. Lurch eased down the heavy cover with a sigh of relief. But Marie, working her piece of wire with frantic haste, was in too much of a hurry. Just as the earring came loose from the hinge, she shot out her other hand to catch it and instead knocked it through the crack and down into the void below. A horrified silence fell, punctuated only by the tinest of plops as the earring fell into the water.

Grimaces were exchanged around the group. Marie was staring at the crack in the hinge as if unable to believe her eyes. Then she jumped to her feet, dragged the trap up by a great effort of will, and threw it open. It hit the floor with a heavy clang. By that time Marie was already into the square opening and climbing down the iron ladder below, hand over hand.

"Stop!" Bez, propelled by urgency, shot across the room and knelt down by the side of the trap. "Come back up here! Didn't you hear me before? (Silly mare)," he added for our benefit. "There's rats down there and God knows what!"

"Alligators breeding in the swamps of the Cross theatre," I observed. "We can test whether all publicity is good publicity."

"I can't see anything," Marie wailed dolefully, her voice echoing off the damp stone. "And there's a horrible smell. . . . Aah!"

Bez rolled his eyes. "What did I tell you? (Rat's got her ankle)," he added to us. "Will you get your arse back up here now, girl?"

Marie's face appeared in the opening, her mobile little features stretched like india-rubber across her bones in shock. The smell of drains and decay rose about her. If it had been a perfume it would have been described as having rich, sweet top notes, with undertones of swamp. For the first time I understood the full significance of the word "miasma."

"There's something down there!" she said, her voice thin and shaky.

"Course there bloody is! Lucky they didn't take a bite out of you," Bez said. "Could you see 'em?"

"What? No, I don't mean rats. . . ." She was trembling. Lurch leaned out to help her up, but she shook off his hand. "It's much bigger than that. . . ."

She ducked down into the opening again. In the silence we could hear her hands moving down the iron rungs of the ladder, which creaked and groaned even under her light weight.

"I just hope that ladder's still OK. Probably more rust than anything else by now," Bez said. "No-one's been down there for donkey's years. What's her name? Marie? Look, Marie, come out of it, will you, there's a good girl." He leant over the edge of the trap. There was no answer, only the sound of water dripping onto stone. "If that ladder breaks you'll go into the water and we'll have to haul you out. Won't be much fun for anyone."

"Unless she gets eaten by the alligator first," I offered.

"I saw a film about that," Lurch added. "They lived in the sewers, didn't they? These crocs, I mean. One got loose from the zoo years back, and they been breeding ever since. Came up through the toilets and bit people's arses off."

"Oh, for God's *sake*," I said, temporarily distracted from the eerie silence Marie was maintaining down in the sump. "How could an alligator get up the U-bend in a toilet? Don't be so bloody stupid."

"They was small, wasn't they?" Lurch persisted. "Specially bred."

"Trained, too, I expect," Bez said sarcastically. "Team of mad scientists down there teaching them how to jump up out of the bog and take a munch on some bloke having a pee—"

Sally, thoroughly exasperated by this discussion, pushed forward and knelt down by the opening himself.

"Marie! Are you all right?" he called.

A long pause followed. Then a small voice, strangely magnified by the echoes on the stone, said:

"It's . . . it's floating not that far from me . . ."

"Where are you?"

"On the ladder. Nearly at the bottom . . ."

"Anyway," I hissed to Lurch, "it would have to be two alligators escaped from the zoo. Otherwise how could they breed? Duh."

"Get a torch, will you, Lurchie?" said Bez. "Dark as the pit down there."

He shone the torch straight down. It picked out Marie's face, which turned up to us briefly, like a fish showing its white underbelly, then dropped again, her dark hair blending into the shadows.

"Try to shine it into the middle," I said. "Marie, why don't you come up now?" She seemed frozen to the spot in terror. It couldn't be vertigo, not after her performance on the mobile—which ruled out the least unpleasant explanation for her state of shock. I thought that Marie had a pretty good idea of what was down there with her.

Bez directed the torch beam away from Marie. Its light hardly kindled a gleam on the surface of the water, which looked as dark and thick as oil. But then it began to pick out something, a pale shape which hung low in the water, its outlines so bloated and swollen that we could hardly see what it had been—

Suddenly Marie started screaming, her cries as sharp and high and unearthly as seagulls after prey. It was a horrible sound. We all jumped, and Bez dropped the torch; it hit the water with a heavy plock and went out. The shape disappeared. Marie's shrieks intensified.

"It's Violet!" she was screaming. "It's Violet and she's dead! She's drowned! Oh—oh—"

There was a scrabbling noise, the rending of iron, and a splash. The screams cut out as abruptly as they had started. Marie had fallen into the water, and it sounded as if the ladder had gone down with her.

"And Marie Lavelle insisted on going down the ladder?"

"She went down straight away, before anyone could stop her."

"Oh, so someone tried to stop her? Who was that?"

"No-one in particular," I said, giving the WPC a very straight look. "But apparently there were rats, and it stank to high heaven. Of course, now we know why. . . . If she hadn't been in so much of a hurry, I'd have suggested that she get a pair of Wellingtons, at least. Though as it turned out she'd have needed waders. It was pretty deep down there."

"Right," said the WPC, scribbling, "let me just run through the order of events. Marie Lavelle goes down the ladder, comes up to say there's something down there, goes back to check, starts screaming when she sees the body in the light of the torch, and falls off the ladder."

"It broke," I corrected. "At first I thought the whole thing had come off the wall, which would have been a disaster. Bez said earlier that it was pretty rusty. But as it turned out, only the rung she was standing on had come away. Bez rigged up an arc light pointing down into the hole so we could see what we were doing, and then I went down with a rope and got it round her. They pulled her up and I pushed her from behind. She couldn't have managed it on her own; all she could do was shiver. They've taken her off to the hospital, haven't they? I hope they're testing her for everything," I added. "That water was unbelievably disgusting, and her head went under when she fell in. She's probably contracted bubonic plague by now."

The WPC closed her notebook. "All right, Miss Jones—"

"Mzzz," I said firmly.

"Ms. Jones, that's all for now. Thank you very much. Would you drop into the station tomorrow to make a formal statement? It shouldn't take long. Say mid-afternoon? Just ask for me at the desk and I'll be straight out."

"Sure." I uncrossed my legs and got down from the work-bench on which I'd been sitting. "I don't envy them trying to get that up," I observed, looking over at the cluster of police officials gathered round the opening of the trap. The longer it was open, the more evident the stench. "I take it we can come back to work in here tomorrow?"

"That should be fine, yes. We'll have the body up by then."

"Rather you than me."

Bez was deep in debate with another PC about the positioning of the winch. Interesting as this was from a technical point of view, I found other considerations kept creeping into my imagination, such as noxious gases stored in the stomach and the inevitable downpour of filthy water and fluids from the corpse as it came up. Looking around the room, I fixed on Sally, who was curled up in a ball on one of the staff room sofas, chain-smoking. The blood had drained from his face, leaving it sallow and unhealthy.

I jerked my head towards the stairs. "Shall we get going?"

He jumped up with alacrity. On the way up we passed Philip Cantley coming down the stairs, Ben at his heels, both of them almost paralysed with shock and disbelief. This followed a pattern I had observed before; under extreme pressure men tended to go numb, while women either became inhumanly practical or went completely to pieces. Marie, obviously enough, was in the second category, while Margery Pickett provided a perfect example of the first. As soon as we had retrieved Marie, Bez had gone to tell Margery to phone the police, and having done that she was downstairs at once, jacket sleeves rolled up, coaxing some hot tea into a near-comatose and trembling Marie.

"I've been meaning to have that basement drained off for years," Margery had kept repeating, in the tones of one who felt that the way to avoid this kind of occurrence was to keep her surroundings so spotless that nothing bad would dare to happen in them. "I should have done it when we had that lottery grant through. . . ."

"Shall we go to the pub?" I suggested to Sally as we went down the corridor. "I could use a drink or three."

He nodded dumbly. I had to give a brief update to the guy at the stage door, who was agog with excitement, before we could push our way out into the street.

"Let's go up to the Angel," I said to Sally, thinking that even a few minutes' walk would do us good. The sun was shining, and though the air was cool it was at least fresher than that in the sump, petrol fumes from Pentonville Road notwithstanding. Slowly we headed up towards Islington, past the playground full of screaming children and chain-smoking mothers staring gloomily at the housing estate beyond, past the little green park where we ate sandwiches in good weather, past Cynthia Street and up the hill. Finally ensconced in the pub on the corner of Penton Street with its comforting, shabby furnishings and chipped dartboard, a Bloody Mary inside each of us and another one on the way, we felt sufficiently anaesthetized to be able to discuss what had just happened without going into hysterical spasms (Sally) or doing a Prince Philip stiff upper lip impression (me).

"This ees not the fairst time you find a *salma,* a—" Sally didn't even try to search for the word; he was beyond that kind of effort and out the other side. Instead he fumbled yet another cigarette out of the packet and into his mouth.

"Corpse," I finished. "No, it isn't. I think I must be Scully and Mulder's bastard love-child. Maybe in my previous life I was a crocodile and hid them all away, and now they're repeating on me. Like raw onions."

"This does not make sense."

"Makes more sense than the average episode of *The X-Files,*" I said, scoring the cheapest of points. I rather missed Hugo, who would have looked down his nose at me and drawled something to that effect.

"Deed they ask you many theengs about Marie?" Sally said, his English slipping like a toupee under stress.

"Mm. They seemed to be checking out whether she'd led us to the body deliberately. But I just don't see how that could be. No-one could stage their earring falling off and rolling into the one place it would need to go, let alone wedging it in so firmly."

"Maybe she puts eet there before," Sally suggested. "When you don't look. She pushes eet down with her foot."

"Goodness, you've got a devious mind, Sal," I said, impressed. "Who would have guessed?"

I drank some more Bloody Mary. The barman stared at us morosely, his jowls drooping like a Sharpei's. The more you drank, the better this pub looked, particularly by daylight, which gave a cruelly accurate account of the red carpet with its swirls of orange and brown, the cheap pine tables and the fraying green upholstery of the banquettes, not to mention the state of the glasses. But not even flatteringly dimmed lighting would improve the barman.

"It weell be impossible to find out who puts the body down there," Sally said gloomily. "There are so many peeple who come and go."

"Not that many," I objected.

"All the crew, the backstage peeple," Sally said, ticking the categories off on his fingers. "The actors, some of them . . ."

"Yes, but only occasionally, like today. Usually people would notice them and wonder what they were doing down in the workshop. And it would be difficult to find a time when no-one was around."

"To take the body down?"

"Maybe. Though don't you think it'd be more likely that she was killed down there? I mean, why kill someone and then start a long trek down flights of stairs dragging a body behind you, when you'd be so likely to be caught? Unless it was unpremeditated, of course. Someone found themselves stuck with a corpse and that was the only way they thought they could dispose of it."

"Why don't they just throw it from above? Say eet ees an incident?"

"An accident, idiot. Throw it down from the fly floor? Well, unless you were up there already, how would you get the body up the Jacob's ladder, unless you winched it up? And besides, I think she was strangled. You couldn't really pass that off as an accident."

"How do you know . . . ?" Sally's voice trailed off as he decided he didn't really want to hear the answer. Finishing his second Bloody Mary in one gulp, he lit another cigarette from the butt of the previous one.

"I saw the marks on her neck when I was down there with Marie," I said. "Bruises. Of course I can't be sure, but—"

"Brrr." Sally shivered, his head and shoulders trembling like a dog shaking off water. "I do not think that they will find this person. I have an instinct."

His hands were continually in motion, fiddling with the nasty stained beer mats under our glasses, peeling bits of wood off the table with his fingernails, tapping the cigarette into the ashtray even when there was no ash to fall. This conversation was making him as jittery as a line of speed on an empty stomach.

"When Marie says that eet ees Violet down there," he said, "I theenk that I am going to—" With a dramatic gesture, he clasped his skinny chest where his left pec would have been if he'd had one, the cigarette in his hand burning perilously close to his jumper. I couldn't decide whether he meant that he'd thought he was about to have a heart attack or a general *crise de nerves* but preferred not to ask for fear of hearing all the symptoms. He was now beating his fist against his chest to simulate palpitations.

"Don't be silly, Sal," I said firmly. "There was no way that was Violet. Believe me."

"You are sure?" Sally said, fixing me with great big imploring puppy eyes.

"By the way it was swollen up, it'd been down there for a long time. Very dead and very smelly," I informed him. This was supposed to be reassuring but just made Sal catch his breath, flutter his eyelashes and shudder like a Volkswagen Beetle with starter trouble.

"Someone ought to ring MM," I suggested by way of distraction. "And the hospital, to see how Marie is."

"You reeng them," Sally said at once.

He fished out his mobile phone and handed it to me. First I tried MM's mobile—she'd be at the church hall with the other actors. It was answered by Matthew, who said in his best important voice that she was directing and couldn't be disturbed, and could he take a message. The note of authority faded as soon as he had heard what I had to tell him, and was replaced by a series of strange gulping noises. Eventually he said he would talk to MM and call me back. Next I rang the hospital and worked my way through the usual series of strained and busy voices till I found one who told me that Marie was basically fine but under sedation for the shock. They were keeping her in overnight for observation.

"I go to collect her tomorrow," Sally said on hearing this.

The phone rang. Sally started nervously and nearly dropped it in the attempt to answer.

"Eet was MM," he informed me when the conversation was over, clicking the off button with still-unsteady fingers that were juggling the phone and his cigarette. "She says we meet tomorrow morning, everyone, to tell what happened. Ten o'clock."

"I'll be there."

"And now," Sally said with decision, "we get drunk."

○○○

I rolled home a few hours later rather the worse for wear, only to find a police car parked outside my studio. As I walked towards it, too slowly and carefully to convey complete sobriety, its occupant got out. He was in plain clothes—very plain: a pair of dark trousers, slightly shiny and sporting a perma-crease down the front, and a brown leather blouson jacket which didn't go with the trousers. This was not a surprise. Nothing would have gone with those trousers.

"Good afternoon, inshpector," I said amiably. "I'm afraid I'm a little dhrunk and dishorderly, but I'm going home now to shleep it off."

I paused for a moment, unable to decide whether I had been putting on a silly drunk voice deliberately. The alternative was too embarrassing to contemplate, so I didn't.

"For God's sake, Sam, it's only six o'clock in the evening!"

I felt my forehead creasing. "Would it be better if it was shix in the morning?" I inquired. "I haven't quite grashped your point." I walked past him with great dignity. "Excusche me now. I must go and lie down."

I fumbled for my keys.

"I'll do that." He grabbed them out of my hand and unlocked the door. "Get in, go on." He hauled me up the front steps.

"Police brutality!" I shrilled, clinging onto the jamb. "Police brutality!"

"Bloody get in!" He detached my hand and shoved me into the studio.

"Bastard! Do you have a warrant? I didn't shay you could come in!" I slumped on the sofa. Not sober enough to remember the precise location of the broken spring, I took it squarely in the small of the back. "Ow! Fuck!" I turned over and surveyed the inspector. By no means handsome, he had a square face with a pugnacious jaw and a nose that had been broken at least once. None of his features quite fit together, but the effect was oddly attractive, and his eyes were a nice shade of blue.

"Fancy a shag?" I said, and found this sally of wit so amusing that I started giggling and couldn't stop.

"Go on, choke yourself to death," Hawkins said sourly, sitting down on the arm of the sofa. "Drunk in the middle of the afternoon. On a Wednesday," he added, as if that made it worse. "And don't go asking me what's so bad about a Wednesday," he said, reading my mind, "or I'll reach new levels of police brutality."

"I'm an artist," I announced self-importantly. "Most artists—schgulptors"—boy, that was a difficult one—"enjoy a little dhrink every now and then. Not to mention bloody policemen," I added, sobering up in a moment of annoyance. "I've seen you put it away often enough."

"Not in the afternoon."

"It's shix o'clock! The shun's over the yardarm!"

Hawkins stared at me in disbelief. I could see him deciding to let it lie. "Yeah, but you started drinking hours ago," he said unanswerably. "I know you, Sam—it takes a lot to get you in this condition. You must have been going at it for a while."

"I wash comforting a friend in dishtresh," I said importantly. "Oh dear." I looked at Hawkins, my face falling sheepishly. I had suddenly remembered why Sally was in distress.

"What is it?" Hawkins said immediately. He can read me like a book. Or maybe that should be a comic strip. "What's happened? Sam? Sam— oh God—tell me you haven't found another dead body. Please!"

"I was preshent at the schene, but only as a witnesh. So don't worry."

"Oh God. Oh God."

"I am the bashtard love-child of Schgully and Mulder," I proclaimed. "And now I think I'm going to shleep."

○○○

Hawkins and I went back a few years. We met when a woman of my acquaintance had her head smashed in with one of her own hand weights (she ran the gym where I worked as a weights teacher) and Hawkins was a humble sergeant. If he kept getting promoted at this rate he'd be a chief constable soon—as long as no-one found out about his connection with me. I was probably on every police red peril list from here to John o'Groats. Had circumstances been different, which was to say had Hawkins not been a policeman or I not a bohemian layabout, we might have taken our affair a little more seriously, but I tended to the theory that the whole point of it was probably the thrill of the impossible. God knew, I didn't have a history of long-term serious relationships. ("Shades of the prison house close/Around the growing girl.")

Also, Hawkins had a girlfriend called Daphne. I was quite grateful to Daphne, who, due to her name and the kind of clothes she bought for Hawkins, I had always envisaged as a sensible, practical, convent-educated kind of girl, with strapping limbs and long mousy hair held back by an Alice band. I suspected that Daphne's existence kept Hawkins from pressuring me into any lunatic, doomed-to-disaster, blood-on-the-wall attempts to make a go of things between us. Still, I had to admit that my mental picture of Daphne sweetened the pill. If she turned out to be a lithe, well-dressed sex goddess with a husky voice and a bosom higher than the Fourth of July, I might not be quite so amused by the situation.

"Sam?" Hawkins' face loomed close to me through the mists of introspection. Still half-comatose, I reflected that this sounded like a good title for a fantasy novel. Book III of the Mists of Introspection series: Zak must brave the bloodthirsty warriors of the Empirical Relativist tribe before he can win through to the Peaks of Comparative Sanity . . .

"I must stop this," I said out loud, sitting up and shaking my head to clear it before my subconscious really started messing with me. The moments just before waking are always the most treacherous. "Ow! Fuck!" I grabbed my head with both hands to quiet down the ironmongery that was rattling round inside.

"Here you go," Hawkins said, holding out a couple of Solpadeine and a glass of water.

"Once more I worship at the shrine of Saint Solpadeine," I said, swallowing the tablets. "You'll make someone a lovely wife, Hawkins. This shouldn't have happened, though. I stuck to vodka and I had lots of fruit juice."

"In Sam language that means you drank three pints of Bloody Marys," Hawkins said.

"With Tabasco. Spicy stuff's supposed to be good for a hangover, isn't it? I meant it as a pre-emptive strike." I sniffed the air. "No complex carbohydrates cooking away?"

"If you mean have I put on any toast, the answer's no."

"Ah well." I got up carefully and went over to the fridge, taking out the packet of crumpets I had been saving for emergencies. Shoving as many as would fit into the toaster, I got out the margarine and Marmite.

"Where have you been, Sam?" Hawkins said, leaning on the kitchen table and fixing me with his best intense blue stare. "I've been ringing you for weeks, but the machine was always on."

"Here," I said. "Working." I gestured to the host of mobiles above our heads.

"Oh, the exhibition! That's not for a while, though, is it?"

"Couple of months. I got swept by the creative urge and did my hermit-in-the-wilderness impression. Who was it that went out into the desert and lived on bugs?"

"I don't remember that one in Bible classes."

"He sat on a pillar and grew a beard."

"St. Simeon Stylites?"

"Could be. No pillars, but I didn't depilate my legs, which is the nearest I could get."

The toaster pinged: the crumpets didn't pop up, because they had been overloaded, but I prised them out with the back of the knife and started smearing them with Marmite.

"I won't even ask you about this latest crisis of yours," Hawkins said nobly. It would have been more noble if I hadn't dimly remembered him pumping me with questions just as I was passing out. He had got enough out of me to check up on it for himself now, which I knew he would. At least that meant he would vouch for me with the investigating officers. God knew I needed it. "I came about something else. Something serious."

"Crumpet?" I said, passing him the plate. "Haha, double entendre."

"I don't know why you insist on using French tags, your accent's terrible," Hawkins snapped while I munched on my crumpet. "Anyway. I came to say that Daphne and I are thinking about getting engaged."

"It was about time you made an honest woman of her. You can't toy with the affections of girls called Daphne forever, you know."

I ate another crumpet.

"It's not as if you haven't had other boyfriends," Hawkins said, ignoring this crack in the interests of harmony.

"I've done my best to mend my broken heart by finding temporary solace elsewhere, if that's what you mean," I said flippantly. "I expect what you're saying is that I'm not supposed to try to seduce you when you pop round to shout at me for being drunk in the afternoon."

"When I'm married, yes."

"When you're married! Hawkins, you hypocrite! You mean it's all right for us to go to bed when you're just engaged?"

Hawkins looked shifty. "It's less bad," he said finally. "It's not good, per se, but it's less bad."

"That's why I fell for you in the first place," I said, finishing the last crumpet. "I knew you were a man of principle."

"Darling, wait till you meet the little boy we're going to be fighting over," Hugo said, strolling up to Helen. "A dark little thing, terribly beautiful—child porn just to look at him. We'll have Esther Rantzen down on us quicker than you can say Childline."

"Where's he from?" Helen said.

"Oh, the usual stage school, but not at all mannered. A real find. Extraordinary, these Shakespearean subtexts. I mean, does anyone ever stop to wonder why Oberon and Titania—the king and queen of the fairies, I mean, *please*—are having a major feud over who gets to keep a pretty little Indian slave boy? Or why such a large proportion of the men only seem able to muster up the energy to do it with girls when they're dressed as boys?"

Bill, who had been talking to Helen and was clearly the main target of Hugo's musings, went straight into his apoplectic beetroot impression. Hugo's lips curled in satisfaction.

"Soph's promised me we can rouge his everything," he continued. "I don't think you fancy him, do you, Helen? I think you're jealous and try to get him away from me to spoil my fun—*not* to protect him from my savage lusts, alas, you're not nice enough for that."

"No, I agree," Helen said intently; once an actor was drawn into specu-lation about their character there was no stopping them. "I think that's why I go for Bottom in such a big way too—obviously you're not inter-ested in me and I've got to get it somewhere."

"It's a shame Marie's a girl, or I could have molested her in a casual sort of way," Hugo mused. "Grope her now and then. She could be one of my boys grown up a bit. Too old for me to find attractive any longer, but still pleasantly nostalgic of happy times together."

Bill made a noise like a head of steam escaping from a kettle.

"Bill! Welcome! I didn't notice you there," Hugo said sweetly, his grey eyes cool. He twisted one of his rings absently, a gesture that called attention to his hands. It was impossible not to notice that he was wearing nail varnish. "Do you like it?" he said, stretching out his long white fingers so that we could appeciate the full effect of the black metallic polish. "It's called Gigolo. Very me, don't you think? Goes with the trousers."

He held his palm flat against one black leather-clad thigh so that we could appreciate the contrast.

"Pansy!" Bill spat at him.

"Oh, is that another colour in the range? A dark purple, I imagine. How fabulous."

"You bloody pervert," Bill said, "it's people like you and that little wop that give actors a bad name—"

"What an *extraordinary* concept," Hugo said silkily. "And I do advise you not to refer to Sally as a little wop within his hearing. Sicilians are strangely touchy about that kind of thing. Silly of them, isn't it?"

Tabitha interrupted at this point, asking Hugo for a light. She was tailed by Francis, the cast lech, a sleazy old git in dirty corduroy trousers who played Quince so well that he had had everyone in stitches of laughter at the read-through. He trotted up to her, a reek of dirty socks floating in his wake, made easier to appreciate by his open sandals. Tut-tutting, he whispered intimately in her ear:

"You *naughty* girl—smoking's bad for you."

Tickled by his beard with its attendant stench of beer, Tabitha flinched away, as MM came over and said:

"Has anyone heard from Violet?"

We shook our heads.

"Everyone's here but her, MM," said Matthew. "And Sally. He's picking up Marie from the hospital."

"Are you sure you spoke to Violet yesterday?"

"Of course I am!" said Matthew indignantly. "Well, I left a message on her machine. I didn't say what it was about, just that you were calling a special meeting for this morning."

MM looked at her watch. "It's ten-thirty already. We'd better get started or I'll lose any chance to rehearse this morning. Bloody Violet," she added. "This is just not good enough."

Coming from MM, this comparatively mild comment had the same power as Oliver Stone getting into a tearing rage and slapping his cast round while screaming insults at their defenceless heads. Matthew took an involuntary step back. Sophie pulled a face. I looked over at Helen. Though her expression was calm, her lips betrayed her; they were curved into an involuntary little smile of satisfaction, her eyes sliding sideways to exchange a smug glance with Bill. Tabitha's face, by contrast, was so blank she might have been a Tory MP.

"Right, everyone," MM said, clapping her hands. The buzz of conversation stilled and died. All the faces turned her way. "I've got something to say, as you've probably all guessed by now. It has very little to do with this production, so no-one panic, please, but you all should know that yesterday at the Cross a dead body was found in the sump below the basement. Marie, unfortunately for her, happened to stumble across it and was very shocked as a result. She should be back at rehearsal tomorrow, though, when she's had a chance to recover."

She paused. If she had gone round the room giving each person present a short blast with a stun gun they could not have looked more dazed.

"As I said, it has very little to do with us. The body has been there for some time, so no-one from this production can have been involved. I doubt that the police will even want to question anyone here."

"The *police?*" said Paul, the Lysander.

"Obviously the police are involved," MM said. "As far as I know they're treating it as a murder investigation."

There was a commotion in the front row of people. Tabitha had clutched her forehead and crumpled to the ground. Paul threw himself to his knees beside her.

"She's down!" murmured Hugo.

"Oi! Give her some air, you lot!" Paul said angrily. "Can't you see she's fainted!"

○○○

"Talk about upstaging everyone," I said later, once Tabitha had had her face fanned and water poured down her throat. I had suggested getting some ammonia from the kitchen and holding it under her nose in lieu of smelling salts, but everyone except Hugo had vetoed the idea. Most of the actors, meanwhile, were discussing in technical terms what a good faint it had been.

Helen sniffed. "I dare say it was effective enough," she conceded, "but she must be desperate for attention. It's sad, really."

"Successful, though, if that was what she was after," I said.

"Little value for purposes of research, however. The crumpling legs were good, but that thock her head made as it hit the floor would be too painful to reproduce on a nightly basis," Hugo observed cheerfully. He crossed his legs, dangling one black crocodile loafer from his toes.

"God, you lot are terrible," Sophie said.

"I notice all the other fairies are keeping their distance from her," Hugo said thoughtfully. "And I don't mean that in the sense of sexual orientation, *pace* Bill."

Helen shot him a nasty look, but couldn't resist a bitching session nonetheless.

"Tabitha thinks she's better than the rest of them, ever since MM got her to read in Hermia," she said. "She's been giving herself airs, and they've picked that up fast enough. They don't hang out with her at all."

She nodded at Mustardseed, Moth and Cobweb, who were gathered in a knot at the other side of the room, giggling together, ostentatiously ignoring Tabitha/Peaseblossom, who was now propped in a chair, sipping some water. Young, slim and fit, they were self-conscious and eager to be noticed.

"Don't they look pretty," Hugo said. "Like a freshly-gathered posy of sweet peas. That blond boy is particularly charming. Mind you, he knows it only too well, which rather cancels out the attraction."

"Tabitha? How do you feel?" MM was saying.

"Oh, much better." Tabitha stood up, swaying slightly. She caught onto Paul's arm to steady herself. "I'm sorry, I must have had a bit of a rush to the head. I can't bear hearing about blood and things."

"Well, let's hope it doesn't happen again."

"Oh, I'm sure it won't. It's just my blood pressure is a bit low."

"And how did the doctor manage to tell her that without her passing out?" I said to Hugo.

"You nasty cynical girl," he said. "Casting aspersions on Precious Petal over there."

"Right, shall we get on?" MM said. As usual, it had the force of a command, those in the scene to be rehearsed next coming forward, the others drifting away to put their coats on. Just then a voice said from the far end of the hall:

"I don't *believe* it! I thought the meeting was cancelled!"

"Violet! Where have you been?" said Sophie urgently.

"Where have I *been?* Well, obviously I'm the only one who's been left out!" Violet said crossly.

"I told you about the meeting yesterday afternoon!" Matthew protested as she skewered him with a glance.

"And *then* you left another message on the machine later on saying that it had been cancelled, so I just came in for rehearsal as normal. I mean, make up your *mind!*"

Wrapped in a long pale coat, her head emerging from the folds of her high-necked matching sweater like a flower from its calyx, Violet looked superbly regal. She stood there, hands in her pockets, still fixing her great purple eyes on the trembling Matthew.

"I never rang you!" he said bravely, his voice faint. "I mean the second time. I never left another message."

"Oh, for God's sake, just *admit* it!" Violet said angrily.

"No, honestly, I didn't!"

"Wait a minute," MM said. "Matthew wouldn't have left a message, Violet—why should he? Are you sure it was him?"

Violet, caught in the middle of a tirade, was visibly bereft of words.

"Well, I *think* so," she said finally. "He said something like: "Hello, this is Matthew, just to say MM's cancelled the meeting tomorrow." I mean, I don't know his voice *that* well, but . . ."

She tailed off for a moment. "Do you mean that someone . . ."

"Violet!" cried Marie from the door. "I'm so pleased to see you!"

She hurtled across the room and threw herself at Violet, hugging her. The huggee, completely taken aback, patted her on the shoulder in a baffled sort of way. Helen meanwhile, unable to bear the spotlight's absence any longer, pointedly engaged MM's attention with some question about her costume.

"She thought you were daid," Sally said, entering at a more measured pace. "When she see the body, eet had hair like yours, and she thought eet was you."

"The face was all swollen up, it was horrible," Marie said, apparently having decided to turn what had happened to her into a bloodcurdling narrative. "I couldn't move, I was too scared, and she was floating towards me. . . . Her hair was all spread out in the water, dark and curly like yours—"

"Ah, Ophelia," Hugo murmured. "Vi'd do a lovely mad scene."

Violet looked extremely shaken. Just then Tabitha let out a little scream. Paul had his hands around her neck and was shaking her back and forwards playfully.

"Ow!" Tabitha said, bursting into giggles. "Watch it, you're strangling me!"

That was the last straw. Violet, stifling a sob, turned and bolted for the door. Sophie, after a moment's hesitation, went after her.

"*Not* the most tactful of interventions," Hugo said reprovingly to Marie and Tabitha.

"*What the hell is going on?*"

It took me a moment to realize that the voice was MM's. Standing in the middle of the room, her face red with anger, she was a terrifying sight: MM with her self-control well and truly lost, even temporarily, not only hushed the occupants of the room into a quivering silence but froze them to the spot like a game of musical statues.

"I will *not* have people playing silly buggers in the middle of one of my productions!" she shouted. The statues stiffened in their poses still further, hoping desperately that she wouldn't single them out. "Someone tell me what just happened! Matthew?"

Matthew scuttled forward.

"Um, I didn't see, MM, I was talking to Bill."

"Hugo?" MM's gaze swept round the group.

"Violet became understandably upset when Marie insisted on comparing her to yesterday's corpse. Paul and Tabitha then compounded matters by doing a lively impression of murderer and imminent murderee, which seemed for some reason to push Violet over the edge. I should say, however, that I doubt they had any intention of upsetting her with what I will charitably call their horseplay," Hugo said with relative concision. "I rather dislike being the school sneak, but under your basilisk gaze, MM, I can keep no secrets. I'm sure that everyone will understand."

MM's eyes narrowed. Her face was still red. "For God's sake, as if we didn't have enough bother without this kind of crap! Right. Tabitha, go outside and apologize to Violet for upsetting her, and make it convincing. You too, Paul, you've got to work with her. Marie, I know you had a hard time yesterday, but *really.* . . . All right, everyone who isn't needed, off with you and try not to shoot your mouths off about this too much. We've only got a few weeks left. But if I find out that anyone—*anyone*—has been playing stupid practical jokes, like ringing people to cancel rehearsals, they're off the production as of that moment. I don't piss around. Right, let's go."

She clapped her hands. The musical statues thawed out in a flash and shot off in various directions, heads ducked as if to ward off blows. I reflected on the power a normally quiet person has when they lose their temper, let alone someone who exudes natural authority. In the space of a minute the church hall had emptied considerably, and the handful of actors still remaining had their heads bent conscientiously over scripts, doing their best to project professionalism from every pore. A few weaker vessels were hiding out in the kitchen area to calm their nerves. Violet had come back in, apologizing prettily for over-reacting. To do her justice she did not seem to be lording it over Tabitha, despite the latter's sulky pout.

MM took Tabitha aside for a short word and then sent her off. Paul, looking shamefaced, went to get Violet a cup of coffee, though she rather ignored him on his return. And now that there were fewer people in the hall I found my attention drawn to Hazel, who had been there all the time, but as usual, chameleon-like, blending into the stone wall behind her till the time came to do her scenes. Did she watch everything that went on, unobserved, hiding in full sight, or withdraw into her own dream world? Someone so unfathomable was either very complex or very simple. I couldn't help wondering which it was.

"Hello? Hello? (Bless the girl, she's in a trance.) Come back from Planet Sam, this earthling wants a word."

I blinked. Hugo was leaning against the wall next to me, following the direction of my stare.

"Fascinated by the dark horse in our midst? I must say, I am too. I can never trust someone who doesn't say anything."

"I know exactly what you mean. I always suspect them of being twisty and secretive when probably they're just shy."

"But she isn't shy, you know. Watch her with Violet. She was overawed at first, but that only lasted till they'd done a scene together. She knows exactly how good she is."

"She is good, isn't she?"

"Very," Hugo said without a trace of jealousy. "Could go far."

"Only could?"

"Darling, this profession is such a lottery. The right part at the right time and you're all set, for a while anyway. If not, it's oh-Hazel-was-so-good-as-Helena, whatever-happened-to-her? Meanwhile, she's off somewhere retraining as a librarian." He yawned. "Are you staying on to watch the rehearsal?"

"For a while. I'm always fascinated by the mood swings."

It was the sight of a group of people concentrating intensely on a scene, so absorbed in what they were doing they were blind and deaf to the outside world. When the section they were working on started at last to take shape, you could have lit cigarettes from the energy in the air. There was an almost audible fizz of concentration, the barely repressed excitement of the actors finding their way at last, relaxing into what they were doing, trying on their characters for size, feeling them stretch out to accommodate them like a tailor-made set of clothes.

Then, snap, the scene would finish and a few minutes later the excitement was over; more, it was as if the breakthrough had never happened. The atmosphere broke down into fragments. MM's attention was already focused on the next scene; Matthew was hovering with his latest list of notes; the actors who were about to start work were busy hyping themselves up while the ones who had finished were putting on their coats and talking about anything but the scene they'd just done, as if it were taboo. And then the same process started up all over again with a new set of people, the cogs grinding slowly at first but gradually meshing together.

I conveyed something of this to Hugo—more than I had meant to say—before breaking off, self-conscious. Chance observations, the way someone moved, a film I had seen, all these things fed themselves into my brain and came out in the sculpture as something so different that only I knew some of the influences that had shaped it; but I hated talking about my work and rarely did so. I was surprised that I had got even this far.

Hugo was looking at me thoughtfully. "Interesting how other people see the process," he said finally. "Cigarette?"

He flicked open the silver case with his thumbnail like Beau Brummell with his snuffbox. I shook my head.

"Are you having a Gauloise day?"

"It was a difficult call," Hugo admitted. "But I finally came down on the side of the trousers. They're definitely not Sobranie."

He struck a pose. The black leather, looking soft as velvet, draped elegantly around his narrow limbs. I had already checked out his bottom, and now found myself hoping that his legs were good. With his build, they might have come out skinny, which I hate. Not much you can do about it, either. One of the hardest challenges in the gym is a guy without calves who wants to build them up. In California they all have implants.

"Exquisitely tailored by Tariq in Brick Lane," Hugo said, "as previously mentioned. I'll take you some time."

"When I decide to give my old pair a decent burial."

"Some kind of pyre?"

"I was thinking more of the Kirk Douglas burning-ship bit in *The Vikings.*"

"One of my favourite films. We must be soulmates. Why don't you come round for tea and we'll watch it together?"

"Any opportunity to see Tony Curtis in leather hot pants."

"You and me both, as our American cousins say so inelegantly . . . though Tariq would have done a much better job with the hot pants. Shall we say tomorrow at four? I'll give you my address."

"Aren't you supposed to be rehearsing?"

"Everyone else is staging a mini-exodus in the direction of the *Doll's House* auditions," Hugo said airily. "Of course, auditions only count for so much. I always suspect directors of having made up their minds already. I'm sure Philip has a very good idea of who he wants, but he does like to string people along."

"People?" I inquired.

Hugo raised one eyebrow. "You're quite right, of course. Young ladies. He has something of a reputation for playing both sides against the middle. I don't think he makes any specific promises, but if they're inclined to be prodigal with their favours, he's certainly not going to discourage them."

"Without following through?"

"Well, let's say that someone who thought she'd been sure of Nora might find herself playing Christine instead. Some day one of them will turn nasty. I rather look forward to that, actually," Hugo added. "Philip's never been one of my favorite people."

He stubbed out his cigarette with a single twist. For a moment his eyes were the colour of steel, and just as cold.

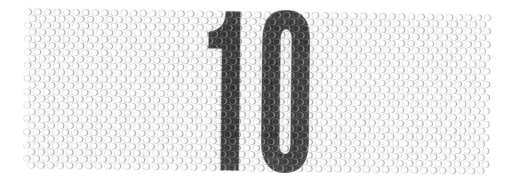

Next morning the theatre was in a state of controlled chaos. Usually the atmosphere at the Cross was so laid-back that it was hard to believe they put on a play six evenings a week, matinée on Thursday, but the finding of the body had affected everyone. Even the assistant stage managerettes—trendy little things with pigtails, flat chests, shrunken sweaters and baggy trousers—were scurrying around like nervous geese. Despite their efficiency, Steve, the stage manager, couldn't stop shouting at them as they hurried past, his usual tetchiness amplified to a full-on temper tantrum. He had them sweeping the stage in relays, not satisfied unless one of them had a broom in her hands. Usually this was his task, which he performed in an obsessive-compulsive sort of way, digging at the floor with sharp stabbing movements. I couldn't help feeling that his moodiness would fade if he had something physical to do, rather than jittering around like a cat on hot bricks. He seemed to be taking the whole affair of the dead body in the sump as a personal insult.

Philip Cantley, crossing the stage, paused to say something to Steve, and I noticed that even the artistic director deferred respectfully to his stage manager. Steve had such a proprietorial attitude to the Cross and all it contained that I think he believed he was the one really in charge of the place, and Philip Cantley just a figurehead brought in to appease the theatre board. If you wanted something done, even the smallest thing, woe betide you if you asked an ASM without humbly checking it first through Steve, who would sniff and then wave a dismissive hand at you, turning partially away to express his contempt at the request.

"What is it?" he would say impatiently. "Don't waste my time, it's money, you know. I'm a very busy man." And once you'd asked him: "Go on then, do it," in a grudging tone. "But just this once, mind."

On my way down to the workshop, I dropped into Margery's office. I admit frankly that my main reason was to gloat. People who live in glass houses with bodies floating in the basement shouldn't throw stones at other people who as yet—thank God—haven't actually found any bodies on their work premises.

"You did say to come in for coffee when I felt like it," I said, putting my head round the door. "Is now a good time?"

She looked up from her desk.

"Oh, Sam! Yes, come in. I'll put the kettle on."

"Are you sure?" I said for form's sake. I was already across the room and lowering myself into an armchair, my eyes on the biscuit tin.

"Yes, it's fine. I needed a break. And I was wanting to ask you about this whole horrible"—she made a gesture with her hands—"*mess*," she finished.

I couldn't blame her for her choice of word. Very few people, in my experience, say "murder" unless they absolutely have to.

"You were there all the way through, weren't you? I mean finding it, of course," she added, standing up and going through into her kitchenette. Sensibly, she stopped talking while the coffee grinder was screaming raucously, and we savoured the rich scent like a pair of Bisto kids.

"If they could bottle that," I sighed, "I'd wear it every day."

Margery put a tray down on the coffee table and sat down opposite me.

"Biscuit?" she said, opening the tin and passing it to me. There was shortbread. I was this woman's slave for life.

She took off her glasses, letting them hang uneasily from their chain, half-resting on her shelf of bosom, half-swinging free. She was wearing one of those cardigans that thinks it's a jacket, loden green, trimmed with grosgrain ribbon and embellished with gold buttons even on the pockets, which didn't need them. Smart yet comfortable. She looked as though *Woman's Journal* had done their "Look for a Lifestyle" makeover on her.

"You've been through this kind of thing before, of course," she said a little too casually.

"Wfhat dfoo—" I swallowed the mouthful of biscuit and started again. "What do you mean by 'this kind of thing,' Margery? People being killed?"

I thought it was rich of Margery Pickett to worry about my exploits causing scandal at the theatre one minute, and the next try to pick my brains for any useful knowledge that I might have garnered while busy exploiting. Still, there was shortbread. And the coffee was excellent.

"Murder," I said aphoristically, "is always unique."

The Pickett didn't look particularly impressed by this piece of wisdom. I think she had been expecting something a little more concrete.

"It's just," she said, leaning forward, "they're going back years, they're questioning everyone to see if they know about a girl disappearing, and if they don't find out who she was, it'll be hanging over us forever."

"Floating under us" would have been a more apt way of phrasing it, but I kept this observation to myself.

"So you *want* to find out who she was?" I said curiously.

She stared at me. "Why shouldn't I?"

I shrugged. "Most people would just sit still and hope it would all go away. And it may well. If they can't find out her identity and they can't date how long she's been down there with any precision, which they probably can't, there's very little the police can do."

Margery Pickett looked genuinely crestfallen. I found this interesting.

"It was a great place to put the body, from the murderer's point of view." I watched her while I said this, and she hardly flinched. "It might have stayed there forever."

"Such a strange way to find it!" Margery said. "She's a nice girl, though. I remember her from an alternative circus company that did a show here, years ago. No animals, of course. She was on the trapeze."

I blinked, then realized who she was talking about. "Do you mean Marie?"

"That's right." Margery smiled. "I have a very good memory for faces. I knew her as soon as I saw her."

"I expect no-one went missing when the circus was in town?" I said as casually as was possible under the circumstances.

"No-one that I can remember," Margery said, sounding rather disappointed. "But there are always so many people around a circus. . . ." she added hopefully.

That, I could see, would be the perfect solution from her point of view.

"Bez was quite friendly with them," she continued. "He might know something."

"Bez has been here since the dawn of time, I gather," I observed.

"Oh yes. Him and Steve, the SM. And me. We're the old survivors' club." Margery brightened up as soon as she said this; she seemed to make no connection between length of service at the Cross theatre and the consequently increased opportunities for strangling some unfortunate girl and bunging her into the sump. "Philip has been here for quite a while, too," she added.

"And Ben?"

"Oh, only a couple of years at the most. He came here straight from university. I was very pleased—he's just what Philip needed, someone who'll take a lot of the organization off his shoulders. It's not really one of Philip's strengths. And he's actually delegating a lot to Ben, which I didn't expect. He's never done that before with his assistants. There's a real change in Philip since Ben came," she said, sounding more cheerful. "He's the first AD Philip's taken seriously. Well, he's a very steady boy. Philip actually listens to his opinions—he's very stubborn usually, you know. But often nowadays he'll say that he won't decide on something till he's run it by Ben first, which I would never have expected. I think he'd like Ben to take over from him, eventually, though of course that's not really for him to decide. Still, it's working out very well. Ben really does seem to have had a calming influence on Philip. He's much less—well, belligerent than he used to be."

"Ben directed *Who's Afraid of Virginia Woolf?*, didn't he?" Once

Margery had got going, I was discovering, all you had to do was prime the pump with questions every now and then.

"That's right." There was a little pause.

"What did you think of it?"

"Oh, he did a perfectly nice job," Margery said.

"You don't sound quite convinced." I poured us some more coffee.

"Oh well . . ." Margery sighed. "He's perfectly competent. But there's a spark missing. You know, most directors in this country are only semi-creative. They're college educated, clever, they can learn how to block a play pretty quickly, but they're not—well, they're not *artistic*. They're no Peter Brook or Robert Lepage. They're predictable, you can foresee their style. The main requirements, really," she said, sounding exactly like a headmistress giving a lecture, "are energy and staying power. Directors crack up like actors do—they lose their confidence all of a sudden and can't get it back. It's a terrible job, really, you're responsible for everything. Homework all night, on your feet all day, expected to fend off every intellectual question the actors can think up. Even in your lunchtime you've got to work out the music, programme notes, lighting. . . . And then you might know in the rehearsal room that what you're doing isn't any good, but it's already too late by then. You just have to plug on anyway, knowing you'll get bad reviews. So demoralizing."

I grimaced.

"Oh, it's awful when that happens," she continued. "A bad production just rolling towards press night, the actors losing their confidence as it goes. And it doesn't really matter what trick you try to distract attention from the mess."

"What kind of thing would that be?" I said, interested.

"Oh, you could underscore a scene—with music, I mean. Or have what they call a design moment that makes the audience ooh and aah over the scenery. Or even bring on all the other actors to watch the scene as a sort of chorus, hoping that'll give it some extra dimension."

This seemed to be the exact parallel of making fifteen big sculptures and then painting them red.

"How do you know so much about that side of things, Margery?" I said curiously. "Did you ever direct?"

"Oh no!" She laughed. "No. I would have liked to, but in my generation things were a lot more difficult for women. No, my husband was a director, before he had his breakdown."

"Oh, I'm sorry."

"He wasn't really suited to the work," she said calmly. "You have to be able to deal with stress, like I said. And he couldn't. Sometimes I worry about Philip, but he always seems to pull himself through. Thank goodness he just took a holiday. Venice, very nice. It'll help a bit with all this trouble now."

"He's auditioning for *A Doll's House,* isn't he?" I said.

"That's right." Margery put down her coffee cup and looked at her watch.

"How's that going?" I persisted.

"Oh, that's Philip's province," she said lightly. "And Ben's, to some degree. I don't get involved in that side of things at all."

She put her glasses back on and smiled at me, the lenses magnifying her eyes rather alarmingly. Certainly, if she had been the director in the family, not her husband, there would have been no stress-induced breakdown. I met her eyes again. Despite her denial of involvement in the auditions, I found it hard to imagine an aspect of this theatre on which Margery Pickett didn't train those lenses.

◦◦◦

Leaving Margery's office, I went, not downstairs, where I should have been—I had three more mobiles to make in two weeks, which was a tight deadline even with Lurch's help—but along the rat's maze of corridors that opened finally into the dark mouth of the wings. It was an hour before the matinée, and things were busy; the ASMs were setting props, Steve was sweeping the stage (clearly not trusting one of them to perform this vital task so near to a performance), the famous actress who played Martha was standing, as she always did, with her back to the cyclorama doing breathing exercises, and Bez was checking that one of the bookcases on the set was secure, as the actor who played George had complained that when he'd leant against it the night before, it had wobbled.

"All right?" I said, strolling onto the stage.

"Hi, Sam."

"D'you want me to hold that while you put the screw in? Phnar, phnar."

"Nice one, ta. Nothing needs doing, anyway," he added crossly for my ears only. "Sturdy as a rock, this bookcase. Waste of my bloody time. Just had to find something to complain about to distract from the fact he needed a prompt, didn't he? Useless git."

"Police let you go, then?"

"Oi, I'm Suspect Number One and don't you forget it." Bez brightened up. "It was a laugh, really. Like on *The Bill*. I mean, I was a bit wild when I was a lad, but I never got given the third degree like that before. They're sharp, I'll give 'em that. You always think the coppers are going to be thick, don't you? Well, not the ones on the murder squad." He whistled a bit of the theme tune from *The Bill*, very badly. It was a tricky one.

The lighting was readjusting itself. One spotlight turned in our direction, blinding us both.

"Oi! Cut it out, you wally!" Bez gave the guy in the lighting box the finger, and the spotlight clicked off again.

"Prat," Bez said sourly. "Does that every time and thinks it's funny." Despite his bravado, he seemed in a worse mood than usual.

"Do you mind keeping it down?" Steve said angrily to Bez. He had stopped sweeping and was leaning on his broom. A tool belt was slung around his lumpy hips, dragged down by the weight of all the odds and ends he carried round with him. He was dressed in baggy black from head to foot and looked like a long-lost member of the Cure.

"You're disturbing Miss Weldon." Steve nodded towards the back of the stage, where the famous actress, hands clasped under her bosom, was panting "Ah! Ah! Ah! AH! AH! AH!" like a trained chihuahua.

"Watch it, Cinderella," Bez said, referring to the broom. "No-one tells me what to do here. Anyway, it'd take a fucking nuclear meltdown to disturb her."

"I'll have you know—"

"Leave it out, all right? Whyn't you take a turn round the stage on Dobbin there?"

"Why, you—"

Steve dropped his broom and advanced on Bez. Since the latter was about ten years younger and much fitter than him, I doubted he had any intention of getting physical, but Bez, to my surprise, dropped his screw-driver and took a step forward too.

"Oh, for God's *sake,*" I said impatiently, but no-one was listening to me.

Just then Steve's deputy, a girl called Louise who always reminded me of a very competent young nun, came smoothly forward and, interposing herself between the combatants, said sweetly:

"Steve, there's a problem with the monitor, could you come and have a look?"

As Louise had doubtless anticipated, Steve immediately transferred his bad temper to her.

"Can't you do anything by yourselves?" he said loudly, stamping off. He had quite forgotten about not disturbing the famous actress, who by now was singing "Oh! oh! oh! Oh! OHH! OHH! OHH! OOOHHHHH!" up and down the scale. Louise took him over to the DSM desk which she ran so capably, discovered, naturally, that the monitor was now working per-fectly, and bent her head meekly to receive the tirade of abuse. Then, once he had stamped off to shout at someone else, she sat down to run through her list of pre-show tasks, having staved off the trouble, eating an apple in perfect calm.

This dissolved immediately, however, as Ben came up on stage and crossed straight over to her desk, saying:

"Well done, Louise! I was in the auditorium just now, too far away to do anything about that—but you were great."

"Really?" Louise caught a bite of apple the wrong way and coughed it down painfully, looking horribly embarrassed. But at least she would be able to attribute her blush to that, rather than Ben's compliment. It was the first time I had seen Louise lose her cool. She looked up at Ben like a fifteen-year-old with a crush on the history teacher, glowing with pleasure at his approval.

"I just wanted to calm them down," she said, still red. "Miss Weldon's doing her exercises, you see."

"You did exactly the right thing," Ben said, smiling at her. He pitched it just right, like the history teacher, well aware of the crush, rewarding a clever pupil, but with just enough detachment not to feed her yearning. "We're all a little tense, I think. It's understandable enough."

"Oh yes," Louise breathed shyly.

"I tell you what. If you think things are building up, you know, tempers getting high, come and find me if you don't feel you can deal with it yourself. Don't bother Philip. He's having a hard enough time as it is."

"Are the police in with him now?"

"No, they've just gone. But he has to make an official statement tomorrow, and God knows what else. I'd better go and see if he's all right. So come to me if there's a problem, OK?"

"Yes, Ben," said Louise, blushing again as she pronounced his name.

He patted her on the shoulder. "Good girl."

Louise stared after Ben with worship as he went off to find Philip. I couldn't help admiring Ben; he had handled her perfectly. Margery was right. He was very capable. I didn't envy him his next task. I had seen Philip Cantley yesterday, looking as twitchy as an alcoholic with the shakes.

It was half an hour before the show went up, and the chief electrician had arrived to do the check with Bez. The state was up and the tabs were in, which meant that the lights were set for the first scene and the house curtains were down; the famous actress pushed off, and five minutes later the stage was empty. At the half it was always like the *Marie Celeste*: actors in their dressing rooms, crew members in the crew room, probably watching a video, Steve and the ASMs, having set the props, in the crew room too, ditto. That was the theory. In practice most people were down the pub. Lurch had told me that when he first started here he thought the half-hour before the show went up was called the half because that was what people snatched in the pub before rushing back to go on stage.

I got myself another coffee from the machine in the SM cubbyhole, careful not to disturb the props so neatly laid out and labelled, and wandered out into the wings, sipping it. I liked this time, when no-one else was around and the stage—lit and unoccupied, half-full glasses laid out on the table—looked eerie, as if all the actors had just this second been beamed up by aliens. I started to imagine the set in a couple of weeks, with my mobiles hanging there instead, and the picture became so vivid that when I heard voices coming down the corridor I ducked back into the SM room, not really wanting to talk to anyone if I could avoid it.

"I think I should take notes this evening," Ben was saying. "You're not really concentrating at the moment."

"Fine, fine," Philip Cantley responded automatically, his voice hoarse.

"Have you had a chance to think about the auditions, Philip? I thought there were some very good possibilities."

"No, of course I haven't!" Philip Cantley snarled. "How could I, with all this going on! For Christ's sake, Ben, how do you think I'm feeling? Questioned by the police for hours! They might call me back! It's all right for *you*," he added bitterly. "*You* weren't here then. But me—I'm in charge. They won't let me forget that. I'm a nervous wreck."

"Well, let me help out, then," Ben said simply, "since you're so distracted. Let me take over casting *A Doll's House*. Only the minor roles, obviously. I mean, Nora and Torvald we know about. Really, Philip. You're too busy with the police to have a chance to think about it and we must make a decision soon. It's important to get this right. I think the girl we saw, the one I mentioned before who's in the *Dream*, would be perfect for Christine. I've directed her in quite a few student productions and she's very good indeed. Then there's the Krogstad to be sorted out. . . ."

There was a short pause. "Do whatever you want!" Philip Cantley said, sounding defeated. "I can't even remember most of the people we saw. . . . I couldn't think of anything but that—that body—and the police keep coming back. . . . What am I going to do, Ben? I can't go on like this!"

He sounded utterly desperate, his voice rising dangerously high, laced with panic. Ben's quiet, sensible tones fell like a cool shower on these excesses, bringing down the temperature of the discussion.

"Relax, Philip, you worry too much about the slightest thing," he was saying reassuringly. "It'll be fine."

"Really?" Already Philip Cantley sounded a little calmer.

"Of course it will. It'll all sort itself out, you'll see. And as far as every-thing goes for the moment, I'll be the soul of discretion. I'll say that I'm just implementing your decisions. Hi, Sam," he said, coming level with the open door of the SM room. "Checking the props?"

"Getting a coffee in a moment of peace and quiet."

Ben grinned. It was a nice smile, brackets forming on each side of his mouth, his eyes creasing up behind his glasses.

"It's strange just now, isn't it? The lights are on but no-one's home."

"I was thinking *Marie Celeste* myself," I agreed.

The first crew members started to trickle back into the wings. Louise was first; she carried a Thermos and a Tupperware box, neatly packed with fruit, which she arranged on a little shelf below the DSM desk. Philip Cantley was waiting for Ben to finish talking to me, fretting at the bit. He looked nervous, unable to keep still, his eyes darting from side to side; even the foulard at his neck was crumpled. As I went past, heading down to the workshop, he stared at me blankly, his eyes seeming to pass right through me. The resemblance to a vampire was still there. Only now he looked like he hadn't had a good pull at a jugular in weeks.

11

Matthew called me the next morning to ask if I could drop by the church hall in the afternoon to discuss a new and exciting idea of Sally's. I agreed, grudgingly, since I was behind with the mobiles, due mainly to my own perversity; what had started out as a simple design had grown more and more elaborate as I experimented with the effects that I had been sketching from the trees in the graveyard. Before, my style had been based on meteors, comets, undiscovered planets, wrapped in wire and hung about with strange rings. But using the ivy from the cyclorama had started me on a new track, aided and abetted by Lurch. He was turning out to have a very good eye and his boundless, seventeen-year-old enthusiasm was infectious. Lucky he'd never been to art school—they knocked that kind of thing out of you at once. I didn't tell Bez what a find his slave was, though, in case he upped the price.

The morning's work went so well that I allowed myself a drop-in at the gym before heading up to the church hall. I had left Lurch with some routine tasks. At least I told myself they were routine. He'd probably have finished the rest of the mobiles better than I could have done by the time I came in tomorrow.

I came up the path to see Titania and her fairies, minus Tabitha, in a tight little cluster formation outside the double doors, sulky expressions on their faces. Hearing my footsteps, they swung round like a bunch of conspirators surprised in the middle of a plot.

"They're waiting for you," said Ranjit, looking almost hostile.

"D'you know what MM called me in for?" I said, less to know than to make conversation.

"Oh yes," said Hugo's blond boy, his pretty mouth drawn into a pout. "*We* know."

The redhead and Helen exchanged significant glances. Ranjit and the blond boy followed suit. I pushed off before they could form a circle round me and do the significant-glance bit as a quartet instead of a duo. Right now they weren't so much fairies as the witches from *Macbeth*, numbers apart, or extras from *The Wicker Man*. They looked as if they were conducting blood sacrifices to ensure the production went well, and I had no intention of being selected as the next victim. I assumed Tabitha had gone first; I had already noted her absence. Or maybe they were reading entrails. In which case I wished the augur good luck with the state of my liver.

The air inside the hall smelt, as usual, of dust, floor polish and cigarette smoke. I paused on the lintel to double-check, but couldn't scent even a hint of freshly spilled blood. Perhaps that was why the fairy queen and her entourage had been so bad-tempered.

"Sam! Hi!" Matthew said, coming forward. "Do you want a coffee?"

"No, I'm fine, thanks. I'm having tea with Hugo later and I try not to mix my drinks."

"Right," he said, looking blank. Matthew never got a joke. If he ever made it as a director he would be well advised to stick, on the comedy front, to Pinter or Gogol. He had as much sense of humour as Strindberg after a particularly nasty fight with the wife.

MM waved at me from across the room, beckoning me over. She was engaged in what looked like a serious conversation with Tabitha, Sally and a tall stringy man with a goatee who was Thierry, the choreographer. I had already met him briefly. He was an ex of Sally's; I didn't know what kind of ex, but probably nothing major. Sal wasn't any better than I was at the serious relationship bit.

"Sam!" Sally kissed me on both cheeks, as usual. "We have a great idea!"

"Yes, I keep hearing this," I said, leaning against the wall. "It makes me more nervous with every repetition."

"No, it really is a great idea," said Thierry earnestly. He and Matthew, as a team, could miss the point for England in the next Olympics. "And all inspired by your mobiles."

"Oh, fuck." I reached for a cigarette and then remembered that I didn't smoke. Bugger.

"I'm going to—" Tabitha piped up, and then fell silent on a look from MM. Clearly she was to be seen and not heard. For someone with her combination of looks and brains, it was an eminently sensible policy.

"The idea," MM said, "is that in the scene when Titania falls in love with Bottom—"

"Act three, scene one," Matthew put in with the air of someone contributing a piece of vital information.

"—she calls all the fairies to come and wait on Bottom. They come in, one by one, and Mustardseed—Tabitha—is the last. When they've all entered but her, she drops down from behind a mobile, where she's been suspended, concealed by it, so it looks like she's jumped down from thin air. Nice surprise. Sally thought of it, clever boy. We decided that Puck should be the only one to ride the mobiles, but it would be nice to have another visual moment with them. As Thierry would say."

"Will she fit behind one?" I asked.

"That's what we want to check. She's the smallest of the lot, and the most agile. Thierry's just been putting them through some contortions and he decided that Tabitha was the most suited."

Thus ensuring pouts all round for the other fairies. The sulking zone outside was now explained. Sally, too, looked doubtful. Tabitha, of course, was radiant with happiness, glowing like a hundred-watt pearlized light bulb. MM's expression, as usual, was pleasantly neutral as Thierry waved his hands around, describing how he had got all the fairies to limber up and perform dramatic feats of skill and daring:

". . . and finally I got them to jump down from the windowsill," he finished triumphantly.

"Sounds like *Peter Pan*," I observed. "Who played the dog?"

Everyone ignored me, which was only to be expected. Thierry put a friendly arm round Tabitha.

"We will work out something great," he said to her.

"So excuse me for breaking in on this love-fest," I said, "but what am I doing here? Or did you guys just want witnesses to your genius?"

MM gave me an unexpectedly amused look. "We wanted to ask if you thought Tabitha would fit behind a mobile as is, or if you needed to make one slightly bigger."

I squinted at Tabitha. "She's pretty small. . . . What happens? There's a blackout beforehand and she gets lowered down behind the mobile, then jumps down on cue? I might not need to alter anything. The mobiles're bulked out already with all the ivy wrapped round them—stumps, boles, God knows what Lurch will have invented this afternoon. . . . Why don't you come into the theatre tomorrow, Tabitha and anyone else who wants to, and we'll do some experimenting? But it should be OK."

"Good!" MM pronounced. "Sort that out, will you, Matthew? Are my next lot here?"

Matthew flicked over some pages on his clipboard.

"Hermia and Lysander!" he announced pompously, as if unaware that Violet and Paul were close by, chatting in a guarded sort of way by the coat rack. They didn't really get on.

"Here, darling," said Violet, flashing such a smile at Matthew that he nearly took a pace back to absorb the effect. She was wearing jodphurs, a white shirt and a silk scarf knotted at her neck and looked like Diana Quick in *Brideshead Revisited,* only even prettier. Paul's ginger handsomeness faded beside her.

"I could see you were plotting and planning," she said, strolling over, "so I didn't *dare* interrupt. I was early, though," she added proudly.

Paul followed in her wake like a tugboat behind a luxury yacht.

"What's going on?" he said rather too jovially. I had already realized how possessive actors were of the director's attention; they were like a group of jealous children, all tugging at their mother's skirts.

Tabitha, still beaming, announced her good news. Somehow under Violet's gaze it came out flatter than it had before.

"So, basically, you're going to do a big jump!" said Paul, unfortunately.

Thierry bridled. "It will be a great entrance," he said crossly. Clearly he had elected Tabitha as his protégée. "We're going to fly her down."

But the damage had been done. Paul stammered out something apologetic that made matters worse. Violet, to her credit, made no comment, not even the arch of an eyebrow, but her presence was enough to make Tabitha wilt still further. She slipped away to the kitchen area, followed immediately by Thierry.

"*Cretino!*" said Sally to Paul. "If she doesn't feel confident about eet, she doesn't do her best."

"I'm sorry—I didn't mean—" Paul blurted, looking horribly guilty. "What can I do? You know, I think she's really good. . . ."

"Leave eet alone," Sally said curtly. "Eef you go to talk to her you will make eet worse."

Paul blundered away clumsily while Sally went off to help reassure Tabitha. Sophie entered on a giant sneeze which she did her best to keep away from the swatches of material she was carrying. She plonked them down on Matthew's desk, the fairies tripping in after her, considerably less grumpy now that they were about to see how their costumes would look. Even Tabitha finally emerged from the kitchen, cheering up to the extent that she seemed to ignore the hostility of the others. Helen, seeing me in my corner, wandered over in my direction. Her mood did not seem to have improved.

"Don't you need to check your costume?" I said politely.

"Oh, I've seen mine already, ages ago, the material too. Sophie's just fiddling round with the colours for the fairies," Helen said dismissively. "Hugo and I are green and silver."

"No togas?" I said, remembering something Hugo had said a few days ago.

Helen ignored this, as she did anything she didn't understand.

"She's done well for herself after all, hasn't she?" she remarked nastily, nodding at Tabitha.

"Only comparatively," I objected. "I mean, as Paul just said, it's only a big jump. You wouldn't have wanted to do it anyway, would you, Helen? You hate heights."

Helen shivered. "That's not the point," she said firmly. "I'm the queen of the fairies. They should have offered it to me first."

"You'd only have turned it down. And Thierry auditioned everyone, didn't he?"

"I didn't think she was as good as they all seemed to think," Helen said dismissively. "Of course, she's *small*. Skinny, really. I suppose that's the point."

I looked over at Tabitha, lithe and nicely curved, and raised my eyebrows. Skinny? Only if you counted Melanie Griffith as being a little on the thin side.

There followed a period of much excited twittering by the fairies as swatches of material were held against their faces. It seemed interminable, mainly because I was jealous that no-one was paying me the same kind of concentrated, clothes-centred attention. At last MM clapped her hands for order; the fairies and Helen collected their things and faded away, Sophie busied herself pinning small swatches of chiffon together and Violet, who had been enjoying herself tremendously pretending to be a Colour Yourself Beautiful consultant, joined Paul in the centre of the rehearsal room.

She was looking rather pale. Putting her hand to her head, she said that she was sorry, but she was feeling a little dizzy and would try to concentrate. The problem, however, only got worse. Violet began to forget her lines and blur the words she did remember.

"She hasn't been drinking, has she?" I said to Sally, puzzled.

"No, of course not." But he leant over and sniffed her coffee anyway.

"Then what is it? You'd think she had sunstroke."

"'If then true lovers have been ever crossed/It stands—it stands—'" Violet broke off. "I'm really sorry!" she said, seeming honestly confused.

"I almost feel as if I've got shun—sunstroke. I've gone all wobbly. I can't think what it is, I was fine till five minutes ago."

"Yeah, right," said Paul with obvious disbelief. "Are you on something?"

"Of course I'm not. Don't be silly." Violet had obviously tried to snap out this retort, but it emerged too slurred to be an effective put-down.

"Well, it looks like that to me."

Sally surreptitiously stuck his finger in Violet's coffee and licked it off. Then he shook his head at me. I didn't see Violet as a secret drinker myself, but you never knew.

"Do you want to sit down for a bit, Violet, while Hazel does her scene with Paul?" MM suggested.

"Yes, maybe. I'm really sorry," Violet repeated, looking dazed. "I don't know *what* can be wrong with me. My head's . . . spinning like . . . a top."

The last words came stumbling out much too slowly. Sophie, concerned, jumped up and helped Violet over to a chair in the flower-arranging room, off the main hall. Hazel materialized into the middle of the room. This was the only way to describe it. I hadn't noticed her come in; nor, when I asked him, had Sally.

"It just came on so . . . *suddenly,*" Violet was saying to Sophie. "Honestly, I'm not . . . making it . . . up."

"Don't try to talk," Sophie said, kneeling down beside Violet, who was half-lying on one chair, her feet up on another. "Do you want a glass of water?"

Violet shook her head.

"It's not that crazy diet thing of yours, is it, Vi? You haven't been—"

Violet shook her head again, more violently.

"Well, let's give you some more room to breathe." Sophie started untying the scarf at Violet's throat. At once Violet shot up a hand to stop her. "I'm . . . *all right,*" she said with an effort. "Just leave me alone! *Please!*"

Sophie stood up abruptly and left the room. I caught her as she came through the doorway, her pretty face creased up as if she had taken offence at Violet's rebuff of her attempts to help. She looked down at my hand on her arm as if she hardly realized who I was or what I was doing.

"Come outside for a minute?" I proposed.

The air was fresh and crisp, the flowerbeds round the little lawn as immaculately maintained as ever. On the far side of the graveyard a woman knelt, clad in Barbour and Wellingtons, her grey hair tossed about by the breeze; the vicar, busy bedding in some plants. I set our pace in the other direction, beneath the great oaks. Looking up into their mass of branches set my head spinning with dizziness, sunlight spilling through the leaves like bright water. For a moment I was in the enchanted forest, a wood outside Athens; and then the scent of Sophie's cigarette, trails of smoke rising through the branches and twining through the sunlight, brought me back to the present place and time.

"I'm so worried about Violet," she said without preamble.

"Don't be. I think I know what it is."

Sophie frowned, looking surprised. "What do you mean?"

"What's wrong with her, of course." I stared at her, puzzled. We seemed to be talking about two different things. "Have you got your anti-histamines with you today?"

"Yes." Sophie patted her pockets and came away with nothing. "Oh, they must be inside. I remember, I left them on the table. I took one when I came in. I always get it badly round here—it must be all the grass and flowers in this churchyard. You don't get much of that in Brixton."

"Well, I think someone's just slipped Violet some of your anti-histamines. Didn't you say before that they make you drowsy?"

Sophie stared at me blankly. "But why would someone do that?"

I shrugged. "Why would someone leave a message on her answering machine pretending to be Matthew?"

"Did they? I mean, I thought it was Vi making up an excuse."

"Do you think she'd have invented something that would get Matthew into trouble? You know her better than I do."

Sophie stubbed out her cigarette inside the empty packet, looking perplexed. "Well, if you put it like that, no, I don't. Vi's a very sweet person, really, when you get past the airs and graces." She was frowning now. "I don't understand. Do you mean someone's got it in for her?"

I raised my eyebrows. "What else? Unless you can think of another reason for her going all wobbly, as she put it. Everyone was milling around the table—it would have been very easy to pop out a couple of your pills and drop them in her coffee. She always uses her own mug, so it would be simple enough to tell which was hers."

"They don't dissolve, the pills," Sophie said.

"It'd only take a second to crush them up in the kitchen with the back of a spoon. We could check that, if no-one's cleared up her mug yet. See if there's any residue at the bottom."

"This is so creepy!" Sophie said, distressed. "I don't like this at all!" Eyes wide, hair pushed back from her little pointed ears, she looked like a frightened pixie.

"What did you mean before?" I asked. "When you said you were worried about her. I thought you meant the dizziness, but obviously not."

"Oh." Now she looked like a miserable pixie. "Vi and men . . . I don't know, she always seems to go for the type that doesn't treat her well. Anyway, when I was trying to undo her scarf, I saw a bruise on her neck. Not a lovebite, a proper bruise. It was sort of yellow and green. That must be why she didn't want me to take off the scarf. And suddenly I thought: she's worn something round her neck all the time I've seen her on this production. Now I know why."

"Jesus," I said slowly.

"Actually, she winced when I got her by the arm as well," Sophie remembered. "I bet she's got bruises there too. I don't even know her boyfriend. I mean, I've seen her with someone a couple of times, picking her up, but that was a while ago. He's pretty well off, though," she added carefully, "going by his car. A banker or something, I think." She turned to me, her voice intense. "What can I do? Should I talk to her about it?"

"I wouldn't. If she didn't want you to see her neck, she'll just snub you if you bring the subject up, and you'll lose her as a friend because she knows you disapprove of what she's doing. You've got to wait till she comes to you." How mature I sounded.

"But Sam, what if she doesn't?" said Sophie, still strung up to a high pitch. "What if she doesn't, and this boyfriend of hers goes too far?"

And I wondered how much Sophie knew about the girl whose body had been dropped into the sump under the theatre: did she know, for instance, that she had been strangled?

○○○

"Dear oh dear," said Hugo quite cheerfully after I had brought him up to date. "Well, this is more fun than *The Vikings*, which is not a statement I make very often. Would you like some more Earl Grey?"

When Hugo invited someone round for tea, he did the thing properly: a bone china tea set, linen napkins and a silver tray.

"All found in Bermondsey market," he had said, gesturing at the table. "Apart from the biscuits, you'll be glad to know. Those I bought fresh. Shortbread and ginger cake—why are you making that revolting snuffling noise?"

"I get uncontrollably excited at the mention of shortbread," I explained. "Now I must have some at once or I'll go into spasm."

"I must say, you quite tempt me to withhold the tin. . . . And by the way, don't you know how fattening shortbread is, young woman?"

"I go to the gym a lot. Give me that tin or I won't be responsible for the consequences."

Hugo's flat was in Spitalfields, the first floor of a pretty little Georgian house. It had obviously been lovingly restored; whether accurately or not I was incapable of telling, but I liked it. Pale yellow walls, hung with black-and-white prints, polished floorboards and delicate wooden furniture which was much more comfortable than it looked. A couple of small tables held a finely judged collection of *objets d'art:* Lalique-inspired glass paperweights, framed photographs and silver candlesticks. I curled myself up on the sofa, which was upholstered in straw-coloured silk, and sipped some tea. Curiously, I had discovered that I had no appetite after all.

"You're not eating much," Hugo observed, leaning back in his armchair and stretching his long legs out in front of him, ankles crossed. He was wearing tweeds, for some impenetrable Hugo-esque reason, and smoking Sobranies.

"I keep expecting you to produce a fob watch," I said rather irrelevantly.

"How dare you compare me to the White Rabbit?" He looked down his long nose at me and blew out a cloud of smoke. "Go on telling me about what happened today. You know I love gossip."

"That's it, really. Sophie and I checked Violet's coffee, and the bottom of the mug was thick with powder. Unless she'd taken something herself, it was the anti-histamines."

"What on earth made you think of them?" Hugo said curiously.

I put down my cup. "Violet looked so surprised by what was happening to her," I said. "She wasn't faking that. And why should she drop an E or even take some prescription drug a minute before she was supposed to start rehearsing? And then I remembered Sophie sneezing when she came in, and thought of hay fever and anti-histamines and general dopiness. . . . It would have been so easy to take a few pills and crush them up in the kitchen with the back of a spoon. None of that lot notices what anyone else is doing. Apart from when one of them's talking to MM, and the rest are going mad with jealousy, trying to hear what's being said. They're all so self-obsessed."

"Very true," Hugo said. "You could probably have strangled Violet then and there and as long as everyone else was distracted by the prospect of their costumes they wouldn't have blinked an eye. So who do you think it was?"

"I have no idea," I admitted. "With Violet, you tend to think of women being jealous. She's such a man's woman. Girls either hate her or, like Sophie, have a sort of crush on her. There's Tabitha, Helen, Hazel. . . ."

"Hazel is a very dark horse," Hugo observed. "Of course, she may be one of those actors who thinks of nothing but their Craft." He gave the last word a capital letter so clearly pronounced that I could almost see it. "And they can be the most ruthless of all."

"It's odd how Hazel leads one to that sort of speculation," I commented, feeling, oddly, that I was talking at random. "I keep seeing her as a chameleon, or an iceberg, practically all of her personality under water. . . ."

Hugo was watching me closely but I had the strangest feeling that he wasn't listening to a word I was saying. And in fact he commented, with total irrelevance:

"You really haven't eaten anything, have you? Well, neither have I, come to that. . . . Do you know, I think I might go and have a shower. Will you excuse me?"

He stood up and went with long, leisurely strides into the bathroom. The door closed and I heard water running; he really was having a shower. I stared after him, baffled by this bizarre behaviour, and then reached for his cigarette case, which he had left on the table. I only smoke in certain, well-defined circumstances, and this was definitely one of them.

After about ten minutes, Hugo emerged from the bathroom, wrapped in a black brocade dressing gown, his hair towelled dry and tied at the nape of his neck. The sun, through the window behind him, caught his fair hair and turned it to gold. Pausing in the doorway, he observed me for a minute in silence. Then, as if he had come to some decision, in one slow, leisurely movement he untied the dressing gown and let it fall at his feet. He was quite naked underneath, as was only to be expected.

"Do you like what you see?" he enquired, his tone of voice level and matter-of-fact. If there had been the least hint of campness, of coquetry, I would have recovered from the shock and made some equally flirtatious remark. But there wasn't, and so I remained absolutely speechless, staring at him, at the long narrow muscles of his thighs, the set of his shoulders, the faint golden glow of his pale body in the light from the window. A small, still-rational part of my mind observed that he did have calves, and registered approval. My mouth was dry.

He started walking towards me. The dressing gown remained where he had left it, a puddle of black brocade on the floor. Behind it I could see the bathroom mirror, opaque, damp with the steam from his shower. Around him rose the scent of Issey for Men, warmed by his skin.

"Hugo?" I said feebly. I had the sensation that I was drowning fast in a sea of incomprehension, catching at anything that would stop me going under. For the first time I knew exactly what was meant by the expression "clutching at straws."

"I know that I've been rather remiss," he said, "leading you to think that I might be gay. But you're so sure of yourself that I couldn't resist the opportunity to catch you off guard. I did enjoy myself for a while. Only now I find it's stopped being quite so much fun. I have had my periods of polymorphous perversity," he added, as if by way of information, "but I infinitely prefer girls. I do hope you're not disappointed."

He was in front of me now, quite unembarrassed about his nakedness. I had used this technique myself before, but it was the first time it had been employed on me. One didn't exactly expect it from a man. But then, Hugo wasn't quite your average male.

He leant forward and started to undo my shirt. The scent of Issey for Men wrapped itself around us both, and under that was Hugo himself, which was just as good. My head was spinning. Hugo's hand slipped inside my shirt and closed around my breast.

"You can't know how long I've wanted to do that," he said calmly. "Goodness, Sam, I do appreciate having you speechless for a change. I expect I'd better make the most of it while I can."

He finished unbuttoning my shirt and began, slowly and with considerable enjoyment, to pull it open.

"Hugo—" I said again without having much idea of what I meant.

"Enough talking for now, don't you think?" said Hugo, suiting the action to the word. "There's a quote for that. I'll remember it later. Only now I'm finding you too distracting to concentrate on more than one thing at a time."

His hands were sliding up my thighs. I closed my eyes and slid back on the sofa, quite incapable of doing anything but taking the line of least resistance.

"'Peace, I will stop thy mouth.'"

"Will you?" Hugo took a long drag on his mauve Sobranie. "Would you terribly mind waiting half an hour or so, darling? I find myself quite drained of energy at the moment."

"Beatrice to Benedick. *Much Ado*. The quotation."

"Oh yes. What a lovely moment that is. The whole atmosphere spins and resettles the other way up after the kiss."

"Rather like you taking your clothes off in front of me. Have you used that manoeuvre before, by the way?"

"I can't say that I have. It was a moment of inspiration while I was soaping my armpits and thinking that really it was time to move things along a bit. I was rather getting the impression that you wouldn't at all mind if I did."

"Just because I didn't eat anything . . ."

"When a girl declares that she is addicted to shortbread and then is only capable of nibbling the corner of a petticoat tail with as much relish as if it were made of sawdust . . . well, there is only one conclusion to be drawn."

"And I smoked two of your cigarettes. If you'd known me better that would have been the final clue."

"I must remember that for future reference . . . Anyway, back to me in the shower, rather dreading making the explanation—it would definitely have been a passion-killer, don't you think?"

"Oh by the way, Sam, I forgot to tell you before—I'm not gay after all, so do you fancy a shag?" I suggested. "Something along those lines?"

"Foul, foul creature," Hugo said, pretending to stub his cigarette out in my navel, "how coarsely you insist on phrasing things. I must break you of this noxious habit. Anyway," he said firmly, "it occurred to me that the best thing would be a dramatic gesture that you could scarcely misunderstand. Followed, of course, by a determined seduction attempt. I think it might have been Modesty Blaise who gave me the idea. She's in the habit of stripping down to the waist when she goes into a room full of hostile men. It gives her more time to shoot them up."

"I see you more as Lord Peter Wimsey than Modesty Blaise."

"*Do* you now," Hugo said, rather too complacently for my liking. "That's a thought. Perhaps if Lord Peter had stripped down to the buff earlier on and chucked Harriet onto the sofa with one of his special judo throws he might have avoided all those boring years when she couldn't make up her mind."

"I don't quite see that approach working with Harriet. It was finishing off each other's sonnets and quoting John Donne that did it in the end."

"So it was. How dire. I can't tell you how glad I am that you're so much more Modesty than Harriet. My poetry is appalling. I wonder what would have happened if Lord Peter had pretended to be gay to lure Harriet into a false sense of security. . . ."

"Talking of which, do you feel like enlightening me about that?"

Hugo lay back on the sofa, blowing smoke rings at the ceiling.

"It was Bill, if you must know. I really do object to raving bigots, and I heard a couple of his cracks at Sally that tipped me over the edge, as it were. I know it can't be easy for a homophobe to be playing Bottom, but after his second crack about bum-bandits—I may have mercifully forgotten the precise expression that he used—I decided that the worst fate that could befall him would be to anticipate being trapped in the dressing room night after night with a raving queen. I *did* enjoy myself. He's had his saggy behind plastered to the wall for the past few weeks in terror. God, as if I'd touch him with a bargepole. I have had my moments, you know," he said, tilting his head to look at me. "Mostly at school. All that raging testosterone cooped up in the countryside, miles from anywhere. I bump into a few of my ex-flames from time to time and we exchange reminiscent glances. But recently I've found girls rather more satisfying, as I seem to remember mentioning just before I had my way with you."

"Either that or you're in denial."

"Oh, is that your theory, madam?"

He stubbed out his cigarette, not on my navel this time, and swung over me in a single smooth movement. Bracing his arms on either side of me, his fair hair falling over his face, he stared down at me, grey eyes cool. I stretched myself out beneath him.

"Are you requesting another round of denial, by any chance?" he said.

I ran my eyes lasciviously down his body. "Go for it," I said.

"I take it that means yes in vulgar parlance. Well, your wish is my command," said Hugo, lowering himself slowly in a blatant attempt to impress me with his biceps. "Actually, this sofa is horribly uncomfortable. Shall we adjourn to my bedroom?"

"Absolutely not. I thought you thrived on a challenge."

"Poor innocent creature, you little know how you are tempting fate."

"Oh," I said, reaching up, "I think I have a pretty good idea."

ooo

Eventually we did move to the bedroom, accompanied by a bottle of sherry and the plate of biscuits. I had convinced Hugo to bring them (he was worried about his figure) by pointing out that we were busy working them off. I felt extraordinarily relaxed and, in sharp contradiction, as if I were tuned up to the highest pitch possible without actually exploding. Both of which states, I dare say, were comprehensible enough.

"Did I say before how much I like your work?" Hugo said through a mouthful of ginger cake. "I probably didn't, for fear of sounding naff and fulsome and as if, as you would no doubt put it, I was trying to get off with you. It's very good."

"Thank you. God knows what Lurch will have done with the latest one by the time I go in tomorrow. He's very excited by the whole thing."

"Lurch? Oh, is that the carpenter boy?"

"I'm rather thinking of buying him from Bez."

"Well, if he's useful enough so that you can leave him toiling and spend your afternoons in bed with me, I thoroughly approve. You can give him his freedom when you're rich and famous."

"Exactly." With Hugo I never needed to spell anything out. It was such a relief. "I'm turning into a post-modernist," I said drowsily. "Having the ideas and getting other people to actually make them for me."

"As opposed to being a craftswoman and insisting on doing all the dreary bits yourself?"

"Mm. Though I can, you know," I said, sitting up again. "I apprenticed myself to a blacksmith after I left art school, and they made me do wrought-iron hooks for a month till I could do them properly. Coat hooks, pot racks . . . then after another month or so I graduated to making tulips for an ornamental gate. Lead. They practically weighed more than I did— why am I telling you all this?"

"Probably the sherry is making you reminiscent. Go on. For some bizarre reason I find it strangely attractive to be in bed with someone capable of soldering ornamental lead tulips, or whatever it is you do with them."

"Are you serious?"

"Mm. Go on."

"Well," I said, propping myself up on some pillows, "ow—brass beds may look nice but they're hell to lean against—what do you want to know? Working with lead? It's very easy. You could melt lead down in a Teflon pan, it liquefies at such a low temperature. It's one of the most sat- isfying metals to work with, so porous—you wax it while it's still hot, with butcher's wax, and it just keeps soaking in. That's how you get that lovely greasy finish. You're enjoying this, aren't you?"

"Can't you tell?" said Hugo lazily. "I adore a touch of role reversal. Oh, and talking about roles, have you heard the latest? Our not-so-shrinking Violet has been cast as Nora in A *Doll's House*. At the Cross. Bodies in the basement notwithstanding. I don't think she'll be superstitious enough to turn that down, do you? And that's not all—guess who's playing Christine?"

"Hazel," I said with unerring instinct.

Hugo looked disappointed. "Did you know already?"

"No. But I heard Ben mention her. He thought she was very good. And I think that he ended up doing most of the casting."

"Ben? Oh, that's Philip's strong right arm, isn't it? Not much of a director, though. Maybe that's why Philip's giving him all those privileges—he knows Ben's never going to threaten him with some burst of creativity. Well, we'll soon know if it was Hazel, won't we? If someone keeps playing nasty practical jokes on Violet in rehearsals for *Doll's House*, it should be clear enough."

"Do you think we should warn Violet?" I turned over in bed. "That someone's up to mischief, I mean."

"I wouldn't. I've known Vi for years and I can assure you it will just make her paranoid and tedious. She wouldn't know what to be on her guard for, anyway." He stretched his arms back, yawning. I leant over and ran a fingernail down from his palm to his armpit.

"Are you ticklish?"

"No, not at all. Do that again, it's rather nice. Mm. Yes. What about moving your field of operation a little further down?"

"Sometimes," I said, "it's uncanny the way you manage to read my mind."

ooo

But it was Gatlinburg in mid-July and
I had just hit town and my throat was dry.
I'd thought I'd stop and have myself a brew.

At an old saloon on a street of mud
And at a table dealing stud
Sat the dirty, mangy dog that named me Sue.

Well, I knew that snake was my own sweet dad
From a worn-out picture that my mother had.
And I know that scar on his cheek and his evil eye,

He was big and bent and grey and old
And I looked at him and my blood ran cold,
And I said: "My name is Sue! How do you do! Now you're gonna die!"

The crowd was cheering and clapping like a wild thing.

Yeah, that's what I told him!

The tape snapped off just as we were reaching the best bit. Without looking up, I shouted:

"Oi! Lurch! What's with the tape?"

"Ms. Jones?" said a voice I half-recognized. "I wonder if we could have a word?"

"*What?*" I switched off the compressor and turned round, still with my respirator on. Both my visitors took a step back at the sight of me with a long black rubber snout. Pulling it off, I said, furiously:

"For God's sake, I'm working! Couldn't you catch me at home or something?"

"We did try to ring," said the constable who had interviewed me before. "I'm sorry to trouble you—"

"I've got so much to *do*." I ran my fingers through my hair, absent-mindedly discarding the metal filings I found en route. There was nothing I could do about the soot; that would have to wait till I got home. Noticing another scorch mark on the bosom of my sweater, I pulled off my work gloves and began to pick off the burnt bits. Force of habit.

"I'm DS Fogarty," said the sergeant rather nervously, "and this is WPC Hamlin."

"Yeah, we met before. Look, what is it? I really haven't got much time."

"We've identified the body that was found down there," said WPC Hamlin, nodding at the trap. She seemed quite unfazed by my Tank-Girl-after-a-nuclear-explosion look. It was always the men who crossed themselves and muttered the Lord's Prayer under their breath.

"How?" I said.

"A couple of pieces of jewellery she was wearing, and dental records. She was called Shirley Lowell and she went missing three years ago, a presumed suicide," said the WPC concisely.

"Well, I had nothing to do with this theatre till about two months ago," I said. "That should be easy enough to check."

"Have you ever heard the name Shirley Lowell before?" said WPC Hamlin.

I shook my head. "Not that I remember. She was strangled, wasn't she? I saw the marks on her neck when I was down there with Marie."

They exchanged glances. "I don't think there's any harm in confirming that," said DS Fogarty cautiously. "And talking about Marie Lavelle, we have information that she was part of a circus company that performed here almost three years ago. There's someone else here who was in the company. . . ."

"Sophie Sandeman," WC Hamlin prompted. "Do you know anything about the circus company at all?"

"Well, Sophie's the costume designer for this show," I said. "I didn't know she'd worked here before. But the only person in this whole place I've known for longer than a couple of months is Sally—Salvatore Santorini, the set designer on the *Dream*," I said. So far that was one evasion and one lie direct. "Now do you mind if I get back to work? I don't want to be rude but I really don't think I can help you, and I've got a mobile to finish by tomorrow."

They trooped off to the crew room to interview any poor souls who might be lurking in its depths. I pulled my respirator back over my head and started grinding down the weld, thinking hard. Shirley Lowell was the name of the girl Hazel had known at drama school, the one who was supposed to have committed suicide like Richey Edwards of the Manic Street Preachers. Chucked herself off the Severn Bridge. Why had they thought that was the reason she had killed herself—was it just because of the copycat method, or had she left a note?

I hadn't wanted to ask either of the police officers. It would have meant showing more interest than I wanted; I have a long-rooted dislike of giving them information, and somehow I had been reluctant to tell them about Hazel's friendship with Shirley Lowell. Others probably would, in any case. So who could tell me what I wanted to know? Questioning Hazel would be as productive as asking a brick wall how its mortar was doing.

Looking down at what I was doing, I cursed. I had ground down the wretched thing too far and now it was uneven. One thing at a time, Sam. Now I'd have to start all over again.

"Sam! Have you heard the latest? The police are here again! They've found out who that bird was that got herself topped!"

Lurch clattered down the stairs, heavy with news.

"Yup, I've just had them in here, bothering me. Look, sort this out for me, will you? I've just cocked it up." I explained briefly what I wanted him to do and threw the respirator at him. "I've got to see a woman about a corpse."

∘∘∘

The police had already brought Margery up to date with the latest discovery and she looked, not to put too fine a point on it, terrible. Clearly she had changed her mind about wanting to find out the identity of the body in the sump.

"Hi," I said, realizing that I could stand in the doorway for hours before she registered my presence. She was sitting at her desk, staring straight ahead of her at the opposite wall, her eyes glassy and unfocused. On hearing my voice she fumbled for the spectacles hanging round her neck, but it took her a few moments to wedge them securely onto her nose. Her face was so pale that her neat, appropriate make-up would have been garish if it had not been so discreetly executed. Still, for the first time, I could see the careful artifice of her appearance. She looked her age. I shivered for a moment with intimations of mortality.

"Margery?" I said more gently. "Are you all right?"

"Oh, Sam. I've just had the police here. It's so awful. . . ." And putting her head down on the desk, knocking her glasses askew, she burst into a flood of tears. I stood awkwardly. The deliberately casual pose I had adopted to seem informal now felt clumsy and forced. When someone as authoritative as Margery broke down, no-one knew what she would accept as comfort and what she would later resent. I almost felt that the best thing to do would be to close the door and leave her to recover in peace, in her pretty room with its peach fitted carpet, matching pastel prints and impeccably tended pot plants; but I wanted to find out if she knew anything about Shirley Lowell's death. So instead I came further into the room, dropping my work gloves on the table, and went into the kitchenette to make some tea, the British prophylactic against disappointments in love, sudden death, bodies in sumps. . . .

Margery had stopped crying by the time I brought her a mug of tea, but that was the only improvement. I had found some aspirins in the kitchen cupboard, and I set a couple down next to her with a glass of water to hand. Then I drew up a chair opposite her at the desk, sipped at my own mug and tried to look as sympathetic as possible. If she were going to confide in anyone it would be an outsider, and God knew I qualified as that.

"Thank you," she said after a while, sitting up and sniffling. She dried her eyes, swallowed the aspirin and then made a great play of cleaning her glasses with a special soft cloth, which she folded carefully into a square before polishing each lens.

"Did you know the girl that was killed?" I suggested, when she had finished. She sat looking down rather helplessly at the now-shiny glasses on the desk, one of those perpetually busy people who, without the next urgent task to perform, are unanchored and adrift. "Is that why you were so upset?"

"What?" She looked at me, her eyes still filmed over. It was as if she hardly knew who I was. "No, of course not. I don't get involved with that side of things at all."

"What side of things?" I said curiously.

"Auditions and so on. She was an actress, the police said. They showed me her photograph. She was so pretty, such a tiny little thing, with long dark hair—why would someone do a thing like that—someone *here*. . . ."

"So she hadn't actually acted here? She just came to audition?"

"No-one can remember her. So I assume she was never in a production of ours, at least. Though she could have been in something like that circus company. Not that one, though. They'd checked." Margery was regaining control of herself.

"Who would she have met, three years ago, if she came to audition?" I persisted.

"Oh, it could have been lots of people," Margery said wearily. "I mean, it might not even have been an audition, I just said that because she was an actress. But she might have applied for a job as an SM, something like that—a lot of them do, they think it's a way to get to know people who could be useful to them if they're not being cast in anything."

"But wouldn't you have met her then?"

She shrugged. "Not initially, only if we actually took her on. It hardly helps, in fact, knowing when she went missing. It just makes us all more tense." Certainly she looked no better. "There was something familiar about her, too. I don't know, maybe she just reminded me of someone. But I can't help feeling—"

"Margery?" said someone from the doorway. It was Ben. "Are you OK?" he said, his voice becoming concerned as he took in her appearance. He himself was the same as ever, square glasses, battered old sweater, steady as a rock. Well, someone had to be, with Philip and Margery going to pieces around him. I had a wave of sympathy for Ben, who seemed increasingly to be the only one at the Cross holding things together. "You look . . ." he started. Out of politeness, he avoided specifying exactly how Margery looked. "Anyway, um, maybe you should go home or something."

Margery sighed. She looked as drained as an empty bottle. "I don't seem to be able to settle to anything," she said. "The police have just been to see me."

"They're with Philip at the moment," Ben said. "Doing the rounds again. They've identified the body."

"I know. I'm supposed to be looking her up to see if we have any record of her on file—CVs, job applications, anything like that. Someone's coming back afterwards to go through everything with me. So I can't go home," she added. "I wish I could." She looked up at Ben wistfully. "It's so out of my control, you see," she said. "There's nothing I can do about it. I feel so—so *passive*. I hate that."

Ben scratched the top of his head, ruffling his hair endearingly so that the lock at the front stood up like Tintin's. "There's nothing any of us can do," he said. "I'm spending twenty-four hours a day as it is trying to calm Philip down. You know how much he hates interviews. Giving statements to the police is like having seventeen arts correspondents crammed in the room with him. It'll take him weeks to recover, and we've got so much to do."

"I heard you've cast *A Doll's House*," I volunteered.

Ben stared at me. "It's not supposed to be public knowledge," he snapped, his good humour fading at once. "My God, the way gossip travels round this place! It's enough to drive you to drink!"

He turned on his heel and left the room. In the silence we heard his footsteps, fast and angry, almost stamping up the linoleum-covered stairs. I raised my eyebrows, thinking that Ben seemed to have his priorities slightly skewed. Still, I was sorry that I'd stepped on his toes.

"Ben's being a tower of strength," Margery said, seeing that I was startled and trying to explain away his sudden surge of bad temper. "He's got so much on his plate. Philip's really gone to pieces—"

But she was interruptd by WPC Hamlin tapping lightly on the open door.

"Would it be all right to go through the files now, Mrs. Pickett?" she inquired with such extreme politeness that it was clear she had every intention of taking the office apart whether Margery agreed or not. Margery heaved another sigh.

"Go ahead," she said, gesturing with one spiritless hand at the filing room.

WPC Hamlin, summing up the situation in a glance, wandered into the stock room and said innocently:

"What an excellent filing system! Did you work it out yourself?"

"Yes. Yes, I did." Margery sat up straighter.

"This all looks very comprehensive. I wonder if you'd mind just giving me a rough idea of how you've organized it and then I won't trouble you any longer."

Margery put on her glasses. "Certainly," she said, pushing back her chair. She went through to the file room with what was almost a spring in her step. "We'll start with the job applications I've kept on file. They're over here, filed alphabetically, of course—"

She had forgotten my existence. I left her office and went upstairs, meaning to get a breath of fresh air before plunging back into the basement depths. On the way I saw Ben going into Philip Cantley's office; he even favoured me with a nod as I passed him. I couldn't help wondering absently about the world view that allowed Ben to be comparatively relaxed about a dead body that had been floating beneath his feet ever since he had arrived at the theatre, and jumpy as a scalded cat about the casting of a play he wasn't even going to direct. Perhaps he was one of those people who liked to know more than anyone else—in which case the theatre was the wrong place for him to work.

I had only been here a few weeks, but already I had learnt that gossip spread like melted butter. Kiss someone you weren't supposed to in Stratford and the whole of the Barbican Centre knew about it within a couple of hours. It might take a couple of days to reach us here at the Cross, but reach us it would. Actors made artists look the soul of discretion. And once those underground lines of communication had been established, it was impossible to switch them off. Everyone in the industry would know now about what was happening at the Cross, that the body of a girl had been found here, strangled, and they would be speculating with morbid enjoyment about what would happen next.

That was something I could have done with knowing myself. It seemed to me that the underground wires were humming, not with news but with tension, strung up as tight as everyone's nerves. Look at the way Bez and Steve had nearly come to blows the other day; Ben, snapping at the oddest things; Margery in tears; Philip Cantley, barricaded in his office as if the light of day would scorch him if he came out. I knew something about sudden death by now, how its wake can spread so strongly that it pulls other people under with it; how one person's fear can breed monsters, seeing danger in every shadow, leaching out to the people around them by osmosis, a nebulous anxiety inhaled with every breath one takes. There was someone in this theatre who was very afraid. I could sense it. And their fear could make them dangerous.

13

"Shirley Lowell?" Janey said vaguely. "Never heard of her. Do you know how many aspiring actresses there are? At any given time something like ninety-five per cent of the profession's out of work. Did she have an agent?"

"I don't know. She was just out of drama school."

"Which one?"

I shrugged.

"Well . . ." Janey said, dismissing further speculation. She leant back on the sofa and tilted her head back to look at the mobile nearest to us. "It's got nothing to do with Helen, anyway. She'd never heard of her either. I'm glad, because she's so nervous now with the production week coming up. The tech—it really gets on her nerves."

"Why?" I said curiously.

"Oh, all the hanging around. Have they told you what happens? It's a nightmare for the actors, all they get to do is top and tail their scenes and stand about for hours while the crew rush about being busy and important. Poor Helen, she always hates it. And poor Shirley Lowell, of course," she added. "I didn't mean to sound callous."

"Well, as long as it was unintentional . . ."

Janey, instead of catching this piece of sarcasm, let it fall to the ground and gave me a peculiarly sweet and rather absent smile by way of response. She was currently not of this earth, but living on *Witches' Peak,* which was the title of the book she had optioned and talked a producer into reading. They had an initial go-ahead to commission a writer to do a treatment and the first episode. Gita, the producer, was apparently confident that the series would eventually get the green light. And since in Janey's opinion Gita and God seemed to be synonymous, Janey was over the moon with excitement.

"It's got everything," Janey had said earlier, bursting into my studio like a bomb. "It's a great thriller, family drama, some supernatural bits—I can't tell you how popular that kind of thing is at the moment—and some really juicy parts for women. We sent a copy of the book to Natasha Richardson's agent and apparently she loves it."

"Natasha Richardson?"

"No, the agent. But it's a start."

"Is there a part in it for Helen?" I inquired casually.

Janey looked surprised. "Oh, there are lots of good parts. I hadn't really—I mean, it'll be a while before we get around to casting it. Helen's doing so well at the moment it hadn't even occurred to me to cook something up for her. She's getting loads of interest," she added.

"But not A Doll's House."

"Oh, she wasn't that keen on it anyway," Janey said airily. "TV pays so much more, and you know Helen. She's up for a part in the new Inspector Grant series. They want a woman sidekick, and she'd be perfect. It would really get her face known."

"The cool, poised new sergeant on the block, melting slowly under the force of Inspector Grant's laid-back Cornish charm and middle-age spread," I said idly. "These endless series with ugly old detective blokes pulling women half their age, not to mention weight. It's all such bollocks, really, isn't it?"

But that was not the right line to take with someone who was already eating, breathing and sleeping *Witches' Peak*, the four-part supernatural thriller-cum-family drama destined to be the highlight of BBC1's autumn viewing. Janey stared at me as if she were a member of the Spanish Inquisition to whom, in a moment of carelessness, I had casually remarked that you couldn't deny that there was a lot to be said for the Protestant work ethic.

"Well, I'm sorry it's not Shakespeare," she said with heavy sarcasm.

"Just because you bumped into someone at Torture Garden who got you involved in something culturally significant for once—"

"Oi! As if my sculptures weren't culturally significant!" I protested. "Wait till you read my catalogue notes. I'm exploring the heaven/earth dichotomy by leaving the viewer perpetually suspended between two worlds, causing him/her to reinvestigate his/her previously conceived notions of stability and balance."

"Who *writes* that shit?" Janey said in horror.

"Someone who would be much better occupied turning out drama series for BBC1."

Janey snorted. "They'd have to put up something better than that before I'd give them a commission. Still," she said, fixing me with a gaze, "I know that you actually do have lots of deep and meaningful theories about your work. You just hate talking about them. I can't say I blame you, but sooner or later you're going to have to."

"Redemption," I said flippantly. "Raising the dead."

"What?" She stared at me till she realized what I meant. Then her eyes dropped.

"I do think it's good you're finally talking about his death," she said, fixing her gaze on her wrist, which instead of its usual clatter of bangles was sporting a single silver twist. Janey was definitely going for the minimal look these days. She turned it slowly, deliberately not looking up at me. "Maybe this way you'll be able to move on."

"From what to what?" I straightened up, insulted. "I mean, what's not working out for me at the moment?"

"Well, your lack of interest in a permanent commitment," Janey suggested.

"Oh, for God's sake—you're the one that's lying on the couch, not me. Look, I was crap at commitment even before him! That didn't change anything!"

"Relationships," said Janey pontifically, "are necessary for the development of the psyche. Only when you've been with someone for at least a few years do you start to learn important things about yourself—"

"Your capacity for boredom," I muttered.

"Actually," Janey corrected me piously, "I was thinking more of compromise and sacrifice."

"*Exactly,*" I said in heartfelt tones. "And I'd like to know who just cast you as Maria von Trapp in *The Sound of Music*. Anyway, I am seeing—well, dating—well, I went to bed with someone the day before yesterday."

"What's that got to do with having a relationship?" Janey protested.

"It's a start, isn't it?" I said unanswerably, getting up to fetch us more beers, and rather wishing I hadn't brought up the subject. To my surprise, however, Janey didn't press me for details, as she normally would have done. Perhaps my amorous vicissitudes looked like mere anthills viewed from the newly discovered dizzy heights of her permanently smug commitment. Certainly this new job was changing her. The added responsibility had gone to her head. I just hoped the effect wore off: I wanted my Janey back, even if that did mean her making me talk about things I didn't really want to.

And I was certainly reluctant to describe my recent encounter with Hugo. The effect he had had on me was extraordinary. He was just as confident as I was, which was nothing new; but his self-control, which at least equalled mine, was something of a revelation. I relished my ability to aggravate men into losing their cool while keeping mine, but Hugo was the first man to attract me so powerfully with whom this manoeuvre simply wouldn't work. I was simultaneously annoyed and fascinated, and I suspected he felt much the same about me. Even in bed we circled each other warily. Most of the time.

And he hadn't rung me since. Normally, if I'd wanted to see him, I would have ignored this and rung him instead; but somehow with Hugo the usual rules I had made for myself didn't seem to apply. I felt as if I were stumbling in the dark. No wonder I didn't want to talk about him.

○○○

"Can we go back one lighting state and leave the sound running?" MM called.

"We're in the Oberon state," said the lights man sourly.

"Yes, well, I want the Titania/Bottom state again," MM said patiently.

The lights dimmed and dipped.

"Could we make it a three-second fade and hang the black just a second more?" she requested.

"Do the lights change before my entrance?" Hugo said from the stage.

"Yes, there's a blackout and—hang on—" MM said, holding up a hand. She was in the centre aisle, on a high stool, with another stool in front of her on which was propped the production book, a ring binder with text on one side and all the business—blocking, cues, set changes, lighting—on the other. Flicking back a page, she checked something out. The composer, in a seat next to the aisle, whispered something to her. She nodded and made a note in the ring binder. Sally, Sophie and I were clustered together on the other side of the aisle, a Thermos of coffee propped between the former's feet. MM called out:

"Yeah, Hugo, there's the blackout and then your music. The Oberon signature tune."

"*Lovely,*" Hugo drawled. "I shall stroll on gently to savour it the better."

"Can we run that again?" The lights faded and died. "All right, on you come."

There was the sound of a stumble and then a vivid curse from Hugo.

"You all right?" Steve said to him from the wings.

"It's so bloody dark out there I need infrared goggles," he said pettishly, arriving onstage.

"All right," MM called, "we're going back to run the scene before, now that everyone's ready. Is Tabitha coming into place?"

"Just hauling her down now," came Bez's voice from high up and far away. The radio headsets were on the blink again and everyone was having to shout, which was not improving the general tenor of the afternoon. Not that you would have known it was the afternoon; even checking the time meant nothing, because time was suspended here. The only thing that mattered was getting the tech right, never mind how long it took. Day for night, night for day.

It was cold in the auditorium without the heating on, the handful of spectators bundled up in sweaters, and every time the stage lights paled to the pearly blue of moonlight, glowing silver on the mobiles, we shivered. The effect was eerie, supernatural, an atmosphere where fairies and spirits seemed the norm and humans out of place. And the colder the images were, the chillier I felt. Watching polar bears on television, you reach for a blanket to wrap around your shoulders. So it was with the set lit for midnight, as black, cold and remote as distant space, the mobiles hanging like strange planets made even stranger by the faint light of their moon.

Helen, as Titania, was discovered lounging on a pile of silvery leaves. Sophie's costumes were fabulous; Helen looked like the Ice Queen from the fairy tale, capable of planting a splinter of ice in the heart of anyone foolish enough to love her. Her wig was so fair it was almost platinum, woven through with strands of silver, her tiny little tiara a Slim Barrett–inspired creation of leaves and diamonds. Bill, as Bottom, wearing his donkey's head, the only part of his costume he had put on, waited beside her for MM's command to start.

"OK, Helen, call the fairies in," came MM's prosaic voice, shattering the magic. "Looking good, isn't it?" she said to Sally and Sophie.

"Peaseblossom, Cobweb, Moth and Mustardseed!" Helen said rather wearily. Ranjit, as Peaseblossom, cartwheeled on, calling: "Ready!" when his head was closer to the ground than his feet; Cobweb, the blond boy, leaning against a flat with his head thrown back, blew a couple of smoke rings before his own "And I!," stubbing out his cigarette and strolling on; Moth, the redheaded girl, ran on, her "And I!" a beat late, throwing herself repentantly at Titania's feet; and still there was no sign from Tabitha. The fairies looked around nervously. Helen remained motionless, waiting. Finally Tabitha's head popped over the top of one of the mobiles.

"And I!" she cried triumphantly, and disappeared from sight for a moment. The jump down was breathtaking, even though I was expecting it. It was impossible to tell that Tabitha was being flown; she made the leap look utterly spontaneous, landing as lightly as a drop of water. The spectators burst into applause and Tabitha, flushed with pride, sketched a little out-of-character curtsy.

"OK, very nice, but it could still be better," said MM, jumping down off her stool and going up on stage. In her jeans and hooded sweatshirt, her clumpy shoes and hair pulled back in an untidy twist, she should have looked incongruous, embarrassed by her own lack of glamour, next to the exquisite little fairies and Helen's regal bearing. Even though the actors weren't made up or in full costume, the magic of their roles clung to them like sequins. But such was MM's assurance that she looked not a whit out of place.

Tabitha, whom she was addressing, had her hands clasped in front of her; she was still glowing with excitement from the success of her jump, her dark eyes sparkling. The others had gone into the actors' slump, bones sunk deep into their sockets, shoulders hunched, arms hanging, looking as if they were nailed between their shoulders to a pole, the rest of their limbs left to droop unsupported. It was the standard pose while they waited for a scene to be blocked or the lighting state to be altered. I had already learnt how much of acting involved hanging around waiting for someone else to finish what they were doing.

"I want you to get your head up there earlier," MM was saying to Tabitha, "so that when you say 'And I!' we actually register that you've been there for a while already, because we haven't seen the movement as you come up. Do it on Ranjit's 'Ready!'—no-one will be looking any-where but at him."

Ranjit, straightening up automatically as his name was mentioned, smirked at this.

"What do you think, Thierry?" MM said to the choreographer.

"Yeah, I told her to do that when we rehearsed it," he called from the back of the auditorium. "She must have got over-excited. The jump was great, though, wasn't it?"

"Great," MM agreed. "Can we run it again? I want to make sure Tabitha gets that head movement right."

There was a collective groan. The guy who was operating Tabitha's line came on stage to hitch her up to it again; the other fairies went offstage; Tabitha was hauled up and disappeared behind the mobile again, and the whole procedure was repeated—not so good this time apart from Tabitha's timing, which was right on cue, and her jump, which was even better than before. Sally was grinning smugly.

"You see?" he said to me and Sophie. "She ees—was—the right one to choose."

And from Tabitha's hundred-watt smile, one could see that she knew it too.

ooo

Marie, as Puck, had already made her triumphant entrance, coming down on the mobile and then leaping off onto Oberon in a sideways manoeuvre that took three operators and no less than four attempts to perfect. By now I felt completely drained. All the bits involving my mobiles were over, anyway. I wandered backstage in the hope of bumping into Hugo. The auditorium was dark apart from the tiny bright orange spots of cigarettes burning away and the small pen lights the spectators were using to follow the action in their scripts. Scrabbling around, I located the door beside the boxes and slipped through it into another world.

The auditorium, built in the 1880s and lovingly restored with lottery money, was a plush little jewel box in crimson and dark salmon with dull gold fittings, thickly decorated with elaborate swags and rosettes in plaster moulding on the domed ceiling and fronts of the boxes. Backstage, in total contrast, the corridors were bare brick: pipes and wiring exposed, neon strip lights running down the centre of the low ceiling. It was chilly and there were ashtrays everywhere. As I came round the corner to the DSM desk the smell of stale beer and cigarettes washed towards me. The wings were full of morose actors waiting for their scenes; this was the horror of the tech rehearsal, where all they were required to do was make their exits and entrances and stand still for any lighting changes that might happen while they were onstage, reduced to puppets for the day that the crew took command. Normally they would be in their dressing rooms, or the pub, but now, with the scenes so compacted and yet so stretched out, they had to be permanently on call, and they hated it.

The fire bucket I passed was as full of fag butts as of sand. Next to it was a huge hamper, large enough for three people to fit inside it comfortably, spilling material. Louise, the DSM, was in her element. Like MM's backstage equivalent, she sat calmly at her desk, checking off cues one by one and keeping up a near-constant stream of quiet talk on her radio headset, which the chief sparks had finally repaired. Before her glowed the unearthly green screen of the TV monitor, showing what was happening on stage. The voices of the actors, crew and occasionally MM, when she went up on stage, echoed round our heads, piped through by the microphone above the stage that relayed the show to the entire backstage area. People working in their offices, or down in the basement, switched it off; everyone else needed it to hear when their cues were coming up.

I went into the little SM office to make myself some coffee. It was cluttered with cans of drink, beakers of stale beer, ashtrays full of banana skins and fag butts, and stacks of paper that looked as if they might be important. The chemical smell of Lysol and carpet-cleaning fluids hung in the air, competing strongly with the cigarette smoke. I had never seen it so untidy.

"God, it's filthy in here," wailed one of the little ASMs, scampering in for a moment and looking around her in horror. "Wait till we have to tidy it up for tomorrow. . . ." She pulled a mini-Mars bar out of her pocket and polished it off in two bites. "I get so bored and sleepy," she said to me. "I just keep snacking, it's terrible. When the show's up and running it's OK, but production week I always put on pounds and pounds." She fluttered out again, distracted. Oh, the glamour of the theatre.

"I thought I saw you come in," said Hugo from the doorway. "You didn't even come and say hello. I was slumped over there on that hamper, chainsmoking. Been there for the last hour." He gestured to a niche next to the dusty, upright piano. "I've rather pissed my territory around it. Access by invitation only."

"Are you inviting me?" I said, more cockily than I felt. He should have looked rather odd, with the top part of his costume pulled on over his stripy trousers, but since all I could think about was how he looked naked, concentrating on the incongruity of his clothing didn't help to summon up my confidence.

"I might be." He looked at me thoughtfully. "You're not pissed off with me, are you?"

"Nope."

"You're not avoiding me?"

"On the contrary."

"Good. Because I was rather hoping to go to bed with you again and if you were avoiding me that would make things rather difficult from a technical point of view."

I stared at him assessingly. "I think it's time you came round to my studio," I said, after a while. "See whether you're up to the full horror that is my life."

"I thought you'd never ask. When?" he said with flattering enthusiasm.

I shrugged. "If you're free tomorrow evening . . ."

"It's a date."

The voices transmitted over the show relay had, for the past few minutes, become increasingly frenzied. Engrossed in negotiations with Hugo, I had tuned out all but their sheer noise; but now, arrangements made, egos reassured, they broke in on us with the force of a hurricane. There was a great buzz of talk through which MM's angry tones sliced like a blunt cleaver:

"Will someone bloody go and find her, then!" she was saying furiously.

"I've looked all round backstage already," Matthew cut in.

"I don't care *where* you've looked—will everyone please go and find Violet! *Now!"*

The last word was practically shouted. It was followed by the artificially magnified sound of lots of feet clumping hurriedly across the stage, off to track down the errant Violet. I looked at Hugo, who was staring vaguely at the coffee machine.

"This is not good," he observed almost to himself.

"Hail, master of understatement," I said sarcastically.

"Mm." He turned, his abstracted grey gaze flickering over me as absently as if he were still looking at the coffee machine, and left the room. Naturally, this piqued my curiosity, not to mention my vanity. I followed on his heels.

He went, not in the direction of the stage, but down the corridor that led to the offices. At the far end was Philip Cantley's, and by the purposeful strides Hugo was taking, that seemed to be where we were headed. I pattered along a few steps behind like a wife in Saudi Arabia on day release from the zenana, feeling as if I should be wearing a chador and looking demurely at the ground.

I was right about our direction. At Philip Cantley's door Hugo stopped and knocked.

"Philip?" he said. "It's Hugo. Look, is Vi in there? They've been calling her for the last fifteen minutes."

"He'll have turned off the stage mike," he added to me in an undertone, "so they might not have heard the calls. . . . Vi? Are you in there?"

"Ssh!" I said, putting my hand over his mouth and rather annoyed by how far I had to reach up when I wasn't wearing heels. The contact sent a little shiver running through me, but I pretended that I was as detached as ever. "I can hear something."

"Well, they'll have to stop," Hugo said through my fingers. He bit one reflexively and then removed my hand. "Vi's in enough trouble as it is."

"No, I don't mean that. Listen."

The unusual happened: Hugo and I fell silent simultaneously. In the unaccustomed quiet, we could hear what sounded like a puppy whimpering faintly on the other side of the door. Hugo frowned.

"What the hell—Vi! Vi! Are you in there?" He turned the handle of the door and pushed it gently. The whimpering seemed to intensify. Hugo looked at me rather nervously.

"Go on," I said impatiently. By now I was consumed with curiosity. He pushed the door further open and edged through it tentatively. Then he stopped dead, blocking the doorway. I had to duck around him to see what was in the room.

It was dramatic enough. Violet was pressed up against a bookshelf with her hands flat behind her, her face white as her shirt. In her beige jodhpurs and silk leopard-print scarf she looked like Gene Tierney in a Forties film, having just discovered a murdered body and convinced that people are going to think she did it. Only Gene Tierney tended to underact, while Violet—well, it would have been cruel to say that she was milking the situation for its histrionic possibilities, but certainly the whimpers issuing from between her perfectly painted lips would have been considered rather overstated in a professional context.

Hugo's first instinct, annoyingly enough, was to rush over and embrace the catatonic Violet. Mine was to swing my gaze round to the owner of the office, slumped back in his desk chair in a manner that tended to signify only one thing, particularly when I noticed the mini-syringe on the desk in front of him. Leaning over, careful not to touch anything, I noticed another two on the floor beside him. His sleeve was rolled up, but no track marks were visible in the crook of his elbow. A streak of sunlight was falling across his face from the open window behind him, but, though he looked even more like Dracula than ever, his expression in death positively saturnine, I somehow didn't think it was the daylight that had put an end to Philip Cantley.

"We should call the police," I said firmly. Violet had draped herself over Hugo and was making little moaning noises, which were beginning to irritate me beyond belief. "Let's get out of here. I'll take Violet down to Margery's office and you go next door and ring 999. Don't let anyone come in till the police get here."

Hugo looked doubtfully down at Violet's cluster of dark curls, now nestled in the crook of his arm.

"Do you think—I mean, shouldn't I . . . ?"

"It's best left to a woman," I said decisively, getting one arm round Violet's waist and hauling her bodily off Hugo. "You wouldn't understand."

"Right," Hugo said, looking unconvinced.

Though I confessed to a twinge of jealousy—most unlike me—on seeing Violet fall into Hugo's arms like the errant wife returning to the forgiving husband at the end of a three-reel spectacular, my main reason for separating the embracees was to give Hugo his hands free to make the telephone call. I had been involved in enough violent deaths for me to be a touch wary of ringing the emergency services to announce merrily my involvement, albeit peripheral, in yet another one.

This could be Hugo's turn. I was capable of tremendous generosity, when it wasn't a question of clasping attractive young actresses to his bosom. He could be the one to take the nice policemen and women on a guided tour of the amenities of Philip Cantley's office, dead artistic director today's speciality. I took Violet down the corridor to Margery's office, parked her there on the sofa and yelled down the stairs to Lurch. I happened to know he was busy repairing one of the chairs for the opening scene which Francis, the drunken old lech with the smelly socks, had stumbled over and broken.

Lurch's head and shoulders appeared at the bottom of the staircase.

"All right, Sam? What's up?"

"Go and find MM and tell her that Philip Cantley's dead and Violet's in shock because she found him, OK? Hugo's ringing the police and everyone should just stay calm. Oh, and send Sophie in here, will you?"

It was a heavy burden to put on the shoulders of a teenager. Lurch's eyes widened and his jaw dropped. His face, already too long, now looked like a tombstone.

"Up, up, come on," I said firmly, "move those feet, come on, Lurch, get going." Sometimes I missed being a weights teacher. I had a knack for giving orders. "That's right, off you go. . . ."

Lurch came up the stairs with a slow, heavy step and his mouth still wide open. I reached up and flicked it shut.

"It looks better that way," I said. "Trust me on this one."

I watched him disappear, wondering what kind of garbled message he would give MM. In this I underestimated the boy; Sophie arrived in five minutes with a good grasp of the situation. She had recently shaved her head and now resembled Sinèad O'Connor's younger, even prettier sister. Cutting off all your hair emphasizes your features and Sophie's eyes, already large, now looked unfeasibly huge, like a heroine in a Manga comic. She was wearing hipster jeans, a tiny top and yet another pair of large ugly trainers. I sighed.

Speech burst out of her like bubbles from a bottle of fizzy water.

"Sam? Lurch said you were in here with Violet. Where's Margery?" She looked around her as if expecting Margery to pop out from under the desk. "What's happened to Philip? They said he's dead. I can't believe it. But then I saw Hugo and he said it was true."

"Where is he? Hugo, I mean."

"Standing outside Philip's office, he won't let anyone go in—"

"Good."

"Where's Margery?" Sophie said again, more insistently. I raised my eyebrows.

"She'll have gone home ages ago. It's nearly eight. Look, I wanted you here because Violet's in a terrible state and you're a friend of hers."

"God, nearly *eight?*" Sophie said in horror. "And we've got so much more to do. I mean . . ." She broke off, looking shamefaced. "I didn't mean that, everything just seems so confused. What's happened to Violet?"

Violet, lying full length on Margery's sofa, stirred slightly at the mention of her name.

"Soph?" she said faintly. "Is that you?"

"Vi! What's been going on?" Sophie dropped to her knees beside Violet. I didn't have a great deal of credence in Violet's near-catatonia; in my experience, people who make scenes about tiny things are often the most cool and collected when a big crisis hits. I was wondering how much of Violet's reaction was genuine shock and how much was camouflage, adopted to play for time.

Sophie, however, would treat everything Violet said as gospel. She had taken one of Violet's small white hands in a reassuring clasp and was tenderly stroking a curl of hair back from her forehead.

"What happened?" Sophie said soothingly. "It's Philip, isn't it? Did you find him like that? It must have been terrible for you."

I observed that any concern Sophie might have for Philip Cantley was thoroughly buried under her more pressing worries about Violet. I could scarcely blame her. Philip Cantley had not been a sympathetic piece of work. And Violet, despite a well-developed capacity for annoying the hell out of her workmates, had a charm as pervasive and powerful as Eighties perfume.

"I went in to talk to him about the play," Violet said, her voice a mere thread, though still audible, each word pronounced with exquisite diction. It was beautifully done. Sophie had now cleared her brow of curls and her smooth white forehead gleamed like a pearl under Sophie's caressing hand. "Not this one, I mean *Doll's House*. I wanted you to do the costumes. My dress for this one is so *lovely*—you understand my figure so *well. . . .*"

I sat down on the armchair and stretched out my legs. This was obviously going to take some time. Sophie, meanwhile, was flushed with praise. No-one could accuse Violet of over-subtlety, but her technique usually hit the spot.

"So you went to see Philip," she prompted.

"He was there already . . . *collapsed* like that . . . oh, it was awful, I knew at *once* he was dead. . . ."

"How come you were so sure?" I couldn't help saying. "I mean, he might just have had a minor stroke or something."

Sophie whipped her head round to stare at me, frowning deeply: Violet was not to be distressed. But she was too late. Violet had already collapsed into misery.

"The needles!" she wailed. "I saw the needles and I *knew*—oh, how could he have been so *stupid?* I told him never to do more than one, I *told* him—*you* know, Soph, I promised you I'd be really careful and I was! He must have done at least *three*. I couldn't believe it, I just didn't know what to do, I couldn't *move*—"

I might not have been in the room; Sophie was focused as intently on Violet as if she had been confessing to having murdered Philip Cantley and, for good measure, Shirley Lowell too.

"Do you mean you gave him some of your stuff? The insulin?"

She sounded so horrified that Violet covered her face with one hand. Clearly deciding that it wasn't enough protection, she retrieved her other hand, which Sophie was still holding protectively, and added that to the first one. Through her fingers she said pitifully:

"I know, I know. But I thought he'd be careful, I really did. Philip was so . . . *controlled*, so sensible about it. *That's* what I can't understand. What happened? It can't have been an accident! I mean—"

Her hands fell to her breast. She stared at Sophie and me with horrified, pansy-blue eyes.

"Do you think . . ." she said.

"Could I just backtrack for a moment?" I suggested in my best reassuring, you-can-tell-me-anything, I'm-a-sculptor voice. "Violet, you were doing insulin for some reason. Does one *do* insulin?" I wondered. "Never mind, let's move on from arid considerations of terminology to the more crucial question of why the fuck you were mainlining the stuff in the first place."

"Oh, you don't inject it into a *vein*," Violet said almost cheerfully. "It's really easy. The dose is all measured out in these little pens they give to diabetics. ActRapid, they're called. Or EpiPens. You just jab them into the muscle, it hardly hurts at all."

"We seem to have lost the plot a bit," I prompted. "I'm still stuck on your reason. I'm sure you had one. You don't strike me as the kind of person who does much on a whim."

"To lose weight!" Violet said, as if it were the most obvious thing in the world. She perked up at once. "It increases your metabolic rate and breaks down the carbohydrates and fats much faster than your body does on its own," she added as earnestly as a recent convert to Scientology explaining its weird inner workings, "so you can eat what you like and afterwards you give yourself the injection. The pens all have the right dose, you see, so you can't take too much."

"Unless you do three at a time," I commented, remembering the ones I had seen on the floor by Philip Cantley's desk.

"Why did he *do* it?" Violet moaned, returned from happy diet secrets to cruel reality. "I don't understand. . . ."

There was a note in her voice that seemed forced. I looked at her carefully. When the thought had hit her earlier that Cantley might have deliberately overdosed, she had been genuinely shaken, but not really surprised. And the only reason for that was that she had some idea of why he might have done it.

"Violet," I said slowly, "I think you know why he might have killed himself."

"Sam!" Sophie said furiously. "That's enough! You're pushing her too far!"

"It's all going to come out anyway," I said. "The police are pretty good at questioning people, you know. They'll get it all out of her. She might as well have some practice at talking about it. Besides, I think I've guessed anyway."

"Do they have to know?" Violet said, blanching.

I shrugged. "What's it to you? He's dead. He can't hurt you. Why not tell them what you think?"

She nodded, paper-white by now.

"What *is* this?" Sophie said, impatient and jealous that Violet and I were talking to each other over her head. "What are you talking about?"

I exchanged glances with Violet. "Violet thinks," I said simply, "that Philip Cantley killed the girl whose body we found in the sump. Shirley Lowell."

Sophie caught her breath. "Oh my *God*," she breathed. "Oh my *God*." She looked as if she were going to go into spasm; she was trembling from head to foot. I frowned, surprised, not having expected the statement to provoke this violent a reaction. What, after all, was Philip Cantley to her?

Then Sophie started crying. Through her tears she said:

"He could have killed you! He could have killed you too! Oh Vi, if anything had happened to you I'd never have forgiven myself—I'd have killed him if he'd done anything to you. Oh God, I don't believe it, I just don't—"

She reached forward and, before Violet could stop her, pulled at the chiffon scarf at the latter's neck. It came away only slightly, but enough for us both to see the pattern of bruises just above the delicate collarbone. Sophie burst into wild wrenching sobs.

"Look at what he's done to you, the bastard! If I had him here I'd kill him myself."

There was a knock at the door. Sophie started; Violet caught her scarf to her neck with one small white hand and pressed herself back into the sofa, head thrown back like Greta Garbo about to face the firing squad in *Mata Hari*; and I said prosaically:

"Who is it?" One of us had to have a sensible reaction.

"Hugo," said Hugo, putting his head round the door. "The police are here. They want to talk to Violet, if she's feeling better."

The ensuing emotional mayhem took about a quarter of an hour to subdue.

"So do you think he topped himself?" Hawkins said.

"I haven't the faintest idea," I said. "I hardly knew him. He sometimes snarled at me as we passed in the corridor, but that was about the level of our interaction. He snarled at everyone; it wasn't just me. He'd been very jumpy recently, since Shirley Lowell's body turned up. Mind you, now one understands why."

"That's just an assumption," Hawkins pointed out. "Even with Violet Tranter's statement. Bloody hell, they always say actors and actresses are a disappointment when you meet them in the flesh, don't they? Not her. We had half the station queueing up to peer at her when she came in."

"Including you, I take it," I said dryly. "Since you're not working this case."

"I may have sneaked a glance or two," Hawkins admitted. "Tiny little thing, isn't she?"

"It would certainly be hard to suspect her of strangling anyone," I acknowledged. "Sticking a needle full of insulin into a boyfriend, however, would be a piece of cake. Philip Cantley didn't leave a note, did he? I didn't see one on the desk."

Hawkins shook his head. "They checked the computer, too, in case he'd left something on there. That's quite common nowadays. But they didn't come up with anything." He sat back thoughtfully. "He'd been out to lunch with an agent. That's been checked. Apparently they did themselves proud. Cantley could have come back, half-pissed, gone to give himself this injection—most stupid bloody thing I've ever heard, frankly, I'd hate to have to take that in front of a jury. Hard to explain something that idiotic. Anyway, one idea is that Cantley, thinking he's overdone it with all he's eaten for lunch, and still pretty much the worse for drink, decides that one injection won't be enough and just keeps going. Doesn't sound very plausible, though."

I pulled a face. "Violet said he was a very controlled person. It's hard to imagine him doing something that stupid."

"I agree. So either it was suicide, or someone killed him."

"Suicide because he'd killed Shirley Lowell and knew your lot were catching up with him?"

"Well, that's just it. There wasn't anything to tie him into her death. Still isn't, apart from the fact that as the artistic director of the theatre he might have been expected to meet would-be actresses. Add to that Violet Tranter's statement that he liked to play rough in bed and scared her rigid on a couple of occasions—I mean, it's still hardly what you'd call having him bang to rights. And he must have known that. Three years can be a long time when it comes to looking back and collecting evidence. There was talk of Shirley Lowell having a new boyfriend, but no-one seemed to know who he was, and that petered out. The suicide theory seemed so obvious no-one bothered to question it too much. She was a real fan of the Manic Street Preachers and took it very hard when that Richey Something was supposed to have topped himself. They found her car parked in the exact same place his was found, with a cassette of theirs in the tape deck. And she was known to have been depressed."

"Which in retrospect might have had something to do with her relationship with someone who liked to play at throttling her in bed, but whom she didn't want to leave in case it meant he didn't cast her in his next production."

"He seems to have made a practice of that," Hawkins commented. "Gave Violet Tranter the lead part in this next play he was putting on. They were on holiday together a month or so ago. Venice. She said he promised the part to her then."

"I thought she seemed a little evasive on the subject of Goa," I said. "So what happens now?"

Hawkins shrugged. "There's no proof he killed her," he said, "and no suicide note. The guy who killed Shirley Lowell might have decided to knock off Cantley to throw the blame on him instead. It's still a murder investigation. And a messy one at that. I'm just glad it's not mine. Look, Sam." He leaned forward in his chair. Our knees were almost touching. "Forget about dead bodies for a moment. I actually came to talk about, you know, the whole Daphne thing. I don't want you to think I was being a bastard last time, I'm just really confused—"

Just then the doorbell rang. The timing was so exquisite it could only have been Hugo.

"Hello," he said, dropping a kiss on my lips and strolling in through the door. "Why is there a police car parked outside your front door? And talking of front doors, a more unsalubrious one I have never seen. . . . My God, look at this place! It's like something out of a 'Before' picture in *Builder's Weekly*."

"It's pretty clean," I said sulkily. "There's just a lot of stuff."

"You can say that again." He stared up at the mobiles. "Hmm, interesting."

Hawkins had risen from the armchair and was taking stock of Hugo, his arms folded and his feet apart, rather as if Hugo had just been brought in for questioning and Hawkins were staring him down in an attempt to break his nerve before starting the interrogation proper. The effect was somewhat marred by the fact that Hugo was congenitally incapable of being intimidated. Besides, my sitting area is underneath the sleeping platform at the far end of the room, and Hawkins was partly in shadow.

"Hawkins, this is Hugo Fielding. He's an actor in the production that I'm doing the mobiles for," I said inelegantly. "Hugo, this is DI Hawkins, a friend of mine."

"A friend of yours?" Hugo raised his eyebrows. "How daringly louche of you, Inspector Hawkins, to befriend this young degenerate. Doubtless you're trying to make her see the error of her ways. Of your own tastes, Sam, I say nothing. I'm still studying them, after all."

He crossed the room and extended his hand to Hawkins, who grudgingly shook it. I noticed with horror that Hugo was still wearing his Gigolo nail varnish.

The two men presented the strangest contrast: Hawkins, large and stocky, in his M&S suit trousers and an acrylic sweater with a tendency to bobble, looked exactly as an off-duty policeman with a girlfriend called Daphne might be expected to look. While Hugo, tall, slender verging on thin, in full dandy mode today, sporting his stripy trousers, a loose silk shirt with a ruffle down the front and a rust-coloured linen jacket nipped in slightly at the waist, resembled nothing so much as an aristocratic rock star with an account at Browns. In point of fact, Hugo had been born and bred in a terraced house in Surbiton, but the height and the nose, not to mention the drawl, all contributed markedly to the impression of leisured and privileged youth that he amused himself by conveying.

"You hadn't forgotten that we had a rendezvous here this evening, had you, my sweet?" he said, turning back to me. "You shouldn't have dressed up, by the way," he added, casting an unimpressed glance over my skull-and-crossbones leggings and short black sweater.

"I was just going," Hawkins said stiffly.

"Don't let me keep you," Hugo said in honeyed tones. "Fascinating though my conversation is."

I narrowed my eyes at Hugo; if he had cocked his leg, sketched a circle around me with his own wee and then started sniffing Hawkins' bottom, growling all the while, he could scarcely have made himself more obvious. Hawkins picked up his brown leather blouson jacket and slung it over his shoulder.

"You must give me the name of your tailor," Hugo observed.

Hawkins, his jaw clamped tightly shut, strode over to me and enfolded me in the kind of embrace with which he was not generally in the habit of favouring me, certainly not in front of witnesses.

"I'll see you soon," he said to me. "When you're alone," he added, glaring at Hugo. He crossed the room and opened the front door. "Remember to put the locks on when he's gone," he said to me, slapping the iron bar that swung across the door. "You can't be too careful."

"I'll remind her of that myself tomorrow morning, Inspector," Hugo said sweetly. "I'm sorry, I didn't realize you were with the local Neighbourhood Watch or I would have plied you with questions about it. I find the whole area of home security rivetingly fascinating."

Hawkins slammed the door. He usually did. I turned to Hugo, not knowing whether to laugh or start throwing things.

"You were shockingly rude," I said severely. "I have never seen a more naked display of jealousy and possessiveness in my life."

"What about when you dragged Violet off me yesterday?" Hugo said sulkily. "If you'd been singing 'Jolene, I'm begging of you please don't take my man,' it would have come as no surprise."

He slouched against the kitchen table, extracting his cigarette case and flicking out a cigarette.

"Who is that man, anyway? And don't try telling me he's just a friend," he said pettishly.

"Well, what about Violet, since you brought her up?" I snapped, surprising myself both by my own delivery and the fact that I was, strangely enough, rather pleased that Hugo was throwing a tantrum over Hawkins. Usually I have the same attitude to jealousy in my boyfriends as I do to syphilis. "She certainly threw herself into your arms without much hesitation. And you knew all about her and Philip."

"Vi and I," Hugo said, lighting up, "had a fling at drama school and have stayed friends ever since. She confides in me, bless her heart. But I'm not really her type. She likes to be dominated and I haven't got the energy to keep that kind of thing up twenty-four hours a day. I prefer to lounge against things, tossing out witty observations. As you may have noticed. Your turn." I noticed that he had cheered up slightly.

"Hawkins and I," I said resignedly, "have an on-again off-again thing. He lives with a woman called Daphne and now they're thinking of getting married, which is getting him all confused. Still, it would never work out between us, and we both know that perfectly well."

"A doomed love," Hugo said, looking pleased with himself. "The artist and the police inspector. I take it you'll go to their wedding, dressed all in black with a little veil, stand at the back of the church and speak to no-one. People will ask him who you were and, gulping back a manly tear, he will reply: 'Ah, the saddest words on lips and pen are those that run "It Might Have Been" . . .'"

I removed the cigarette from his mouth, stubbed it out, said:

"Peace, I will stop thy mouth," and kissed him.

"I take it that's the definitive answer?" he said, emerging some moments later with his jacket off and his shirt half-unbuttoned. "I mean, I'd hate to feel that you were working off some frustrated passion for PC Plod on me. If you like, we could hire a uniform. It would suit me better than him. He hasn't really got the build for it."

"*Hugo. Shut up.*" I grabbed him by the hair. He looked at me docilely, his eyes gleaming with mischief.

"What is it, darling?"

I made a noise of extreme frustration, let his head go and started undoing his belt instead. There was one sure and certain way to make him stop talking.

I was awoken at the unearthly hour of nine the next morning by a repeated pounding on the front door. My would-be visitor either couldn't find the doorbell or was exhibiting a tender consideration for my nerves by choosing to waken me in a more gradual manner. Wrapped in my kimono, I made my way down the ladder and across the room, still drunk with sleep, peering through the spyhole with bleary eyes. Then I started the long process of unbolting and unbarring the door, my hands slipping clumsily on the locks.

"Finally!" Sally said, coming in and kissing me on both cheeks. "I have brought some breakfast."

"Oh, good. If I were awake that would be great." I stumbled into the kitchen and filled the percolator with coffee. Sally pulled out a plate from the cupboard, looked at it with barely concealed disbelief and washed it carefully under the tap with the hand soap. I had run out of detergent longer ago than I cared to remember. He dried it on his own handkerchief, placed it on the table and produced from a paper bag a mound of pastries, which he piled on the plate. I went into the bathroom to brush my teeth and wash my face and emerged a few moments later, exfoliated and shiny, to find Sally pouring coffee into three mugs.

"I take some up to Hugo," he announced.

I stared at him, drawing the belt of the kimono more securely around my waist.

"How did you know?"

"I see—saw—heem last evening, when he was going home. He said he was coming to see you. He looked," Sally added, "very happy."

"Sal?" Hugo called from upstairs. "Is that you?"

"We have breakfast," Sally called back. "Do you want some?"

"Try to keep me away." A few moments later Hugo came downstairs, swathed in a navy silk spotted dressing gown which I had bought second-hand and never worn because being man-size, like the tissues, it presented a hazard going up and down the ladder to my sleeping platform. "I like this," he said thoughtfully, smoothing down the skirts of the dressing gown. "I think I shall adopt it. It's much too big for you. Ah, coffee. No milk?"

"In thees howse," Sally said, navigating the complicated vowels with aplomb, "eef you want something you bring eet yourself."

"Not necessarily," said Hugo, smirking at me. "Thanks, Sal."

He sipped some coffee. I finished working myself round a *pain au chocolat* and drew a deep breath.

"I theenk thees ees a very good idea," Sally announced. "You and Hugo. You are both very annoying and thees way you break each other's balls instead of breaking ours."

"I *am* a little sore this morning," Hugo agreed. "If I'd known that was what she was up to I would have stopped her earlier. What have you come for, Sal? Are you just being our good angel, come to bless our union with the holy gift of Danish pastries—"

"French," I muttered.

"—French pastries, I stand corrected—or have you come to talk about dead people? I suspect the latter."

Sally's face fell immediately. "Thees ees so terrible," he moaned. "For a moment I have forgotten and now you make me remember."

"Well, you'd remember as soon as you got to the theatre," I pointed out. "It must be swarming with police by now."

"Positively no-one will be able to prove an alibi," Hugo said, lighting up a cigarette and emitting a hacking cough.

"That's attractive," I commented.

He ignored me, continuing: "We were all just milling about. I, of course, was on my hamper the entire afternoon, when I wasn't trotting about on stage, nearly breaking my ankle to satisfy the whims of some power-crazed lighting supremo, but who's going to testify to that? Not a single person will be able to prove that they didn't have a chance to pop into Philip's office and shoot him full of insulin."

"What about MM?" I suggested. "She's right in the middle of things."

Hugo looked at me pityingly. "Don't tell me she didn't go to the loo, or backstage to check something. No-one's going to be able to account for every minute. I for one," he added, taking a long pull on the cigarette, his cough abated by now, "would be extremely suspicious of anyone who did manage to prove an iron-clad alibi."

"I was there all the time!" Sally protested. "Weeth Sam and Sophie!" He turned to me. "You saw me, Sam, no?"

"Well, yes," I said. "Till I went backstage. But I couldn't swear to it that you didn't disappear for ten minutes or so. I mean, I was watching what was happening on stage."

Sally looked mortally offended. "I am going to the theatre," he announced, standing up and pushing the plate away with a gesture of repudiation. "I weell talk to Sophie and we weell see that she remembers that I was there sitting next to hair."

"Yes, but—" I began. It was hopeless. Sally stalked to the door, looking as if someone had ruffled his feathers up the wrong way.

"Sophie," he said coldly, "ees my friend. She weell remember where I was. You weell see."

The door slammed behind him. I pulled a face.

"Bugger it, I didn't mean to wind him up. But what could I say? I mean, I *think* he was there all the time. . . ."

"You see what I mean?" Hugo said. "Be suspicious of the person who proclaims a perfect alibi."

"Oh, don't be silly. Not *Sally*. Besides," I added, "it's not just a question of someone having the opportunity to slip into Philip's office. It must have been someone he could trust reasonably well, to let them get close to him."

"Apparently he'd been drinking like a fish at lunchtime," Hugo commented. "He might have been having a little snooze on the desk and not even noticed someone coming in."

"How do you know?" I said.

Hugo held up his hands pacifically. "No, darling, you haven't caught me out. I was on my hamper, like I said. The person who happened to have been plying Philip with drink was my agent Ronnie, who's not a great one for holding back with the post-prandial brandies. He rang me yesterday all worked up—he'd heard Philip was dead, but not how. Thought he might have stuffed Philip with so much pig's trotter that he'd had a heart attack."

"Pig's trotter?" I said in revulsion.

"It's the latest thing."

"Blech."

"He said," Hugo informed me, "that Philip was definitely not himself. Drinking like a fish, even by Ronnie's highly elastic standards, and seeming very stressed indeed. It adds weight to the suicide theory. Guilt about Shirley Lowell and imminent arrest playing on his nerves."

"But his arrest wasn't imminent. And he didn't leave a note."

"Details, details." Hugo waved a hand majestically.

"You'd better touch up your nail polish," I observed, "it's chipped. Anyway, just supposing that it wasn't suicide for a moment, your idea is that Philip Cantley had passed out when the First Murderer entered with the syringe? But you know, that's another thing that points to it having been done by someone who knew him well. He was injected with his own supply of needle pens. I can't imagine he told that many people about his new diet discovery. Violet, obviously. Sophie knew about Violet, and she might have guessed that Philip Cantley was doing it too. But I doubt she'd have wanted to incriminate Violet."

"I knew about Vi's insulin connection," Hugo put in helpfully. "She told quite a lot of people, actually. And even if she hadn't told me, I'd have had a pretty good suspicion that she was seeing Philip. I mean, they were a little obvious. Holidays taken at the same time, then she gets cast as Nora. . . . I'd be pretty surprised if other people hadn't worked that out too."

"Sophie told me Violet was going out with a banker."

He shrugged. "She'll have said that to cover up for Vi. Wouldn't want anyone to think Vi got Nora through any but the most above-board methods. Though she might well have got it anyway. She'll probably be very good," he observed.

"Who'll direct it?" I asked. "Ben?"

"Don't know. Maybe, as a stopgap, while they're busy appointing a new artistic director. Ben won't get that—he simply hasn't got the pedigree. It's a shame for him Philip's dead, actually. He was very good at handling Philip; if that had gone on for another couple of years he'd have built up a nice little backlist of productions. Now he's in a rather precarious position and I'm sure he knows it—Ben strikes me as someone who keeps his eye firmly on the ball. Whoever gets the job will probably want to bring in their own assistant director. Bad luck for Ben."

He looked at his watch.

"Jesus, I should be at the theatre. It's the dress rehearsal today. *What* fun we're going to have." He paused, as if an idea had just struck him.

"I can tell you're thinking something," I observed. "That noble brow, furrowed with the effort of reflection . . ."

"Oh, it's nothing much," Hugo said, standing up. "I should have a shower."

"What was it?" I said, fired up with curiosity.

"Just about clouds and silver linings," Hugo said with a hint of reluctance. "Ben may be imminently out of a job, but it's worked out nicely enough for MM. Philip dropped in on a run-through last week and took her out for a drink to make some suggestions about how it was going. Standard procedure, nothing unusual, but MM loathes having anyone from outside seeing her productions until the last moment. And he liked to think he knew better than anyone else. I think he threw his weight around a bit and she rather resented it. Can't blame her, really. He could be very annoying."

"And she's very stubborn," I observed.

"Oh, a positive mule. Anyway, this means of course that Philip isn't going to be hanging around driving her mad during the dress and previews, for which I'm sure she'll be extremely grateful. Of course, there are things to iron out, but she knows what they are better than anyone else. I have," Hugo said, "great faith in MM. She's so understated you don't realize how much she's doing with you till all the bones are already laid nicely into place. It's going to be very good, this *Dream.*"

"Scarcely much of a motive for murder," I said, "wanting to get the boss out of the way so you can carry on putting the final touches to your production in peace and quiet."

Hugo raised his eyebrows. "Certainly not," he said austerely. "And now I think I'll go and have that shower."

He disappeared in the direction of the bathroom. I stared after him, even more thoughtful than before.

○○○

After Hugo left, I immersed myself in a hot bath, having decided not to go to the gym. The activities of the night before tended to perform much the same function, when done properly. I still didn't know what I thought about Hugo, so I took an executive decision to try not to think about him at all. We hadn't made plans to see each other again in private; there was always a moment at parting when we looked at each other, the words on both our lips, but neither of us was prepared to swallow our pride and be the first one to propose another meeting. Very juvenile.

I scrubbed myself thoroughly, applied face masks, hair treatment creams and depilatory lotions—the equivalent of servicing a car, really—and finally, all my pores opened and breathing, hair wrapped in a towel, skin pink and resentful at everything it had just had to endure, I curled up on the sofa and rang my agent Duggie to tell him that he could come round and see the new batch of mobiles.

He sounded pathetically pleased to hear from me, poor thing. Duggie didn't like it when his artists went AWOL for a couple of months.

"You haven't answered *any* of my messages," he wailed. "I was so worried. I mean, darling, artistic temperament is one thing but not picking up the phone for months on end is quite another. Finally I thought, well, she's obviously in bed with someone new and much too busy to ring me back, but it wasn't that much of a consolation."

"No sex, just lots of mobiles," I said succinctly, which was the only way to talk to Duggie: he could prattle for Britain.

"Excellent!" Duggie was sounding happier and happier. "When can I come and see them? We've been having some marvellous ideas for the installation. Do you remember that ghastly assistant Willie foisted onto me? Adrian? The one who wears the pale pink suits?"

"I don't remember pale pink—"

"I *assure* you. Exactly the shade of that revolting American wine they advertise in the colour supplements. White Zinfandel, only it's blush-pink. Oh, the horror of it all. I'm always terrified that people will think he's my boyfriend, it would be so shaming. Anyway, he turns out to have rather a good eye. He did one of these courses in installing exhibitions, which of course you know I totally *despise*, but actually he turns out to be rather good despite all the idiocies with which they've filled his nasty little head. He thought we could have one of the mobiles actually coming through the ceiling. Maybe I'll bring him round when I come. Then we can pack him off and have lunch somewhere nice, what do you say?"

We arranged a date for next week and I hung up, grinning. I hadn't talked to Duggie in so long that his particular style of conversation, rather than being enervating, had acted on me like a pick-me-up. I dried my hair and went up the ladder to my sleeping platform to decide what I was going to wear today. As always when I came out of a full-on work binge, the bliss of getting up every morning and picking out an outfit which did not consist of layered holey sweaters and stained jeans took weeks to fade. I was still in the euphoria stage. Finally I settled on my new vinyl hipsters, a tight little T-shirt with "Barbie Is a Slut" scrawled over the bosom area, and a chenille cardigan, piling my hair up with a lot of blue diamanté hairclips. Then I went down to the bathroom and painted on some fudge-coloured lipstick. I was ready to face the world. Whether it was ready for me was a different matter altogether.

ooo

I parked outside the stage door and paused, after locking up the van, to have a monarch-of-all-I-survey moment. The sun was bright and clear and the relatively small section of the sky that I could see was blue—not a bad combination. Add to that an extremely pleasant post-coital buzz and the knowledge that now I had handed over my mobiles to the whims of the technicians I was no longer responsible for any glitches that might occur with them, and the sum of my mood was positively exalted.

I strolled past Viv on the door, who blinked at my appearance—it had been a while since he saw me dressed in something that actually fitted— and down the maze of corridors to the stage, humming a happy little tune to myself. It was lovely to have the right to walk through this place as I wanted without actually having to do any work to justify my presence.

The actors' voices echoing down the Tannoy reached me a good few minutes before I arrived backstage. By now, like everyone else, I was so familiar with the play that I could identify most scenes by a short snippet of dialogue. The only exceptions were those featuring the rustic comedy interludes, which frankly had never cut it for me. Shakespeare's Dog-berries and Quinces and gravediggers always seemed like challenges for the gamest of actors rather than parts that anyone could actually be pleased to be given.

Hermia and Helena, a.k.a. Violet and Hazel, were working each other up into a fine frenzy on stage. Hermia was quite unable to believe that both her suitors had abandoned her for the previously despised Helena, and was accusing her of having bewitched them; Helena was convinced that this was all a set-up to rub in the fact that neither of the men found her remotely attractive, and was becoming increasingly upset at what she saw as their mockery. The scene was degenerating into a series of insults. Hermia, con-vinced that Helena was mocking her lack of height, flew into a frenzy:

> How low am I, thou painted maypole? Speak!
> How low am I? I am not yet so low
> But that my nails can reach unto thine eyes!

I had seen them blocking this scene and knew what came next. Her voice reaching a scream on the last words, Hermia leaped at Helena, her hands formed into claws. Lysander dragged her back and Demetrius caught Helena, swinging her up into his arms. Hermia got loose and came at Helena again; Demetrius threw Helena over Hermia's head to Lysander, in an attempt to save her, and was knocked to the ground by Hermia's furious charge. Lysander, catching Helena triumphantly, held her over his head like a trophy. It was a lubricant-slick piece of business, choreographed by Thierry and depending on split-second timing and the fact that both men were strong; Paul, playing Lysander, worked out regularly and swung the nine-stone Hazel up above his head as easily as if she were a rag doll.

Over the Tannoy came a series of quick scuffling footsteps and then, instead of Hazel's next line, a muffled cry. Everything went still.

"Hazel, are you all right?" Fisher, the Demetrius, was saying.

"My eye," Hazel said, her voice still stifled. "I think she caught it with her nail. . . ."

"You didn't take the step back in time!" Violet protested, her voice shrilling up the scale. "I couldn't help it!"

I rounded the last corner and came level with the DSM desk. Louise, ensconced in front of it as always, had her head tilted back, watching the action on the eerie flickerings of the greenish screen above her head. Steve, grumpy as always, was demanding: "What the hell just happened?" as if Louise were personally responsible for each and every catastrophe at the Cross.

"Oh, Violet did her jump at Hazel and the timing was out," Louise said peacefully. "I don't think it's serious."

"Bloody *hell*, Louise," said Steve, as crossly as if she had been the one to try to scratch out Hazel's eye, and stomped away, his tool belt jingling. He had a bottom like a flour sack full of softening potatoes.

Quite unaffected, Louise flashed a smile at me as I went past. I slipped into the wings to observe the scene. Hazel, her eye watering, was surrounded by concerned amateur practitioners of medicine, while Violet sulked downstage right, ignored by everyone.

"Can you go on?" MM said finally, after one of the ASMs had got Hazel some TCP ointment and applied it to the affected spot.

"Of course she can," muttered Violet, not quietly enough. Fisher rounded on her.

"*What* did you say?" he demanded. "Do you know she's got a scratch right next to her eye?"

"Well, I didn't *mean* it!" Violet protested. "It wasn't my fault! If you'd pulled her back sooner it wouldn't have happened."

"Oh, for God's sake—"

"Right, that's enough," MM said firmly. She clapped her hands. "I want to take that again, OK? And this time everyone knows exactly where they're supposed to be. We've just seen what sloppy timing can do."

"If that's meant for me—" Violet started. MM gave her a long hard look and, miraculously, Violet's voice trailed to a halt. "I didn't mean to hurt you, Hazel," she said crossly. "I mean, *obviously* I didn't. Are you OK?"

Fisher emitted a small, humourless laugh with the air of one who thinks that too little has been said too late. Paul, hands shoved in his pockets, pointedly refrained from making any comment at all. Hazel, however, neatly folded up the tissue she had been pressing to her eye, stowed it in her costume and, in her small, rather prim voice, said quite naturally:

"I know you didn't mean to, Violet. We'll have to watch that one. It's very close."

"All right, we'll run it from 'Fine, i'faith!,'" MM said. "Everyone where they were."

"Clear the stage, please!" Matthew said, trotting after MM as she went back down to her stool in the centre aisle. The ASMs faded into the wings, chattering excitedly in hushed voices: "Did you see it happen?" "No, did you?" "She had her hands right out, like claws. You should see the scratch!" and Hazel said, her voice now snapped back into Helena's youthful, anguished tones:

Fine, i'faith!
Have you no modesty, no maiden shame,
No touch of bashfulness?

As always, I was taken aback by the actors' ability to spin in a moment from one person to another. Fisher, who at the beginning of rehearsals had seemed just another good-looking young space-filler, was giving a very intelligent performance, which shouldn't have been a surprise to me. You couldn't talk to Fisher for long without realizing that he wasn't just a pretty face. He had looked hard at the text and his Demetrius was a nasty piece of work to start off with, deliberately cruel to Helena, aggressive and threatening, but so broken-down and confused by the happenings in the wood that by the end of the play he had been shocked into becoming a better person. In the scene they were rehearsing now, he, Hazel and Violet sparked so well off each other that the fight, which was usually done as a piece of knockabout comedy, had a genuinely dangerous edge to it.

The only weak link was Paul, who always played himself, giving a straight reading of his lines without any interest in developing his character. He was a magnificent figure of a man, tall and broad, a redhead with that wonderful characteristic milky-white, lightly freckled skin, but he was the kind of actor one kept for show rather than for use. If his agent were sensible he'd move him over into TV and get him his own series playing a doctor or a policeman, garnering sacks of fan mail from admiring female groupies.

I watched the scene all the way through. This time the whole sequence of movements went fine, though it lacked the spontaneity that made me catch my breath when I saw it done perfectly. Everyone was being a little too careful, except for Hazel, who launched herself into the air with as much energy as ever. For her it was as if nothing had happened, and maybe for her it hadn't. Nothing mattered to Hazel except the performance; the scratch didn't interfere with that, so it was instantly forgotten. It was an admirable trait.

But, watching her, and moved despite myself by the poignancy with which she said her lines, I found myself thinking of Shirley Lowell. Hazel could suffer and bleed for Helena, who wasn't even real, but when we were talking in the church hall she had dismissed, almost casually, the suicide of a girl she had actually known. How did Hazel feel about it now that she knew Shirley had been killed? I determined to ask her about it. Very probably she would just say something noncommittal in her small quiet voice and change the subject; but I would ask, all the same.

In the light of subsequent events, this was not one of my better decisions.

The actors came off stage in that loping run they all used when their scene was over and they needed to clear the stage quickly. I wondered if it was taught specially at drama school. Once in the wings, they pulled up short. Oberon and Puck's voices rang out from the stage. Violet, the last to exit, was poised on one foot like a hunted doe. She looked around her anxiously.

"Sophie?" she said in a fretful little voice. "Sophie!"

Sophie was already hurrying towards her.

"Vi! What happened? I heard it on the Tannoy. Are you all right?"

Violet threw herself into Sophie's arms with the abandon of a sex siren in a silent film.

"I've got to go to the police station after this," she sobbed, "and give my statement. I'm so *frightened*, I can hardly concentrate, and then the scene just went wrong and everyone's so *cross* with me. . . ."

Louise turned round from her desk and hushed her, politely but firmly. Sophie's eyes met hers above Violet's head.

"Sorry, Louise," she whispered. "Vi, come on, we're in the way. Let's go round for your next entrance and we can have a little chat while you wait."

She led Violet off. Steve, the stage manager, glared after them.

"Ought to know better than to make that kind of row backstage, she ought," he said crossly to Louise.

She flicked a switch and contemplated the board for a moment.

"Demetrius to stage right, Demetrius to stage right, please," she said quietly into her radio mike.

A *Midsummer Night's Dream,* by now a machine turning itself over without too many cogs slipping out of place, continued onstage. I felt as if I were standing in the control room of a battleship; the real action was taking place elsewhere, excited people rushing in and out to give updates on what was happening, but this was the still centre of the spinning world, Louise and her desk, bathed in a little pool of yellow light, the rest of the backstage area in near-darkness. Walking away from it felt like leaving the fulcrum for a lesser part of the action.

Paul, leaning next to a fire bucket and tapping the ash of his cigarette into it with quick, jerky movements, buttonholed me as I came past.

"What d'you reckon to that little performance?" he said sarcastically, though he kept his voice adequately hushed. "You're a friend of hers, aren't you?"

"Do you mean Violet?"

"It was a fucking shambles back there," he said, hardly paying attention to what I'd said; he just wanted to let off steam to the first person he saw. "Vi was well out of order. It wasn't Haze's fault. Haze never gets anything wrong. It can get to you when you're rehearsing with her and you keep cocking up, but you're grateful in the end."

He lit another cigarette from the butt of the first one.

"It's not really me, y'know, Shakespeare," he said. "I trained at drama school and all that, did me stint, but I only said I'd do this *Dream* cos my agent said it would be good for me to work with MM. She's going places, in't she? Anyway," he said, sucking on the cigarette as if it were an oxygen supply, "I'm not enjoying it that much, to be honest. Can't get me tongue round the verse. I reckon I'm a more naturalistic type of actor, you know what I mean?"

"I was just thinking that you'd be really good on the telly," I said, truthfully enough.

He brightened up at once. "Really? I'm up for something at the moment, actually. Kind of drama crossed with sitcom. Young hero and all that. Did you see my chocolate commercial the other night? I was the boyfriend that gets stood up while the girl pisses off to eat chocolate in the car by herself. Stupid, really, but a nice little earner."

"I must have missed it."

"Oh, it'll be on again," he said carelessly. "To be honest, I even preferred that to this. Shouldn't say that, really. But I'm at my best on camera. That's just the way it goes. Though I like all the horsing around we do," he added. "Me catching Haze and all that. That's a laugh. When Vi isn't fucking up big time."

"So you think it was her fault?"

"Course it was. Came at her too fast, didn't she? Haze didn't have time to get out of the way. I mean, I know Vi's boyfriend's dead and all, so she's upset but he's not exactly a loss, is he? Never much of a charmer in the first place, not to mention what's coming out now. They reckon he did that girl they found, don't they?"

I shrugged. "It's one theory."

"Yeah, he did her and then topped himself. Charming, eh? I don't think Vi gave a monkey's arse for him. She was just hanging out with him to make sure she got that part in *A Doll's House*, wasn't she? I bet she's pissed off Haze got Christine. She's incredibly fucking competitive, Vi. Needs taking down a peg or two, if you ask me."

"You seem to have a lot of time for Hazel," I observed.

"Yeah, she's all right," said Paul, but so casually that it was clear his interest in Hazel was merely friendly. "She's really good but she doesn't rub it in your face, know what I mean? There's plenty that would. Mind you," he added to salvage some pride, "I don't reckon she'd be much cop on the telly. Not very photogenic. Nah, she's not my type."

"Oh?" I said.

But Paul declined to comment further on what his type might be. Instead he returned to bad-mouthing Violet: she gave herself airs; she thought she was better than everyone else; she wasn't actually that good an actress, she relied too heavily on mannerisms. This last observation was an all-purpose actors' insult when you had run out of other criticisms.

"Do you wish Tabitha was still playing Hermia?" I said, to see what would happen.

Paul looked away. "Yeah, I suppose so," he said less easily, "Tabs is all right. We had a real laugh when she was reading in for Violet. But, y'know, that's the way it goes, isn't it? We're stuck with her. Vi, I mean. Oops." He cocked his ear to listen to the Tannoy. "'Scuse me." Stubbing out his cigarette in the fire bucket, he shot back on stage, bellowing:

"Where art thou, proud Demetrius? Speak thou now."

I wasn't surprised that Paul had been so open with me. Hazel, buttoned-up and self-composed, was very much the exception to the rule which said that actors were invariably gossipy and forthcoming to the point of indiscretion. Probably that was why I was enjoying myself so much hanging out with them; I can never get on with people who suffer from emotional constipation.

Left unceremoniously beside a fire bucket which stank unattractively of stale cigarette smoke, I decided that a change of scene would do me no harm. I would drop down to the basement and see what the boys were up to. As I passed Margery's office, however, her voice fluted out to me, light and cheerful.

"Sam! How's it going out there?"

She was sitting behind her desk, computer on, papers piled up in her filing trays, looking the picture of health and efficiency in a bright pink jacket and patterned blouse. Her glasses were propped on the end of her nose, and her hair, blown dry and styled with care, looked a little shorter than usual.

"Have you cut your hair?" I said.

She put up one hand in an instinctive gesture, patting down one of the waves.

"Yes, I had it done this morning. Do you like it?"

"It's very nice," I said politely. "You look much better than when I saw you last."

She looked, in fact, positively blooming; it was as if Philip Cantley's death had functioned on her like a dose of salts. Her lipstick was a shiny pink and her cheekbones glowed with blusher, her eyes bright and clear as a healthy dog's. I refrained from testing to see if her nose was wet.

"I do feel better," she admitted, rather shamefaced at the admission. "Awful though it is. I always find uncertainty terribly difficult to deal with. I'm very organized, you see, I hate situations where I have to be passive. So at least the silver lining is that we know what happened to that poor girl and Philip finally did the decent thing."

"Fell on his sword," I suggested.

She nodded. I decided not to challenge her conviction that it had been Philip Cantley who had killed Shirley Lowell.

"Also," she was continuing, "I'm obviously very busy talking to the theatre board about a new artistic director. Ben will hold the fort quite capably till we can appoint someone, but really the sooner we sort things out the happier everyone will be."

"Apart from Ben," I offered.

Margery pulled a face. "Well, we'll have to discuss that. I mean, the person we do appoint might be very happy to work with him as Philip did. Certainly it would be very useful from their point of view to have someone who knows the ropes round here. Alternatively, if they wanted to bring in an assistant of their own . . ."

She left the sentence hanging.

"Doesn't he have a contract or something?" I asked.

"Oh, everyone's on short-term contracts now. Even Philip only had a three-year contract. Everyone else's comes up for renewal each year." She shrugged. "It's the Nineties."

"What about you, Margery?" I asked, to tease her.

As I had expected, Margery's back stiffened slightly. "Well, I *am* the administrator," she said defensively. "We couldn't go chopping and changing every year, could we? It would be very confusing for everyone." She gestured to her filing room. "Imagine setting up a new system every few years!"

"No, it would be ridiculous," I agreed docilely. Clever Margery had doubtless written her own contract of employment: a job for life, no messing around.

"We're very impressed with the *Dream*," Margery said, obviously wishing to change the subject. "Ben's very enthusiastic about it, and a couple of the board members are sitting in on the run-through at this moment. Philip would have done that normally, of course, but as it is . . . Your sculptures look wonderful, Sam, by the way."

"Oh, thank you," I said, still demure. "So how does it work, finding a new artistic director? I don't imagine you can just run an ad in the *Guardian*."

"Oh *no*," Margery said, a little shocked. Although she was not humourless, she was quite incapable of catching anything but the literal meaning of a statement. Undercurrents and irony sailed past her and disappeared through the wall as if in a painting by Magritte. "We would approach suitable candidates and see, informally at first, if they were interested. Then we set up an interview process. It does take quite a while to do well," she added regretfully. "But one has to follow proper procedure."

"Absolutely," I said. "Well, I'll let you get on. I'm sure you must be up to your neck in work."

She flashed a smile at me and adjusted her glasses more firmly on her nose.

"I *am* rather swamped," she admitted. "And I'm coming to the first preview tomorrow night, so I'm in a bit of a rush."

I sketched a goodbye wave and went downstairs. It was deserted, apart from the chief sparks' charge hand, who was watching a dirty film on the video and nearly jumped out of his seat when I greeted him amiably. Once recovered—that is, when his colour was starting to return to normal and his voice wasn't squeaking—he informed me that Bez was up on the fly floor. I removed myself, saying sweetly:

"Enjoy your film. Sorry I interrupted in the middle of a good bit."

The poor boy coloured up all over again, tried to say something, caught himself in time and froze with his mouth half-open. Or half-shut, depending on your world view. I left him there and went back upstairs, grinning to myself.

I approached the fly floor by going up two flights of stairs, through a hatch and back down the Jacob's ladder which ran up the back wall of the theatre. I could have saved myself a few stairs by simply climbing up the ladder from backstage, but there were a lot of people milling around and I didn't feel like explaining myself to everyone. I was on the last few rungs when someone caught me from behind and swung me down to the floor.

"Couldn't resist the chance to grab those trousers," Bez said cheerfully as I turned round. "Makes a change to see you dressed properly for a change." He read my T-shirt and burst out laughing. "I take back the properly. Oi, get a load of this," he said to the three flymen, who were ranked along their respective hawsers, radio mikes on their heads. "Guess what Sam's got on her T-shirt? 'Barbie Is a Slut.' Good one."

"You being sponsored by the Sindy fan club?" said the nearest flyman.

I grinned. "How's it going, Bez?"

"Not too bad. Not bad at all. Apart from the blood being spilled down there." He nodded to the stage below.

"It was an accident," I said reproachfully. I didn't carry a torch for Violet myself, but I couldn't help feeling sorry for her in this case, despite her lack of remorse. Gossip spread here like a forest fire in August; soon people would be saying that Violet had had to be forcibly restrained to stop her performing an impromptu version of the eye-putting-out bit in *King Lear*.

"Yeah, yeah. I know. And I wouldn't blame her if it hadn't been. That Hazel's a sly one, if you ask me. Comes and goes like a shadow, you don't notice she's there half the time." He looked thoughtful. "I was going to say butter wouldn't melt in her mouth, but it's not that exactly. She's just— she's always on time, on cue, where she's supposed to be. Like an acting robot, that girl. Drive anyone to drink."

"But she's really good."

"Makes it worse, dunnit," Bez said unanswerably. "Look forward to seeing them two in the *Doll's House*. Sparks'll fly."

The scene was changing; the lights dipped and faded, the actors' voices silenced. The flymen were hauling on their cables and three of my mobiles floated down into the dark space below us, glimmering like satellites. I lost myself for a moment in contemplation of what I had wrought; Sam looked on her works and she saw that they were good.

"They're fucking brilliant," Bez said quietly. We had been speaking in near-normal voices; I was always surprised by the volume of noise that could be made backstage. His hushed tones were more a compliment to me than a necessity. I felt a smile spreading across my face.

It was the last scene. Hugo, as Oberon, was giving the penultimate speech.

"Now he's very good," Bez said approvingly. "One to watch."

I had already noticed how well tuned the crew were, not only to the actors' performances, but also to their potential. If you wanted to know what an actor was like, or if he or she would do well, you could do worse than ask Bez, or the chief sparks, or even one of the flymen; they had seen so many of them come and go by now that they had sharp eyes for a possible success.

"Going to the National next, isn't he?" Bez said.

"Edmund in *King Lear*. And a couple of other things as well, I think."

He nodded. "Yeah, they do a season. He'll have been cast in *Lear* and then a couple of other directors pick you out of the pool, see, to do something for them as well. Nearest thing to rep there is now."

"It must be an administrative nightmare," I said. "Margery'd be in her element."

Bez snorted. "You'd never get old Margery away from here. They'll have to carry her out on a stretcher when she goes. Whoops." He looked at me, a great grin on his face. It wasn't just his crow's feet and the lines around his mouth; all his features creased up with laughter. He had one of the most infectious smiles I had ever seen. "Could have said that better, couldn't I? We've had enough bodies carted out of here already. Nah, Margery's as much a part of the Cross as I am. You get attached to a place, you know?"

"She was saying that she's busy trying to suss out a new artistic director."

"Yeah, they'd better get on with that pretty quick." He leant back against the pin rail, serious again. "Know what I heard? Rumour doing the rounds? They might be going to ask MM if she'd be interested in interviewing for the job."

"Really?" I said, surprised. "But she doesn't have any experience running a theatre, does she?"

Bez shrugged. "Get that by doing it, don't you?" he said. "Philip hadn't run a theatre before, either. He'd acted for years, done a bit of directing. But nothing like this." He whistled. "Who'd have thought it, eh? Old Phil a murderer. I still can't get my head round it." He paused for a moment, as if taking it in. "Anyway, nothing's certain. But this"—he nodded down towards the stage, where the Pyramus and Thisbe playlet was in full swing—"is a fucking success if ever I saw one. MM's on the spot, they're in a hurry to find someone. . . . I mean, of course they'd prefer someone better known, but you never know."

"But I think she's booked up for a while," I said.

"You never know," Bez repeated gnomically. "Just thought you'd be interested. Wouldn't half put young Ben's nose out of joint. Bad timing for him, Philip doing himself in like that."

"You're not the first person to say that to me," I observed.

"Well, it's the truth, innit? If Philip'd stuck it out a few more years, Ben'd have stepped into his shoes, no problem. As it is . . ."

"But he must have just as much experience as MM. She's only a few years older than him."

"She's an old soul, that girl. You can see it," Bez said. "More important, she's got the spark. You know?"

I leant against the pin rail, next to him, watching the play come to its triumphant conclusion: "Give me your hands, if we be friends,/And Robin shall restore amends," Marie piped.

Further along the fly floor, the last flyman had started to haul down the curtain. It occurred to me to wonder, in the light of what Bez and Margery had said, whether Ben had an enemy at the theatre, someone who disliked him enough to kill Philip Cantley, knowing how insecure that would make Ben's position . . . then I realized that I was being ridiculous. The more tortuous the theory, the more unlikely it is. After all, if someone disliked Ben that much, why wouldn't they have cut out the middleman and just killed Ben instead?

I swarmed back up the ladder and through the hatch at the top. Jumping down to the linoleum-covered floor, I stood for a moment, dusting myself off and contemplating the dressing room door directly in front of me. On it was a small card, tucked into a little frame, bearing the legend: "Miss Hazel Duffy/Helena." Yielding to impulse, I knocked.

"Come in," Hazel's voice said.

I opened the door and put my head round it, saying, not wholly untruthfully:

"I was passing and I just wondered if you were all right."

The dressing room was tiny, like most of those at the Cross. There were a few slightly larger ones in which people doubled up, and Hugo and Bill maintained an uneasy truce in the star dressing room, which was simply two smaller ones knocked together with a sink in the middle. But Hazel's was the classic model: a cubbyhole, the white paint yellowing with age, peeling away where an endless series of actors had pinned up cards and photographs, bits of Blu-Tack and drawing pins still fixed in place, holding on grimly to the torn corners of whatever poster they had once supported. A small and unsafe-looking electric fire stood in the far corner; a low shelf along one wall, a mirror above it, surrounded by naked lights, a clothes rail and two chairs comprised the rest of the furniture. The carpet was so frayed that it caught in the door as I shut it behind me.

"Cosy," I said, looking around me.

"It's all I really need," Hazel said, composed as ever. She had already taken off her costume, which was hanging on the rail. Dressed in a shirt and jeans, she was sitting in front of the mirror taking off her make-up with some Boots baby lotion squirted onto a piece of tissue. The cosmetics stacked beside the mirror were Spartan in their simplicity. I bet Violet used Lancôme make-up remover and the finest cotton wool money could buy.

"Does that sting your eye?" I asked, to show how concerned and caring I was.

"A bit. I'll put on some more TCP cream afterwards. It was nice of you to come to see how I was."

"Oh no. I mean, I'm at a bit of a loose end now anyway. The fun's just starting for you lot. All my work's done, really." I put as much pathos into this as I could. "It's going very well, don't you think?"

"I'm pleased with it," Hazel said, her eyes meeting mine in the mirror. I didn't know whether she was talking about her own performance or the play as a whole. Make-up removed, she unpinned the hairpiece she was wearing and started brushing it out with neat little strokes. Then she placed it on a stand and attended to her own hair with much less care than she had given to the fake ponytail. It occurred to me that this summed up Hazel perfectly.

"All this upset doesn't seem to have damaged the play too much, thank goodness," I said, ploughing on doughtily. "Apart from Violet, of course, but that's understandable. I mean, she found him. And he was her boyfriend."

"Violet didn't mean it," Hazel said placidly. "Didn't mean to scratch me, that is," she amplified when she saw that her comment had puzzled me. Again, she had chosen to answer only the part of my statement that related to her, or to the play. "She's just a bit upset, like you say. I'm sure she'll be more careful. It was a nasty shock for her too."

"How are you finding all this?" I said, deciding that the only way was to be direct. "I mean, you knew her, after all. Shirley Lowell. You were a friend of hers, weren't you? I remember you saying so at rehearsal."

"Yes, we were at drama school together when she disappeared," Hazel said, her tone of voice, her eyes, not altering in the least. She could have passed any lie detector test. "I expect she was a friend of mine," she added rather doubtfully, as if she wasn't quite sure what a friend was.

By now she had caught her hair back in a ponytail and was smoothing some more baby lotion into her face and neck. I watched her slow, careful movements, the way she observed herself, not assessing her own appearance as I would have done, but treating her face simply as another tool that served her as an actress, requiring regular maintenance and attention. I had never really looked at Hazel before, never seen her for herself rather than for the person she became while acting. She had mouse-fair hair, a wide brow and neat features, which, while not mobile like Marie's little monkey face, seemed capable of infinite transformations. Her eyes, wide set and grey, would have been greatly improved by a few coats of mascara on her long lashes; but as I watched she dabbed on some powder, more to take off the shine than for any other aesthetic purpose, and turned to face me, obviously considering her beauty routine fully performed. I thought of Judi Dench, of all the actresses who, with average looks and forgettable faces, manage, through sheer bravura, to convince an audience of their beauty and grace.

"Shirley was an odd girl," Hazel said reflectively. "She was quite a good actress, but limited, I thought. We went out for a meal after class every so often. She lived just round the corner from me. She wasn't a very happy person. When she went missing, I was surprised. I mean, she was really serious about acting and I thought it was funny she'd miss classes. Then they told us they'd found her car, and that she'd killed herself. That surprised me too, a bit. But not that much, when I thought about it."

I stared at her blankly, feeling sorry for the police officer who had had to take her statement; you could ask Hazel questions all day and still have no idea what kind of person she was describing, who Shirley Lowell had really been. Probably Hazel didn't know herself.

"What was she like?" I asked, curious to hear what she would say.

"Oh, good, but she didn't have much of a range, like I said," Hazel responded.

"I meant as a *person*, not as an actress," I said gently.

"Oh." That brought Hazel up short. After a short pause for reflection she said: "She was all right. Easy to get on with. Ambitious. I expect that's why she had the affair with Philip. She didn't really like men. She'd have done it because he could help her career, not because she really wanted to."

I stared at her. "Did you know she was having an affair with him all the time?"

"Oh no. I mean, I don't know for sure even now. It's what the police think, though. They asked me if I could remember her ever mentioning his name, but I couldn't."

I wasn't surprised; it was hard to imagine anyone confiding in Hazel about their love-life. Involuntarily I wondered what Hazel herself did about that. She was as sexless as an amoeba which reproduced by splitting itself down the middle. Passion she kept for the stage.

"It would make sense if she'd been seeing him, though," Hazel was continuing. "She looked a lot like Violet."

This rang a bell with me. I remembered Margery saying that Shirley's photograph had reminded her of someone; it must have been Violet. Philip Cantley had clearly had a definite type.

"She dressed quite smartly, too," Hazel commented. "Though not like Vi. Vi always looks like a film star." She said all this without a trace of malice or envy. "I'm looking forward to working with her on *A Doll's House*," she added. "I think she'll be very good as Nora."

"Would you have liked to play it?" I inquired.

"Oh yes." Hazel's eyes brightened. "There's so much you can do with that part . . . But I'll be understudying her. And Christine's a very interesting woman to play. It's fair enough, Violet getting Nora. I mean, no-one really knows me yet. I'll play her one day," she said with such assurance that I believed her completely.

Just then someone knocked on the door and, not waiting for an answer, opened it slightly. Ben's head appeared round the doorframe.

"How are you, Hazel?" he said amiably, acknowledging me with a friendly nod. "Thought I'd better check up on you in my august role as acting head of this place."

"I'm fine, thanks."

"As long as you mean it," Ben said, coming in. "You're the kind that goes on acting with a broken ankle. Hi, Sam. Come on a mission of mercy too?"

I spread out my hands. "Yes, but it didn't last long. Hazel and I were just having a chat."

"It's very nice of you both to be concerned," Hazel said, tranquil as ever. "But it's really OK. Look, you can hardly see it." She tilted her head towards us. There was a faint red line running away from the corner of her right eye. "I don't know why the boys made such a fuss. Letting off steam, I suppose."

Ben pulled a face. "Well, that's understandable. It can't be the best atmosphere for all of you—bodies everywhere, the police in and out. I had to give my statement this morning, and I was pretty intimidated, even though I hadn't got anything to confess. But somehow you feel like you do, you know? You want to blurt out about the Mars bars you shoplifted when you were fourteen."

"I expect everyone feels like that," Hazel said. "That's why Violet was so tense. She's got to go along there after MM gives us her notes."

"What did the police ask you about?" I said to Ben.

"Oh, the usual. I mean, nothing I didn't expect." He leant against the wall, shoving his hands into his pockets, his glasses perched on the bridge of his nose. Like MM, his clothes were almost deliberately nondescript, as if it was a considered policy of theirs that directors should be heard and not seen: an old pair of corduroys that didn't suit his square frame and a battered Aran sweater that reminded me for a moment of my friend Tom, who was currently travelling in India with his nightmare of a girlfriend.

"They wanted to know where I was when Philip killed himself, that kind of thing," Ben was saying. "To which all I could say was, probably halfway round the Angel on a 73 bus. . . . And had I ever heard anything about Shirley Lowell and Philip, which was another no. I mean, I got here about a year after she went missing and although Philip and I got on pretty well, he wasn't exactly going to start confiding in me about having strangled her, was he?"

"You think he did it, then?" I said curiously. Ben had spent a great deal of time by Philip Cantley's side; he probably knew him as well as anyone here.

"Yes, I do." Ben's eyes, clear and brown behind the lenses of his glasses, met mine properly for the first time. "There was something not quite right about Philip. I couldn't have put my finger on it before, but I knew it was there."

"But do you think—"

"I should really be getting down," Hazel said, standing up. "MM's got to give us our notes."

We left the dressing room in a small group which was soon swelled by other actors issuing from their dressing rooms, back in their own clothes, faces shiny with make-up remover or carefully made up again, flooding downstairs to the stage. As we passed the large dressing room on the first landing the door opened precipitously and Bill shot out as fast as a human cannonball, his girth contributing to the image.

"Darling, don't leave me this way!" Hugo's voice followed him through the door. "You've still got a tiny touch of mascara on your left eye. Let me pat it off for you."

Yielding to impulse, I detached myself from the stream of people and slid through the door. Hugo had one foot propped up on the dressing table and was doing up the buckles of his boot. He was looking very smart in a tight black polo neck and a pair of navy and black checked hipster trousers.

"Hello, my sweet!" he greeted me. "I heard you were around. Come here. No, wait, has Bill gone? All right, then."

He pulled me into his lap and kissed me very thoroughly.

"You're looking very gorgeous," he said, smoothing back a bit of my hair that had just come loose. "Mm, I like kissing you in front of a mirror. Very sexy. I've always wanted a mirror over my bed."

We regarded ourselves in the mirror for a moment, Hugo's chin resting in my curls; both our expressions were horribly complacent.

"I could rig it up for you, if you've got the mirror," I offered, turning to bite his neck.

"I forget you're such a handywoman," Hugo said, taking one of my hands and turning it over, "until I look at your poor scarred little paws. You must sleep in cotton gloves and cold cream for a week. After you've put up the mirror. I think that's a very good idea. Mm." His hands slipped under my T-shirt and eased it up, still watching our reflection.

"The difficulty, as always," he said into my breasts, "is deciding what we want to do first. . . ."

"Hugo!" Someone was knocking on the door. It was one of the ASMs; she called nervously: "Um, they're all waiting for you onstage."

"Bloody damn," said Hugo as I pulled down my T-shirt and slid off his lap. "The Perils of Pamela, to be continued. We leave Pamela in the clutches of the evil Baron von Fielding. Tune in next week to see if she can escape from his foul embraces before her honour is smirched forever."

I took a deep breath and readjusted my hair in front of the mirror. "Or if she'll finally manage to get a shag," I finished, pulling Hugo to his feet and giving him a long, slow kiss with my hands tangled in his hair. "Come on, Baron, your public awaits."

Hugo slapped my bottom. The vinyl trousers made a very satisfying noise.

"I must get a pair of trousers like these," he said, following me to the door. "His and hers outfits for the pervert couple. The family that plays together stays together. Oh hello, Liz," he said to the ASM hovering outside. "I should say thank you for coming to get me and I'm sure that when all my parts have subsided I'll be grateful. At the moment, however, I find myself still in a rather pettish mood at the disturbance."

We clattered down the stairs, Hugo hanging back a little so he could watch my bottom.

"I know what you're doing," I said over my shoulder. "It's not big and it's not clever."

"I shall eschew the obvious response," Hugo said loftily.

"For once."

"*How dare you.*"

"Oh, Hugo, thanks for joining us," MM said sarcastically as he made his way onstage, where two semicircles of chairs had been arranged for the actors.

"Not at all," Hugo said with charming aplomb, hitching up his trousers and sprawling into a chair.

I slunk round the back way and emerged through the pass door into the auditorium, where I took a seat at the back. After a while, as my eyes became used to the change in the light, I noticed a man and a woman sitting equally unobtrusively a couple of rows in front of me; I didn't recognize them, but they weren't scruffy enough to be anything but the members of the theatre board who Margery had said were watching the run-through. Onstage MM's quiet voice ran through a series of points. She had set up her two-stool combination, perched on one while on the other, directly in front of her, was propped the ring binder in which she had scribbled her notes. Matthew was seated on a chair, placed with suitable deference below and to one side of hers, while Sally, Sophie, Thierry, Steve, the composer and several other people I didn't know were gathered stage right in a little huddle of chairs.

Every so often one of the observers from the board would lean to the other and whisper a remark, to which the addressee would nod vigorously. Occasionally they would bob their heads in unison, like a pair of coordinated nodding dogs hung from the rear-view mirror of a Ford Escort. The spectacle rather palled after a while, but MM was nothing if not concise, and it only took her twenty minutes or so to complete what she had to say. The actors rose and stretched theatrically, competing with one another to see who could do the best Pilates-influenced shoulder-untwisting. A group of ASMs, like a bunch of alternative fairies in their second-hand jeans and tiny little T-shirts, scampered on to help move back the chairs; Matthew possessed himself of both MM's stools at once, clearly wanting to be the only person who touched the sacred seat where the holy bottom had deigned to rest; and the two board members stood up and made their way to the front of the auditorium. I followed after them.

"Ms. Marsh?" the woman said. "I'm Denise Sholto, from the theatre board. This is Brian Fitzpatrick. I believe you knew we were sitting in on the run-through."

"Oh yeah. Hello," MM said, looking slightly distracted. She ran one hand through her hair, pushing back the untidy fringe.

"I think I can speak for both of us when I say that we enjoyed it very much," Brian Fitzpatrick chimed in, to the accompaniment of another series of pizzicato nods from Denise. "We were wondering if you might be free to go for a drink and talk about how you feel things are going."

"Yeah, fine. Sure." MM looked at her watch. "Could you give me a quarter of an hour? I just have a few more things to go over and then I'm all yours."

"Fine, we understand," Denise said. "We'll meet you in the foyer in fifteen minutes, then. Or would you like a little longer?"

"No, that's OK," MM said rather blankly; when she said a quarter of an hour, that was what she meant. Denise and Brian pushed off down the centre aisle and Hugo vaulted elegantly off the stage and jumped to earth beside me.

"Drinks," he said. "And then dinner. And then perhaps we could pick up the saga of Pamela and the Baron where we were forced to leave off. Did you come here in your revolting vehicle?"

"Yup." There was no point arguing that one.

"There's a rather nice restaurant near me. I'll take you there if you provide the transport."

"Sounds like a good deal to me," I said cheerfully. Hugo's bone structure, his beak of a nose and high cheekbones, which was so photogenic, could look over-bony or extremely handsome, depending which angle you saw him from. Just now the light was in his favour and he was dazzling. I wouldn't tell him that, however. He would lap it up in an instant and beg for more. There was no point spoiling the brute.

○○○

Hugo's restaurant of choice turned out to be a very elegant affair in the heart of Clerkenwell, set on the corner of a bank building, all polished wood floors, opaque glass tables and padded black chairs with what were doubtless supposed to be aerodynamic backs. A young man in a black Nehru jacket, standing at a high uncluttered curve of pale wood, took our coats and showed us to a table, after the obligatory tut-tutting at Hugo for not having booked. Hugo waved the reproaches away imperially.

"I come here so often this is practically my *kitchen*, Kenji," he said firmly. "And it would be silly to make a reservation in my own kitchen, wouldn't it?"

Kenji, slightly mollified, said:

"Does the lady know how everything works?"

"I'll explain it to her," Hugo said. "We'll queue up straight away, we're both starving. In the meantime, could you bring us a bottle of that Australian Chardonnay I always have?"

"You flash bastard," I muttered to him as Kenji glided away.

Hugo flashed me an unexpectedly beautiful smile, open and simple. It was extraordinarily endearing.

"When I'm in the money," he said cheerfully, "I am an extremely flash bastard. Believe me, you would be too if you'd grown up poor in Surbiton. Come on, let's get something to eat."

He stood up. I followed suit.

"Where are we going?"

He led me round the tables to the far side of the restaurant, where a mass of well-dressed diners were gathered round what looked like a long, double-sided salad bar.

"Oh good, it's an upmarket Pizza Hut," I said sarcastically. "How sophisticated."

"You little animal," Hugo said. "Pick up a bowl, fill it with what you want and then, if you ask them nicely, the gentlemen over there will cook it for you."

He indicated a couple of big, burly Oriental guys in white uniforms, who were ranged behind a waist-high semicircle of ferocious gas outlets capped from above by an enormous stainless steel vent into which great clouds of cooking steam were rising. It reminded me of an installation I had liked a lot at the Saatchi Gallery a few years ago. Running just above the cooking area was a little shelf on which the customers, queueing in the best polite English fashion, placed their bowls of food. I examined the contents of the food bar more closely and had to admit that I was impressed. Apart from all the different kinds of noodles and rice, there were raw prawns, squid, snapper, and as many varieties as Heinz boasted of meat and vegetables, all diced and sliced with exemplary neatness.

"Put the noodles in first, and any meat or fish on the top, and don't take too much, otherwise you won't have room to come back," Hugo recommended, hovering over my shoulder to check I was following his instructions as I selected soya noodles with prawns, ginger, spring onions, waterchestnuts and a strange kind of fungus which I picked to avoid seeming limited in my food choices. As we queued to have our bowlfuls cooked I ran my eyes down the list of sauces posted behind the grill: spicy peanut, teriyaki, sambal, sweet and sour. . . . I chose lemongrass and Hugo sweet chili. The chef flicked the prawns and then the vegetables into a wok seared black with hard labour; instantly there was the sizzle of food searing. A minute later he emptied in the noodles, stirred them in with a few quick twists of the chopsticks and let them heat through. As he poured in the sauce the bubbling lemongrass combined with the other ingredients to rise in a single cloud of sweet-smelling vapour. I sniffed it in appreciatively. Then he flicked the entire mixture back into my bowl without a speck of sauce landing on its sides.

"Thank you," I said, heading back to the table with all speed. I sat down and shoved in a mouthful practically simultaneously.

"How is it, greedy-guts?" Hugo inquired patiently, sitting down opposite me at a more leisurely pace.

"Mmn." I swallowed and took a swig of wine to wash it down. "Delicious. The wine too." I had some more of both.

"It's good, isn't it? I'm gradually working my way through the combinations. And it's great if you're watching your weight, which I always am, alas."

"You don't need to lose weight! Don't be ridiculous," I said, sending down the next mouthful. "You're thin enough already."

"Television puts on about *half a stone,*" Hugo said in sombre tones. "Need I say more?"

I pulled a face. "I'm so glad I'm not an actress."

"So am I," Hugo said in a very heartfelt way. "Don't tell me you've finished that already!"

"I was hungry," I said, abashed. "I'll wait for you to finish before I go back."

"Absolutely not. I don't want you sitting here watching me lift my chopsticks up and down to my mouth like some starving pauper trying to make me feel guilty. Go on, off you go."

No sooner said than done. I was queueing at the grill with my bowl full once more (rice with white crab meat, bamboo shoots and beansprouts) when someone behind me ruffled my hair. At first I thought it was Tim, a journalist friend of mine who worked at the *Herald,* whose offices were just down the Clerkenwell Road; I had already noticed a few familiar faces from the paper and had been half-expecting to bump into him. But when I turned round I found myself face-to-face with Janey, half his height and certainly more than his girth, small, plump and pretty, smiling at me.

"What are you doing here?" she said, rather unflatteringly surprised.

"Oh, I'm not trendy enough? Or not yuppie enough?" I gave her as much of a hug as I could when both of you are carrying bowls stuffed to the gills with food. "I came with a friend who lives round the corner. What about you?"

She indicated the person behind her. "Gita brought me. She says she's in here all the time. Gita, this is Sam, one of my oldest friends. Sam, Gita's the producer I'm working with. I must have mentioned her already."

She flashed a smile at Gita, who was tall and dark, dressed in a semi-transparent leopardskin-print shirt and snug chocolate shantung silk leggings. These finished mid-calf, the better to show off Gita's impossibly narrow brown ankles and faux-leopardskin high heels. In her ears were large, slender, gold hoop earrings and her heavy eyelids were shaded with carefully blended gradations of brown, right up to the palest of beiges below the delicate arches of her eyebrows. The effect was highly studied and deliberately exotic in the way only Asian women can carry off; a Western woman wearing the same outfit would have looked as cheap as an It girl.

The chef was beckoning for my bowl, so I put it on the bar as Gita held out her hand to me, the fingers laden with gold rings. No-one I knew had worn gold for a decade, but on her it looked wonderful, setting off the dark olive of her skin. Her wrists were as thin as her ankles, projecting fragility together with the strength of tensile steel. I shook her hand and realized that I disliked her without having a clear idea of why. Maybe it was the way she was looking at me, coldly assessing, as if she were working out whether it would be worth her while to get to know me.

"You're a sculptor, aren't you?" Gita said.

"How did you know that?" Janey exclaimed.

"You told me, ages ago. I have a very good memory for what you tell me." Her voice was low; I bet she had worked hard to deepen its register. I really had taken against her. "Sam, look, your food's ready."

I took the bowl as Janey and Gita handed theirs over to the chefs.

"I'd better go and eat it while it's hot. Where are you sitting?"

"Over there," Janey said, indicating a table by the window on the other side of the room.

"Come over and say hi later."

Hugo wasn't at the table when I returned; he appeared in a while, bearing a bowl of beef and rice with red peppers and peanut sauce.

"Who was that you were talking to?" he said.

I filled him in. He looked interested. "Not only do I get to meet Helen's doubtless long-suffering girlfriend, but also a producer and commissioning editor at the BBC. I must take you out to dinner more often."

"You've already exhausted my range," I said, grinning at him. "Janey's my one and only posh friend. Oh, and there's Tim. He's on the *Herald*."

"Not a reviewer. I don't recognize the name."

"No, features mostly."

A trio of girls from the *Herald* Sunday colour supplement passed the table, all dressed in black and looking high on life. I knew them; we'd been out drinking together a while ago, and they were girls who knew how to drink. We'd rolled out of a lock-in at two in the morning and one of them had fallen over, ripped her Agnès B trousers and thrown a major wobbly. It gave us the same bond as battle-scarred survivors. They waved at me as they went past. I always thought of them as the three witches from *Macbeth*, capable of frightening a man to death at twenty paces.

We were just finishing the wine when Janey and Gita appeared, accompanied by Helen. I found it interesting that they hadn't mentioned her presence earlier. Hugo, his manners impeccable, immediately stood up and looked around for a waiter.

"Could we have a couple more chairs, please?" he said. "Our friends are joining us for a drink."

With Janey and Helen side by side on the banquette there was just enough room for us all. The waiter cleared the plates and brought another bottle of wine. Gita had seen Hugo in *Ghosts* and told him he had been very good, which, judging by his modest smile, he was already aware of but was happy to be told again. Hugo had seen a play Gita had produced for BBC2, and some episodes of a drama series Janey had worked on at her last job, and made all the right noises about them both. Everything was going swimmingly.

"I didn't know you and Hugo knew each other so well," Helen snidely observed to me.

"Oh, catch *up*," I wanted to say. Hugo remarked instead:

"We don't, Helen. That's half the fun."

"How did you think the run-through went today?" Janey said to him.

"Oh, pretty well. No major hitches."

"Helen told me about the Violet thing. Did you actually see it?" Janey said. "I mean, did she really go for her?"

Hugo very deliberately avoided looking at Helen. I found myself remembering what I had thought before about gossip taking on a life of its own the further it goes from the source, like a stream swelling gradually into a river.

"It was a storm in a teacup," he said equably enough. "Everyone's timing was a little out."

"It's the tiniest mark," I chipped in supportively. "I dropped into Hazel's dressing room to ask her how she was and you could hardly see it at all. She didn't give a toss about it."

I felt Hugo's gaze on me, but he refrained from comment.

"Oh well," Janey said, sensing that she had put her foot in something, "that's a relief." She turned to me, obviously about to change the conversation; but Helen wouldn't let it go at that.

"Oh, come on," she said fretfully, her green eyes contracting into slits. "It's more than that. Really, I think Violet's jinxed. I mean, if you look at everything that's happened—turning up late for rehearsals, throwing a fainting fit, not to mention Philip—I heard she knows more about that than she's letting on. And now this thing with Hazel. I'm sure it wasn't just an accident."

"Oh, you were present?" Hugo inquired with ominous calm.

"No," Helen said defensively, "but Bill was. He told me. And I know you and Bill don't get on, but I think he's very reliable."

Hugo's eyes were as cold and grey as a winter morning.

"Hazel told me," I volunteered quickly before Oberon could lean across the table and start throttling Titania to death, "that she was looking forward to working with Violet on *A Doll's House*. If she obviously doesn't feel angry about it, why should anyone else?"

"Well, it remains to be seen if that will go ahead, doesn't it?" said Helen venomously. "I mean, now Philip's dead."

"But surely the production will go on," Gita said patronizingly. "It's in their schedule, Helen." She pronounced "schedule" the same way a bornagain Christian might have said "the Bible." "They couldn't possibly change it now."

Helen looked sulky. "Well, I heard it wasn't certain," she said defiantly, though she refused to say where she had heard it. "And if you ask me, it would serve her right."

"But no-one did ask you, did they?" Hugo said with deceptive smoothness. "At least, I can't remember it." He looked round the small group, clearly about to inquire if any of us had put the question to Helen in a moment of his temporary inattention.

"We should probably be going, Helen," said Janey, finishing her wine and rising from the table in one long stretch of movement. "I've got a very busy day tomorrow."

"We," corrected Gita, smiling at her, "have a very busy day tomorrow."

"How's it going?" I asked.

"Gita will tell you," Janey said quickly, wanting to avoid any further confrontation by getting Helen away as fast as possible. "Helen and I should've been home an hour ago. Thanks for the drink, Hugo. It was nice to meet you. I look forward to seeing the play; I'm coming to the preview tomorrow."

"Oh, shall I come with you?" I volunteered. "I still haven't seen it all the way through."

"Great. I have to see so many plays on my own, and I always hate it. When does it go up?"

"Seven-thirty," Hugo said.

"Shall I meet you in the foyer at seven, Sam?"

"Fine with me."

Helen had stood up while Janey and I were talking, avoiding Hugo's stare; there was the usual round of kisses goodbye and then Janey, winding her arm lovingly through Helen's, waved a farewell and was gone.

"I should really be going too," Gita said, sitting back in her chair. "It's been a long day."

"Do you live nearby?" Hugo asked. "Why don't we walk you home?"

We left Gita at her front door. She offered us drinks or coffee with polite formality which we duly refused, all of us going through the accepted motions of social intercourse. The door shut behind her.

"Alone at last," I said.

"Not quite," Hugo said as a car passed, "but nearly. And I for one can't wait. Come on, Pamela. I'm going to tie you to the bed and force you to do all kinds of unspeakable things. I shall expect you to flatter my vanity by protesting in horror and finally succumbing in ecstasy."

"I can guarantee to do the first bit," I assured him. "But if you're going to tie me to the bed, the rest is in your hands."

"Literally," Hugo said with an anticipatory smile.

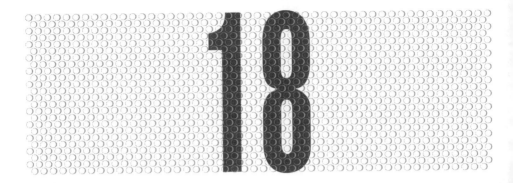

Janey made only the obliquest of references to Helen and Hugo's contretemps of the previous night when we met up in the foyer of the Cross. It was a lovely, clear evening, and if it had been the Royal Court or any of the theatres on the Aldwych the clientele would have been milling around on the steps, soaking in the last rays of sunset, imbued with a pleasant sense of virtue for doing something culturally rewarding. But although the Cross didn't actually have people dossing down on the steps at that very moment—usually they arrived later, when they'd finished their stint of begging at the station—the atmosphere was scarcely Sloane Square in all its glory.

The view down the road was a slice of the Thameslink station and a bus stop with its glass shattered spectacularly over the pavement, the thick crystals like a flood of ice. Beyond it was the corner of the once-glorious Scala cinema, now closed. I had heard that the pool hall next door was using a part of it to expand its premises. What really rankled was the way the landlords would close down cinemas, complaining that the rents were too low, and then do nothing with them; the frontages remained to taunt you as you passed the Scala, the Plaza or even the now-multiplexed Parkway, with memories of late nights, spilling out onto the Camden pavements, heart beating with the film, looking for somewhere to go that would keep that excitement alive. And I didn't mean the Electric Ballroom.

Janey picked up her ticket from the box office and we went into the downstairs bar to get a drink.

"You looked very pensive," she said.

"I was mourning the Scala."

"Oh." Her face fell. "I know."

We observed a moment of respectful silence. Then Janey said:

"D'you know, I'm actually looking forward to this. Usually the thought of seeing yet another *Dream* makes me shiver with boredom, but the word is that it's excellent."

"It should be," I said, sipping my gin and tonic. "Though I've only seen bits and pieces. Almost all of the lovers' scenes, for some reason."

Janey picked up on this at once.

"So what are they like?" she said curiously. "How is Violet? You know Helen doesn't really rate her."

This was the closest she would get to mentioning last night's scene in the restaurant.

"Very good," I said simply. "Not that I know a lot about it, but I think both of the girls are very good." I paused for a moment. "Hugo and Violet are old friends," I said, "from drama school. He's quite protective of her."

Janey nodded understandingly.

"I look forward to seeing what he does with Oberon," she said. "Gita was saying today that she wants to come and see it too. I'll probably be back again, so I might come with her."

She took a sip of her Bloody Mary and looked around her. I stared at her, baffled. She wore a white linen sheath, ankle-length, with several strings of amber at her neck, and her hair was arranged not only very prettily but a good deal more tidily than usual. I would never have called Janey elegant before this recent transformation, but now it was the first adjective that popped to my lips. Surprising: working at the BBC usually had the opposite effect on people's wardrobes. It wasn't the change from a Janey trailing clouds of drapery and layered shirts, to a new model careerist in fitted linen, however, that had really taken me aback. Before her move across and rise in status—BBBC, as it were—if Janey had bumped into me at a restaurant with a man I hadn't previously mentioned to her, she would have rung me the next morning to shower me with questions about him. I had to admit that I was slightly piqued at her reticence on the subject of Hugo; now that things were going so well, I had been looking forward to the opportunity to drivel on a bit.

"Have you lost weight?" I said, examining her more closely, searching for clues to the change in her. "You have, haven't you? Are you dieting?"

Maybe that was the reason; she was so starved that nothing was capable of holding her attention but a cream cake bulging with calories and raspberry jam. She shook her head, smiling faintly, as if I were very far away.

"No. I mean, yes, I have lost weight, but I'm not dieting. I think it's the job. I've been wanting to film this book for years now, and finally it looks like it might be happening. . . . I'm so excited I can't even think about food."

"Hey, if it works for you—" I finished my gin and tonic. The five-minute bell was ringing. "Shall we go in?"

My heart was pounding to the degree that it usually reserved for death threats or imminent sexual intercourse as we filed into the auditorium and took our places. I had been trying not to think about the moment when the curtain would lift and I would see my mobiles hanging in space; and as the lights dimmed and the curtain began to rise I found, ridiculously enough, that I had closed my eyes. Around me I heard people catching their breath and then, after a moment, whispering comments to their neighbours. I opened my eyes again cautiously, and my own breath stopped for a moment. Janey had taken my hand and was pressing it tightly.

"Glad you did it after all?" she murmured in my ear.

I gulped and nodded, not trusting my powers of speech. The cyclorama was dark as velvet, dotted here and there with tiny star-like points of light; in the foreground the mobiles floated, the glimmering steel-blue of platinum, almost haloed in their own light, seeming neither organic nor planetary but some strange new hybrid. Trails of silver ivy twisted around and through them as if they were meteors which had fallen into a magic forest and become entangled with enchantments.

"It's wonderful," Janey said, still pressing my hand, as the lights changed, becoming richer, the mobiles rising now to become chandeliers, and the stage flooded suddenly with people. For a moment I had a vision of the fly-men, pulling away at their hawsers, a series of quick commands and adjustments running down their radio mikes as the mobiles slid into perfect alignment; then the first words of the play were spoken and the familiar rough magic worked again. I was held by the shapes and sounds before me, by the deliberately planned illusions, and forgot to think of the reality of work gloves on calloused hands, tugging at steel cables, let alone all the people I knew as they were offstage. They were their characters instead. It only takes a few minutes to make the adjustment, especially when the performances are so confident, so unfaltering. I had thought it might be strange to see Hugo on stage, after spending a large part of last night exploring a Donne-ish range of prepositional possibilities together, but he was so convincing that I found myself taking it for granted almost at once.

The run-through yesterday had been as jerky as a spastic colon. But now, watching the first scenes unfold, I couldn't spot the joins; MM had welded together and ground them down so smoothly that the transitions between scenes, between entrances, seemed effortless, the play flowing like water. The lovers fled from Athens; Oberon and Titania quarrelled; the rustics started to rehearse their play-within-a-play; and at Marie's triumphant descent on the mobile, leaping off it into Hugo's arms, a child some rows ahead of us said "Ooh! Wow!" in awestruck tones, and a great ripple of amusement ran through the audience.

Now Puck was casting an enchantment on Titania so that on awakening she would fall in love with the first creature she saw. The blackout in which Tabitha descended had been a matter of moments, but she had to hang there for a while, curled up in a ball behind the mobile to avoid being seen, as the rustics arrived and Puck clapped a donkey's head on Bottom. His friends fled in terror at the sight of him; Titania awoke and stared at Bottom, already captivated, and, in an effort to keep him with her, promised him the service of her fairies.

"Peaseblossom, Cobweb, Moth and Mustardseed!" she called.

Everyone was inspired tonight. Ranjit did his cartwheel, bowling across the stage like a hoop, calling "Ready!" as he went; tall, blond Cobweb, tossing away his cigarette, strolled across the stage like a model on a catwalk, drawling "And I!" in a lazy voice; and the girl who played Moth, throwing herself to her knees, skidded the last few feet and stopped perfectly a few inches from Titania, so that Helen's outstretched hand needed only to drop a little way to stroke her head.

There was a pause, and I caught my breath, waiting for Tabitha's jump down, thinking how much it would excite the little boy in front of us.

"And I!" came a voice from behind the mobile. For a moment there was dead silence; then all the fairies looked up in unison, like puppets pulled by strings. There was nothing to see; Janey turned and looked at me, perplexed. Then Tabitha's head popped up above the mobile. "And I!" she said again, a faint tinge of desperation in her voice.

"Oh my God," I said. "She's stuck."

"*Stuck?*" Janey hissed.

With mounting horror, I realized that none of the fairies could actually see Tabitha from below, not unless they went right under the mobile; it effectively blocked her from view for everyone but the audience. Mercifully the scene was a short one, and Tabitha delivered her few lines with aplomb. Somehow she had managed to wriggle round the side of the mobile, moving it with her body, so that we could see her head, neck and one arm, with which she made extravagant gestures, as if to compensate for being strung up fifteen feet off the ground with hardly any range of movement.

The fairies, professionals all, recovered themselves and continued, and perhaps it was only my familiarity with their performances that meant I noted a certain level of desperation in their voices. Ranjit was supposed to exit grabbing Tabitha and swinging her round by one arm and one leg, and there was a horrible moment of suspended animation as I saw the realization dawning on his face that he was going to have to invent something else. In the end he cartwheeled off again, but this time his gymnastics were all too earthbound, lacking the almost inhuman lightness that they had had before his confidence had been broken.

Helen and Bill were the only ones who seemed unaffected by the catastrophe. Helen, very sensibly, made no effort to crane her head round the mobile in an attempt to see Tabitha; instead she lounged back still further on her bed of leaves and addressed her as if, being the queen of the fairies, she could see straight through the mobile to her servant beyond. It was this display of sangfroid which helped the rest of them, less experienced and more prone to the jitters, to pull themselves together, and I commended her for it. She hadn't even registered surprise when she had understood what was happening. Bill, meanwhile, strolled round the mobile and called bluffly up to Tabitha the speech he was supposed to give her.

"Come, wait upon him," Helen addressed the fairies, "lead him to my bower. . . ."

She stood up and indicated that Bill should precede her. In a moment of inspiration, he gave poor Tabitha a wave, as if to say that he would catch up with her later, and followed the other fairies offstage. A blackout promptly ensued, this one unprogrammed. I hoped to God they were managing to get Tabitha back up; apart from the humiliation, she must be suffering cramps by now. The blackout extended and, suddenly violently uncomfortable, I tapped Janey's arm, nodded at the stage and whispered: "See you in the interval," before slipping out, treading on several unwary feet in my escape.

Leaving the auditorium, I went quickly round the corner of the corridor, down a flight of plush red steps with gold handrails and through the pass door at the far end, into a stone-walled passageway with bare strip lights overhead. The shock of the contrast between backstage and front of house was as strong as ever. I passed the ASM stationed in the wings, twitchy as a caged prisoner, pulling with short neurotic tugs on the curtains; she looked up at me with wild eyes as I drew level with her.

"Did you *see* it?" she whispered.

I nodded and kept going. Paul, sitting on an upright chair, was muttering his lines, too early for his cue, working himself up into a fine state of nervous tension; every so often he looked up and checked his appearance in front of the huge stained mirror that hung at an odd angle directly in front of him. This seemed to do wonders for calming him down. I turned the last corner and came on the DSM desk. Louise was talking urgently into her headset. From the stage came Marie's voice, giving one of her long speeches. She sounded higher and much more nervous than usual.

Beyond the desk, a little to the left, was Steve, screaming almost silently at the crew member who operated Tabitha's line. The object of his abuse was standing in place, his hands still around the line, his face white with shock. He hardly seemed to hear Steve at all, which was as well, because Steve was being particularly savage, his hands planted on his hips in the way he did when his exasperation was pushed beyond the limit. His heavy stomach hung over his tool belt like a kangaroo pouch.

"What the fuck just happened out there?" Steve hissed, his voice sounding as if he had burned the inside of his throat and was forcing the words out in extreme pain. "What the fucking fuck just happened? Fuck!"

For a moment I lost myself in appreciation of Steve's way with words. The operator looked lost, too, but not quite for the same reason, I imagined. I took a few steps past them, till I could get a clear view up above, and tilted back my head. Tabitha's small figure was walking along the narrow fixed bridge, towards the fly floor. If they couldn't get her down, at least they had managed to take her back up again. As I watched, she swayed slightly and then caught at one of the waist-high hawsers for support before swinging herself over the pin rail onto the fly floor and disappearing from sight.

"It wouldn't fucking move!" the operator was saying to Steve, having finally recovered his voice. "There were two of us hanging off it by the end like a pair of bloody bell-ringers, and it still wouldn't bloody move! Going up was OK, thank fuck. Otherwise that poor little cow'd have been stuck there till the interval."

Steve's brand of eloquence was corrupting those around him, I noticed. "Well, what the hell was it?" he demanded.

Winding the line round its hook, the operator said impatiently over his shoulder:

"We're going to check it out straight away, aren't we? The lads up there'll be on the case already."

"Did you feel anything wrong with the line?"

"Of course I didn't bloody feel anything wrong with the line!" The crew member swung round, face creased in fury. Clearly he had been paralysed with shock and was only just starting to recover. I imagined that shouting at Steve, even sotto voce, was a welcome release for the pressure that had built up while he was tugging impotently on Tabitha's line. "D'you think I'd just have gone ahead and not said anything if it didn't feel OK? What d'you think I am, a fucking moron?"

"Don't you bloody talk to me like that, sonny boy!" Steve yelled back, his temper rising still further. I noticed, impressed, that despite their tempers neither of the men's voices rose beyond the limits of what was acceptable backstage. These habits die hard.

"Steve? Steve!" Louise called from the desk, her voice as soothing as ambient music. "Why don't you go up and have a look yourself?"

"I will. I'll do just that," Steve said, staring malevolently into the operator's eyes, as if he were threatening him with the decision. "And then we'll see what we will see."

With these magnificently meaningless words, he stalked over to the far wall and started hauling himself up the Jacob's ladder, one painstaking rung after another. He was so out of condition that his bottom sagged down almost to the back of his knees.

The operator turned, shaking now with stress, and caught my eye.

"It was stuck!" he said rather pathetically. "I couldn't do anything about it!"

I nodded sympathetically and tilted my head back to see what was happening above us. One of the flymen was advancing along the fixed bridge; he reached the centre and stood there, craning his head back, trying to see what had happened to Tabitha's line. I heard a fuzzing through the headset of the operator who was standing next to me, a voice smudged with static, coming from the bridge above. He was asking if the operator had noticed anything odd about the line.

"Nothing. Bloody nothing! Ran as smoothly as always, I swear to God!" the poor man insisted.

The flyman was swivelling now, circling his head. The flymen always insisted that they could tell as soon as they started to pull a cable whether it was wrongly weighted, or tangled up in something; they were so used by now to the precise feel of it running through their hands. If it had been a bar that had got stuck, it would probably have been a simple matter of it being wrongly rigged and catching on the fly rail, or another bar, and although it would have been equally disastrous for whatever was happening onstage, it would be much easier to see and adjust at the interval. But a line, running through pulleys and other lines high up on the grid, was as difficult to spot when it went wrong as it was to untangle the strings of a puppet.

The flyman had given up and was walking back down the bridge as lightly as if he weren't thirty-five feet off the ground on what was effectively a narrow beam with a couple of hawsers running along each side. His voice buzzed again down the headset.

"Yeah, OK, mate. I'll be there," the operator said in answer.

He turned to me. "He can't see anything, but it wasn't likely he was going to. It's not down here and it's not on the fly floor. The problem's got to be up on the grid. He'll check it in the interval."

I nodded; it was what I had assumed already. "Marie's line was fine, though," I said. "Or was it? Did you have any problems when she came down?"

He shook his head. "Smooth as silk. Me and Jack down here and Trev up doing the mobile. And that one's much more complicated—she's got a tracking system to take her sideways for the jump off the mobile. No, that went fine." He was cheering up visibly with the memory. "No problem at all."

There was nothing for me to do here. I slipped back into the auditorium, deciding to take one of the spare ushers' seats at the back rather than cause more distraction by grinding a few more feet into the carpet on my way back to my own seat. Besides, it suited me to sit at the back, neither a part of the audience nor of the crew, watching the play with a detachment that was habitual to me. I liked always to be a little on the outside of a situation, and this was perfect: alone in the dark, the wall at my back, neat rows of heads stretching in front of me to the edge of the stage, the actors beyond. I found my mind sliding away from the action onstage to the puzzle of what was happening at the Cross theatre. By now it was a challenge to me, as intricately tangled up as Tabitha's line and just as difficult to unweave. I reminded myself to be careful. I always do. But I always forget, too, that just reminding myself is never quite enough.

○○○

At the interval I bought Janey a Bloody Mary and then promptly abandoned her to go backstage, too curious about what had happened to Tabitha's line to wait till the end of the play to find out. Janey had, as always at the theatre, already bumped into a couple of agents she knew and was chatting away to them.

The atmosphere backstage was charged with excitement and something else, a kind of heightened ghoulishness; by this time people had given up trying to predict what fresh disaster would befall them and were simply waiting, nerves charged up, to see what it would be. Swarming up the Jacob's ladder, I emerged through the square hole cut into the fly floor to find it jammed with people. Besides all the flymen and the operators from down below, there were MM and Matthew, Sally, Thierry, Bez and Ben. The last-named was looking distinctly shaky, staying as far back from the edge as he could, despite the height of the parapet. The mere knowledge of how high up he was obviously sufficed to send his head spinning. It couldn't have been easy for him coming down the ladder. I rather admired him for making the effort; no-one would have blamed him if he'd stayed away.

Everyone was watching a lone flyman, high up in the grid like a spider in its web, clambering hand over hand towards the pulley through which Tabitha's line ran. Everyone, that is, apart from Ben, who was looking straight in front of him and swallowing hard. One of the flymen was giv-ing him a running commentary, as if he were blind.

"Nearly there now," he was saying. "Oops—nah, he's all right, don't worry." Ben had started like a rabbit seeing a dog.

"Why's he up here at all?" I said quietly to Bez.

He shrugged. "Says he's responsible in the end, cos he's in charge. Nonsense, really. Does the lad credit, though."

Far above us the flyman bent and hooked one hand around the pulley. Steve put one hand to his headset to steady it as a stream of words poured out.

"OK," he said. "Sort it out and come on down, all right?"

He turned to us, his pudgy pale face puffed up with news like a tropical fish with poison.

"Well, come on, mate, let's be having it!" Bez said impatiently. "What is it?"

I noticed that this was universally considered as the problem of the the-atre, and not of the production of the *Dream*. MM and Matthew were nat-urally present, but the responsibility lay squarely on the shoulders of the Cross theatre crew.

"He says there's a jubilee clip on the line, isn't there?" Steve said sav-agely. "Someone's only gone up there and put it on so the line can't bloody run through the pulley! No wonder it got stuck!"

"You mean," MM said implacably, "that someone has sabotaged Tabitha's line."

"That's right," Steve said. "No way that could have happened by accident."

"This is very serious," Ben said. He was still paler than usual but his voice sounded relatively normal. "After the show goes down I want a full meeting of every single person in the theatre. Not front-of-house staff, obviously. But everyone who could have had the opportunity to tamper with the pulley, or who might have seen someone else doing it."

"Wouldn't they have said by now if they'd seen something funny going on up in the grid?" Matthew volunteered.

"They might not have known what it meant," I said. "They might just have seen someone whose job it was to be up there, and not thought any more about it."

"I can tell you for a start that none of the flymen'd have pulled something like this," Bez said. "They'd never tamper with a line. Right, lads?"

The flymen were nodding. The guy who had been up on the grid, temporarily forgotten in the shock of the news, came down the ladder behind me like a fireman, using only his hands, protected by the thick gloves, to slide down the sides of the iron ladder.

"You told 'em then, Steve?" he said, looking round the group. "That wasn't no accident. I reckon it happened just after the half. No-one's around then, cos everything's been checked already. It wouldn't take long to do."

It was true. Backstage was deserted for a good quarter of an hour after Bez and the chief sparks had done their safety checks. The cast would be in their dressing rooms, the crew in the pub or the crew room; there might be the odd ASM flitting round the deck, or Steve pacing back and forth, but Steve had obviously seen nothing, or he would have said so. And anyway, from the deck it would be impossible to identify someone fifty feet up on the grid.

From behind me came a stifled cry. We all swung round, which, in the cramped space, wasn't easy to do; Matthew tripped over a weight and would have gone down if we hadn't been squashed in like sardines. As it was, he staggered into Bez, who toppled slightly onto Ben, who instinctively grabbed onto the wall for support, his hand going through the cables. One of the flymen let out a yelp of concern and bounded forward to save the cables, scattering bodies in his wake. The other flymen who had been beside him immediately started clowning around, knocking into each other like human dominoes, clattering over the floor, everyone eager to let off steam after the tension of the recent discovery.

In all this confusion the exclamation from the new arrival had been temporarily forgotten. Trying not to giggle, I focused harder on the back wall of the fly floor where the Jacob's ladder ran; the wall was in shadow and it was hard to make out the person who was standing there. As if realizing this, she came forward a few paces, the light picking out her face. It was Tabitha.

She must have come down the ladder from the hatch above while we were talking. The horseplay continued behind us for a little longer, the flymen still jostling each other. I had noticed they were taking the opportunity to push Steve round a bit in the spirit of fun; he was too bossy and self-important to win any Mr. Popularity contest. But I had fallen silent, and so had those around me. From her expression, it was clear that Tabitha had heard what had happened to her line.

"Someone deliberately sabotaged it?" she said, faintly but clearly. Good voice projection, I noticed. "Why would anyone want to do that to me?"

"Tabitha—" said MM, starting forward.

She had already covered her face with her hands. "I don't believe it!" she was sobbing. "Why would someone do that? It was so scary! I was stuck up there! I didn't even know if I could get down!"

MM was patting her shoulder in a heartening way.

"We'll make sure that nothing like this happens again, I promise," she said firmly. "From now on we'll double-check your line every night. Don't worry."

Sally, pushing through the crowd, reached Tabitha and put his arms around her.

"You wair very good," he consoled her. "You handle eet very well. No-one een the audience knows what ees happening."

He looked up at MM, signalling her with his eyebrows to add to the reassurances.

"I've already told Tabitha how good she was," MM said. "Haven't I, Tabitha?"

The latter uncovered her face, beaming up at MM. Next to her, Tabitha looked very small and fragile; but at those words of praise she was transformed, her eyes shining, huge and dark, her lips parted.

"Thank you," she breathed. "Do you really think so?"

"Absolutely."

Thierry was flanking Tabitha's other side by now, concerned in case the incident might have made her lose her nerve.

"So you'll be all right for tomorrow?" he said, not perhaps as tactfully as one might have wished. Sally caught my eye and rolled his own theatrically.

But Tabitha was still basking in MM's praise.

"Oh yes!" she said happily. "If MM thinks I can do it . . ."

She was still staring up at MM as worshipfully as if she were a shepherd girl from the Balkans and MM an idol who was due to start streaming tears of blood any minute now.

"Of course you can," MM said simply. "You're not going to let yourself be fazed by someone's stupid little joke. We can run through it tomorrow afternoon, if you'd like."

"Whatever you think," Tabitha said subserviently.

"Now you'd better be getting back," MM said, frowning. "The interval must be nearly over."

Thierry and Sally escorted Tabitha up the ladder, one before, one after her, like a palace guard. The rest of us, recalled to immediate considerations of time, started shuffling in that direction. The flymen detached themselves from the general movement towards the ladder and bunched together in a mass at the far end of the fly floor, heads together, talking quickly. One of them kept shooting glances over at our group.

"Sam?" Ben said, bending over and picking something up from the floor. "I think this must be yours."

He stretched out his palm to me. On it lay a hairgrip, silver with a tiny diamond star at its end. It was a pretty little thing and I could see exactly why he had thought it was mine; I had a few not unlike it. Only it didn't belong to me. MM was the only other woman who was up here now, and she would have looked like a man in drag if she'd worn diamanté. That only left Tabitha, and she had been in costume. Besides, she hadn't come that far down the fly floor.

I let the hairgrip sit for a moment on Ben's palm, waiting to see if anyone else identified it as something that must have fallen out of their pocket. No-one did, though MM and Matthew, who were just behind Ben, both glanced at it.

"Thanks," I said. "I must have dropped it just now. Or maybe it fell out earlier." I put my hand up to my hair. "I can't remember missing it before. . . ."

"Wasn't here before," Bez said. "We were up here at the half and I didn't see nothing. I'd have noticed it for sure."

MM was saying to Steve: "I meant what I said to Tabitha. We'll have to make sure the lines—hers and Marie's—are double-checked every night, and then keep someone around during the half to make sure no-one tampers with them."

"Nothing like this," Steve said ponderously, "has ever happened before in this theatre. And I've been here a good twenty years now."

His head swivelled to MM and Matthew, taking me in as it went. The implication was clear enough. Steve was putting the onus of responsibility on someone who was involved with the production of the *Dream*. My hand closed round the hairgrip in my pocket, feeling the points of the diamond star in the centre of my palm. The worst of it was that I thought he might well be right.

As might have been expected, the bulk of suspicion fell squarely on the fairies. They were known to have been hostile to Tabitha, and in fact it emerged that they had effectively been sending her to Coventry for the past week or so. I was never really surprised by how petty adults could be to one another, but even so this seemed exaggerated. After all, Ranjit had a scene with Puck at the beginning of the play which was larger than the rest of their roles put together, and he was also Marie's understudy, and neither of these facts seemed to have made the others jealous of him. But then Ranjit was not the kind to lord it over the others. They clearly took it for granted that he should have been preferred. Besides, he had been cast that way from the start, making his privileged status a fait accompli. Tabitha, on the other hand, had grabbed her chance to stand in for Violet, and apparently had wittered on at great length about the many and varied compliments Thierry had paid her gymnastic abilities. If it had been the fairies who had sabotaged her line, clearly they had thought she was asking for it.

They had no alibi, or rather their alibi was collective; it transpired that Liza, who played Moth, had been sharing the boys' dressing room rather than the one she had been allotted with Tabitha. They said they had all been in there together during the half, and no-one had seen them outside. Still, as people were all too ready to point out, the hatch to the Jacob's ladder was very near the door of their dressing room, and it would have been easy enough for them to sneak out.

A side order of suspicion, however, fell on Violet. This was orchestrated, I suspected, by Helen and Bill. Helen, of course, loathed Violet cordially, and Bill followed her lead; Helen and the three fairies also shared a good deal of antipathy towards Tabitha, and she was thus bound to defend them against any accusations. The trouble, in a way, was that no accusations were actually being made. Everything simmered just below boiling point in a manner that was much more stressful over a period of time than a proper explosion would have been.

The informal investigation set in train by Ben and Steve threw up nothing. None of the ASMs had been in the wings, which had been the best hope for witnesses; they had set their props and then retired to the local café for a quick sandwich. Ben had been with the front-of-house manager, and the crew, naturally enough, had been down the pub, with the exception of Steve, who said he had been doing a series of last-minute checks without specifying exactly where. Bez said witheringly that he knew perfectly well Steve had been down in the crew room watching a dirty video, but he wasn't going to admit to it.

It was hard not to reach Steve's conclusion that the culprit responsible was someone connected with the *Dream*. I found it easier to believe that one of the fairies had been playing a nasty practical joke to cut Tabitha down to size than that Violet had bothered to scramble up to the grid and rig up a shackle on Tabitha's line. Put simply, I couldn't see Violet getting her hands dirty. Besides, it was hard to see what motive she might have; she had emerged victorious out of her and Tabitha's little tiffs.

Then another thought struck me. What if Violet had found out that it was Tabitha who had arranged for that message on her answering machine and later dosed her coffee with anti-histamines? Might she not have decided to get her own back, once and for all? The suspicion had even crossed my mind some time ago that Violet might have set up those incidents herself so that people would sympathize with her rather than resenting the fact that she had been nearly a week late for rehearsals. It would have been so easy to lie about the message and drop a couple of anti-histamines into her own mug. Sophie had said that Violet had been very distressed when Sophie told her about the latter incident, but that proved nothing. I thought Violet might well be capable of staging the two events. Certainly it was an extreme measure, but people who are desperate for attention will use extraordinary methods to obtain it. I couldn't rule out that possibility. It left her, however, without a motive for sabotaging Tabitha's line; unless there had been some recent encounter between them that I didn't know about. That, again, was all too possible.

I didn't share these last thoughts with Hugo. Instinct rather warned me against it. In any case, as the first night drew close he was becoming increasingly nervy and distracted. The other two previews had gone without a hitch; Bez and I had taken to using that phrase to one another in an ironical way, to mean specifically that no-one's rope had been fouled. He had explained it to Lurch, who thought it was the height of wit, bless him. One of the flymen had been delegated to check the lines just before the half, and after he had given the all-clear, Steve, Bez or the chief sparks would patrol the area, making sure that no-one could tamper with them.

"It only helps up to a point, though," I observed to Hugo the evening before press night. "I mean, if someone's running around playing silly buggers, there's no limit to the kind of stuff they could get up to."

This was not what Hugo wanted to hear. He muttered something about my being an insensitive idiot and pointedly turned his attention to the TV. We were watching a crappy late-night American thriller, which was perfect for Hugo's needs as the acting was so bad and the script so poor that he was not required to feel jealous of anyone connected with the production and could lounge back sneering instead. By the time it had finished he had completely recovered his good humour, though he was rather tired.

As we went to bed he apologized for his exhaustion and said, in a smaller voice than usual, that he didn't think he'd be up to anything that evening, and did I mind. I was so touched it didn't even occur to me to tease him; he fell asleep almost at once, as if he had been turned off at the mains. I stayed up reading for a while. Hugo turned over and curled around me, still fast asleep, one arm heavy over my waist. It brought such a lump to my throat that I had to put the book down and turn out the light. Somehow it seemed more permissible to feel sentimental in the dark.

○○○

"That *poor* girl," Violet said sympathetically. We were having a late lunch in Islington, Hugo, Violet and myself. That evening was the press night, and both of them were rather on edge. Talking about Tabitha's misfortune had cheered them up, however. Nothing like discussing someone else's disasters to make you feel better about your own impending reviews.

"The bright side," I offered, "is that she's getting lots of sympathy and TLC. Thierry and Sally are hovering over her like guardian angels. And MM's been very reassuring."

Hugo pulled a face. "Scant compensation," he said. "I can assure you that after that contretemps, no-one's getting me into a body harness as long as I live. I mistrusted those contraptions anyway and now I have a cast-iron reason for refusing."

"Oh, I don't know," said Violet lightly. "It was a one-in-a-million chance. That kind of thing hardly ever happens."

"Scarcely chance, Vi," Hugo said sharply. "Or maybe you meant that it's extremely unlikely that someone would dislike you enough to play that kind of prank on you. Which, as we know, isn't true."

Violet stared at him. "Do you think it was the same person who left that message and put the anti-histamines in my drink? I never thought of that!"

"It's possible, isn't it? More likely than that there are two practical jokers milling around as completely independent contractors. That does rather beggar belief."

"I thought that was all over with," Violet said, distressed. The waitress brought our food and she automatically favoured her with a blinding smile and a murmured "Thank you" in her best smooth voice. When Violet turned on the charm, it was lethal at twenty paces; the waitress reeled back slightly, visibly dazzled.

Hugo tucked into his steak with gusto. Violet was staring down at her plate, still miserable.

"Oh, come on, Vi, cheer up," Hugo said bracingly. "Obviously the practical joker has turned their attentions elsewhere. You should be grateful. Unless you're jealous, of course."

"*Jealous?*" This, as Hugo had known it would, brought Violet's head up with a start. "Why should I be jealous?"

"Of Tabitha," Hugo said, washing his bite of steak down with a judicious mouthful of wine. We had ordered a bottle on the understanding that I would drink the lion's share. ("*Lots* of calories in wine," Violet had said mournfully. "Besides, we don't want to get tipsy at lunchtime. Or rather, we do, but we mustn't.")

Now he said mischievously to Violet: "Jealous that the prankster has lost interest in you, darling. It's like having your stalker decide that he wants to go after someone off *EastEnders* instead. Most unflattering."

Violet bridled. "I really don't think I need to be jealous of *Tabitha*," she said firmly.

"No, if anything it should be the other way round," Hugo mused.

Violet, restored to form, started in on her food. We were in Café Flo on Upper Street, one of Hugo's favourite haunts; it was his usual practice, when due at the theatre that evening, to eat a large lunch at about two. This was his main meal of the day. After the play he would have nothing but salad, cheese and fruit, since he maintained that eating late at night put on weight which was impossible to shift.

"Look at opera singers," he would say ghoulishly. "I don't want to be the obvious choice for Sir Toby Belch in twenty years' time."

Violet was tucking into her poached egg and chicken frisée salad with as much enjoyment as if it were a giant plate of chips. She had already favoured my own giant plate of chips with a disapproving gaze.

"Hey, I don't have to go on television," I pointed out. "No worries for me about the camera putting on seven pounds."

"It's more like *ten* when you're small-boned," Violet said dismally.

"You wait till you're being interviewed on late-night review programmes," Hugo said to me. "You'll come running to us pleading for diet tips."

Violet perked up. "The insulin injections really do work, you know," she said. "I swear by them."

"What I don't understand," I said, "is that they're supposed to break down carbohydrates, right?"

"And sugars."

"But you hardly ever eat carbohydrates. I mean, look at your salad. There isn't a carbohydrate within several miles of your plate. Apart from my chips." I waggled one at her before putting it in my mouth.

"She has a point, Vi," Hugo said. "God knows what they're doing to you, those injections."

Violet looked sulky. "Well, I don't use them every day," she said, pouting. "Just when I've been a bit naughty."

"Like Philip," I said, "after lunch with Hugo's agent."

Violet's great eyes fired up. "That was *not* an accident," she said, leaning towards me across the table, a forkful of chicken breast abandoned on her plate. "Philip would *never* have made that kind of mistake. *Never.* No matter how much drink Ronnie poured down him. I wouldn't have given him a supply if I'd thought there was any danger of that."

She looked at both of us, her face falling.

"Oh, I've just remembered," she said. "Oh *no.*"

"What?" I said, curious.

"A trouble shared," Hugo said encouragingly, "is a trouble halved. Or tripled, in this case. No, hang on, that's not right. What would the word be for something divided by three? Thirded?"

"Hugo," I said, "shut up. You're losing it."

"Yes, darling." He leant back in his chair and steepled his fingers in front of him, contemplating his rings.

"When I had to give my statement," Violet said, lowering her voice for extra effect, "the police asked me how many needle pens I'd given Philip. And I wasn't exactly sure, but I knew it was at least five or six."

"So?" Hugo said.

"Well, when they found him, he'd taken three. But there weren't any left over. They looked everywhere. In his flat as well."

"Well?" Hugo said impatiently. "He might have taken the others already."

Violet was shaking her head. "I only gave them to him a couple of days before. And we were together. I'd have known if he'd had any. He was very careful anyway, like I said. He wouldn't have done them every day, or anything like that." I noticed that she was too worried to remember the accent she usually affected, with its emphases on key words and upper-class intonations. I much preferred her this way.

"Do you mean," I said slowly, "that there are probably another two or three needle pens still at large?"

"At least," Violet said.

"Which is enough to kill someone," I said. "So that if Philip didn't kill himself, whoever did it has made sure they've got another supply in case they want to do it again."

Violet was nodding. I looked at Hugo.

"A cheerful thought," he said, pushing his plate away from him and reaching for the wine bottle. "On second thoughts, Sam, maybe you won't have to finish this by yourself after all."

He filled his own and Violet's glasses once more. We all drank deeply. Shallow and limited as we obviously were, it seemed the only adequate response to Violet's latest piece of news.

○○○

Hugo insisted on picking out my outfit for that evening. We went back to my studio and he amused himself tremendously by flicking through everything on my clothes rail, commenting with increasingly arcane and Shakespearian swearwords on the selection it had to offer, and finally flinging a few things on the bed, ordering me imperiously to try them on. My cover story for going along with this display of masculine authoritarianism was that I could see how stressed he was at the thought of the press night fast approaching, and was happy to help distract him, whatever form that might take; but actually I rather enjoyed myself. It was such a treat to have a straight man—a boyfriend-type person, no less—actually interested in what I was wearing rather than simply looking approving when I put on something short, tight and black.

Since this was my usual fall-back position, I had an awful lot of short, tight, black garments, all of which Hugo rejected. Instead he picked a long, white sheath with spaghetti straps and a slit up one side, which I had bought on sale and never worn.

"Doesn't it make me look fat?" I said, pivoting distrustfully and trying to look down at my bottom over my shoulder, regretting the giant plate of chips at lunch.

"No. You're in rather good shape for someone who eats like the hero of *Babe*."

"I was hungry," I said defensively. "And anyway, I work out a lot."

"I can tell, darling. I am familiar with the state of your inner thighs."

Lounging on my futon, Hugo looked like a pasha surveying one of the newest recruits to the harem. Now I realized why I had all those pillows. It was so Hugo could prop himself up on them and look at me down his long nose, eyelids heavy, a lock of his fair hair tangling over his forehead. He was temporarily distracted and would push it back firmly as soon as he realized, but I liked it; when someone's grooming is so perfect, these little flaws fill you with a kind of speechless tenderness.

I blinked and swallowed in an over-ambitious attempt to dam the flow of slushiness that was threatening to overwhelm me.

"Are you all right?" Hugo asked sympathetically. "I only wonder because you seem to be going into spasm."

"Fine," I said, recovering. "I was just wondering what shoes to wear with it."

"Those silver sandals you got at the second-hand shop on Upper Street last week," Hugo said simply. "The Fifties ones. And put your hair up so it doesn't all fall down halfway through the evening. Now take that frock off and come here. I always need to make love the afternoon before a press night and you're the closest woman to hand."

"Undeniable," I said, unzipping the dress. "But I warn you, the futon isn't as adaptable as your bed. I'm not going to tie you up to it. It couldn't take the strain."

I let the dress fall to my feet. I had been changing behind the clothes rail previously and Hugo, being, after all, a man, hadn't realized that I wasn't wearing anything underneath it. I was pleased to see that I was capable of rendering him speechless.

"Or maybe I should go like this," I said, advancing on him. "What do you think?"

"It's definitely my favourite," Hugo said, making a stab at recovery.

I pinned him down and kissed him. He slid back on the pillows, sprawled happily beneath me.

"Prove it," I said.

Well, I hit him hard right between the eyes
And he went down, but to my surprise
He come up with a knife and cut off a piece of my ear.

But I busted a chair right across his teeth.
And we crashed through the wall and into the street
Kicking and a-gouging in the mud and the blood and the beer.

I tell you, I've fought tougher men
But I really can't remember when.
He kicked like a mule and he bit like a crocodile.

I heard him laughin' and then I heard him cussin',
He went for his gun and I pulled mine first.
He stood there looking at me and I saw him smile.

"Hi!" I said, coming down the stairs gingerly on my heels, holding onto the railing for support. Lurch, who was whistling between his teeth to the song in progress, swung round and nearly bit off the tip of his tongue, which was lolling out the side of his mouth.

"Sam?" he said in amazement. "You look like something out of a perfume ad."

"Thank you. I think. Look, did you put all the presents in the dressing rooms? I forgot to ring today to remind you."

"After all that work we done? Course I did!"

Lurch and I had spent the past few days making first-night presents for the cast and crew, after I had learnt from Hugo that it was considered obligatory to give everyone a good-luck card, if not a present. Having time on my hands, I had enlisted Lurch, and we had pottered around happily collecting scraps of metal, wire, nuts and bolts, soldering them onto plaques of metal to make key-rings. On the back we had etched the name of the play and today's date. Our creations had got more extravagant as the hours wore on; some of the key rings were definitely more decorative than practical.

"Cut your 'and up reaching into your bag for this one," Lurch had said, holding up the last effort, so heavily crusted with soldered-on fragments of metal it looked like we'd put down a magnet in the middle of the work-space and let it attract half the debris in the room. "Who're we going to give it to?"

"Bez," I said. "That'll get him back for taking the piss out of the first one we made."

We had wrapped the presents in brown paper and sealed them with wax. I was rather pleased with the result. At least it was different.

"Look," I said now, producing a bottle of champagne from behind my back and waving it in the air. "Round up some mugs and we'll have a drink. Where's Bez?"

He emerged from the crew room. "I can smell a bottle of booze at fifty paces," he said cheerfully. "Come on, let's be having some. Champagne, is it? That's what I call starting the party early."

"You're coming to the party, ain't ya, Sam?" Lurch said anxiously. "It's at Matthew's house."

"She knows that, moron," said Bez, cuffing him round the head. I opened the champagne with a loud, satisfying pop. "Course she's coming. Why d'you think she's dressed up like a dog's dinner?"

"Thanks very bloody much," I said with hauteur, filling the mugs. The chief sparks and his charge hand gathered round as well.

"Oh, have you heard the latest?" Bez said. "MM's been asked if she wants to apply for Philip's job. The board had a couple of people sitting in on a run-through and they really rated the production. Well, they bloody should."

The thought of running a theatre, with all its conflicts of interests and demands, egos to soothe, punters to pull in, not to mention plays to direct, sent a shiver of horror down my spine. But MM could cope with it if anyone could.

"That's great news," I said, drinking some champagne. "I hope she gets it."

"So do I," said Bez.

"That's just 'cause it'd be her first time running a space like this and you could take the piss," said the chief sparks cynically.

"Don't talk rubbish," Bez said with unexpected emphasis. "I don't see anyone taking the piss round here, do you? She knows exactly what she's doing. That's why I'm all for her. And she's got no airs and graces. Not like Philip. He was a right one for putting his nose in the air."

"If MM gets the job," I said thoughtfully, "would that mean Matthew would get Ben's?"

"I'd bring him in if I was her," Bez said. "She can pick them all right. Works all hours, never complains, everything you ask him about he writes it down and checks it out and gets back to you—yeah, I reckon I'd keep Matthew on. Only it'd get on my tits a bit having him follow me round like that. You'd think she had him on a lead."

"Practically does," piped up the charge hand. "He'd do anything she asked. If she said, 'Matthew, go and jump off the fly floor without a line,' he'd just go: 'Right, MM,' and off he'd pop." Intoxicated by his own invention, he continued: "If she told him to go and lie down in the middle of the road—"

"Yeah, all right, we got the idea," said the chief sparks witheringly. The charge hand subsided, still flushed with his own eloquence.

I poured out the last of the champagne. We polished it off with indecent haste.

"Feel like the party's started already," said Bez.

"There's just the small matter of a play to be got through first," I pointed out.

"Oh yeah." Bez grinned. "Always a spanner in the works, isn't there?"

○○○

The party was already raging by the time we arrived. Matthew's house turned out, in strict point of fact, to be his parents'. They were apparently, and one hoped for their sakes definitely, staying at their Wiltshire house for the weekend, leaving the cast, crew and hangers-on of *A Midsummer Night's Dream* to run quite literally rampant through their luxuriously appointed Chiswick home.

I had never been to a party where both surroundings and guests had displayed such uplifted aesthetic standards. Certainly the cast were a peculiarly good-looking bunch: young, hungry for success and well aware of the necessity to make the most of their natural advantages. As we walked towards the house, Paul and Tabitha, sitting on the steps outside with their arms around each other and their heads together, made a *Hello!*-worthy couple, with the added bonus of their ethnic differences: Paul, tall and red-headed, was one of the rare people who actually has white skin, as opposed to the rest of us who are various shades of murky yellow. And Tabitha, ethereally slender in a little navy slip dress, her dark shiny hair piled on top of her head in a style I suspected her of copying from Violet, was the exact shade of Donatella Versace's wrinkled, leathered permatan. Only on Tabitha the colour was real, her skin smooth and perfect.

They looked up as we passed them, Tabitha giggling. No accidents for her tonight, no problems with her line, and her jump had been perfect. She was flushed with her success and with Paul's proximity and looked more relaxed than she had been for weeks.

"Hi, everyone, hi!" she said, so effervescent I could practically see the bubbles rising from her lips. "Isn't it a great party?"

"We don't know," Hugo said, "because we haven't gone in yet. But if you meant the question purely rhetorically . . ."

"I'll take him away," I said, pushing Hugo up the steps. "I do apologize."

Hugo had had a triumph; resounding applause, compliments from all sides and an ecstatic response from his agent. He was floating thirty feet up without the benefit of artificial substances. My job tonight was to act as the rope that tethered the helium balloon to the ground.

The front door was ajar, though difficult to open further, due to the press of people in the hall. At first glance the party looked impossibly glossy, like the photographs for gossip magazines taken at angles which leave out all the poorly dressed people. After a while, however, my eye became more finely tuned, as it does when you enter a darkened room, and I began to spot the scruffier members of the *Dream* entourage. Prime among them was MM herself, wearing a skirt for the first time in my acquaintance with her, a drop-waisted dress in dark red which suited her even less than her jeans and didn't matter at all, because with MM her clothes never mattered. I rather envied this higher, Zen-like state while knowing that I would never attain it and, secretly, didn't really want to. I smoothed down my white satin-backed crepe column as if to reassure myself.

Hugo wasn't too high on Cloud Nine to miss this gesture.

"You look lovely," he said, bending down to kiss the top of my head. He was wearing a white linen suit with a pale beige T-shirt underneath; on his wrist was a chunky silver bracelet which looked rather like my necklace. We even had matching nail polish: Uzi, by Urban Decay, a glittery blue-grey. Hugo was a label junkie and wouldn't listen when I told him you could get the same colour for a third of the price from Boots. The paparazzo from the *Evening Standard* had picked up on the synchronicity of our outfits and, overruling me, had insisted I join Hugo for the photograph. It wasn't that I was worried about stealing the limelight; on the contrary, my main objection had been that I was sure he would come out better than I would.

"Not fair," I had said crossly, "making me wear white and then stand next to someone twice as tall as me, not to mention thinner. I'll look like one of those church candles."

"Darling," Hugo had reproved. "No-one could call you *squat*. Hourglass, yes. Squat, no."

Certainly one of the advantages to wearing white was that everyone turned to look at you. This must be what it was like to be blonde. Janey glided through the crowd to hug us both, Helen just behind her. Helen was prettier than I had ever seen her, glowing like a nuclear reactor; the adrenaline-charged atmosphere had infected her, too. It would be interesting to see how far its effects reached. I doubted, for instance, that she would start to say nice things about her fellow actresses.

"Have you heard?" she said. "They've offered MM the artistic director job! Isn't it brilliant?" She was wearing her usual ankle-length black Lycra tube, which showed off her narrow hips and hid her less-than-perfect legs. I had to admit that if you didn't know about the lumpy calves it was very effective.

"Offered her the *job?*" Hugo said doubtfully. "I think they've just asked her to interview for it."

"Oh really?" Helen looked disappointed. "I heard they'd offered it to her. . . ."

"Chinese whispers are never to be trusted," Hugo said. "Amazing how these things get distorted when they reach the fifteenth person in line."

"Actually, I heard it from Bill, and he got it from someone very close to the board," Helen said, bristling at the suggestion that her contacts needed polishing. "Isn't that right, Bill? Bill!"

Duly summoned, Bill trotted over. He had gained weight during rehearsals and looked more lardily pale than ever, his skin the dirty white of uncooked lamb fat. His trousers were splayed with creases round the crotch, deep as canyons, and his shirt was swollen and straining over his paunch. Out of the corner of my eye I saw Hugo look down complacently at his own flat stomach. He had been to the gym that afternoon, working on his six-pack. Bill was a perfect example of how contradictory actors could be; offstage he was such heavy going conversationally that William Hague would seem like Stephen Fry by comparison. Yet his performance tonight, notwithstanding the fact that I had seen it many times before, had not only made me howl with laughter but also won my sympathy. Suspension less of disbelief than of dislike.

"All right," he said, nodding round the group. He was holding a puff pastry canapé piled high with prawns, and now he bit into it with such delicacy that the pastry hardly flaked at all. I was impressed. Useful Social Skill number 149.

"I was just saying," Helen said brightly, "that apparently MM's been offered the artistic director job." She looked at Bill expectantly.

"Well, not exactly," Bill said, shifting uncomfortably from side to side. "I mean, they've asked her to interview and they're really impressed by the *Dream*. So, y'know. . . ."

His voice tailing off, he fitted the rest of the canapé into his mouth and closed his jaws over it, chewing with long slow movements, his cheeks as puffed out as Marie Helvin's.

Helen, let down by her accomplice in gossip, flushed an angry pink.

"It'll be very interesting to see what happens," said Janey swiftly. "MM's certainly on a roll at the moment. Practically everyone who matters came to see the show tonight. Look, there's Trevor Nunn."

All the actors present perked up as sharply as if someone had applied a cattle prod to the base of their spines.

"Where?" Helen said eagerly.

"Over there, talking to MM and Ben."

"Trust Ben to sidle his way into that conversation," Helen said nastily. "He's a sly one."

Hugo rolled his eyes to heaven. "Well, if you mean that he's looking out for himself, surely that's fair enough?" he drawled. "I didn't know you considered that kind of behaviour so beneath the pale, Helen. Oh, look at Tabitha and Paul over there with their tongues down each other's throats. How charming. I must say, this production has been a hotbed of couplings. Probably the atmosphere of the play—all that rushing about in a wood being passionate with the first person to emerge from the nearest bush. I doubt *King Lear* will be quite as frenzied." He contemplated this for a moment. "Though you never know, all that blood and mutilation works like a charm for some people . . . So do you have your eye on someone, Bill?"

"Oh, I'm a married man," Bill said evasively. "Does anyone want another canapé?" He waddled off as fast as an elephant which has suddenly realized that all its companions have been hoovering up the watering hole for the past ten minutes. Helen turned on her heel pointedly and went after him.

"He used to fancy Tabitha, but now I think it's Liza," I said, naming the girl who played Moth. "He's always leering at her."

"Lucky, lucky Liza," Hugo sighed. "If only Bill had deigned to favour me with a leer or two, how happy I would be. That I should love a bright particular star. . . . Meanwhile, Liza and the boys are doubtless busy menage à trois-ing it all over their dressing room. That I would like to watch. I must ask Steve to install a closed-circuit camera in there. I hear he rather enjoys watching dirty films."

"They all do," I said.

"No, my sweet, you haven't quite followed me. I hear Steve *really* enjoys it," Hugo said significantly.

"Blech," I said elegantly. "Now I need a drink."

"I'm going to wash that taste right out of my mouth, I'm going to wash that taste right out of my mouth," sang Hugo. "Where's the bar in this godforsaken sub-Chelsea chinzfest?"

We were in such high spirits that I had hardly noticed Janey's near-silence. Looking round for the bar, I caught her gaze and realized how subdued she was.

"Are you OK, Janey?" I said, calming down for a moment.

"Yes," she said, managing a smile that didn't reach anywhere it should have done. "I'm just a bit thoughtful this evening."

"Oh, that's absolutely not allowed," Hugo said firmly. "But don't worry, we have the antidote."

"Darlings!" Violet descended on us, a bottle of champagne in one hand and a cluster of glasses in the other. Always beautiful, tonight her grooming was so perfect that she looked as unreal as a model: her make-up was exquisitely executed, her hair massed in smooth coils at the back of her head like a Greek goddess in a frieze, diamond earrings sparkling with the slightest move she made. "You're not *drinking!* Here!" She handed out the glasses and promptly filled them.

"Saint Violet of the Perpetual Bottle," I said, drinking deep. "Thanks."

"That's right, Vi, if you keep performing errands of mercy maybe no-one will notice you came out in your underwear," said Hugo.

"Hugo! This is *Dolce and Gabbana!*" Violet, said giggling. Her dress was a little black wisp with fitted cups and lace-trimmed straps, not unlike Tabitha's slip. Only Violet's was the real thing and Tabitha's was a high-street copy. The difference wasn't hard to spot. "I modelled this for the *Mail* last week and the Dolce people said I could keep it," she said complacently. "Wasn't that nice of them?"

Her ethereal figure contradicted the implications of the dress; she managed not to look as if she were planning to pop round the back of King's Cross later on tonight and hang out underneath a lamppost, jutting out her hips at passing cars.

"When does the article come out?" said Janey, whom I rather suspected of fancying Violet. Her spirits had risen visibly, and I didn't attribute it to the champagne. Janey was a red wine drinker.

"Tomorrow," Violet said. *"Perfect* for the play."

"What is it, Vi, life, love and skincare?" Hugo asked.

"Mostly," Violet said. "They tried to get me to talk about Philip, obviously, but after all that tabloid stuff last week I said I wouldn't answer questions about him."

The tabloids had revelled gleefully for a few days on Philip Cantley's death. It was the combination of Violet and the insulin—though, without any evidence, they had been unable to link the two except by implication. Much enjoyment had been derived at the theatre from such headlines as: "Is This How Sexy Fuchsia Girl Keeps Her Figure?"; "The Killer Who

Loved TV Babe Violet"; "I Luvvy You To Death" (the *Sun*. I thought that one was rather good). Violet had sensibly refused to be interviewed and so they had cobbled together the facts of Shirley Lowell's murder and Philip Cantley's death with as much suggestiveness as they could find. The fact that Philip Cantley had played the baddie in the latest *Prime Suspect* series, thus making his face vaguely familiar to readers of the tabloids, plus Violet's relationship with him, plus Violet's penchant for going out in public wearing frocks which looked, even at a second glance, like an upmarket version of what the girls wore down Goods Way when hanging out round lampposts, made it a story, and they played it up for all it was worth.

All the speculation had of course been illustrated with shots of Violet as Fuchsia, looking no more than sixteen, all wide eyes and curls and a pout—Violet Elizabeth Bott as a stroppy teenager, I had said sourly to Hugo. To do him justice, he had found it amusing. However, the papers had particularly gone to town with some sexy photographs of her which Violet insisted had been taken years ago by someone she trusted who had taken advantage of her naïveté. Actually she was no less covered in them than she was by tonight's frock, but the poses were definitely more risqué than she favoured now—unless in tomorrow's *Mail* she was lying on her back with her legs apart and one hand halfway down her cleavage. Somehow I doubted it.

"We're starting rehearsals for *Doll's House* soon, you know," she said.

Hugo raised his eyebrows. "That's a long rehearsal period."

"It's a very complex play, darling," Violet said airily. "And what with all the *turmoil*, we thought we'd better start sinking our teeth into it as soon as possible. Just me and Jeremy at the moment." This was the actor who was playing Torvald.

"Ben's directing, isn't he?" said Janey.

Violet nodded. "I'm *so* looking forward to working with him. He absolutely agrees with the way I see Nora, which is *vitally* important. I think she's quite manipulative," she added thoughtfully. "And sometimes she can be downright *rude*. You know, the way people are when they rely on their charm and you don't quite notice what they're saying. She's a complete cow to poor Christine. I want to bring that out."

Despite myself, I was impressed. This was a side to Violet I had hardly seen before; when she talked about her work seriously she was actually interesting.

"Hazel Duffy's playing Christine, isn't she?" Janey knew this perfectly well. I wondered if she were stirring. "Your fight tonight was very good."

"Oh my God! Did you hear about me nearly scratching poor Hazel's eye out?" Violet exclaimed. "Yes, I'm sure Helen told you," she added a trifle maliciously. "Hazel didn't bear me any grudge, thank goodness, because really it was a close thing. I'm so glad you thought it worked, because I was being *frightfully* careful tonight and I was worried it wouldn't look good enough."

This was a technique I often used myself; admit upfront to all the embarrassing things you've done in order to head off someone else mentioning them. After her initial discomfiture about her near-maiming of Hazel, Violet seemed to have recovered remarkably well. But then the police had been wanting to question her every two minutes; it was understandable that she should have been on edge. I realized that I was making excuses for Violet. I must be warming to her.

"I think we need some more fizz," said Hugo, finishing his. "Stay here, ladies. I'll deal with this."

He disappeared into the crowd. Violet followed him affectionately with her gaze.

"I'm so glad you're with Hugo," she said to me.

"Oh really?" I was cautious. In my experience ex-girlfriends never meant this statement; it was simply a preliminary to a comment they intended to make as cutting as possible. "Why?" I added.

Violet fixed her huge eyes on me. When she did this to you it was impossible not to feel as if you were falling into them.

"Well," she said, "he needs someone . . ." She paused. It was either a search for the right word or a deliberate attempt to heighten the insult that was about to follow. I braced myself for the worst. ". . . *clever,*" Violet said finally. "Someone who can keep up with him. I mean, I'm not a *fool*, but he's very intelligent. He has what they call a wide frame of reference. And you always know what he's talking about, Sam. Also you don't take him too seriously, which is terribly important. Hugo can get horribly pompous if people think he means everything he says and treat him with too much respect."

I hadn't been expecting this at all. I stared at Violet with my mouth open. Not only was she absolutely right in her analysis of Hugo, but she was paying me a very gracious compliment. This was unheard of. Either everything Hugo had said was true—that he and Violet were old friends who by now, years after their affair at drama school, cared about each other like brother and sister—or she was a very devious person indeed.

"And lucky you," Violet said, giving me a very naughty smile. "He was absolutely *fabulous* in bed years ago and I bet he's only improved with age."

To my even greater surprise, that was what clinched it. I burst out laughing, having decided that Violet was immensely endearing. She was giggling too.

"Girls, girls! This is not the sixth-form dormitory of St. Trinian's after lights-out! Stop that unseemly sniggering!" Hugo reproved, returning with another bottle of champagne. Suddenly wary, he looked from me to Violet and then to Janey. "What are you giggling about? May I be permitted to know?"

"Sam and I were just discussing what you're like in bed, Huge," Violet said cheerfully.

"Oh great," Hugo said with withering sarcasm. "Just avoid any subjects that could really embarrass me, won't you, like how many sugars I take in my coffee or whether I sleep on the left or the right. I mean, talk about the size of my cock all you want. In front of me. Feel free." He opened the bottle with a violent pop.

I winked at Violet. She pulled a face back. We were practically Thelma and Louise by now.

"Hi!" Sophie said, squeezing through two tall men who were standing next to us and popping out like a little Munchkin on the near side. She was wearing a knitted dress in stripes of vivid colour; down its over-long sleeves ran the kind of extruded triangles found along the spines of dinosaurs. Weirdly enough, it suited her. She had shaved her head in hon-our of the party and it made her eyes look as big as saucers. "I saw Hugo with the bottle and hunted him down like a dog," she said, holding out a glass.

"Take a number," Hugo said sourly, filling her glass. "There's a queue forming over here."

Seeing Sophie's shaven skull reminded me of something I had to do.

"Oh, Violet." I reached to the back of my head and extracted a hairgrip from among the many holding up my curls. "I think this might be yours."

Violet's face lit up.

"Wonderful! I've been looking for that *everywhere!*" she said, taking the grip from me. "It's one of a pair. I thought I'd lost it in my dressing room."

"Isn't it pretty!" said Janey, reaching out to touch the diamond star sol-dered to the head of the grip. "Where's it from?"

"Harvey Nicks," said Violet airily. "Where did you find it, Sam?"

Watching her face, I said: "Matthew picked it up on the fly floor and gave it to me. He thought it was mine."

"Oh well, thanks anyway," Violet said, slipping it into her bag. "It's a mystery how I lost it. They never usually fall out. On the *fly floor?*" she added, looking bemused. "How bizarre."

Sophie, standing next to her, had gone white; her eyes were two huge hollows in her small face. If Violet didn't know what that meant, Sophie certainly did. She looked at me for a moment, quite stricken, and then dropped her gaze. Violet, of course, was happily oblivious to this by-play. She favoured us with another blast of smile.

"I think I might just go and see if I can ooze my way into a conversation with Trevor. I'm sure there's a queue a mile long by this time."

"Wrong thinking," Hugo said with authority. "We go and have a lively conversation next to Trevor and wait for him to say hello to us."

Violet nodded. "All right. Coming?" she said to me and Janey.

I shook my head. "I'll circulate. Good luck."

They pushed off in the direction of Trevor Nunn, chattering loudly, careful not to look at him as they approached. Sophie stared after Violet, looking very worried indeed.

"She's actually very nice, isn't she?" Janey said, staring after her. "I think Helen was a bit over-the-top about her."

I hardly heard what Janey was saying. My thoughts were concentrated on the diamond star hairgrip now lying in Violet's bag. Should I have pointed out to her the significance of the place the hairgrip had been found?

As it turned out, it didn't matter at all; it wouldn't have made the slightest bit of difference if I had dinned into Violet's thick head that her hairgrip had probably been left on the fly floor by the person who had sabotaged Tabitha's line. She would just have thrown a fit and no-one would have been any the wiser. Occasionally I do actually make the right decision.

I introduced Sophie and Janey, who said hello to each other politely. Then I was unable to resist reaching out and running my hand over Sophie's scalp. It was as compelling as feeling pregnant women's stomachs.

"It's a Number One," Sophie said, temporarily distracted. "I haven't had it this short for ages. What do you think?"

"It suits you," I said.

"Definitely," Janey chimed in appreciatively.

Sophie acknowledged the compliments rather distractedly.

"I didn't know you'd done costumes for a circus," I said, remembering something the police had told me days ago. "It must have been fun."

"Oh, it was," Sophie said, brightening up. "It was great. A bit like Archaos. They just threw everyone on stage whether they wanted to or not. By the end of the run I was up on the trapeze dressed like a dragonfly. Marie was amazing—she can do anything, you should have seen her. She's wasted not doing acrobatic stuff all the time. But she wants to get into serious acting, so . . ." She shrugged. "Do you think Vi's OK?" she said to me, snapping back to the only subject that really interested her at the moment.

"She seems fine," I said firmly. I had the instinct that Sophie was the kind of person who preferred her friends to be in trouble, so that she could comfort them; she needed to be leaned on. Or perhaps it was only Violet that she wanted to console. However it ran, I never thought that kind of pathology should be encouraged.

"Oh right," Sophie said again, sounding deflated. She drooped, her head at a downward angle like a flower needing water.

"I loved the costumes you did for the *Dream*," Janey said politely.

"Did you?" Sophie's head came up again as if someone had just recut her stem and put some aspirin in her vase. "Thank you! I think they turned out OK. The fairies were the trickiest—"

"All that cavorting around—" Janey suggested.

"Exactly, they had to have lots of room to move—"

They were off. I slipped away, not looking for anyone in particular, just itchy to circulate. What bliss it was to be at a party where you knew so many people that you didn't have to make conversation with a stranger or a bottle of vodka. The first person I bumped into was Matthew, and I blinked. He was positively exalted by what was, by now, the obvious success of the production, and it gave a colour to his face it had previously lacked. And he wasn't wearing his glasses. Without them, he was almost handsome. It was the first time that I had seen him in anything other than the standard director's wear of badly fitting jeans and a shapeless sweater; he had on a pair of nicely cut trousers and a shirt, open at the neck. I realized for the first time that he had a very good body. How that observation could have eluded me before I didn't know. I must be slipping with age.

"Well hello, Matthew!" I said with enthusiasm. He was looking slightly dazed. "Is everything all right?" I enquired.

"No, it's just—well," he said with boyish embarrassment, "I haven't seen you all dressed up before. You look really good."

"Thank you!" I said, before the penny dropped and I realized that Matthew had been having the same reaction about me as I had about him. I would have snarled if he hadn't been blushing, which always disarms one. "I was thinking just the same about you," I said evilly. "I never realized you had a body under those ghastly clothes you usually wear."

"Oh—I—I—" Matthew stammered, flushing still further. I smiled with my mouth shut. That would teach him not to appreciate me until I had on my best Wallis evening dress.

"Hello, Sam," said MM from behind me. Matthew's eyes lit up when he saw her. Nor was this reaction merely gratitude that she had saved him from a tête-à-tête with me.

"I hear the people from the theatre board really liked the production," I said to her. "Congratulations."

"Yes, it went very well," MM said. She had had a few drinks and it showed; everyone was charged up tonight, high on success, and the director was no exception. As usual, she looked like a librarian, but now it was a librarian at the annual Readers' Night party, with her little gold chain round her neck, matching small gold earrings and the previously-mentioned frightful dark red dress. I wouldn't have been surprised if she were wearing Birkenstocks just to complete the look. Matthew, however, was gazing at her as if she were the Venus de Milo come to life with the full complement of arms included in the price. And there was more than professional interest in the look she gave him in return. A switch clicked on in my brain.

"Do they want you to interview for Philip's job?" I asked, to gain time while I observed them both.

"Oh yes. But I don't think I want it," she said simply.

"You don't want it?" I said incredulously. Everyone had been saying what a great opportunity it would be for her.

She shook her head. Her hair had been plaited and pinned up in concession to the occasion. It looked just as dowdy as ever.

"Is it the stress?"

MM looked blank, as if she weren't sure what I was talking about.

"The *stress?*" she repeated. "Oh no."

Matthew had moved to her side now and was looking down at her proudly.

"Too much administration, not enough directing," she elucidated, seeing that I hadn't taken her point. "I do want to run a theatre of my own some day, but not one like the Cross. More a workshop space with a floating group of people who can come in and out. That kind of set-up keeps you fresh. The Cross is very monolithic, frankly."

"Did you tell the board that?"

She nodded.

"It just made them keener," Matthew said eagerly. "Isn't that ridiculous? They thought she was playing hard to get. As if MM would behave like that. Or compromise her vision to do something that wasn't right for her."

MM smiled up at him fondly. His gaze was positively worshipful, his hand reaching out for hers. I wondered how long this had been going on. Had they always been an item, keeping things discreet during rehearsals, or had it sprung up more recently?

"I'd be very interested in working with you again, Sam," MM was saying to me. "I think the mobiles have worked excellently."

"Wonderfully," Matthew echoed.

"So are you going to do the interview?" I asked curiously. I still found it hard to believe that she would turn down the job if it were offered to her.

She shrugged. "Can't hurt. And they know what I think already, it's not false pretences."

If this were a tactic—which, cynically enough, I couldn't help suspecting—it was a very well-judged one. There was nothing that would interest a jaded theatre board as much as some young, up-and-coming director who might have been expected to leap at the offer saying instead that she didn't actually want the job.

"Sam, *carissima!*" Sally hugged me from behind. "I am so 'appy! Eet goes so well! Are you pleased now that we meet een the Rubber Neeple and I bully you into doing the play?"

"It was the Torture Garden, Sal," I reminded him.

"Oh yes, I remember now. Come weeth me, I take you to meet someone."

Pulled away by Sally's insistent hand, I left MM and Matthew to their own devices and followed him as he threaded his small wiry body through the room, yodelling greetings to most of the people we passed. We filed upstairs, trying not to tread on any expensively upholstered feet as we went, down a long beige-carpeted corridor, through a deeply impressive bedroom with a Japanese screen on the back wall and lots of lacquered cabinets, and into an equally smart bathroom with black-tiled walls and a whirlpool bath.

"Lovely," I said as Sally locked the door behind us, "you've brought me here to meet your friend Mr. Jacuzzi."

Sally produced a wrap of paper from his pocket and put it on the marble shelf next to the sink.

"Mr. Charles Jacuzzi," I corrected myself. "Nice one, Sal."

Sally beamed. "I have a gram for Hugo too. He ask me to get heem some. But we do some now of mine."

"We certainly do," I said.

◦◦◦

Ten minutes later we left the bathroom as fizzy and effervescent as Tabitha had been earlier. I wanted to dance and jump about and throw things in an exuberant fashion at the nearest wall, shouting: "Wheee!" Fortunately I was experienced enough by now to know that what I truly needed was a drink to level out my balance. Pausing for a moment on the landing, we looked down at the seething mass below, taking our bearings.

"That," Sally announced, pointing to someone in the crowd, "ees what I am taking home tonight."

"Who?" I said, trying to squint down the line of his arm. Our senses were so heightened that every little gesture seemed extraordinarily important.

"Feeshair," Sally said complacently. "I look forward to eet for a long time."

"Fisher?" I said, surprised, looking down at the object of Sally's affection. He was wearing a pearl-grey suit with a V-necked T-shirt underneath in stripes of pale blue and brown, the T-shirt tight enough to show off his nicely rounded pectorals and flat stomach. I admired this trend in men's fashion. The more ogling possibilities it offered, the better. "I didn't know he was gay," I commented.

"But *he* does," said Sally with a smug little smile. "Wheech ees the important part."

"Does he know you're taking him home?" I inquired.

Sally's smile intensified. "He weell soon."

Now I thought about it, Sally had always preferred men twice his size. Perhaps he liked to feel small and masculine.

"Go with God, my son," I said, making the sign of the cross in the air. "Just bring him back in one piece, OK? They need him for the play. And don't mark his face."

Sally swatted me across the bottom.

"How about you?" he said. "Do you leave any marks on Hugo?"

"I do my best," I said, grinning.

"He ees a very nice guy," Sally said more seriously. "I know heem for a long time. You make a good choice."

Sally tortured the vowels in the last word within an inch of their lives. Still, since he was being sympathetic, I didn't point this out to him. Instead I said:

"He chose me, actually. Maybe that's why—"

"*Cosa?*"

I hemmed and hawed. "I dunno. I'm just more used to jumping on people than being jumped on. Too cocky for my own good. Maybe that's why I'm feeling a bit insecure. I dunno."

Boy, Sam, I thought, you're wasted in the visual arts: with your extraordinarily lucid gift for communication you should write novels or go into politics. . . . Sally looked at me, his mobile little face twisting itself up more expressively than any Anglo-Saxon one would ever be able to manage.

"You like heem a lot, no?" he said.

I nodded. There was an awful pause.

"Right, that's enough soppy stuff," I said, regaining my emotional balance. "Dr. Jones prescribes alcohol and flirting, not necessarily in that order. *Avanti!*"

"Your accent," Sally said, with the air of one pronouncing judgement, "ees terreebull."

○○○

The first people I saw as we descended the stairs were Ben and Hazel. She had her back to the newel post and was sipping a glass of wine, her expression as calm as ever; Ben was standing very close, almost touching her. One arm was propped on the banister beside her, hemming her in. He was talking fast and earnestly, leaning forward so that his glasses were slipping down his nose and he had to push them back with one finger every so often. I remembered Helen saying that Ben had a crush on Hazel, and as we went past I tuned myself into the conversation:

". . . but at the same time she's very *strong,*" Ben was saying with conviction. "Look at the way she persuades Krogstad to change his mind. From being a little mouse she turns into this force for good at the end— moral, but without being heavy about it. And we've got to *see* that change happening. It's vital that we don't perceive her as being interfering when she insists he leave the letter for Torvald. . . ."

I had to grin. Ben was in full *Doll's House* rant mode. Perhaps Helen had confused Ben's enthusiasm for Hazel-as-Christine with a more personal interest in Hazel-as-Hazel. Certainly Helen saw sex and plots everywhere. She should be starring in one of those convoluted BBC1 family dramas where everyone double-crossed and took to bed everyone else, preferably simultaneously.

Meanwhile, Hazel was nodding placidly. Doubtless she would make her own mind up about Christine's character and was humouring Ben for the sake of a quiet life. And as always, I couldn't help wondering if Hazel's life really were as quiet as she let people understand; maybe she was a dominatrix in her spare time, or attended swingers' parties in Bromley. . . . As I passed she took another sip of wine and wiped her lips when she had swallowed it. Very neat and tidy. Ben was still going strong.

Sally had already located Hugo, who was following him into a quiet corner of the room, the French windows overlooking the garden. They turned their backs, ostensibly to admire the night sky, and the changeover of money and drugs happened so discreetly that if I hadn't known what was happening I would have noticed nothing at all. Sally peeled off in Fisher's direction with a purposeful glint in his eye, and Hugo, gazing around the room with the lofty dignity of someone over six foot with a long nose to look down, finally noticed me by the staircase. He forged his way through to me. Some girl trailed her feather boa over his shoulder as he went, giggling up at him coquettishly. You couldn't strangle someone with a feather boa; it would snap. She should count herself lucky.

"Can I tempt you into accompanying me to the bathroom?" Hugo said suggestively.

"Already been. But thanks for the offer. You really know how to show a girl a good time."

Hugo cuffed me lightly round the back of the head.

"Wait for me here, then. I won't be long." He strode upstairs.

"All right, Sammy!" Bez and Lurch hove into view, half-cut and happy. Bez offered me a joint, but I shook my head.

"Not right now, thanks. What I need is a drink."

"Lurchie!" Bez snapped his fingers. Lurch brandished the nearly-empty bottle of champagne he had been carrying and looked around him for a glass.

"Well, go and get her one!" Bez said impatiently. "Go on!" Lurch vanished on cue.

"It's great having him around," I said enviously. "Can we arrange a sort of Lurch timeshare?"

"He's handy, isn't he?" Bez was having some difficulty getting the words out. I revised my view of his state: he was wholly cut. "Did some good work for you on those mobiles."

"Exactly. I wouldn't mind borrowing him every so often."

"I'm sure we can work something out. Just you and me. We'll put our heads together," Bez slurred, leaning towards me in what a sexual harassment councillor would call an inappropriate invasion of my personal space. Long experience had taught me how to deal with male friends who become amorous after too much drink; I reached out and righted him again, saying warmly:

"So how's Jill? Did you bring her along tonight? Or did she need to stay home with the kids?"

Jill was Bez's wife. I had seen photographs of her and the children.

"I was looking forward to meeting her," I went on cheerfully. "Finally see the woman crazy enough to put up with you."

"She's crazy all right," Bez said bitterly. God, men who had been married more than five years shouldn't be allowed out to parties on their own. Just then Lurch arrived back with a fresh bottle of champagne and a glass for me.

"Good one!" I said appreciatively, reaching out for my glass.

"Oh, thanks, Sam," he said, ducking his head and grinning sheepishly. He fiddled nervously with the bottle till I showed him how to open it.

"Ease it out gradually," I said. "Only wallies pop out the cork. It's very naff."

It was pretty to see Lurch's expression of pride as he gentled out the cork and saw the pale vapour rising from the bottle neck. He tilted the bottle as delicately as if it contained nitroglycerine.

"Pour it like it was beer," I instructed, "down the side of the glass."

He observed the result with considerable pride. I held up my glass to him.

"Thanks for all your help with the sculptures, Lurch," I said. "You've been brilliant."

"Oh, it wasn't nothing," he said. "I mean, I really enjoyed myself, know what I mean? Didn't really feel like work. We had a good laugh, didn't we? Expect you won't be coming back no more."

He looked wistful.

"I was just asking Bez if you could come and help me sometimes in my studio," I said.

"Really!" Lurch brightened up in an instant. "Wicked!"

"Yes, she is. It's one of the attributes I actually like about her," said Hugo, descending the stairs. "I'm going to take her out now and show her the garden. Do excuse us."

He extricated me neatly from Bez, who staggered forwards muttering something about giving me a goodbye kiss.

"Bez is rather merry tonight, isn't he?" Hugo observed. "When he goes for it he does it so thoroughly he comes right out the other side."

"Nothing you can't handle, though," I said breezily. "He doesn't mean any harm."

Hugo shot me a look. "Sure of that, are you? Oh well, never mind."

He was leading me towards the French windows. Beyond them was a small terrace with a wrought-iron balustrade and, at the far end, a staircase leading down to the garden. The outside lights were not turned on. I couldn't decide whether this was an oversight or thoughtful consideration for amorously inclined guests, but after the brightly lit party it took a little time to accustom my eyes to the gloom. Under the terrace, in deep shadow, I could hear the laughter, murmurs and occasional shrieks of a couple of people deepening their acquaintance with each other; Hugo was already moving across the lawn, his pale suit like a beacon, looking over his shoulder to see if I was coming. The moonlight caught his fair hair and turned it to silver.

The garden was beautifully landscaped. Against the far wall I could hear the cascade of a miniature fountain and the plosh of water overflowing the sides of the stone bowl below. A light breeze played through the trees and a white rose bush loomed up on my right, the flowers gleaming with their own radiance, so flawless they looked almost artificial. Beyond them a wash of scent hit me, strong as a spray of perfume, enough to make me dizzy. It came from a bed of white lilies, high as my waist, the shape of fluted champagne glasses with a frilled edge, opaque and waxy, their perfection eerie. The stems were so dark they disappeared into the gloom and the flowers seemed to be floating, suspended in space. I stared at them, hypnotized.

"Sam!" Hugo said from across the lawn. "I'll take you to the Chelsea Flower Show next year, OK? Now haul yourself over here, will you? I didn't know you were so interested in horticulture."

"You can take a whore to culture but you can't make her think," I said, catching up with him. "Dorothy Parker."

"Did she say anything about gazebos?" Hugo said, leading the way into the one in question. It was built around a corner of the garden wall, made of arches of wrought-iron meeting in a cupola at the top, roses and creepers trained up the sides in a curtain so thick that from the terrace I hadn't even noticed that the gazebo was there. I assumed this was precisely what made it attractive to Hugo. A wooden bench ran around the two sides of the wall. I jumped onto it in a rush of energy.

"I feel like Liesl in *The Sound of Music*. 'I am sixteen going on seventeen, innocent as a rose—'"

Hugo was overtaken by a fit of coughing at this point.

"'—bachelor dandies, drinkers of brandies, what do I know of those? Totally unprepared am I to meet the world of men—'"

"You need someone older and wiser telling you what to do," Hugo said firmly. "Get down from that bloody bench."

"Won't."

Hugo looked at me consideringly. "All right, maybe it's not such a bad idea," he said, taking off his jacket and throwing it on the bench. Then he started to unbuckle his belt.

"*Hugo.*"

"Could you try to say that with wonder and awe in your voice?" he suggested.

"*Hugo.*"

"No, if anything that's worse. I'm obviously not cut out to direct. Never mind."

He picked me up and put me on the ground, with my back to the iron structure of the gazebo. Instinctively I reached up and grabbed onto the railing for support. Hugo was kissing my neck so comprehensively that I didn't notice his hands till my skirt was up against my waist.

"Very sensible of you," I said, "no grass stains—"

"Peace," said Hugo, settling his hands firmly around my bottom, and looking down at me in a way that made me take a tighter grip on the railing of the gazebo. "I will stop thy mouth."

And he did.

○○○

It was some time later that we heard the screams. Apparently they had been going on for some time, directly preceded by a violent scuffle, but at the time in question we would have been oblivious to anything short of a Brixton-type riot complete with cars ram-raiding the gazebo. The screams had dimly percolated my consciousness, but since they had merely seemed like projections of the kind of noises I would have been making myself if Hugo hadn't had his hand over my mouth, they had failed to register any deeper significance.

"Hugo," I said finally, my voice faint, opening my eyes. Hugo looked so beautiful that, if he hadn't secured my wrists to the railing behind me, I would have let go my clasp on it out of sheer visual pleasure; his eyes were wide and dazed, his features blurred as if I were seeing them through a soft-focus lens.

"Hugo? *Hugo!*" His arms were locked in place around me, my legs around his waist. I didn't want him to move at all; still, someone did sound like they were screaming, not too far away. . . .

I tugged harder at the belt round my wrists. It came loose and fell to the ground with a dull slither. Reaching down, I clasped Hugo's arms; they were still rigid. He tilted his head from side to side, heavy movements like someone shaking water from their hair in slow motion. I leant forward and laid a kiss on his swollen mouth.

"Hugo, there's someone screaming in the garden."

He let me down. My legs would hardly support me; I stumbled back a half-step against the gazebo, dragging in a deep breath. Slowly, like sleep-walkers, we tidied ourselves up and refastened everything that needed it. Hugo picked some leaves out of my hair. I retrieved his jacket from the bench. We were incapable of speech. Outside in the garden I could hear people running, the screams slowing down, voices raised. Music was still rolling out of the windows, Freak Nation and Jamiroquai, but nothing seemed to have anything to do with us. We were in another place entirely.

"Are you OK?" Hugo said to me. I nodded. He ran his hands through his hair, trying to restore it to some sort of order. "All right," he said slowly, "let's go and face the crisis."

It was strange that we shared the instinct to go out and see what was happening; probably the most sensible course of action would have been to hide out in the gazebo until the storm had passed. Hugo took my hand. I almost flinched with the contact. We were in that state where you are almost frightened to touch each other's bodies, as if you might let off another explosion; your own still feels so sensitive, almost bruised with what has just happened.

"My wrists hurt," I said irrelevantly as we took a step together through the arch, out into the garden.

"My lip hurts. And my hand. You bit it."

He turned it to show me. I kissed it. Our eyes met above his palm and a shiver ran through me, deep as a rope pulling inside me. His eyes were huge and grey and open as the sea. There was a moment of suspended animation; then we both took a breath together and turned to go back inside again, our fingers tightening on each other's.

"Hugo! Sam!" It was Sophie's voice, from across the lawn. She came running towards us, panting for breath, totally incongruous in that Chelsea Flower Show garden with her shaved head and sturdy boots. She skidded to a halt in front of us and I realized she was trembling from head to foot.

"Someone's just tried to kill Violet!"

Violet was lying in a crumpled heap under the terrace, a group of people clustered round her. Janey was trying to make her sit up, but Violet was resisting, moaning something about her head. Finally Janey managed to lift her so that she was half-resting in Janey's lap, leaning back against her. Someone turned on the outside lights and the lawn blazed into a sward of oddly phosphorescent green, the flowerbeds surrounding it a haze of colour. The stretch of patio under the terrace, however, remained unlit, and Violet's skin seemed unnaturally white against the dark background, her face and shoulders seeming to float in the shadows like the clusters of lilies.

"What happened?" Janey was saying gently to her. "Can you talk?" She stroked a lock of Violet's hair back from her forehead. They looked like a Pietà; Janey made the perfect madonna, her pretty face full of concern. Her arms supporting Violet were soft and white and rounded as the rest of her. It was a style of beauty that was old-fashioned in a time when we were all encouraged to hit the gym and work on our muscle tone, and even more attractive for that.

Matthew came clattering down the steps and swung round the side of the patio, MM just behind him. Someone must have called him; he was the host, after all.

"What is it?" he said, sounding worried. "Did Violet have a fall?"

"Someone attacked her!" Sophie cried, her voice as high and thin as a bird's. She threw herself to the ground beside Violet. "Vi? Vi! What happened? It's me, Soph. Are you all right?"

Violet raised her head slightly.

"Soph?" she said, her voice groggy. "God, my *head*." She sounded quite genuine, I noticed; there was no exaggeration in her voice, no playing for sympathy.

"Someone get her some aspirin or something!" Sophie said, looking round impatiently. Matthew stood indecisively for a moment. Not a great self-starter, he was much better at taking orders; when MM leant over and gave a whispered prompt, he shot away on the errand, looking glad to have something to do.

"I just came down for a breath of fresh air," Violet said plaintively, sitting up a little more and wincing with the movement. She put one hand to the back of her head. "Nothing broken, thank God. It doesn't feel like it. I'll have a huge bump, though."

Delicately, Janey traced the outline of the bump for confirmation.

"We should get an ice pack on that," she agreed.

"I'll do it," Sophie snapped. "You don't have to bother."

Oblivious to this by-play, Violet was continuing:

"He grabbed me as soon as I'd come down the steps—"

"Who grabbed you?" Sophie insisted.

"I don't know," Violet said helplessly. "I didn't see him. He came up from behind and it was dark."

"Did he follow you down, Vi? Or was he already here?" Hugo said, dropping to his knees in front of her.

"I don't know. I mean, I said I was going out into the garden and I expect someone could have heard me—come out and waited for me. . . ."

Someone switched on the patio lamps. The whole area was suddenly bathed in light, abrupt and unexpected. Matthew slid back the glass door that led into the basement; Helen, who had been standing with her back to it, jumped and then moved aside. He was carrying a glass of water and a couple of white pills. I had the crazy instinct to reach forward and check that they were what they were supposed to be.

Violet sat up further, still supported by Janey, and swallowed down the aspirin. I noticed that her hands were shaking.

"I'd come down the stairs and I was just going to walk around a bit," she said. "Not on the lawn. I had to be careful of my shoes." Automatically she stuck out a foot, clad in a Manolo Blahnik which was so perfect it would probably end up in the V&A, black suede with a tiny diamanté clasp at the toe and a heel so high and spiked that any antipathy it felt towards the lawn was sure to have been mutual.

"Anyway, he grabbed me from behind and pulled me back, under here." Violet's voice was trembling. She reached out her hand; Sophie's was already closing round it. I saw Violet's knuckles turning white as she held on tightly to Sophie's square little hand. "He had one hand over my mouth so I couldn't scream. I didn't even think of it at first, it was such a shock. I mean, we're at a *party*! I was paralysed for a minute, I couldn't believe what was happening. Then I thought it was a joke, but he wouldn't let me go. I started to struggle, but he was very strong. And then I felt . . . I felt . . ."

She took a deep breath. I could see that she was trying not to cry. Matthew, standing awkwardly behind her, looked horrified and shame-faced. Bless him, he probably felt in some way responsible for what had happened to Violet in his parents' house.

"He had a needle—it must have been one of my ActRapid pens—he stuck a needle in my arm—" Violet started sobbing. "I felt it pricking my skin and I panicked, I knew what he was trying to do." Still holding Sophie's hand, she subsided into the cradle of Janey's arms, crying with all her strength, a powerful catharsis. Janey was stroking her hair and whispering comforting words close to her ear. I looked up and caught Helen's unguarded expression. Her mouth was drawn into a thin, narrow line. Suddenly I could see what she would look like in thirty years' time. Personality etches its own design on the face, and Helen's was there for all to read.

"Do you mean he actually injected you with insulin?" Hugo said urgently. "Had you taken some already this evening? Vi, this is crucial! We should ring for an ambulance."

"No," Violet said, beginning to calm down. She wiped her eyes with some tissues Sophie handed her. "I hadn't had any. And he didn't manage it properly. So I'm OK, Hugo, don't worry. I'm not going to go into a coma or anything."

From what I understood of insulin, it would already be too late for her if Violet's attacker had managed to inject her with enough of it; a couple of those penfuls and she would have slipped into an irreversible coma within about five minutes. Philip Cantley had taken—or been given—three, but Violet was a tiny little thing. Two, for her, could well be fatal.

"Are you sure it was a man?" I said.

Violet looked puzzled. "Well, I—yes, I think so. Though I didn't see who it was."

"Then how do you know?" I persisted.

Violet closed her eyes in an attempt to concentrate. "He was much taller than me, I think. Though actually now I'm not sure. It all happened so fast. . . ."

"Try to remember the details. What was he wearing?"

"Don't pester her!" Sophie protested. "Can't you see she's in shock?"

But Hugo silenced her: "Sophie, leave it. This is important. Go on, Vi."

"Shoes," Violet said. "Men's shoes. Well, sturdy, like men's shoes. I stamped on one and then I kicked back at his leg. He was wearing trousers, I think. That hurt him and he pulled back, so I got my arm free from him and the needle fell. I was swinging round and he grabbed me and shoved me hard into the wall. I lost my balance and knocked my head on it. And my arm." She held it up for everyone to see. There was a long raw scrape down the forearm, as if she had taken a vegetable peeler to it. "No," she said, correcting herself. "Actually I hit the wall with my arm first, and fell sideways and hit my head."

"Do you remember anything else about him?" I said rather helplessly. Violet seemed better able to recall the sequence of her own injuries than the physique of her attacker. "What gave you the idea that he was tall?"

"Well, he *seemed* tall," Violet said petulantly. "And he was very strong."

"What about his hands? Did you see them? Or was he wearing after-shave or anything like that?"

"What is this, *The Bill?*" muttered Helen.

"Sam's asking Violet some very important questions," Hugo snapped, "and no-one needs to stick around if they don't want to hear the answers."

"I resent that!" Helen said furiously.

"Helen, *please,*" Janey hissed.

Violet ignored this whole interchange. Her forehead was puckered with the effort of remembering, colour returning to her face. Certainly it was doing her no harm to be the centre of attention.

"There's nothing really special, I'm sorry," she announced. "I mean, his hand was the normal size, if you know what I mean, and he didn't really smell of anything strong. Not the Comme perfume or something like Angel for Men that you recognize at once. There was some sort of after-shave, though, now I think about it. Maybe CK One."

"Oh, brilliant," Hugo sighed. "That really narrows it down."

"He was white, though," Violet offered. "I'm pretty sure. I mean, it was dark, but I think I would have noticed if he'd been black, from his hand."

"Unfortunately that doesn't help as much as it should," Hugo said wearily. "You might be sure it wasn't Fisher, who's pretty dark, but I doubt you'd have been able to tell the difference between me and Ranjit, for instance, down here without the lights on."

"No, I couldn't swear to that," Violet said, looking solemn. "Oh God!" Her choice of words had made her think of something. "We don't have to call in the police, do we? I couldn't bear all that again! MM?" Her eyes searched the group for MM, who came forward. "I don't have to, do I?"

"But Violet," said MM with considerable self-control, "it looks as if someone's just tried to kill you."

"But you know—what I was saying to you just now—" Violet twisted round to look at MM. "All the *scandal*—I mean, it's all right for someone like Liz Hurley, who can't act, she positively *thrives* on publicity, but what I was saying to you, about being taken *seriously*—I've got Nora coming up and I really want it to work, at the moment people just know me as the girl who was Fuchsia or that awful beer ad. . . ." Violet had gone into an emotional tailspin, but her speech patterns were back on track; she had turned back into the double-barrelled Chelsea Sloane from the more normal Susan Higson she had once been. "It'll just mean more headlines, the wrong sort, and they'll never catch whoever it was anyway."

"But aren't you scared it might happen again?" MM said, sounding by now frankly incredulous.

"Well, yes!" Violet conceded. "But the police are so *useless*, I told you just now, they keep *besieging* me with stupid questions, like wanting to know where I get the insulin from, which hasn't got anything to do with it anyway because Philip got it from me, I've told them that already, I don't see why I should have to tell them where *I* get it from, do you? But they seem to think there's things I'm not telling them, they won't leave me alone *now*, just imagine if we report this. And I don't enjoy them asking all sorts of questions and trying to catch me out, Hugo would *love* it, actually, he'd have loads of fun with them, but it's just not me."

"Is it true?" came a voice from the staircase. It was Tabitha, palpitating with emotion. Having secured our attention, she came running down the stairs, hands held out. When she reached the bottom of the staircase she crossed them at her bosom instead and trod lightly through the group of people, which had parted for her in an impromptu simulation of the Red Sea.

"Oh *no!*" she breathed, staring down at Violet. The latter, by now sitting up straight, hardly leaning on Janey, seemed to have needed only Tabitha's intrusion to restore her to full fighting form. Her cheeks had regained colour and her movements were much brisker.

"Violet," Tabitha was continuing, "I'm so, so sorry. I can't *tell* you how sorry I am!"

I wondered how much of a coincidence it was that Tabitha was talking so much like Violet. It seemed that she had taken her for her model in more than just her dress sense.

She knelt down in front of Violet, raising her eyes appealingly to the victim's like Linda Darnell at the end of *Blood and Sand*.

"Will you ever forgive me?" she said, her voice a mere thread.

"Tabitha, are you saying that it was you who attacked Violet?" Hugo said, dry as a vermouth-free Martini.

Tabitha whipped her head round. Paul had come down the stairs behind her and at Hugo's question he took a step forward, saying aggressively:

"What d'you mean by that?"

"Exactly what I meant," Hugo said with chilling calm. "Tabitha seems to be accusing herself. I wanted to know precisely what she thinks that entails."

"Of course I didn't do anything to Violet!" Tabitha protested to him. On closer examination I could see that her eyelashes were layered in dark mascara with silver applied at the tips. It looked very striking. "I didn't mean *that*," she was continuing. "I'm just really sorry that poor Violet got mixed up in all of this."

"Poor Violet," said the person in question, standing up rather shakily, "would be *fascinated* to know what you're talking about."

Tabitha stood up too. Most other people backed away a little nervously. The women were perfectly matched, of a similar height and build, not to mention the fact that their dresses, hairstyles and shoes echoed each other's. This had clearly not registered with Violet before, and now I watched her taking it in. Her reaction was a mini-drama in itself; she registered surprise, contempt and pity with just one lift of her eyebrows.

"Don't you *see!*" Tabitha burst out. "The way we're dressed . . ."

Violet rose magnificently to the occasion, even if it meant appropriating an earlier comment of Hugo's. "Oh, you're *dressed*," she said, looking at Tabitha as if she were something on the X-Files found disintegrating inside a body bag. "I thought you'd just come out in your Top Shop nightie. There's a thread hanging loose from your hem, by the way."

Hugo was trying manfully not to laugh. I knew how he felt.

Tabitha set her jaw and stared back hard at Violet. She was much more attractive when she stopped doing the little-girl-lost act.

"If you can't *see* what's happened I don't see why I should bother to tell you," she said angrily. "But whoever attacked you didn't want you! They wanted to get me! First my line being fucked up and now this! Can't you see that someone's trying to *destroy* me!"

And she burst noisily into tears.

○○○

"I expect we should be grateful that she didn't pull a faint this time," I said a little while later.

Hugo shrugged. "Ringing the changes. This time we got a demonstration of crying on cue. Tabitha thinks life is one perpetual audition."

"Always when MM's around," I added, looking at the person in question. "She's perfectly normal when there's no director hovering."

Violet was upstairs in Matthew's parents' bedroom, Sophie in attendance applying ice packs to the bump on her head. Tabitha had been removed by Paul, following MM's polite but firm instructions; she had worked herself up into such a state that it had been easy to insist that she be taken home to recover. Everyone else at the party had been told that Violet had taken a fall and hit her head, and they were too busy having a good time to do more than make concerned noises and carry on getting plastered while chatting each other up. The consequent sounds of mirth and revelry washed around our enclave as the rest of us—Hugo, me, MM, Matthew and Janey—gathered in Matthew's mother's office to hold what amounted to a council of war. Violet was still insisting that the police not be called, and though we disagreed, it would be pointless to summon them only for Violet, eyes wide, to recite a story of how she had simply slipped on her Manolos and she was terribly sorry that everyone else was making this totally unnecessary fuss.

"There's obviously no way to convince her of the mistake she's making," Hugo said, lighting a cigarette and looking round for an ashtray. The room was as well appointed as the deluxe hotel lounge it rather resembled, all chintz sofas, framed watercolours of birds and occasional tables, personalized to some degree by the silver-framed photos distributed over every possible surface. The only incongruous note was the business-like computer, covered very properly with a pale grey plastic hood, on the cherrywood table by the window. "Violet's as stubborn as a mule," he went on, locating a cut-glass ashtray and propping it on the arm of his chair.

"We have to do something, though," MM said decidedly. "This can't go on."

"I agree," Hugo said. "Though what we're going to do is a little harder to pin down."

"Why would someone attack Violet at this party, with all the risks of being caught?" I mused.

"Maybe they were relying on all the confusion to cover what they were doing," Janey said. "Or maybe it was someone who couldn't see her at any other time. This was their one opportunity."

I shook my head. "That doesn't make sense. Anyone involved with the production would be able to find a way to see her in private. All you'd have to do would be to go round to her flat during the day, making some excuse. And it must be someone on the *Dream*. So why here?"

"What do you think?" Hugo said.

I took a deep breath. "I think that something happened this evening that made whoever it was see Violet as such a risk that they couldn't wait to try to get her out of the way. They were hoping it would look like an accident, maybe even a suicide, perhaps with the idea that Violet killed Philip. Anyway, there wouldn't be a shadow of proof as long as they cleaned their fingerprints off the needles."

Janey shivered. "I can't believe this," she said in a voice so thin I could hardly hear her.

"Violet was talking to me earlier," MM said slowly. "About Philip's death and the police pestering her."

"That they thought there was something she wasn't telling them?" Hugo asked.

"How did you know that?" Matthew said abruptly.

"She said much the same thing in the garden," Hugo said, looking at him. "Someone might have heard what she was saying before and pan-icked. . . . So you were there too during the conversation?"

"Of course I was!" Matthew said, moving closer to MM on the sofa.

"And where were you later?" Hugo inquired. "When someone was attacking Violet in the garden?"

Matthew bridled. "In the kitchen, getting more glasses. If you must know."

"Are we sure," I suggested hesitantly, "that someone actually *was* attacking Violet in the garden?"

There was a long and thoughtful pause. I had been expecting Hugo to turn on me immediately and ask me what the hell I was talking about; that he didn't I found suggestive, to say the least.

"She does like to be the centre of attention," MM said finally.

Everyone gave tentative nods of confirmation.

"She's not the only one," Janey pointed out. "What about Tabitha? Did she really think that someone mistook Violet for her?"

"It would be perfectly possible," I observed.

"But Tabitha might just have exploited that as a way of taking the spotlight off Violet," Hugo pointed out.

"Still, after what happened with Tabitha's line, she has a right to be a little paranoid," MM said fairly.

"Yes, and who did that?" Matthew broke in. "And who telephoned Violet cancelling the rehearsal, and put anti-histamines in her coffee?"

"And what about Philip?" I added for good measure. "Did he kill himself or was he pushed? I tend to agree with Violet that it couldn't have been an accident."

Another silence fell.

"God," said MM in a heartfelt voice, "this is such a bloody mess."

Just then the door opened. We all looked towards it eagerly, as if hoping that Hercule Poirot would make an entrance and tell us exactly what had been going on. However, it was only Helen, looking distinctly aggrieved.

"So here you all are!" she exclaimed. "I've been looking for you everywhere!"

"Come in," Matthew said unnecessarily. He stood up and shut the door behind her. Helen plopped herself down next to Janey, scowling.

"I don't know why you felt you had to leave me out," she said sulkily.

"It wasn't deliberate, darling," Janey said, putting a consoling arm round her shoulders. "It was just that we found ourselves all together after getting Violet upstairs and we thought we'd better have a bit of a talk about it."

"You could have come to find me," Helen said, slightly mollified.

"I know. Big sorry. Forgive me?"

"OK." Helen's pout subsided somewhat. "So what were you saying?"

There was yet another pause.

"God," Hugo drawled at last, "I've always avoided doing Pinter and now I know why."

"I was saying what a bloody mess this all is," MM remarked. "Which seemed to sum things up for everyone."

"Well, I'd look pretty closely at Violet if I were you," Helen said, getting into her stride. "And Tabitha. Both of them," she added, in case we hadn't quite grasped this concept yet. "I don't know if I believe this whole story about being attacked. I mean, what proof is there? No-one saw anything apart from Violet herself."

"I scarcely think that Violet banged her own head and scraped her arm down a stone wall," Hugo said coolly. "She's too careful of herself to go to those lengths."

That was a good point, I had to acknowledge. "But what if she was worried that people suspected her of killing Philip and staged that to draw suspicion away from her?" I suggested.

"Then she would want the police to be called," Hugo said.

"Not necessarily," I objected. "She might not want them to pick holes in her story. It might be us that she really wants to convince."

I knew that this wasn't what Hugo wanted to hear, but I was stubborn enough to say it anyway. Unfortunately for me, Helen jumped in at once with both feet.

"I think that's very true," she said. "Besides, how do we know that anything's really happened to her at all? She could have made it all up—the phone call, the anti-histamines. . . ."

"How do you know about that?" Hugo said sharply.

"Oh, everyone knows," Helen said airily. "And not many people believe her, let me tell you. It's all so far-fetched, isn't it?"

"Sour grapes." Hugo's tone was dismissive. "If you'd been cast in *Doll's House* instead of Violet you wouldn't be trying to undermine her."

"I'd have got the part all right if I'd been sleeping with the director!" Helen hissed at him. "And she's not the only one! I could tell you a few things about that!"

"Do you mean that Philip was having an affair with someone else too?" I said curiously.

"I'm not going to listen to this anymore," Hugo said, pushing back his chair and standing up in one sharp, angry movement. "The rest of you can do what you want. I'm going to see how Vi is."

He didn't even look at me as he passed. The door closed behind him with a bang. I felt as if he had slammed it in my stomach.

23

I woke up the next morning sober but with my stomach in a tight little knot. There hadn't been much more to say after Hugo left; still, the rest of us had juggled for a while with the series of possibilities without reaching any conclusions. Not having any certainties to use as a base, it was all we could do. I had the instinct that just a couple of hard facts would be enough to start unravelling the tangle. But until we had them, we would be slithering around, unable to get any purchase on what was happening. In a way I understood Violet's reluctance to go to the police, if the reason she had given was the real one. It gave me a headache just to imagine having to explain, painstakingly, the anti-histamines in Violet's coffee, the sabotaging of Tabitha's line, not to mention all the interconnected rivalries between members of the cast, to a couple of police officers with their eyes bulging out from the effort of trying to keep track of all the people who were being named.

Strangely enough, despite the incipient headache, this line of thought was doing me good. It was distracting me from the aforementioned knot in my stomach, which had been there ever since Hugo had, as I saw it, walked out on me. I had glanced round the party later and, not seeing him, had assumed he was upstairs taking his place in the line of admirers waiting to console Violet. So I had left, not willing to go and find him, feeling that he had chosen her over me. Pride—my besetting sin—was sitting on my back and whipping me on.

On the way out I had bumped into Sally and Fisher coming out of the downstairs toilet, very rumpled and pleased with themselves. Misery loves only the company of others who are equally miserable and I had snarled at their smug, happy faces when they tried to persuade me to stay, their arms wrapped around each other, barely managing to keep their mouths off each other's necks. Instead I had gone out and hailed a taxi. At least in that area they weren't hard to find. At two in the morning in my neck of the woods you were infinitely more likely to be offered Class A substances than a black cab for hire. Actually, now that I thought about it, that held true whatever time it was.

Taxi and minicab drivers were always, predictably, first surprised and then horrified by where I lived, but this one was particularly so. I assumed it was the contrast between the pick-up in Chiswick and the destination in Holloway, not to mention my smart frock and fake-fur wrap. Usually I looked scruffy enough so that the bare, windowless, concrete frontage of the studio seemed, if deeply uninviting as a residence, at least a plausible port of call for someone looking like me. Initially the driver asked if he should wait a few minutes, looking rather sly; obviously he thought I was a Sloane who preferred to get her kicks slumming it while scoring rather than make her dealer come to her. When I said that this was where I lived, he stalled the taxi in shock. It's notoriously difficult to shock a black cab driver. So I had achieved something last night, however meagre it might be.

I hadn't even hit the vodka when I got in and barred the door behind me. I was half-expecting Hugo to ring, or come round, and I didn't want to be drunk if and when he did. So I finally fell asleep on the sofa, still in my dress, with the bizarre, energetic inanities of late-night TV flickering across the room and weaving themselves uncomfortably into my dreams. There must have been a slasher movie showing, because Hugo was chasing me down a corridor with a hunting knife; he was wearing a balaclava, but I knew it was him. I ducked into a niche and hit him over the head with an iron bar as he passed, and I remembered thinking in a moment of lucidity that dreams have a wonderfully convenient ability to provide you with iron bars at a second's notice. He fell like a stone, the knife tumbling from his hand. Kicking it away, I knelt down beside him, scrabbling to pull off the balaclava. My heart was racing; I hoped against hope that it wouldn't be Hugo underneath.

But it was. Blood was dripping down his forehead and into his eyes. He opened them and said to me:

"Violet! Are you all right?"

And that made me so angry that it jolted me awake. I sat up, furious and shaking. By now the television was fizzing as if with static. It was six in the morning and Hugo hadn't rung. I crawled up the ladder, stripped off my dress and curled up in bed like an animal in its lair, wrapping the duvet so tightly around me that not a chink of light or air could penetrate it. After a while, cocooned, protected, I managed to sleep, and, mercifully, if I dreamt this time, whatever I saw behind my closed eyelids was not powerful enough to wake me up.

ооо

I had two simple choices: I could get up and try to trick my depression into slipping away by concentrating hard on something else, or I could lie here and feel miserable for the indefinite future. Option A was a touch more appealing. Besides, by getting out of my studio I could distract myself while hoping that Hugo would have left a message by the time I returned. I pulled on a short T-shirt, an equally short V-necked chenille sweater and my old leather jeans, feeling a twinge at the pit of my stomach as I thought of Hugo saying severely that they didn't fit me any longer and I should get a new pair made. Through the belt loops I threaded a belt with an enormously heavy silver buckle, hoping that it would weigh down the front of the jeans enough for them to look a little like hipsters. Ideally a tiny slice of stomach should be showing above the buckle and below the sweater. On reflection, however, I was grateful that the jeans weren't hipsters. I hadn't done any sit-ups for weeks—though I had been having sex, which sort of counts. I blocked out this thought and any that could lead to Hugo, applied dark plum lipstick, black eyeliner, a silver choker and my favourite boots: I was as ready to face the world as I would ever be.

I got in the van and headed for Kilburn. A straight line down to Camden, looping into Delancey Street, round Regent's Park and up to the rarefied heights of St. John's Wood; along the Edgware Road, growing steadily shabbier, till I reached the new hotel which had been converted optimistically and at great expense and which doubtless declared itself on its brochures to be at the heart of Maida Vale. It would just work, as long as none of its clients ever turned right when they exited, because in less than twenty paces they would find themselves in Kilburn, rough and filthy and poor and teeming with much too much life for the tourists and business travellers the hotel was planning to attract.

I crawled down Kilburn High Road behind a 16 bus, traffic backed up behind me, slowed down by a series of mothers hefting double pushchairs up and down the steps and trying to control two screaming children simultaneously. Besides making me profoundly grateful for being unattached and baby-free, the delays gave me time to look around. I'd always liked Kilburn, with its litter thick on the pavements, its roaring ethnic mix, everything from spit-and-sawdust Irish pubs with IRA rumours perpetually hovering around them to West Indian travel agencies and hairdressers, to the best and cheapest South Indian restaurant in London. . . . As our convoy of cars passed the partially boarded-up shopping centre, now colonized by a thriving collection of market stalls, I looked left to see if the Asian woman who preached at a trestle table under the frontage of a closed-down Irish bank was still there. She was. Her accent was as difficult to understand as ever, and the megaphone didn't help. However, today she seemed to be confining herself to easily comprehensible soundbites.

"JESUS LOVES YOU!" she shouted at a couple of girls passing by, who weren't expecting it and jumped in shock. They both had their hair gelled and straightened into thick, shiny, black bobs, fake-looking but exuberant.

"MISERABLE SINNERS!" she added for good measure.

"I don't bloody *believe* her," said one of the girls, loud enough for me to hear it. The other one couldn't stop giggling. I stopped at the traffic light and they crossed in front of me, the first girl saying:

"I'm going to use that on Frenchy the next time he's coming up on one, I'll go 'MISERABLE SINNER' really loudly in his ear. Betcha I die laughing—"

The lights changed. I pulled away and turned left by the McDonald's, down towards Brondesbury, a long series of narrow streets with little houses clustered tightly together and cars parked up on the pavements on either side so that passing anything wider than my own Escort necessitated a series of ducking and diving manoeuvres. Reaching the railway bridge with both my wing mirrors mercifully still in place, I crossed over into nobody's-land. The roads were wide here, but for the most part eerily empty, lined by broken-down, shuttered-up shops and the occasional dodgy second-hand car dealer. Here the colonization by young urban would-be yuppies stopped dead. No-one wanted to live here, so near to the estates, if they could help it.

I turned into the estate entrance and parked as close to the central precinct as possible, between two reasonably well maintained cars. The idea was that if anyone was going to vandalize or simply nick a vehicle, mine, in this company, would look the least tempting option. I noticed quite a few Suzuki Vitaras; they were very popular around here. A local drug dealer must have started the trend.

Getting out of the van I looked round, trying to orient myself without looking too obviously lost. I had always loathed big estates; finding your way round them was worse than Hampton Court Maze, which at least had a trick to it and someone sitting on a platform above shouting instructions if you needed them. It took me nearly twenty minutes to locate William Wordsworth House and another ten to circle round it and find the set of buzzers which included number fifty-eight. Most of my researches I conducted under the stares of a group of boys who looked so bored they might have been slumped in front of an invisible TV, their eyes as dull and withdrawn from the world as if they were watching *Richard and Judy,* a numb disbelief to the sag of their shoulders. They should have had "Is This All There Is?" tattooed on their foreheads. It wasn't even a consolation to reflect that at least they weren't hassling me. In a way I would almost have preferred that to this sad graveyard shift of zombies.

I buzzed up to number fifty-eight, not knowing whether there would be anyone in, or if they would want to speak to me even if there were. But almost at once there came an answering dull whirring, the sound of the door lock releasing. I pushed the door open, struggling for a moment under the shock of its weight; it felt as if it were reinforced with concrete. I pitied all the inhabitants of the block who didn't pump iron at least three times a week.

Once inside I hesitated, looking at the unpromising grey and dented lift doors, then pressed the button to call the lift, deciding to see what it looked like inside before making up my mind. When the doors slid open it was clear that more than a few of the residents in William Wordsworth House appeared to have taken art therapy classes as a means of getting in touch with their inner children. Maybe it would be more appropriate to say their inner babies, because they seemed to have advanced no further than the pre-Oedipal stage—obsessive fixation with genitalia and bodily functions. Or perhaps they had just been reading too much Kathy Acker. It's so easy to be influenced by someone else's writing style.

I was grateful that at least the urban poets had limited their outpourings to the walls of the lift, perhaps having decided that it would be overkill to accessorize the floor with used syringes, condoms or a selection of the many and varied human waste products referred to in their writings. Still, by the time the lift had cranked itself up to the fifth floor, I felt I knew much more than I needed to about the private lives of individuals variously known as Carl, Silla and Brian. In fact, I didn't think I could have looked them in the eyes if I had been introduced to them.

I saw Hazel as soon as the lift doors opened; she was standing in the doorway of her flat, her posture ambiguous.

"Sam?" she said. "I got your message. . . ."

Her voice tailed off. She was waiting for me to say why I had wanted to see her. Clearly I was going to have to talk my way into the flat. She had positioned herself in such a way that, without seeming hostile, she was blocking the entrance. Still, she had buzzed me into the building. I was halfway there already.

"Shall we go in?" I said, deciding to act as if I took it for granted that she would allow me into the flat. "We can't really talk for long out here."

"I haven't got a lot of time," Hazel said. But she moved back slightly.

"That's all right. I don't want to bother you. But it's quite private . . ." I let the words hang in the air. There was a long pause; then Hazel breathed out a sigh of assent and stood aside, gesturing me through the door.

It was a typical council flat, poorly designed and cut up into as many small rooms as possible. The door opened onto a short, narrow central corridor down which I could see a series of doors, set close enough together to signal the cramped size of the rooms behind them. The first door on the left was the sitting room, and Hazel led me into it. Opposite was a tiny kitchen, little more than a galley. Why the architect hadn't set the corridor down one side of the flat so that it didn't split the kitchen and living room was a mystery; knocked together they would make a nice-sized space.

Hazel didn't offer me tea, or anything else. She just sat down on the sofa and folded her hands in her lap, watching me as I took a seat opposite her. No chat, no social niceties. The tactic was a good one; it made it harder for me to introduce difficult subjects. I gained time by looking around me. The room was furnished so neutrally that it revealed practically nothing about the person who lived there, lacking a colour scheme or attempt at a personal style that would give some clues to Hazel's taste. Instead it looked as if she had kept on whatever had been left by the last inhabitant and added to the furnishings merely out of necessity, buying the most basic items possible. The table, sofa and upright chairs were all such generic examples of their kind that you forgot what they looked like as soon as you took your eyes off them. Behind the sofa were a couple of bookshelves, lined with play texts, dust-free and alphabetically organized. Everything was neat and clean and functional, like Hazel herself, and like Hazel herself the flat seemed perfectly contented with that.

Hazel was still waiting for me to speak. At last I said lamely:

"Everyone's quite worried about what's going on at the theatre. Especially what happened to Violet at the party."

"Oh yes. I heard about that this morning. I didn't stay long. I wasn't there when it happened."

"Who do you think it was?" I said. I had already learnt that there was no point beating around the bush with Hazel.

She didn't blink. "I don't know. I wish it would all stop, though. It's very distracting." Her pale face remained quite calm as she spoke.

"What about Philip Cantley?" I asked. "Do you think he killed himself? Or that he killed Shirley Lowell?"

Hazel kept her gaze fixed on mine. "I do think he killed Shirley, yes," she said rather unexpectedly. "I thought he was capable of it, anyway. I saw him once with Violet and he wasn't treating her well."

"Helen said something last night that suggested you might have been having an affair with him too," I said, stirring things up. I wasn't really stretching the truth, either; Helen hadn't actually named Hazel, but who else could she have meant? Hazel was the only other woman in the cast of A Doll's House, unless you counted whoever was playing the maid or the nurse.

For the first time in my knowledge, Hazel showed a powerful reaction. She looked, quite simply, flabbergasted.

"Helen said *what?*" she asked incredulously.

I spread my hands wide. "Just that, really."

"I don't know what to say." Hazel was still in shock. "Helen said that I—I mean, I know she gossips, but that's just nonsense." She stared at me as if trying to read in my face some explanation for this baffling statement, and it occurred to me that she was taken aback not only because of the suggestion that she had been going to bed with Philip Cantley, but just as much at the idea that she would want to go to bed with anyone.

"Why would she say something like that?" I asked.

"Oh, Helen says a lot of things," Hazel said, sounding more resigned. "But usually they're true. That's partly why this really surprises me. When she was telling me about Matthew and Tabitha I wasn't sure, but then I realized she was right. In fact, now I come to think about it, she hasn't ever told me anything that wasn't true. She tells me quite a lot of things," she added reflectively. "I think it's because I don't gossip myself. So she can let off steam a bit and know it won't go any further."

"Hang on a minute," I said. "What about Matthew and Tabitha? Are they seeing each other?"

"Well, they were. At the beginning of rehearsals. Not any more though."

"How do you know?" I said curiously.

"Oh, the way they are with each other. I can always tell. I expect it's because I'm not very interested in that kind of thing myself," Hazel observed placidly. "But I always know about other people. There are lots of little signs. Anyway," she added, "it was mostly Tabitha making the running. Matthew's had a crush on MM ever since he met her. If he'd asked me I could have told him to wait till the first night. She'd never have started anything while she was in rehearsals because she wouldn't want to be distracted."

Hazel didn't seem to mind my bombarding her with queries; in fact she seemed to have got happily into her stride. Someone uncharitable would have said that she was enjoying showing off her superior knowledge, but I thought that Hazel was profoundly interested in what made people tick. She was a born observer, noticing the slightest gestures, the oddest little quirks of behaviour, in order to channel them into her work.

"Do you know MM well?" I said, trying to find a question that wasn't just "How do you know?" again. I like to ring the changes.

"No, not really. She was in her last year of the director's course when I started at drama school. And I've worked with her a couple of times since then. But I can see what she's like. She only really cares about whatever she's working on, and she doesn't mind what she has to do to get there."

There was a faint shade of approval in Hazel's voice which I recognized immediately. I had the strong sense that she saw MM as a kindred spirit. I stared at her, my brain racing with the attempt to find some way to put what I wanted to ask. Finally I said rather clumsily:

"What else did Helen tell you that turned out to be true?"

Hazel looked thoughtful. "You mean things I wouldn't have thought of myself? Well, what she said about Bez, I expect. He seems so nice. Sometimes you can't always sense that kind of thing."

"What kind of thing?" I said carefully.

"He used to drink too much and hit his wife. Quite badly, I think. Finally someone, a neighbour, called the police. They cautioned him and he got counselling for it. He's better now, apparently."

"Still drinks too much, though," I said, thinking of Bez's red, swollen face last night. There was something particularly unattractive about men with his light colouring when they tied one on; it was the contrast of the blue eyes with the bloodshot veins standing out against the white, the fair skin flushing red as a beet right up to the roots of the hair. I pulled a face. "I sort of wish you hadn't told me that," I admitted. "It changes how you see someone. Even if he has got himself together now."

"I know what you mean," Hazel said seriously. "But if you're going to keep working with someone and you have to get on with him, the best thing is just to forget what you know, if there's nothing you can do about it. And mostly there isn't. You can't change people." Her voice had gone a little quieter, as if she were thinking about something very important. "But some men are like that," she added more casually, "especially ones who drink. They change personality when they're drunk. Jekyll and Hyde."

"He was a bit over the top last night," I said. "More amorous than anything else, though. Staggering around trying to hug all the prettier girls in the room."

"He didn't try to hug me," said Hazel quite composedly. "But then there were a lot of girls much better-looking than me. I dare say if he'd been desperate, towards the end of the party, he might have had a go."

"The last time I saw you, you were talking to Ben," I said.

"Yes, he said some quite interesting things about the play—*Doll's House*, I mean—which is why I came home early, before all the fuss happened. I wanted to have a think about Christine."

I noticed this reminder that, according to her, she had left the party before the attack on Violet, and wondered whether she had dropped in the reference deliberately. She looked at her watch.

"I should be getting off," she said. "I've got to go and see some producer at the BBC, so it's all the way to White City and back this afternoon."

I stood up, prompt to take my cue.

"Thanks for talking to me, anyway," I said. "I hope it wasn't too much of a nuisance."

Hazel stood up and led the way to the door. I followed her down the little corridor, so narrow that she had to open the front door and precede me out onto the landing to give me room to pass without our jostling each other.

"Oh, that's OK," she said neutrally. "I hope I helped."

That was the first false note she had struck during the whole conversation. She ducked back inside the flat as soon as I was through the door, not even waiting to say goodbye. I stared after her as the door closed in my face. For some reason I was perfectly sure that Hazel had just said the exact opposite of what she really thought.

There were a couple of girls in the entrance hall as I got out of the lift, one huddled up against the wall, crying and clutching her bag to her chest, the other one trying to comfort her. Both of them wore school uniform, pleated grey skirts and white shirts, which they had customized by adding high stack heels, sheer black tights and big puffa jackets over the top. The look was oddly effective. If Anna Sui or Marc Jacobs ever saw them it would be flying off New York catwalks next spring. The girl who was attempting to cheer up her friend had the adolescent thinness of two sticks tied together, with long skinny legs and the pleats of the skirt hanging straight down where her bottom should have been. Her hair was caught into a series of tiny curly black knobs tight to her scalp, which was the colour of chestnuts in autumn.

Her friend was still snivelling as I passed.

"Why's it always me?" she was sobbing.

"Oh, pay no attention. They're a bunch of racists, Steff, you know that. They always pick on white girls. At least they didn't get your bag this time."

"Oh, fucking brilliant," Steff snapped back, cheering up a little. "What, I should be grateful or something?"

"That's the spirit. Here, have a Silk Cut."

Lighters snapped, the girls inhaled deeply, and I wrestled the door open.

"Makes you see why Lisa got her gang together," Steff said sullenly, blowing out smoke. "Maybe I should ask her if I could join. Get some respect."

Going out, I heard the girl who wasn't Steff say:

"Don't be so fucking stupid. That lot are all maniacs, you know that. Look, you want to watch *Xena: Warrior Princess*? I taped it on Saturday. Watch some rank bastards getting their arses kicked."

That girl should set up in practice as a therapist one day: she'd make a fortune. As I headed for my van I eyed up the group of boys hanging around on the wall, but on reflection I came to the conclusion that they were very unlikely to have been the ones hassling Steff. Most of them could barely keep their eyes open. Or perhaps they were simply bored by me. I dismissed this as a possibility at once. It was a positive thinking day.

There were a few messages on the machine when I got home, and I switched it to Play even before I had closed the door, sure that one, at least, would be from Hugo. There were a couple of hang-ups; at the last one I braced myself. My disappointment on hearing Sally's voice instead was intense.

"Sam? I am reengeeng to see how you are. You seem—seemed"—giggling, he corrected himself here under prompting from someone—"you seemed upset last night and we wondair—wondaired!"—more giggling—"eef you are OK. Also I wanted to tell you something about Helen. I do not like that girl at all. But I saw her in the garden last night and later I hear about Violetta, and I think, oh, that's funny, so—what?" He broke off for a second. *"Thought!* I *thought* eet is funny! I go now because Fisher is breaking my balls weeth all thees grammar. He salutes you."

The message ended with another onslaught of giggling. I kicked the door shut and, still unsatisfied, seriously contemplated smashing the answering machine against the wall. When your own love-life is in shreds and tatters, you should avoid at all costs friends in an advanced state of romantic bliss. I wondered if I knew anyone whose marriage had just broken up. What I really needed was to hang out with someone with a serious drug habit or a large selection of the kind of complexes that prevented them ever forming a meaningful relationship; someone, in short, who would make me feel better about my own lot. What else were friends for?

I erased Sally's message immediately, in case I listened to it later by accident and was driven to take a crowbar to the answering machine. That's the trouble with being a sculptor—you tend to have a wide selection of tools lying around, providing a temptation for those moments when you act first and think later. A wave of anger against Hugo swept me; if I saw him at this moment I would definitely follow my instincts without referring them at any point to my thought processes.

The phone rang. I caught my hand as it went for the receiver and made myself wait for a few rings before picking it up. I didn't want to look like the kind of sad and desperate person who has been hovering over the telephone, waiting for a call.

"Hello?" I said, trying to sound totally uninterested in the question of who might be ringing me.

"Modesty darling," drawled Hugo, "it's me."

If this was an attempt to charm me, it would fail dismally. I glared at the phone.

"Look, darling," Hugo continued, "I really need to see you."

"Oh *do* you," I said coldly.

"You're cross with me, aren't you? Come round and let me apologize in person. I'll grovel, I promise."

"You could have rung me last night," I said sulkily.

"Look, let's talk about that when I can actually see the face you're pulling. Come round straight away."

There was an edge to Hugo's voice I didn't understand. It was consistent with his still being cross with me, or even giving me the brush-off; but then why had he rung me, and why was he so insistent that I come round? Something didn't tally. Slowly I said:

"Is everything all right?"

"Of course it is, Modesty. Right as rain. Apart from the fact that you're pissed off with me. So come round and we'll make it better."

"All right. I've just got something to finish here first. I'll be round in about an hour."

"As soon as you can make it, my sweet."

I hung up and stared at the wall, bemused. Though Hugo usually talked in a flip, facile way, he always sounded relaxed when he did so, which, after all, was part of the point. But just now he had seemed as tense as a bowstring, a gaping lack of connection between his words and his manner. And why had he called me Modesty?

Picking up the phone again, I dialled Hawkins' direct line. By some miracle, he was at his desk. He sounded busy, though this altered as soon as I identified myself. Now he sounded suspicious.

"Don't be like this," I said reprovingly. "This isn't a nice way to be. Try to sound happy to hear from me."

"Why should I? You're only ringing me because you want something."

"You wouldn't sound any more cheerful if I said I was ringing because it was you I wanted," I pointed out.

I had taken the wrong tack. Hawkins' voice softened. "Is that why you rang me up, Sam? Do you want to see me?"

"Well, yeah, in a way. I mean, it would be great, but actually there's just something else I have to clear up before I'm free to get together." I was floundering badly. "If you wouldn't mind helping me with that first . . ."

"The thing that really pisses me off," Hawkins said, "is not how pathetically obvious you are but how you know that you don't need to bother being subtle because I'll go along with it anyway. I must need my head examined."

"Hawkins," I said firmly, "bitter is not attractive. Remember that. Anyway, sometimes I'm helpful. Look what happened at that merchant bank."

"That wasn't my patch. And all we managed was to send someone down for dealing, not murder. You didn't get a shred of proof on that."

"God, you're picky today. What is it?"

"You don't want to know." This statement is always followed by the piece of information that you apparently don't want to know: I waited and it duly came. "Wedding stuff. Daphne and her mother keep trying to get me to look at hotels for the reception, and whether I think we should have cold salmon for the buffet, and rubbish like that. I just haven't got the time."

"I don't know why they're bothering to involve you at all. They should just get on with it by themselves. I mean, they'll have much more fun that way."

"That's what I keep telling Daph, but she says she wants me to be a part of it. I mean, I'm marrying her, aren't I? How much more a part of it can I be than that?"

He gave a long, slow sigh, full of gloom and despondency. I knew a Doberman once which used to sigh like that. It was the saddest sound in the world.

"Look," I said cunningly, "you need distracting. Why not throw yourself into your work?"

Hawkins sighed again.

"All right," he said, sounding beaten down by life. "I'll bite. What the hell is it this time?"

○○○

Nearly an hour later I pulled up outside Hugo's house. Parking round here was not too much of a problem yet; give it ten years and Spitalfields, not to mention Clerkenwell, would be as cluttered as Kensington. Even alternative-lifestyle yuppies, the ones who wore black to work and spent their leisure hours discussing layouts in glossy magazines, liked their cars. At least my Escort van fitted in here better. I was thinking of upgrading and spent most of my driving time eyeing up Corsa vans lustfully. What I really wanted was a pick-up, but then I'd have to move country to find weather to go with it, and it seemed a little much to have to accessorize your home to the demands of your vehicle. Not too much. I was a machine freak. But a little.

I rang the bell and was buzzed in straight away, without a word over the speakerphone. Inside it was as quiet as the tomb, and as I climbed the stairs to the first floor the leather of my jeans and the creaking of the wooden boards made a racket loud enough to raise the dead. The door to Hugo's flat was ajar, which did not surprise me. Gingerly I pushed it open in one slow movement. Usually there would have been music streaming out and down the stairs. Hugo's taste was so eclectic that it was impossible to predict what the music might be, but the fact of its existence had been, up till now, a given. And he never left his door open.

I waited for a few moments before crossing the threshold. Underfoot the bare boards rasped against each other, struck down by the blakeys on my boot heels. He would know that I was here in any case, since he had buzzed me in. But somehow I wished that the floor was unfashionably carpeted. To announce my arrival this noisily seemed horribly unsubtle. And I hate being obvious.

Hugo was in the living room, sitting on a chair, facing me. He was wearing a facial expression I had never seen before and which, if he had asked my opinion, I would have had to say frankly did not suit him. I couldn't blame him, however. I doubted that, if I were tied to a chair with someone standing over me holding a syringe perilously close to my arm, I would look any less tense, nervous and all the other adjectives manufacturers of headache pills use to identify your state prior to whopping down a couple of their codeine-laced products.

The only real surprise was the person holding the syringe. Actually it wasn't a syringe, but an EpiPen, small and white and entirely devoid of menace. I had to keep reminding myself of what it contained in order to take the threat seriously. Hugo probably took it seriously without this effort, but then it was a lot closer to him than it was to me.

"Ben," I said, almost experimentally. "I wasn't expecting to find you here."

Ben looked as likeable and normal as ever. Maybe it was the wire-rimmed glasses and the sensible sweater, or the reassuringly square face and nice set of his mouth, which had probably lured a number of people into an entirely false sense of security.

"Sit down, Sam," he said, his voice pleasant. "We're not all here yet. I don't have to tell you what'll happen to your boyfriend if I inject him with this, now, do I?"

"He's not my boyfriend," I snarled. "And you'd have to give him at least two of those to have any effect."

"Actually," Hugo said, clearing his throat, "he's thoughtfully given me one already."

Ben smiled at me over Hugo's head. "See?" he said. "I'm very thorough."

"I know I'm repeating myself, but I wasn't expecting you," I said, pulling a spindly yellow silk-upholstered chair towards me and leaning on the back of it in a compromise that I hoped would appease Ben. I really didn't want to sit down. "I thought it might have been MM. Silly of me, wasn't it?"

"MM?" Ben said blankly.

I pulled a face. "Hazel told me she'd been at drama school with her, so she would have known Shirley Lowell too. I never thought anyone but Philip killed Shirley, but clearly someone else knew about it and was using it to keep a hold on him. I expect the most obvious person for that was you. But I hate being obvious."

At this Hugo, momentarily forgetting that he was in immediate danger of death by insulin coma, fixed me with a stare of incredulity and pity, nicely blended.

"So why did you kill him?" I said to Ben. "You did kill him, didn't you? It was such bad timing for you, though. Out of your job with no prospect of being given his."

"He was panicking," Ben said simply. "The police kept calling him in to question him. They could see it too. It was only a matter of time before he broke down and told them he'd killed Shirley. He'd got to that stage where it'd be a relief for him to confess. It was a clever tactic of theirs."

"Cribbed from Dostoevsky," Hugo murmured.

"Who probably got it from some Moscow policeman he went drinking with," I pointed out. "This copper's downing vodka and banging on about how he's trying to wear down some suspect they can't get enough evidence on, and Fyodor thinks: "Wow! I can get a good six hundred pages out of that!"" I cleared my throat and got my voice down to a serious note again. "So, Ben," I said, sounding rather too like a daytime TV interviewer, "you were worried that when he confessed he'd tell them you knew about it all along?"

"He'd have enjoyed that part the most," Ben said bitterly. "Dragging me down with him. Ungrateful bastard. I practically ran that theatre for him."

"You knew Shirley from drama school, didn't you? Hazel told me in a way that you'd been there with her, but it didn't connect. Did she confide in you?"

"Yeah, Shirley and I were pretty close. I was the only one she told about Philip. We sort of cried on each other's shoulders."

"She about Philip being violent, and you because of Hazel?"

"That's the point, don't you see?" Ben said intensely. "It was all for Haze. All of it. I could get her an audition for *Doll's House*, I could make sure she got the part. If I were running the Cross, or a theatre like that, I'd be able to do so much for her. Then she'd look at me differently. Before I was just Ben. We've known each other for too long for her to think of me like that. But the better I did as a director, the more she'd need me. . . ."

Hugo, face shielded from Ben, was looking extremely dubious. I concurred. This was the paradox of being in love; on the one hand you were hypersensitive to the slightest move of the loved one, your nerves constantly on edge, your stomach fluttering like a bird, and at the same time you bound your eyes up in cotton wool and charged headfirst through all the warning signs, wilfully indifferent to the most glaring signals that the person who obsessed you was not who you thought she was. If Hazel hadn't needed Ben at the beginning of her career, she needed him much less now that she was already making a name for herself. And she was a much better actress than, by all accounts, he was a director. But Ben had obviously been nurturing this fantasy for years. When he had schemed his way to the artistic directorship of the RSC, Hazel would fall into his arms with a list of parts she wanted to play. Maybe they could put that in the wedding vows: honour, cherish and direct as Lady Macbeth next season on the main stage at Stratford.

"How soon did you realize that Philip had killed Shirley?" Hugo asked.

"Oh, practically as soon as she went missing. Shirl'd been ringing me every day in a terrible state. She was frightened to leave him. He kept making promises about the roles he'd give her if she stayed with him and put up with it, and then he'd say that if she left him she'd never work again. I told her not to believe him, but she was never that intelligent. And then this idea about her having topped herself like that bloke from the Manic Street Preachers. I mean, it was ridiculous. You'd have to have been a really obsessive fan to do that, and Shirl wasn't."

Ben was speaking calmly enough, gesturing with the hand that wasn't holding the EpiPen; but the other remained where it was, poised just above Hugo's upper arm, which was secured firmly to the back of the chair. Ben was not allowing himself to be distracted.

"So when I heard about it I got on the next train and went straight down to see Philip. I was in Edinburgh at the time," he explained. "So was Hazel. We had a play on at the Festival. Cast-iron alibi, which was useful later when they found her body. Otherwise, what with me working there, it might have looked a bit too suspicious. Anyway, Philip and I had a nice little talk. He was easy," Ben said contemptuously. "Pathetic, really. Got his kicks strangling women, but when I confronted him he collapsed at once. Even let slip where her body was, can you believe it? So he sacked his AD and I walked into the job after Edinburgh. I was good at it, too. It wasn't like I was dead weight or anything. In a couple of years he was going to resign and make sure I got the job after him. It was going perfectly. And then everything fucked up. They found Shirley, and Philip went to pieces. I had to kill him. At least I knew no-one would ever suspect me; I only lost out by his death."

Apart from getting to direct *A Doll's House* with Hazel in it, I thought. But no-one would consider that sufficient motive for murder.

Ben was staring at me.

"Is that why you thought it was MM?" He pronounced her name with tremendous hostility. "Because they asked her to interview for Philip's job?"

"Well, I did wonder. She was quick to say that she didn't really want it."

"Oh, she doesn't. Bloody stupid, isn't it? I'd have killed for it."

Hugo opened his mouth. Then, very sensibly, he took a moment to reflect and shut it again.

"And it was you who tried to kill Violet?" I suggested.

"That was stupid, too. I'd had too much to drink. I heard her say that she was going outside and I just acted on impulse—got down into the garden before her and waited for her. It was crazy. Someone could have seen me so easily. I even heard some people in the gazebo, which unnerved me, but they wouldn't have heard a bomb going off. I thought they'd have it down around their ears."

Hugo quirked an eyebrow at me. I attempted to keep my face as blank as possible.

"But Violet'd been banging on for ages about being questioned," Ben was saying. "I thought Philip had confided in her. I was sure there was something she knew that she wasn't telling. And the more they kept pulling her in, the worse it got for me. I felt like they were doing Chinese water torture."

I toyed with the idea of asking the group if this expression should now be considered politically incorrect, and then, not without regret, abandoned it.

"But did she know about you? Did she know that you'd killed Philip?" I said instead.

"I don't know!" Ben half-cried. "But she knows something. And I can't bear it any longer!" His eyes were shifting nervily around the room, his whole body jittery.

"Philip was so easy," he added, as if he felt the need to explain. "He was slumped on the desk already, practically asleep. All I had to do was inject him. I used two needles at once. It was all over in less than ten minutes. But when I grabbed Violet at the party—I must have been drunker than I thought, I can't believe I was careless enough to have tried that on—and she struggled, I was completely panicked. I was sure she'd be able to identify me. So . . ." His voice trailed off.

"Now we come to the part that interests us directly," Hugo said to me, as if he were bringing me up to date with what had happened on *EastEnders* last week. "Ben found out that Violet stayed here last night. She was scared," he added quickly as I stiffened in anger, "she didn't want to go home because she was afraid the person who'd attacked her might try again. So I brought her back here. Ben's waiting for her to get back from the shops. And by the way, Ben, I know I've said this to you before, but you're vastly over-estimating Vi's capacity to be interested in anything that doesn't directly affect her. She's completely absorbed in herself and her own career. Anything else passes right over her pretty head. Even if Philip did say something to her about your having a hold on him, she'll just have said vaguely, 'Oh, fine, darling' and forgotten about it the moment afterwards. I know her."

Ben looked a little confused by this assertion. Then he pulled back his shoulders and said: "Well, it's too late now. You're all going to overdose together." He looked at me. "I'm sorry, Sam. I liked you. But I can't take any risks."

I stared at him in disbelief. How on earth did he think that he was going to get both me and Violet to stay still while he injected us with insulin? Only the immediate threat to Hugo kept me where I was, and as soon as he left Hugo's side I could do what I wanted. Could he really be so stupid as to think that just because I was a girl I would stand still dutifully and let him stick me with the EpiPen, not once but twice?

"Have you got enough for all of us?" I enquired. "Because Violet said there were only about three pens left."

"I've been to her doctor and got some more," Ben countered. "I got the address from Philip ages ago."

"But they'll be able to track you down through that," I pointed out.

"I rang up and said they were for Violet," Ben said smugly. "Then I went and picked them up disguised as a motorcycle courier. I didn't take the helmet off so they couldn't see my face."

"Violet really should have turned that doctor in," Hugo said disapprovingly. "That's the most sloppy, unprofessional thing I've ever heard."

"And why do you want to kill me too?" I asked curiously. "I mean, I can see Hugo, because Violet might have confided in him—"

"Gosh, thanks for that," Hugo muttered.

"—but why me? I'm too far down the food chain to be important, surely."

"Hazel rang me this morning," Ben said. "Apparently you went round to her flat and asked her lots of questions."

"Yes, but I didn't even suspect you. And besides . . . Wait," I said more slowly. I had just remembered that as soon as I had mentioned Ben's name, Hazel had slid away from the subject, looked at her watch and said she had to be going. At the time I had thought that she had simply used my reference to him as an excuse to stress that she had left the party too early to have killed Violet. I stared at Ben, saying:

"Do you mean that Hazel *knew* about you all along?"

A host of things tumbled through my brain: Hazel happy to talk to me in general but ending conversations as soon as Ben came into the room, or his name was mentioned; Hazel's apparent absolute lack of interest in the events surrounding Philip Cantley's death, which was extraordinary even for someone as detached as she was; Hazel's reference, this morning, to a situation when someone you knew had done something bad, and all you could do was just get on with things and try to forget it had ever happened.

Ben looked, suddenly, very weary. For the first time, the hand holding the EpiPen relaxed a little.

"Hazel," he said, "is just like Hugo described Violet. Only even more ambitious. She's like a heat-seeking missile when it comes to her career. And she doesn't—she doesn't care about anything but that." There was a horrible sadness in his voice. "So no, she doesn't *know* anything about me for sure. But she's always been very good at seeing what people are like, what they're capable of. It's because she stands so far back, she never gets involved. She has a very clear perspective. I don't think she's ever had a boyfriend, you know? I don't think she's ever let herself go with anyone. When we were in Edinburgh I slipped her an E. I know you shouldn't do that kind of thing, dose someone without their knowing, but I was desperate. I thought it would loosen her up, but it hardly changed her. I mean, she had a big smile on her face, and she was sort of swaying with the music, but when I tried to touch her she just picked up my hand and put it back on my lap. I couldn't even get close to her then."

Visibly affected by this touching confidence, Hugo had stuck his tongue out and screwed his face up as if he were retching. I ignored him, knowing that it was a kind of inverse macho: look at me, I'm not really scared! Hugo couldn't resist playing the fool even when his life was in danger.

"But she wanted to warn you about me, so she must care about you, Ben," I said, sounding as gentle and caring as I possibly could. It wouldn't have been remotely plausible to anyone who knew me; in fact, out of the corner of my eye I could see that Hugo's face-pulling had intensified. "Doesn't that make sense?"

There were tears in Ben's eyes now, but when he spoke his tone was bitter.

"The only reason she rang me was that if I go down the production of A Doll's House might collapse. Don't you see? She'd never have bothered if it weren't for that. Oh, she wouldn't want to see me in prison anyway. I could still be useful to her. But she knows she's going to be very good as Christine. And she's understudying Violet. She wouldn't want anything to happen which would jeopardize that."

"I'm sure you're under-estimating her," I said consolingly.

"Do you really think so?" Ben looked at me anxiously.

At that moment a great deal of things happened all at once. The door, which I had left ajar, was pushed further open. I turned to see who it was. Violet stood just inside, looking horrified. She rushed forward, crying:

"Ben! *No!*"

While Ben was momentarily distracted by the sight of Violet, I removed one of Hugo's expensive glass paperweights from the small table on my right. It was round and heavy and fitted very nicely into the palm of my hand. Violet had come to a halt just in front of Hugo's chair, and Ben was telling her to get back in increasingly shrill tones. I caught Hugo's eye and jerked my head back slightly. He shot a quick glance at the paperweight in my hand and nodded.

"Violet, step back! Then go and close the door!" Ben half-screamed, one hand rising to push the air in front of him, as if he could shove Violet away by sheer force of will. He was trapped; though he was holding us with the needle poised above Hugo's arm, if he shot it home the threat would evaporate. His face was a mask of panic. I nodded at Hugo. His long legs shot up as he tipped the chair violently backwards. In the same instant my arm swung back and I threw the paperweight straight at Ben's head.

Ben, partly behind the chair, had been knocked sideways by it and the paperweight was off-target as a result, catching him a glancing blow on the right temple. He stumbled back, already losing his balance. I was already on him, kicking one of his kneecaps as hard as I could. He went down, but the force of my kick had sent him spinning round and he fell over the chair, trying to catch at it to save himself, crashing heavily on top of Hugo. The needle, still in his hand, disappeared under their bodies.

Terrified now that he would inject Hugo with more insulin, even by chance, I grabbed Ben by the scruff of his neck, like a dog, and hauled him up again before he could get his bearings. He must have pushed himself up off his good leg, because he came up with a bound, shaking my grip on him loose. The needle was nowhere to be seen. Violet was wailing like a banshee. And two police officers came through the door at a run, pulling up dead at the sight of the chaos.

"Do something!" Violet screamed at them, waving desperately at Hugo, prone on the floor. "He's dying! He's dying!"

Hugo must have hit his head as the chair went over; he was groaning but conscious. Still, none of us knew if Ben had injected him a second time, and I couldn't see where the bloody EpiPen had ended up. Ben made a rush for the door. I caught hold of the back of his sweater, and as he swung round I backhanded him across the nose. He aimed a punch at my face which half-connected, though I ducked, catching it partly on my forearm. Still, it glanced off my cheekbone hard enough to send me staggering back a few paces, the impact juddering through me like a drill. Hands clapped to his face, Ben looked round desperately, seeing the doorway blocked by the policemen. One of them was kneeling beside Hugo; the other was impeded by Violet, who was hanging on to him in full hysterics.

My head was reeling. I caught my breath and saw that Ben, his nose bleeding, was heading for the bathroom, limping slightly. I launched myself across the room to stop him and promptly skidded, the metal blakeys on the soles of my boots making me unstable on the wooden floor. Ben kicked out at me with his good leg, wincing with the pain of balancing on the other one. Still, he sent me off balance long enough to reach the bathroom door. By this time the second policeman had dumped Violet on a sofa and was charging towards us. As he lunged forwards Ben held up an EpiPen above his head, waving it as frantically as if it were a white flag.

"Don't touch me!" he screamed. "I've already injected myself once! If I do it twice it'll kill me!"

We all froze for a moment, as if someone had hit the Pause button. The policeman swivelled his head to me and mouthed: "What the *fuck?*" his whole body sparking with adrenaline as if he had just been let off a leash. The suicide threat held us for a bare second, and in that moment Ben slammed the bathroom door behind him and shot the bolt. The policeman, cursing horribly, threw himself against it almost at once. Wood splintered loudly, drawing a stifled protest from Hugo. But I could hear other sounds from inside the bathroom, a sash window being pulled up. . . . I dashed to the living-room window and threw it open just in time to see Ben clambering out onto the windowsill, manoeuvering himself round to catch at the drainpipe.

"He's got out the bathroom window!" I shouted.

There was a mass dash for the door.

"Hugo!" I bent down next to him. "Did he inject you again?"

Hugo shook his head, looking dazed. "No, just the once."

"Are you *sure?*"

"Positive."

I breathed a sigh of relief and ran out of the door after the policemen. By the time we reached the street, however, the only sign of Ben was the screech of a car pulling round the far corner of the road, too far away for me to see the make or colour.

"Do you know the registration?" said the policeman who had been breaking down the bathroom door. His colleague was already in their own car, jabbering urgently on the radio.

I shook my head.

"But I bet I can tell you where he's going," I said.

○○○

I returned upstairs to find the situation somewhat calmer. Hugo had liberated himself from his ropes and was slumped in an armchair nursing his head. As I came in he looked up and gave me the most beautiful smile I had ever seen.

"Modesty," he said. "Are you all right? I'm going to start calling you that seriously from now on. You've got a bruise starting on your cheekbone, poor thing. Come here."

I bent over and felt the back of his head.

"Does it hurt? Did you lose consciousness at all?"

"Yes and no."

I squinted into his eyes. "Your pupils look OK, which means you're probably not concussed. Is your sight blurred at all?"

"No."

"D'you want to go to the hospital anyway? Or call a doctor?"

"Absolutely not. I want a stiff drink and a ton of aspirin, in that order. And then I want—"

"Hugo? Are you all right?" Violet had self-resuscitated and was stirring to life on the sofa. It was probably unfair of me to think that she looked like a snake uncurling itself. "Sam!" she said, sitting up slowly. I had to admit that there was nothing but concern in her voice. "What *happened?* Is everyone all right?"

"Well, Ben is currently being chased at high speed towards north-west London, so let's hope no pedestrians get in their way," I said. "Hugo isn't concussed, and if there were any bones broken he'd have been shouting about it by now."

"I am a trained actor," Hugo said pompously. "I have been taught how to fall."

"It was so *frightening!*" Violet said, starting to cry again. "Hugo tied to the chair like that—and he would have done it, he would have *killed* you, Hugo, he'd already killed Philip. . . ."

"I think killing Philip was done completely on impulse," I said reassuringly, wanting to avoid another display of unbridled emotion. "Ben came into the office and saw Philip snoring on the desk. The perfect opportunity.

There's a big difference between that and injecting a conscious victim in front of two other people."

"Oh, that's your considered opinion, is it?" Hugo snapped. "Ben was calm enough when he stuck the first one in my arm. You weren't around to pronounce on that."

"Yes," I said, looking him straight in the eyes. "I'm not saying he might not have panicked. But I doubt he'd have gone through with it. I mean, what was he thinking of doing with me and Violet? He could never have got us both to stand still to be murdered. None of it made sense."

"I don't know how you can talk about it so calmly," Violet said faintly. "We could all have been *killed!*"

I shook my head. "Not all of us. Hugo was the only one who was ever in danger. And like I said, I don't think Ben'd have had the nerve for it."

"Well, we must both bow to your superior knowledge about killers, Sam," Hugo said, salting each word with enough sarcasm to harden my arteries for life.

I stared at him, my eyes narrowed in anger. I had only been trying to deflate Violet's dramatic excesses and restore some much-needed calm; but Hugo was taking my words as some kind of macho declaration.

"You should," I said. "I know more about them than you ever will."

And now he'd taunted me into saying something really macho, which annoyed me past bearing. Violet was staring at me, horrified, big purple eyes wide, girlie beyond belief. I turned on my heel and swung out of the room. Hugo yelled after me at full pitch:

"That's right, Sam, save the damsels in distress and then just walk out. Make sure you keep your bloody cool! You really do think you're bloody Modesty Blaise, don't you?"

I slammed the front door so hard behind me it saw stars.

25

"I just don't believe it," Sophie said for about the seventeenth time that afternoon. "Ben! I just can't get my head round it! He seemed so . . . so *nice!*"

Murmurs of agreement ran round the group. Two days had passed since Ben's dramatic flight and a small inner circle of interested parties connected with the production were sitting in Patisserie Bliss at the Angel, drinking cappuccinos and eating chocolate croissants. I had ordered a cheese and tomato one but when it came I could only pick at it listlessly. I was off my feed. Soon I'd be lying down to sleep. If I was lucky they'd shoot me in the head before they dragged me off to the knackers' yard.

Sophie reached out and, gently as a feather falling, touched my bruise, which was now fading to an attractive pale chartreuse with streaks of yellow.

"I brought you the cover stick I said I would," she added. "It's brilliant. Just moisturize a bit and then pat the stick over the bruise. I can't believe he actually punched you, the bastard."

"Well, I did hit him first," I said fairly. "I think I broke his nose for him."

Sophie's hand shot back from my face, as if I might bite it. Sally was staring at me in horror. And Matthew choked on his cappuccino.

"Sam's been the heroine of the hour," MM said. She and Fisher were the only ones who seemed quite unfazed by my admission. "Sam, I expect it would be too much to ask you if you've got any idea who was playing the practical jokes? Though I shouldn't call them that, since they weren't remotely funny."

I stirred my coffee, cutting the milk froth with my spoon and watching it dissolve in a chocolate-flecked whirlpool, gaining time to decide what to say.

"I'm pretty sure it was Tabitha," I said at last. "I don't have any proof, though. But I bet she'll confess everything, and throw a major scene of repentance into the bargain, if you tell her you know it was her. In a way she doesn't mind what an idiot she makes of herself as long as she's got you for an audience. It's a kind of actors' Münchhausen's syndrome, I expect."

Everyone was staring at me. Fisher exclaimed:

"But sabotaging her own line! I know she was desperate for attention, but that's too masochistic to be true. I can't believe someone would do that to themselves."

"No, you're quite right," I agreed. I'd always thought Fisher was pretty smart. "Nothing Tabitha did was very serious. Phone messages, antihistamines in a drink; she wasn't risking much. It was the same with all the faints and scenes she pulled. They were just to make Violet look bad and keep herself in the centre of attention. She didn't mean to injure anyone, least of all herself."

"Do you mean it wasn't Tabitha who sabotaged her line?" MM said slowly.

I shook my head. "I thought it was, at first," I admitted. "But then, when we were up on the fly floor just after it had happened, she came down to see what was going on, do you remember?"

MM nodded.

"We were larking around and in the confusion I heard something clatter across the floor. I didn't think anything of it at the time. But then Ben picked up a hairgrip he thought was mine. Actually, it was Violet's. And there wasn't any reason for a hairgrip of Violet's to be on the fly floor. She never needed to go there."

I looked across the table at Sophie, who had seen me give the hairgrip back to Violet and known at once what it might mean. She looked at me imploringly.

"Do you mean *Violet* . . . ?" MM said what everyone was thinking.

"No." Out of the corner of my eye I saw Sophie relax. "I can't see Violet being silly enough to wear diamanté in her hair if she were clambering about on the grid messing up Tabitha's line. It was an incompetent attempt to frame her. Tabitha must have gone to Violet's dressing room while we were all on the fly floor, taken the hairgrip and then, while everyone was shoving each other round, skidded it across the floor so it landed near Ben. Actually I think it would have been noticed at once if it had been there from the beginning. All the flymen have very sharp eyes, not to mention Bez and Steve, who's obsessed with sweeping the floor. One of them would have spotted it as soon as they came back to start the show. I can't see how it could have lain there for most of the first half without someone seeing it."

"But that doesn't mean Tabitha didn't do it," Matthew objected. "Rig up her own line, I mean. She might have thought of the hairgrip afterwards."

"Come on!" I said impatiently. "The whole point of sabotaging her own line, if it was Tabitha, would be to make Violet look bad—and have a nice time with everyone feeling sorry for her. She'd have made sure to take the hairgrip and leave it there as soon as she'd put the shackle on the line. The only reason there could be for her having to get it from Violet's dressing room later was that, as soon as it had happened, Tabitha herself assumed it was Violet paying her back for the anti-histamines and the message on the answering machine. She couldn't tell people that, because it would mean confessing to what she'd done herself. But she wanted to make sure everyone realized it was Violet. Hence the hairgrip. It was pretty feeble, really, but worth a try." I looked at MM. "Tell Tabitha you know everything and I bet she'll spill the beans," I advised.

I drank some coffee, though it was cold by now. I didn't really care. I was deep in anomie. Dropping my eyes, I found my gaze resting on my croissant. For a moment I stared at it with a kind of blank surprise, unable to see what the point of it might be.

Matthew had paled slightly when I had referred to Tabitha telling MM everything. But if Hazel had been right and his fling with Tabitha had only been at the start of rehearsals, he had no need to worry. MM certainly wouldn't. It would keep him on his toes, however, which was never a bad position for a boyfriend to be in. This made me think of Hugo and I pushed the croissant away from me in revulsion, as if the two things were somehow connected. No-one had mentioned Hugo; they all knew we'd had a fight.

"But who rigged up the shackle on Tabitha's line, if Violet didn't?" Fisher persisted.

"I don't know," I lied. "But I'm pretty sure it was a one-off. I mean, I don't think you need to worry about it happening again, MM."

"Why not?" she said, eyes boring into mine. I glanced at Matthew, sitting next to her; he still looked horribly uncomfortable.

"Just an instinct. But I'd trust it."

MM stared at me hard. "Was it Paul?" she said.

"I bet he was the one who left the message that was supposed to be from Matthew," I said evasively. "He wasn't any keener on Violet than Tabitha was. But I really don't know who rigged the line."

MM was utterly dissatisfied with this reply, but I wasn't going to say any more. Fisher's eyebrows were raised so high they nearly disappeared into his hairline. Sally ordered another coffee from the waitress. Unusually for him, he had hardly spoken a word since he had got here.

"Well, at least that's sorted out," Fisher said finally, seeing I wanted the subject changed. He glanced thoughtfully round the table and then squeezed Sally's hand. "And the whole murder thing's over. There won't need to be a trial."

"Have they unplugged Ben yet?" I inquired.

MM shook her head. "Soon, though, I think. Margery said that his parents were going to make the decision today."

Everyone fell silent, contemplating this. Ben had, as I had guessed he would, headed straight for Hazel's flat that afternoon, closely pursued by the two policemen. It had been a last-ditch attempt to throw himself at her feet: look at what I've done for you, I've even killed for your sake. The sequence of events was unclear, but, Hazel's reaction apparently falling short of what he had hoped, Ben had promptly injected himself with two more EpiPens, bringing his insulin total up to twenty international units, the same amount which had killed Philip. Only Ben hadn't died. Hazel, acting quickly, had poured most of a bottle of Coke down his throat as soon as she knew what he had done, trying to get some sugar into him fast enough to reverse the effect of the insulin. Hazel had always been practical. By that time, however, Ben was already slipping into a coma. It took only five minutes to come on. And the result was that by the time the police arrived, with the ambulance called by Hazel only shortly behind, Ben was effectively a vegetable. What Hazel hadn't known was that giving sugary drinks to someone in an insulin coma doesn't fully cancel out the process. Ben had irreversible brain damage.

"How's Hazel?" I finally asked.

It was MM who responded.

"Like a zombie offstage. And even better than before when she's on."

"It's going to be incredibly uncomfortable working with her from now on. I mean, I know she didn't actually do anything herself, but I'd be amazed if she hadn't had some sense of what Ben was doing for her sake," observed Fisher, to a heartfelt chorus of agreement from everyone else.

"Poor Violet's going straight into rehearsals for *Doll's House* with her!" Sophie said.

"Better Violet than anyone else," Fisher said, lightly sarcastic. "She has a wonderful capacity to block things out."

Sophie bridled at this.

"Hazel's the most unlikely *femme fatale* in the world," he added quickly to ward off Sophie's defence of Violet. "I just can't see the attraction myself."

"I'm glad to hear eet," said Sally, perking up slightly.

"There is something about Hazel, though, something quite fascinating in a strange way," I said thoughtfully. "She's so complete in herself; she doesn't want anything from the outside world except people to study and the opportunity to work."

"She's very centred," Sophie said, conferring reluctant praise.

"It's more than that," I said reflectively. "Apart from on stage, Hazel's quite sexless. It's as if she's a hermaphrodite, d'you know what I mean? She has everything she needs right there and she's totally content with it."

"Actually that's true," Fisher volunteered. "There's this enormous sexual charge coming off her when you act with her, and as soon as you've finished a scene, boom! It switches off just like that and she's this little mouse again. Most people are the opposite—they work themselves up for a scene and then they're all charged up afterwards and don't know what to do with it."

"Hence all the backstage affairs," MM said dryly, looking at him and Sally.

"I help you any time weeth your energy," Sally said flirtatiously to Fisher, batting those extraordinary eyelashes.

"Sal," I said, unable to resist asking, "do you use mascara at all?"

"Yes, clear mascara," Sally said, going immediately solemn as he did with any discussion about clothes or make-up. "Eet geeves them definition but you don't see I am wearing eet."

"I should be getting on," MM said, finishing her coffee. "I've got auditions starting in an hour."

MM had refused an offer made by the board of the Cross to take over the direction of A *Doll's House;* she was already booked up now till the end of the year. More interestingly, she had also turned down the job of artistic director, which they had tried hard to persuade her to accept. I had to admit that this had impressed even me. A prestigious job with a very nice salary plus the ability to play God on a large scale, and MM had turned it down because she wanted instead to establish her own studio space which would probably pay a quarter of the money the Cross were offering, if she was lucky. Still, she was riding the wave at the moment. Every theatre wanted her as a guest director, and the fact of having refused the Cross job only added to her prestige. If ever there was a time for refusing to compromise your personal vision, this was it.

The only fly in the ointment for me was that Helen had been right again about MM being offered the job. But then, awful as it was for me to admit, Helen did usually seem to be right. I didn't remember if she'd predicted that the production of A *Midsummer Night's Dream* would be the raving success that it was, however. It was fully sold out already, and not just because of school parties booking group excursions to see a GCSE text in performance: queues regularly formed every night for returns. The board was already trying to organize a West End transfer. They had found the theatre already; the problem was jockeying round the schedules of all the actors involved.

Plastered all along the outside of the Cross, boards vaunted Hugo's Oberon ("definitive. I will not see a better one in my lifetime"—*The Sunday Times*), Helen's Titania ("The Ice Queen melts down like a nuclear reactor"—*Time Out*), Marie's Puck and all the fairies ("breathtaking acrobatics which hold the audience spellbound"—*The Guardian*), and the four lovers ("split-second timing and delightful grace. I have never seen these scenes played better"—*Mail on Sunday*). Hazel in particular had been singled out for praise ("Hazel Duffy's superb Helena takes a normally thankless part and turns it into a starring role. Watch her. She will go very far indeed"—*The Independent*).

Everyone, in short, was very happy. Sophie's costumes and Sally's set designs had triumphed and Duggie, my agent, was rubbing his hands with glee over all the cuttings which praised my mobiles. I am too modest to quote them here but suffice it to say that they did not go unheralded. Apparently he had already had a great deal more interest in my work, and the play had been running for barely a week. It looked as if I would be able to afford designer drugs and Absolut Blue vodka for the foreseeable future.

We settled up the bill and wandered out onto the pavement. Traffic was roaring past, mainly buses and lorries racketing along at dangerous speeds to beat the traffic lights at the Angel, pollution spewing out from exhaust pipes in great black trails like factories during the Industrial Revolution. In a strange way I quite liked the effect. I had the theory that if you lived in a city you might as well make it a proper one, a capital throbbing and heaving with life and filth, where even the fittest only survived with their lungs permanently contaminated.

To my disappointment, everyone else but me turned out to have places to go and people to see. The success of A *Midsummer Night's Dream* had conferred on all of those involved with it a particular lustre of desirability, in career terms at least. Sally and Sophie were negotiating job offers to try to fit in with MM's next set of plans; Fisher was being called up for a long series of auditions, including a TV series he would never have been considered for before the *Dream* had become what the *Express* had rather horribly called "London's latest must-see play"; and the cast of *A Doll's House* was currently in discussions with the theatre board about which director would be most suited to take over the play. It had to go ahead. As Gita would say, once something was in the schedule it was fixed in stone.

With the speed of light, the group of croissant-eaters dispersed to their next appointments. MM in particular gave me a firm handshake and a stare that told me she hadn't been deceived; she knew I had a theory about who had sabotaged Tabitha's line, no matter how much I denied it. Fisher and Sally gave me a big wave and crossed the road to the tube station, Sally still looking a little subdued.

"Sam?" Sophie said behind me. I started and turned round.

"Soph! I thought'd you'd gone to the bus stop."

"I came back. I just wanted to say thank you." She hugged her arms across her chest self-protectively, looking sheepish and slightly pink with shame. "I know you know it was me that messed up Tabitha's line. I could tell from the look you gave me just now. Thanks for not telling anyone. It was really nice of you."

"I think Fisher's guessed too. He's a clever guy. And he knows how much you care about Violet."

Sophie ducked her head in embarrassment. "I just couldn't resist it, you know? Tabitha was flouncing around making such a big thing of that scratch Vi gave Hazel—and it was only an accident! I wanted to get her back for being such a bitch. It was completely on impulse."

"And you'd done some trapeze before, with that circus. So you weren't afraid of heights, and you knew how to rig up the shackle."

"It was a mistake telling you about having done trapeze," Sophie admitted. "I realized as soon as I'd said it that you'd know what it meant."

She took my hand and looked at me with great pleading eyes. "This will be our secret, won't it? I promise I'll never do anything like that again. I was so scared afterwards, for myself and in case people thought it was Vi, which didn't even occur to me at the time. And I felt really guilty. Poor Tabitha. She didn't deserve something that bad to happen."

"I won't tell anyone," I said, squeezing Sophie's hand back. "Just be good, OK?"

She flashed me a beautiful smile. "Yes, boss! Promise! And you look after yourself. No more getting punched. Or punching people," she added.

I made the sign of the cross in the air.

"Do my best."

"Try out the cover stick when you get home. Just breathe on it slightly to warm it up a little first."

"OK. And thanks."

"Don't be silly! Look, I've got to run." She gave me a hug. "Thanks again, Sam, you're a real friend."

And she dashed off to the bus stop, rucksack swinging off her shoulder, her face lit up with relief, not only that I would keep her secret, but that she had confessed and been absolved. I liked Sophie a lot. If she could just get over her crush on Violet things would be much easier for her.

Sophie jumped on a bus and was gone, leaving me marooned on the pavement, traffic blaring behind me. I found myself staring into the pawn shop window, feeling rather lonely now they had all gone off, trying not to think about Hugo. I had never pawned anything in my life but somehow it had been nice to know that this place was always here, majestically bestriding the corner across from the tube station, just in case of need. Now I was apparently going to be making a decent amount of money, for a change, and I wouldn't need the pawn shop back-up option. This reflection failed to cheer me up. The prospect of imminent financial success didn't seem to have sunk in at all. In fact, the only thing that had sunk was me, into an advanced state of gloom.

○○○

And he said, "Son, this world is rough
And if a man's gonna make it, he's gotta be tough
And I know I wouldn't be there to help you along.

"So I give you that name and I said 'Goodbye'
I knew you'd have to get tough or die.
And it's that name that helped to make you strong.

"Yeah," he said, "now you have just fought one helluva fight
And I know you hate me and you've got the right
To kill me now, and I wouldn't blame you if you do.

"But you ought to thank me before I die
For the gravel in your guts and the spit in your eye
Because I'm the ***** that named you Sue."

In the end I had done the only thing there was to do. I caught a 73 to Oxford Street and went on a shopping binge. Then I met Janey after work for drinks. She was brimming with news and could only give me an hour or so before rushing off to dinner, but by that time I was twitching to get my purchases home and try them all on again, so it fitted in nicely. I was upstairs on my sleeping platform modelling a long suede hipster skirt, slit to mid-thigh, and a rather snug little silky vest when the phone rang, blaring importunately through Johnny Cash.

It was at moments like this that I wished I'd installed a fireman's pole for quick descents to the main studio. If my ladder were vertical, like the Jacob's ladders in the theatre, I could have slid down it in approved flyman style, one hand on each side; but then I wasn't wearing work gloves. . . . Extraordinary how many things can rush through your head when you're nearly breaking your neck to get to the phone. It was lucky the skirt was slit so high or it would never have made the trip in one piece.

As soon as I picked up the receiver and said "Hello?" the line went dead. My reaction was not pretty. It took me a little while to calm myself down, though in my defence I should plead that I didn't smash either the phone or the answering machine. Instead I stubbed my toe quite badly kicking my welding mask across the studio and then stomped upstairs, hissing invectives. It was pretty damn lucky that I had plenty of new expensive clothes to gorge myself on by way of distraction.

Twenty minutes later there was a ring at the doorbell. When I finally threw the door open, however, there was no-one there. I was about to scream insults down the street and slam the door again when I noticed, to my considerable surprise, a large pitcher sitting on the top step. I looked at it for a long moment and then bent over it rather suspiciously. It was filled to the brim with frozen strawberry margarita and looked very much as if it had come from the Finca tapas bar on Pentonville Road. I toyed with the idea of grabbing the pitcher and nipping inside to drain it dry in peace and quiet, leaving a pause for long enough that—I hoped—he would be starting to panic: then I said:

"Hugo? You can come out now."

He emerged from around the corner of the studio. I could see that he had made an equal effort with his clothes as he had with the cocktail; he was wearing the black leather trousers he knew I liked, with his tight black Dolce and Gabbana sports shirt, the cap sleeves fitting snugly over the start of his biceps, and his belt with the dull silver buckle. On his wrist was his favourite silver bracelet and on his face was an expression simultaneously smug—because he knew that I was incapable of resisting a pitcher of frozen margarita—and sheepish, because he also knew that I was still pissed off with him. He followed me in, shutting the door behind him. I was already at the kitchen cupboard, removing a couple of glasses.

"Do you know the episode of *Cheers* where Sam's on holiday in Mexico?" he said, accepting a full glass. "They ring up from Cheers to ask him to come back—he's working in a bar there—and he's got a cocktail pitcher in his hands. He says: 'Hang on a second, guys, let me just finish making this margarita.' Then he puts the phone down, leans over the bar to where this girl's sitting, and says: 'So, Margarita, what are you doing later on this evening?' Are you still cross with me?" he added through my snorts of amusement.

"Your timing's out," I said. "You should have waited to ask that till I'd finished laughing."

"I must be nervous," said Hugo coldly. "God knows why. Perhaps, on reflection, it might be the thought that you're perfectly capable of throwing some household object at me, knocking me down and then kicking me to death if I say the wrong thing."

"Would you rather I hadn't bothered to save your life?" I said with equal *froideur*.

"On the contrary. You were wonderful. I mean that in the old sense of the word. I just find it hard to imagine that a girl who can handle herself like that could get her knickers in a twist for even a moment over the fact that I put up an ex-girlfriend for a few nights because someone was trying to kill her. I didn't sleep with Violet, you know. She was in the spare room."

I wasn't about to admit that I had taken a good look into Hugo's spare room while I was in the flat and checked out the rumpled bed and evidence of Violet's occupancy. I merely sniffed in what I intended to be an ambiguous sort of way, and said:

"You stormed out on me at the party. In front of everyone."

"Sam," Hugo said, sounding increasingly exasperated, "I was pissed off with Helen and you weren't helping much. I just needed to get out of there and when I came looking for you half an hour later you were gone. I think we're pretty equal in the storming-out stakes, don't you?"

Responding to that would have been beneath me. I refilled our glasses instead.

"And you'd never have rung me," Hugo continued. "I know you. Pride is your most irksome characteristic. It would have killed you to pick up the phone. You made me do it instead."

"You only rang me because Ben had you tied to a chair!" I said more crossly than I had meant to. "I can't tell you how flattered I feel!"

"Well, I was really glad that he gave me the excuse to ring you!" Hugo snapped back.

We stared at each other angrily for a couple of seconds before the idiocy of what we were saying came home to us.

"How did Ben manage to tie you up?" I asked curiously.

"I went into the kitchen to get us a drink and he hit me over the head from behind," Hugo said. "I came back to life to find he'd hauled me onto the chair and was pressing the phone to my mouth. When he'd turned up, he told me he wanted to talk to Vi about *A Doll's House*, so of course I said he could come in and wait for her. It was bloody lucky she wasn't in when he came round or we could really have been in trouble." He looked at me. "How did you get the police to go along with it?"

"Oh, um, my friend the detective inspector," I said, embarrassed. Hugo must have been feeling contrite, because he didn't pick me up on this. Not even a jealous twitch contorted his face. "I could tell that something funny was going on by the way you were talking so I took a risk and asked him to send over a couple of coppers to listen in. They were there when I arrived, waiting round the corner. I left the front door open for them."

"And then Violet turned up and barged her way in," Hugo said. "She said she'd been listening for a while till she decided it was the right dramatic moment to make her entrance. I imagine the coppers had no chance of stopping her once she'd made her mind up."

"Oh, she didn't mess anything up," I said fairly. "Actually it was quite a useful distraction."

Hugo put down his glass. "She's gone back to her flat now," he said. "She went that evening. I was waiting for you to ring and see if I was all right. I thought you'd use that as an excuse. But you didn't even care enough to see how I was."

"Well, I knew you were OK," I muttered. "Everyone told me."

"You're as stubborn as a mule," Hugo said, with the air of one pronouncing judgement. He looked at me closely. "Tell me, is it the latest fashion to wear the price tags outside your clothes or have you been on a shopping spree? That skirt is very nice, by the way."

"Yeah, I just think it's going to be tricky to sit down in," I said, pulling at the slit. I am always easily distracted by talk about clothes.

"I don't see the difficulty. You'll have a nice air circulation going. And the next time you get your knickers in a twist about nothing at all I'll be able to tell at once."

"True." I drank some more strawberry margarita, feeling as if a heavy weight were dissolving from my shoulders. And it wasn't just the tequila. "I had a drink with Janey earlier," I said. "She's left Helen."

"Great!"

"For Gita."

"Not so great."

"You didn't like her either?"

Hugo shook his head. "Fake as Val Kilmer playing the Saint."

"Those are harsh words," I said.

"I stand by them nevertheless."

"And to think I was so pleased that Janey was smartening herself up and looking so great," I said gloomily. "It was all for Gita."

"Looking good is never wasted."

"No, I know, but . . . And she was being so affectionate to Helen. I should have known that meant she was going to dump her."

"The cynicism of the girl!" He coughed. "I thought we might go out and get something to eat, and then maybe check out Submission. I wore my leather trousers specially."

"Oh, and I thought that was just because you know I like them."

"Go upstairs," Hugo said, "put on something perverted enough to get you into Submission but not too over-the-top to get us banned from Café Pacifico, and don't take more than half an hour." He looked at his watch. "I'm counting down."

"Oh good, we're eating Mexican?"

"The margaritas seem to have worked so far. Only a fool would tinker with a winning formula. Go. Now."

"I'm going!" I refilled my glass to take upstairs with me. Then I rewound the tape to catch the end of the song.

"What could I do? What could I do?" Johnny Cash was asking the assembled crowd as I ascended the ladder.

> *I got all choked up and I threw down my gun.*
> *Called him a pa and he called me a son,*
> *And I come away with a different point of view.*

> *And I think about him now and then*
> *Every time I tried, every time I win*
> *And if I ever have a son I think I am gonna name him*

> *Bill or George—anything but Sue!*

"And next time," Hugo called through the roars and applause of Johnny Cash's hugely appreciative audience, "it's your turn to come round and make up."

I pulled my vinyl miniskirt off the clothes rail and stared at it thoughtfully, wondering if it would work with the new little vest top I had just bought.

"Hey," I yelled back. "I'll freeze your margarita any time."

"Bollocks! Bollocks!" This was Lex, in a near-seamless continuation of his previous ejaculation. Only by now it was many hours later, we had changed venue, and he was shouting the words over an insistently fast and thumping bassline. "How can you possibly fucking say that my work doesn't inspire emotion? You should have seen people reacting to that piece I did at Black Box last year! They were all over the place!"

I sneered at him.

"I'm sorry," I said, or rather shouted, as coldly as I could under the circumstances. "I really don't see that a load of lads spitting out diluted cough syrup all over the floor counts as emotion, except perhaps in the most literal sense—"

"It wasn't just sodding cough syrup! It was syrup of figs! It took me ages to get hold of that! And there was flat beer and tea, mixed together, in the Tallisker bottle, and vodka in the water—*and*," he added with great pride, as if this would clinch the argument, "I left the chartreuse as it was! No one was expecting that!"

"Oh, for God's sake, Lex!" I was exasperated by now. "Just because you lined up a load of bottles on a table with different stuff in them from what it said on the labels, and some idiot boys were fool enough to taste them—"

"It's about challenging people's perceptions of the real!" Lex insisted. "Breaking down our standard assumptions and showing how much we depend on labels—"

"Of course we bloody depend on labels! Take all of them off the tins you've got at home and then try finding the baked beans!"

"Well, that bit was more about mass-marketing," Lex yelled across an increasingly loud break of sound, "how we expect certain things from a particular brand, because of advertising—"

"Then what you should have done," I said, sighing, because it was so obvious, "is bunged a lot of bottles of vodka, say, on the table, right from supermarket brands up to Absolut or Finlandia, to see if people could taste the difference."

Lex's eyes went absorbed and distant for a second, "Nah," he said, "that would be—"

"What?"

"That would be too practical!" he shouted. "So, what, you're saying your stuff actually provokes emotion?" He put huge and sarcastic stress on the last two words.

I was drunk enough by now not to be embarrassed by the turn the conversation had taken.

"I dunno! I'm just saying that the emotional range you go through while swilling your mouth out to get rid of the taste of cold beer and tea mixed together and cursing the so-called artist at the same time—"

"I don't bloody call myself an artist! Well, only as a convenient short-hand—"

"ANYWAY—that kind of sensation's about as shallow as you can get. People probably experience a much more complex array of feelings watching *Babe* on video."

"I can't hear a word you're saying! Let's go and sit on the stairs, OK?"

I nodded. Lex turned and shoved his way through the crowd of people milling around the bar. I followed the shoulders of his battered fawn suede jacket as they jostled a path for me over to the staircase on the far side of the bar. Earlier I had taken one look at the dancefloor and beat a hasty retreat. A battery chicken would have sized up the situation and returned with relief to its cage, finding it pleasantly roomy and well-ventilated by contrast. Still, it was better than the last drum and bass club I'd been to, just behind Regent Street. There no track had been longer than ninety seconds—without a tune there wasn't anything else to sustain it for longer—and every time the DJ put a new one on he stopped dead and blew a whistle several times, at which everyone screamed and waved their arms around and joggled back and forth. A basic mathematical calculation will find that in ten minutes this had happened roughly six times, which was about how long I lasted.

And there had been the added handicap that practically everyone had been wearing puffa jackets tied around their waists, even while dancing, for some quirk of fashion whose reasons were obscured in the mists of time. Maybe Goldie had turned up at a club once looking like that and everyone had copied him, not realizing that after about half an hour he'd taken the jacket off and stowed it somewhere sensible. So it was almost impossible to move because of all the duvets with sleeves slung at waist height, slipping against one another, scratching at any exposed passing flesh with the teeth of their zips. And the dancers, jerking up and down like Duracell rabbits in their little white vests, were sweating heavily under the low ceiling, the sweat running down their bodies and soaking into the channels of the puffa jackets. . . .

"So, what were we saying? Whoah, I can almost hear myself when I talk normally—that's got to be an improvement." Lex dropped down on a stair and patted the tread beside him invitingly. I joined him, chugging back some of my beer, and then had to squeeze in closer because someone was coming downstairs. "Yeah, what were we saying?" he repeated. "Nah, fuck it. Enough of that."

He drank most of his whisky chaser and turned to look at me directly. My thigh was pressed up against his jean-clad one, and the contact was very pleasant. Automatically I glanced down to check his footwear and made a mental tick against Caterpillar boots, rather sloppily laced. Under his suede jacket he wore a denim one with a T-shirt under that, a look I've always approved of. His hair was dark and cut short; I had the impression that it would be curly if he let it grow. His skin was a clear pale olive, his eyes big and dark. Indeed, he looked much as I might if I'd been a boy. Only his eyelashes were much longer than mine, the bastard. When he opened them wide, as if he were protesting his innocence, they framed his eyes in great dark spikes Twiggy would have been proud of. And he knew exactly how pretty he was.

Mel and Rob had left already, the former, I thought, distinctly reluctant to leave me and Lex alone; my instinct in matters of sexual attraction has been finely tuned over the years. But she and Rob had boyfriends or girl-friends or pet gerbils waiting for them at home, and those claims must have taken precedence.

Lex's thigh was pressing ever more insistently against mine and, enjoy-able though it was, in the big picture this was not a good situation. We had a show to get through together, and in principle I was firmly opposed to shit-ting on one's own doorstep. I decided to finish my beer and leave. Halfway down, someone else pushing past us jogged me and the beer would have gone everywhere if Lex hadn't righted the bottle in time, his fingers deliber-ately closing over mine for much longer than the emergency warranted.

"Whee!" I said when I'd got my breath back. We were both cackling with laughter, for some reason. Clearly we were drunker than I had real-ized. I cleared my throat and mentally slapped myself around the face.

"I've got to go," I said resolutely, impressed by my own maturity.

"Oh, what? No way! Come on, Sam, don't wimp out on me." He grinned. "I've heard all about your staying power."

"Is that a challenge?" I said, rising to it immediately.

"It's a fact." He looked at his watch. "Shit, it's only one! You can't bot-tle out this early!"

"I really do need to go home," I said feebly.

"Tell you what." Lex batted his dark silky eyelashes at me. "Let's go do a line of charlie. That'll keep you going."

It was the drugs and not Lex's eye-work that persuaded me to stay. I swear it on my life.

○○○

The minuscule cubicle in the women's toilets were painted a pale yellow. The walls were filthy, thickly encrusted with graffiti—some of it quite witty—and peeling like a terminal case of psoriasis. I made an amusing little crack about them having had too much AHA cream which Lex, being a boy, didn't understand. Too many scientific terms for his tiny mind. In mitigation, however, it could be argued that he had his mind fully on the wrap he had produced from one of his jacket pockets. Unfolding it, he tapped out a steady stream of white powder onto the equally white cistern. I noticed that the wrap was cut out of a football magazine. He might as well have had "New Lad" tattooed on his forehead.

"Ladies first," he said, gesturing to the cistern.

"All right if I go instead?" I said satirically. Bending over, I hoovered up a line. It cut sharply at the lining of my nostrils.

"A bit speedy, isn't it? Not," I hastened to add, "that I'm complaining."

"Yeah, it's nice," Lex agreed, bending over in his turn and thus providing me with the kind of view I could have watched for much longer than the sadly brief few seconds it took him to snort the other line. He ran his finger over the cistern and smeared anything left, together with most of the dirt and grime that had been there already, over his gums. New Lad, new hygiene.

"So," he said, looking at me, "here we are."

And then he kissed me.

It wasn't a tentative buss; it was full-on, shove-the-girl-up-against-the-cubicle-wall, hands-all-over-the-place. PG Wodehouse would have called it the Stevedore, as opposed to the Troubadour, approach. The only word for it, frankly, was snog, and I am sorry to admit that, mainly but not entirely due to these shock tactics and my advanced state of drunkenness, I found myself responding with enthusiasm, despite the proven uncleanliness of his gums. We crashed back into the small space between the toilet and the wall, radically disarranging each other's clothes, tongues wrapping themselves around tonsils with abandon. My head knocked back against the wall. I heard the ageing plaster crumble under the pressure. Lex's hands were closing around my bottom, smoothing the shiny material around my hips enthusiastically.

"Mm, sexy," he purred into my neck, kneading the skirt like a feeding kitten.

For some reason the way he said it struck a false note. There was something self-conscious about it, as if we were making a porn film and he was talking for the benefit of the camera. I pulled back a little and caught such a smug expression on his face that my fingers snapped back from one of his fly buttons as if it had given me a short electric shock. No one ever takes me for granted.

"Close," I said. "But no cigar."

I pulled my sweater down again. With the increased vision this permitted me I was happy to see that Lex's face had wiped itself clean of anything remotely resembling smugness; for a moment it was blank—which quite suited him—and then his lips parted in disbelief. He looked very fetching when he pouted.

"What? Bollocks! Come here!" He dragged me towards him and ground himself against me. The tender romance of this caress softened neither my heart nor any other part of my anatomy.

"Sorry, gorgeous. Got to go."

"What?" he repeated. "Sam, you can't do this to me! Come on, baby, it was going so well—"

How Seventies of him. "You sound like the singer in Hot Chocolate," I said, adjusting my skirt and picking a couple of pieces of yellowing plaster out of my hair.

"What's wrong with that? Hey—" He started kissing my neck. This was very pleasant, but I ignored it womanfully. "It needn't change anything! We can still be friends afterwards—"

I always loathe it when someone says that.

"Who says we're friends now?" I inquired, and stepped neatly past him and through the door. A couple of girls had just come in, sweaty from dancing, their eyes bright. They were both wearing the ubiquitous puffa jackets round their waists and the cladding was enough, in the small space, to cause a traffic jam of M25 proportions. As I was squeezing past one of them said, separating out her words for emphasis:

"God, I am so fucking up for it it's not true. I could've grabbed him right there and given him what for, and I don't even fancy him that much, know what I'm saying?"

"You're on heat!" her friend bawled, giggling madly.

I had a flash of inspiration.

"Well, someone in there could do with it," I broke in, nodding to the cubicle. "If you don't mind finishing what I started."

They broke into noisy and raucous laughter.

"All right, Shaz, what about it?" the first girl said as I left the toilets. She was the size of a house even without the jacket bulking her out. Lex had better get out of there quickly if he wanted to remain unmolested; once she cornered him between the toilet and the wall she'd have him bang to rights. I hadn't warned her about his hairy back. It had felt like he was wearing a mohair sweater under his T-shirt. Oh well, she'd just have to find out for herself. You opens your cubicle door and you takes your chances.

ooo

The brief amusement I felt at the way I had handled my exit faded fast, the smile on my lips spreading wide into a silent scream. I rolled over in bed whimpering and biting the pillow, and not, I stress firmly, because the memory of Lex's tongue halfway down my throat had rekindled any passion in my loins. Oh, the shame, the horror. It was worse than anything I could have imagined. I had kissed—no, Sam, look the brutal truth right in the face without flinching—I had *fumbled in the Blue Note toilets with a young British artist*. How I was going to live with myself after this I didn't know.

And what on earth was I going to tell Hugo?